THE
INNOCENT
SLEEP

*Coming soon from DAW Books

SEANAN McGUIRE

THE INNOCENT SLEEP

AN OCTOBER DAYE NOVEL

DAW BOOKS

New York

Jacket illustration by Chris McGrath

Jacket design by Adam Auerbach

Interior dingbats by Tara O'Shea

Edited by Navah Wolfe

DAW Book Collectors No. 1948

DAW Books
An imprint of Astra Publishing House
dawbooks.com
DAW Books and its logo are registered trademarks of Astra Publishing House

Printed in the United States of America

Library of Congress Cataloging-in-Publication Data

Names: McGuire, Seanan, author.
Title: The innocent sleep / Seanan McGuire.
Description: New York : DAW Books, 2023. | Series: An October Daye novel ; #18
Identifiers: LCCN 2023026650 (print) | LCCN 2023026651 (ebook) |
ISBN 9780756416805 (hardcover) | ISBN 9780756416829 (ebook)
Subjects: LCSH: Daye, October (Fictitious character)--Fiction. |
LCGFT: Fantasy fiction. | Novels.
Classification: LCC PS3607.R36395 I56 2023 (print) |
LCC PS3607.R36395 (ebook) | DDC 813/.6--dc23/eng/20230609
LC record available at https://lccn.loc.gov/2023026650
LC ebook record available at https://lccn.loc.gov/2023026651

First edition: October 2023
10 9 8 7 6 5 4 3 2 1

For Diana.
Take a breath and count to ten:
I swear I'll get us home again.

ACKNOWLEDGMENTS

Writing two of these acknowledgments in one year is a new experience for me, but I did it to myself: I'm the one who went and decided that I needed to approach an event of this size from two directions at the same time, meeting in the middle. Getting it to fall together the way I needed it to forced me to up my game in some ways I'm very proud of, and the challenge was super fun. I hope you had a nice time.

This book is dedicated to Diana Fox, my agent, who has been with me from the beginning, because when I started conceptualizing it, she was the one who essentially ordered me to sit down and write it properly, rather than just tooling around with it for a while, getting distracted, and deciding to do something else with my time (probably playing a bunch of Magic the Gathering at my local game store). She gave me another anchor to hang my year on, and in so doing, saved my remaining sanity. Thanks, Diana! Have a book!

The downside of doing this twice in quick succession is that not much has changed. Here's where I give my thanks to the people who deal with me in daily life, including my various D&D parties, who continue to be very good about my insistence on only playing Tiefling magic-users, my Magic draft and command pod, everyone at Zulu's Board Game Cafe, PFER, the Machete Squad, the team at DAW Books, and my new personal assistant, Terri Ash, without whom my inbox would be even more of a nightmare than it already is. Keeping me going where you need me to go is a challenge and a calling!

Thanks to Mike and Marnie, for being wonderful; to Manda, for making sure I eat even when everything but salad is just too much trouble; to Wish, for keeping me from climbing the walls and crying out of isolation, and to Blyss, for both massage work and making me aware of butternut squash lasagna. Thanks to all my gaming companions, and to Kyra, for quickly becoming a delightful partner in crime and bringer of endless chaos. Thanks to Shawn and Jay and Tea, to Phil and Mars and a whole list of people, all of whom I adore utterly.

Thanks to Joshua Starr for his patient wrangling of my endless administrative needs, and to Kayleigh Webb for being the publicist of my dreams. Diana Fox has retained the ability to Discord message me at midnight, while I continue to love Chris McGrath's covers beyond all reason. All of my cats are doing well: Elsie, Thomas, Verity and Megara all thrive on my being home constantly, and finally believe that they're getting as many Rocking Lobster cat treats as they properly deserve. I have added a fifth cat to the clowder: Kelpie, who is a cousin of my lost, lamented Alice, and is gracing my days with kitten antics and with joy. Finally, thank you to my pit crew: Christopher Mangum (website), Tara O'Shea (dingbats), and Kate Secor (offsite sanity maintenance).

My soundtrack while writing *The Innocent Sleep* consisted mostly of the Amazing Devil's full discography, endless live concert recordings of the Counting Crows, and the soundtrack to the Beetlejuice musical. Any errors in this book are entirely my own. The errors that aren't here are the ones all the people listed above helped me fix.

Now come on. There's a mist in the trees, and a fire on the hill beyond, and there's so much to be done before the tale is ended . . .

OCTOBER DAYE PRONUNCIATION GUIDE
THROUGH *THE INNOCENT SLEEP*

All pronunciations are given strictly phonetically. This only covers types of fae explicitly named in the first eighteen books, omitting Undersea fae not appearing or mentioned in the current volume.

Adhene: *aad-heene*. Plural is "Adhene."
Aes Sidhe: *eys shee*. Plural is "Aes Sidhe."
Afanc: *ah-fank*. Plural is "Afanc."
Annwn: *ah-noon*. No plural exists.
Arkan sonney: *are-can saw-ney*. Plural is "arkan sonney."
Bannick: *ban-nick*. Plural is "Bannicks."
Baobhan Sith: *baa-vaan shee*. Plural is "Baobhan Sith," diminutive is "Baobhan."
Barghest: *bar-guest*. Plural is "Barghests."
Blodynbryd: *blow-din-brid*. Plural is "Blodynbryds."
Cait Sidhe: *kay-th shee*. Plural is "Cait Sidhe."
Candela: *can-dee-la*. Plural is "Candela."
Coblynau: *cob-lee-now*. Plural is "Coblynau."
Cu Sidhe: *coo shee*. Plural is "Cu Sidhe."
Daoine Sidhe: *doon-ya shee*. Plural is "Daoine Sidhe," diminutive is "Daoine."
Djinn: *jin*. Plural is "Djinn."
Dóchas Sidhe: doe-sh-as shee. Plural is "Dóchas Sidhe."
Ellyllon: *el-lee-lawn*. Plural is "Ellyllon."
Folletti: *foe-let-tea*. Plural is "Folletti."
Gean-Cannah: *gee-ann can-na*. Plural is "Gean-Cannah."
Glastig: *glass-tig*. Plural is "Glastigs."
Gwragen: *guh-war-a-gen*. Plural is "Gwragen."

Hamadryad: *ha-ma-dry-add*. Plural is "Hamadryads."
Hippocampus: *hip-po-cam-pus*. Plural is "Hippocampi."
Kelpie: *kel-pee*. Plural is "Kelpies."
Kitsune: *kit-soo-nay*. Plural is "Kitsune."
Lamia: *lay-me-a*. Plural is "Lamia."
The Luidaeg: *the lou-sha-k*. No plural exists.
Manticore: *man-tee-core*. Plural is "Manticores."
Naiad: *nigh-add*. Plural is "Naiads."
Nixie: *nix-ee*. Plural is "Nixen."
Peri: *pear-ee*. Plural is "Peri."
Piskie: *piss-key*. Plural is "Piskies.'
Puca: *puh-ca*. Plural is "Pucas."
Roane: *row-n*. Plural is "Roane."
Satyr: *say-tur*. Plural is "Satyrs."
Selkie: *sell-key*. Plural is "Selkies."
Shyi Shuai: *shh-yee shh-why*. Plural is "Shyi Shuai."
Silene: *sigh-lean*. Plural is "Silene."
Tuatha de Dannan: *tooth-a day du-non*. Plural is "Tuatha de Dannan,"
    diminutive is "Tuatha."
Tylwyth Teg: *till-with teeg*. Plural is "Tylwyth Teg," diminutive is
    "Tylwyth."
Urisk: *you-risk*. Plural is "Urisk."

The innocent sleep,
Sleep that knits up the ravell'd sleave of care,
The death of each day's life, sore labor's bath,
Balm of hurt minds, great nature's second course,
chief nourisher in life's feast.

—William Shakespeare, *Macbeth*.

ONE

June 13th, 2015

EXITING THE SWEET SAFETY of the shadows for the warmer, softly lit solidity of the bedroom I shared with October was, as always, something of a shock. She pushed against my chest to be released and I let her go, staying where I was and watching as she stepped away to catch her breath and brush the ice from her hair, remaining within reach. We were both, I think, too shaken to move very far from one another.

She shot me a look, wearily amused, and pulled her fingers through her hair, coming away with flecks of frost clinging to her skin. The Shadow Roads did treat her harshly, even after all this time.

"When I said to get me out of there, I assumed we'd wind up in the Court of Cats or something," she said.

I raised an eyebrow, and asked, "Why in the world would you assume that when home was right here, waiting to serve as a perfectly lovely option?" It had been so many years since I'd considered any point outside the Court a home. Now that the option was once again open to me, I was more than happy to exploit it.

She smiled, slow and warm and perfect and *mine*, offering me her hands. "You know, when you put it like that, I have no idea."

I took her hands, raising both eyebrows to cover the fact that I badly wanted to start kissing her fingers, to reassure myself that we were both here, and solid, and safe, operating under our own control and not the control of an ancient and terrible Queen. "Why am I concerned that whatever it is you're about to say will be in some way distressing?"

"I genuinely hope it's not going to be," she said. "I mean, we've talked about it before."

"We've discussed a great many things." I eyed her warily. "Many of them involve knives, blood, and screaming."

"I think two of those are likely to be involved." She took a deep breath, visibly steadying herself. "I'm pregnant."

I knew the words. I understood the words. And in that moment, the words meant nothing to me; they were only sound, signifying nothing. Slowly, I frowned.

October attempted to pull her hands from mine, clearly intending to move farther from me. I tightened my grip, refusing her retreat. Puzzled, I cocked my head and continued to frown at her.

"I'm sorry," I said. "I do believe I must have misheard you."

Suddenly insecure, she stopped pulling against me. "Um, if what you heard was 'I'm pregnant,' you heard correctly," she said. "We've talked about this. You said you wanted to have kids. Did you not? Want to have kids?"

"You said we would have to wait until you had finished risking your life in a casual fashion," I replied, keeping my voice as even as possible.

"I said I wasn't willing to start *trying* until I was finished risking my life in a casual fashion," she said. "Apparently, the universe had a different idea."

All my attempts at remaining calm were slipping from my grasp. I allowed my frown to fade, face relaxing as I watched her. "You're pregnant."

"Yes. That's what I've been trying to tell you."

"And you told Simon first." I could accept the man as her father, I could. In many ways, I already had. But I was her husband, and the order irked me.

Her eyes widened slightly, pupils dilating. "He was dying. I shared my blood to save him. He must have picked up the thought from what he was swallowing."

"So you didn't tell him?"

"Not intentionally, or using actual words."

"A baby." The smile I had been fighting to contain finally escaped. I had been waiting so long for . . . oh, oak and ash. My eyes widened. "But before, when I—"

"You mean, when Titania." October's voice was iron, and not the killing kind. She pulled one hand free, reaching up to lay her fingers against my cheek. "You didn't do *anything*. She forced you, and I'm fine. I'm fine, and the baby's fine, and we're both going to be fine."

I put my hand over hers, trapping it where it was, keeping her close to me. "You know how my first wife died." Sweet Anne had been as mortal as the morning. She would have been long gone even had all things played out perfectly.

But I would still have changed the past, had I been able to do so. Even now.

"And you know I'm basically unkillable." She stepped closer, until I could smell the salt-sweet of her skin. "Can we try to be happy? Please? For me? For us? So I can be in a decent mood and not totally terrified when I go to tell Quentin and May? Oh, ash and oak, and Raysel. Is she going to think we don't have room for her? That we want her to lea—"

I pulled her into my arms and pressed my lips to hers, silencing her anxieties with a kiss. It wasn't the sort of thing that would work for long; her worries would catch up with her soon enough, as they always did. But for the moment, all I wanted was to kiss her until she was breathless, then pick her up and do it over again. A baby. *Our* baby. A child we had made together, coming into Faerie already safe and loved, with no need to fear rejection as we had both done. She was already a mother, but I had never been a father to a child that lived, and the thought was dizzying and heady.

I took a step back, pulling her along with me; and sat down on the bed, placing her in my lap as I continued the all-important task of kissing her anxieties away. My little fish had many anxieties. This could take a while.

When I finally stopped kissing her, it was to lean back and smile without letting her go. "A *baby*," I breathed. "*Our* baby. I've never been a parent before."

I had come close, down the years, had taken the uncle's role at every opportunity, but a child of my own, to love and raise in safety and in joy, had never been a part of my life. October snorted, like she wanted to argue, then leaned over, resting her head against my shoulder. "Our baby," she agreed. "I guess it's time to start talking about names. Oh, and there's that whole Sleeping Beauty story thing. Do purebloods have any weird 'Hey we have a baby now' traditions that I need to know about?"

I swallowed my laughter. "Well, there won't be a christening, if that's what you're asking. There will be a party, however, to present the infant to the local nobility, and to allow them the opportunity to provide gifts. It's traditional for the Firstborn of the parents to be invited. They never attend, of course."

"Except that in my case, they actually might," she said, with a groan.

"That's a problem for tomorrow," I said, and leaned down to kiss her again. This seemed like an excellent way to pass the next several hours.

That was when she screamed and jerked away, almost falling out of my lap. I held her where she was, staring wordlessly as she spasmed and thrashed, clearly caught in the web of some agonizingly painful physical reaction with no visible source.

She kept screaming. I stared at her, trying to find the words that would take her pain away, trying to figure out what enemy was attacking her so. The bedroom door slammed open. May burst into the room, her eyes gone wide and wild, and air around her crackling with the scent of cotton candy and ashes.

"Toby?" she demanded, a note of shrill terror in her voice. Her eyes snapped to me. "What's wrong with her? Why is she screaming?" Then: "What did you *do*?"

"Nothing," I said, and I could hear the horror in my own voice. "I was kissing her, and she just—"

October was struggling to breathe, even as she continued to scream.

It seemed impossible that her body should still be producing sound, that she should be anything but silent and unconscious from a lack of air, all apart from whatever was happening to her. Quentin appeared behind May in the doorway, his eyes fixed on October and a short sword already drawn and in his hand. Jasmine, close behind him, was just as visibly horrified as the others. None of them seemed to have any better idea than I did why this was happening.

I couldn't let her go, couldn't go looking for whatever was causing her such endless pain. All I could do was hold her fast, keeping her from falling to the floor as she screamed and writhed.

Finally, after what seemed like an eternity, she managed a break in her screaming long enough for her to catch her breath. Silence fell, broken by the soft sound of footsteps on the stairs. She looked to May, gasping as she struggled to speak. "Is that . . . Raysel?"

"She's asleep in her room," said May. "She was exhausted. I know that seems odd, given the whole 'cursed to sleep for a century' thing, but magical sleep and real sleep aren't the same thing. She's fine."

October took another breath. It sounded painful. It sounded like a dagger in my own heart.

"Someone . . . on . . . stairs," she said.

May looked at her in horror before she whirled to stare at whoever was coming down the hall. She paled at the sight, taking a half-step back, putting herself more firmly in the bedroom door. "You can't *be* here."

October tried to stand. I didn't let her go.

Quentin turned. "You!"

This time, when October tried to stand, I allowed it, and stood with her, close behind, putting my hands on her shoulders. Not to hold her in place—to be sure she knew that I was there, for anything she needed. She drew her knives, keeping them low by her sides, and I shifted slightly to make it easier for her to strike if the need arose.

The smell of roses wafted down the hall, woody and wild and tantalizingly familiar. I wanted to follow those roses, to sniff at them until I understood where they were coming from. October stepped forward, and I let her, lowering my hands as she left me behind.

"Quentin," she said.

Her squire ducked his head as he hurried into the room and moved to stand beside her. May remained in the doorway, eyes on our unseen intruder.

"Child of mine," said a female voice, familiar and not, all at the same time. I saw May stiffen, and I knew who had come for us. "Child of mine, you cannot stand against me. Stand aside."

May glanced at October, agonized, before she moved out of the doorway to make way for the woman who appeared in her place. Titania stepped into the room, looking flatly at October. Her expression was almost neutral, more dismissively unimpressed than anything else. Her hair and clothing were once again impeccable, all signs of the earlier battle washed away. I couldn't look at her directly. She was so much more than we were, and she had caught me so easily before this . . .

"You can't hurt me," said October, my brave girl. "You can't hurt any of us. You're not allowed to harm my family."

"True, child," said Titania, voice sweet. "But you forget how young you are. You forget how much more time I've had to play this game. So much more time than any of you. Only the distorted child of mine comes anywhere near to me, and hers is a dilute and unwarranted claim to her age. I know the way of ward and wording. I know the roads through riddle and restriction. Do you truly think my husband can stop me from doing anything I want to do?"

"Get out of my house," said October, with cold finality.

"I can't hurt you." Titania smiled. "But I can make you someone else's problem."

The smell of roses grew stronger, filling the room. My nerves jangled with the sudden awareness of danger, and I moved to wrap myself around October, to protect her and our child from the threat Titania represented. As for Titania herself, she watched me begin to move, expression entirely serene.

"Uh-uh-uh," she said, shaking a finger. "Naughty kitty. You'll not ruin this for me. You'll not ruin this for her, either, or for anyone. I don't think there's a place for you in what I'm doing."

October's knives clattered as they slipped from her hands and fell to the floor. I couldn't move. I couldn't do anything but glare in futile, frozen hatred at the woman who was meant to be the mother of us all. The air turned pink with sourceless brilliance, then red, crimson and carmine, as if the entire world were bleeding.

This is how October sees the world, I thought, and my mental voice was the accent of my childhood, of a London that passed centuries ago, and for a moment, it dazed me, and in that moment, everything went away.

I never even saw her disappear. She was simply gone. They all were, and I was alone, plummeting through endless, burning white.

TWO

THE BLAZE LASTED FOR some immeasurable amount of time until, as abruptly as it had begun, it ended, and was replaced by the sort of blurry darkness that comes when the eyes have yet to adjust to a sudden change. I blinked repeatedly, trying to chase the afterimages away. The scene began to clear.

Whatever I was looking at, it wasn't the bedroom I shared with my wife, or any other part of our home. I realized I was sitting down. I had been standing a moment before, hadn't I—? But now I was seated on something soft but flexible, and when I shoved myself to my feet, it creaked dangerously under the pressure of my hands. I squinted at it, hoping closeness would give me a better view of the object, and saw it for a stack of wooden shipping pallets covered by empty burlap sacks of the sort that coffee beans are often packed in. I blinked again, then turned to survey the rest of my surroundings.

I was in a cavernous, familiar room. It had been the center of the local Court of Cats several times over the previous decades, falling in and out of favor in keeping with our number. The Eureka Valley Station was an underground edifice originally constructed for the use of San Francisco's streetcars, and enjoyed decades of service before it had been sealed off and forgotten, allowing it to slip into the spaces occupied by the lost things—the spaces that belong to us.

The mortals still had access to their own version of the station, of course, and should they ever reopen it to such a degree that whatever arcane force marked the space as "lost" decided it had been found, our own iteration of the space would dissolve and fade away. For now, however, it was stable, and there had never been any indication that it would become otherwise. Still, at times it was too large to suit us, and it offered few comforts, being comprised of concrete platforms and open track beds. There were offices and the like, but when we had need of a place that could contain us all at once, they were useless to the point of irrelevancy.

My eyes were continuing to adjust. I realized my stack of pallets was far from the only one, although it was the tallest by several feet, as befit my station: more stacks had been pushed against the station walls, while the tracks were blunted with piled-up mattresses and heaps of fur, only some of which was attached to the curled-up, dozing bodies of cats. Crates and old, clearly scavenged posts covered in carpet and sisal dotted the scant remaining open space. From the looks of it, this had been a primary gathering space of the Court for years, which was . . . wrong.

For nearly a decade, the Court had been meeting mostly in a walled-off alley that had managed to slip into our control, choosing to risk the small chance that we might be observed in order to hold our courts beneath the open sky. The air was clearer there, and sometimes rats would stumble into our company, providing a pleasant diversion during a dull debate on some topic or other. We had abandoned Eureka Valley almost as soon as the alley had appeared in my domain.

So why were we here now?

My eyes finished their adjustment and, between one blink and the next, it was as if the room had been suddenly populated with cats. They were everywhere, curled or lounging on every surface, prowling between the pallets, sharpening their claws on sisal. Almost none had chosen the limitations of a bipedal shape, not here, not among their own kind and in their private spaces. I was considered something of an oddity by my own people for my favor of the form.

Much of Faerie disdained us for going about in the bodies of beasts. We pitied them for never having the opportunity. Spending a life locked into a single shape meant they were cutting themselves off from other perspectives.

Perhaps that was why my little fish was so intriguing. She belonged to the Divided Courts, one of their static daughters, and yet she had spent a long period looking through other eyes, even if it had not been by choice, and not been suited to her desires.

And none of that mattered right now, because she wasn't beside me. I shook my head, trying to clear away the last, clinging cobwebs of the flash that had somehow moved me from the safety of my home to the confines of my Court. Half the cats I saw were unfamiliar, and all of them seemed indolent to the point of resignation, draped over the surfaces they had claimed as their own.

A colony of cats—or a Court of Cats—is a living social organism, with its own internal structure and politics. One cat will always be superior to another, and perhaps inferior to yet a third. It's a more fluid structure than the Divided Courts tend to adhere to, but its very fluidity made the scene around me a strange one. Some opportunistic kit should have been looking for a better sleeping spot, or trying to reintegrate with a family unit that had decided they were old enough to sleep safely on their own.

The stillness was a sign that something was wrong, if not as clear a sign as my presence was.

I have been San Francisco's King of Dreaming Cats since the late 1800s, when I took the crown from the former Queen, who had wearied of its weight and sought to move inland in pursuit of a quieter life. I don't know what became of Cornelia after her relocation; I received a few postcards informing me that she was thinking of settling in Highmountain, where there were few Cait Sidhe in general, and no royal cats had yet chosen to stake their claim. I've always assumed she set herself down there, establishing a new kingdom among the airy mountains, and found herself as content as she was ever going to be anywhere.

It took me well over a century to find myself a probable heir. Royal cats are rare at the best of times, and the centuries since Maeve's disappearance have not been the best of times for the shapeshifting lines among the fae. Our children vanish without explanation; our animal kin find themselves hunted and worse, leaving us without the ability to conceal ourselves among them. When one among my subjects sired a son, a boy who already showed the sparks of power that would one day make him a Prince, and perhaps even a King, I had seen my eventual freedom in the kit's still-clouded eyes.

Perhaps it was unwise of me to allow Samson and Kamini to remain with their child when they brought him to me, but I had been very weary in those days, trapped in an endless maze of responsibilities and rules, and I had remembered my own kittenhood all too well. Children should be raised with love whenever possible. I could have taken Raj from his parents, raised him as my own son and not my nephew, and I would have loved him as well as any kitten had ever been loved, but his mother's affection for him had been evident and unfeigned, and I had been unwilling to steal him from her side.

That choice brought me a boy, and eventually a betrayer, when Samson thought to put his son in power sooner than the normal march of time allowed. But Kamini was long dead by then, done in by Oleander's cruel machinations, and while I had always loved the boy, his father had seen him as a tool rather than a child. In the bloody clash for the Court, Raj had chosen me, and still stood as my heir when his father stopped his dancing.

In the days since then, I had presented my suit to Sir October Daye of the Court of Shadowed Hills, and she had accepted it, showing the flagrant lack of common sense for which she was perhaps best renowned, agreeing to become my wife and tie her dancing to my own. We had faced many dangers and overcome them all, some through luck, some through skill, most through my lady's occasionally heart-stopping ability to stand up again after suffering an injury that should have left her for the night-haunts.

And in the midst of all those changes, other adjustments had been required. Samson had been able to raise his rebellion in part because his claim that my attention was split between the Court and my lady had contained a grain of truth, and a King must put his people first. When it became clear that I could no longer do that, I had gone to Raj and asked him if he was ready to carry the crown.

He was not, nor had I expected him to be, but he was eager to help my happiness in whatever way he might, and had agreed readily enough when I proposed going to my old friend, Jolgeir, King of Whispering Cats, to ask if he might be willing to grant us the loan of his second-born daughter. Ginevra had been born a changeling, like my lady, and had grown to her adulthood in that happily balanced state, beloved of both her parents, powerful enough to change her form, but not much else.

A meeting with my October had changed that—had changed everything, for all of us. For when Ginevra had requested to be made fully fae, the removal of her mortal blood had revealed her to have the strength necessary to stand as a royal cat. She would one day be able to take her father's place, when the time came for him to stand aside, and thus his freedom was assured.

But my time to release the crown would come well before his, and so Ginevra had traveled down the coast to stand Regent for Raj, allowing me to step down in all but name. For the better part of two years,

I had been living with October and our small, eternally evolving family, and had barely stepped inside the Court of Cats.

For me to be here was an aberration. For me to be here and none to make comment on it was an impossibility.

And for me to be here now, alone, when I had been with October only moments before . . .

That was an offense. Someone was going to suffer, just as soon as I could figure out what had happened.

I approached the nearest platform, where several cats were curled in a heap of multicolored fur and unending indolence. It is not a crime to wake a sleeping cat. It should be. The slumber of cats is a sacred thing, worthy of respect, and even in my anger, I winced as I drove my hand into the pile and scruffed the first neck I found, dragging a drowsing, one-eyed tabby to the top. I gave him a small shake. He opened his remaining eye and blinked at me quizzically, hanging heavy in my hand.

"Your King requires your attendance," I informed him, and let go, allowing him to drop back into the pile.

Slowly, he stood and stretched, with all the casual dismissiveness he could muster. Then he leapt to the ground, pushed himself up with his front paws, and stood a second time, rising in a man's array, the smell of dust and squash blossoms accompanying his transformation.

"Sire," he said, bowing slightly at the waist.

From one among the Divided Courts, I would have taken the shallowness of his bow for an insult. Under the circumstances, all I could do was scowl, and demand, "Where are we? Who are you? What's happening?"

Looking bewildered, he blinked at me, and replied, "The Court of Dreaming Cats, Sire, as I would expect you know quite well; I am Grimnir, and I wouldn't expect you to know that at all, as I have done nothing to distinguish myself in your eyes; and as to what's happening, gloriously nothing at the moment. In a few hours, it will be feeding time, and the halls will descend into the frenzy."

I frowned, eyeing him. In my experience—which is quite extensive, where the Cait Sidhe are concerned—the one-eyed toms are the most aggressive about hunting their own prey, continuing to fend for themselves even when injury or illness makes it unwise in the extreme. Yet this man spoke of being fed like he was a pampered housecat, and seemed to see no strangeness in it.

Something was very wrong. "Is it not strange to see me so?" I asked.

His bewilderment deepened. "Why would it be strange to see a King within his Court? We may be the last Court of Cats in all Faerie, but still we know the ways of things."

"I . . . see. You may return to your bed, and be glad of it, for I am done with you." I turned away, unable to shake the feeling that the world had shifted several feet to the left, and was stubbornly refusing to return to true.

The next step, naturally, would be to attempt to leave. I walked toward a corner where the shadows gathered thickly, reaching into them with the part of my magic that always knew how to access the Roads, and they parted when I pulled against them, allowing me to step into the comforting dark.

The Shadow Roads were a gift from Oberon to the Cait Sidhe. We have always been able to access them—good luck to anyone seeking to keep a cat out of a place where it has reason to pass—but they weren't always ours to keep and care for. Since they passed into our keeping, their anchors depend on us. The more we use them, the more stable they remain, and they connect all of the Summerlands and mortal world in one long, glorious passage.

We call them "roads" out of habit and in description of their function, but really, passage through the shadows is more like running into a vast, dark field from which any point in the world can be accessed, if only you know how to feel your way through the space you occupy. There are no routes nor passages; you run in infinite space, listening to the world around you, letting it choose the direction, letting it tell you when the time has come to drop back into the light.

Running the shadows is an art and a gift, and I have been practicing it since I was a kit.

It was difficult for me once, when I was much younger. The air is thin in the shadows, and to those who aren't feline born, it seems entirely absent; our passengers regularly choke and gasp during the passage, unable to catch their breath. It can be thus for kittens as well. There was a time when my own breath sought to stop, but now, as I stepped into the dark, I felt only as if I were going home.

The shadows around the Court were a strange, unusually dense tangle, folded over and over on top of themselves, until I nearly lost my way several times. A weaker cat might not have been able to navigate it at all. I certainly wouldn't have been able to transport a passenger, not even my October, who by this time had been so often in the shadows that they almost recognized her right to passage. I fought my way through, and by the time I passed into more settled territory, I was bristling and uneasy, my every nerve alert to coming danger. I had already known something was terribly wrong—how else to explain my sudden relocation?—but now it seemed that whatever had gone awry was even greater than I would have guessed. For something to disturb the *shadows* . . .

I tried to put the thought aside and ran faster toward the home where I dwelt with my beloved.

The route was familiar: when I arrived at what should have been my destination, the shadows shifted around me, and I stepped back into the bedroom I had left only a few minutes before.

At least, I stepped into the physical shell of the bedroom. There were no wards. While October had long since adjusted the house wards to accommodate my comings and goings, as well as those of Raj and Ginevra, I should have *felt* them as they considered whether to allow my passage. Wards are spells intended to function semi-autonomously. As they're built up over time, they develop personalities, almost, attitudes and quirks entirely their own. October's wards were wary and warm, like October herself; they knew me and welcomed me as a member of their family.

And they were gone. There were no echoes of magic in this place, nor of our life together. The room was empty save for dust and cobwebs, with no sign that anyone had lived here in years. The light through the window was glaringly bright in the absence of October's favored black-out curtains, illuminating the dust motes dancing in every sunbeam. I moved toward it and looked out onto the street below.

That, at least, looked relatively normal, although the garden was filled with dead, neglected plants in place of May's thriving flowers and herbs, and October's car was absent from the drive. I took a step back, looking uneasily around, and moved to open the bedroom door before I dropped to all fours.

Better to investigate this place in feline form, in which my senses were sharper and my presence less likely to attract attention, if I somehow caught the eye of our nosy mortal neighbors. Prying into the affairs of those around you has never been a purely fae pursuit, and humans are well skilled in observation and gossip.

The hall was dusty, and there were no signs that anyone had been here in years upon years. I prowled with my ears flat and my tail bushed out to more than twice its normal size, seeking some sign—any sign—that I had ever been here before, or that my lady had existed at all.

Neither of those things presented themselves. The front and back doors were both closed. I considered, for a moment, returning to bi-pedal form and unlocking them, only to dismiss it as a poor idea. The neighbors would surely see and notice if I did something so blatant. Instead, I stepped into the shadows and emerged, still feline, from beneath one of the bushes in the yard.

Here, too, there was no sign of habitation, or that the garden had ever been tended. I was about to turn away and go looking for some-one who could tell me what was happening when I heard one of the only sounds a King of Cats is incapable of ignoring.

A cat, meowing in distress.

Quickly, I circled the house to the front door, where two elderly colorpoint cats sat on the step, their faces turned toward the door it-self, yowling their unhappiness to the air.

"Cagney! Lacey!" I called, in the half-spoken, half-understood lan-guage of cats, which fae and mortal felines share. They turned to me as I bounded toward them, and for a moment, the three of us moved as one organism, rubbing cheeks against bodies, twining tails together as we stepped lightly around each other.

"Mother!" wailed Cagney.

"Mother is *gone*," added Lacey.

I stepped back, and they watched me go, their matching blue eyes bright with fear and heavy with resignation. "What do you mean, *gone*?" I asked.

The sisters were mortal cats, adopted by October from an animal shelter shortly after her return from the pond, when she had still be-lieved me to be an enemy. That she had taken cats into her home even when she knew they might spy for a man she mistrusted was one of countless small things that had endeared her to me. Being mortal, they were somewhat less astute than their Cait Sidhe cousins, and not al-ways equipped to understand complicated concepts. What they called "gone" could just as easily mean "visiting the Luidaeg" or "at the gro-cery store."

Although I was direly afraid they meant neither of those things.

"Gone," repeated Lacey. "We slept in our bed—"

"Safe, warm, good."

"—and then we were outside, alone, and all trace of Mother was gone. We've gone around the whole house, and she's not here. Who will feed us? Who will pet us?" In a moment of rare complex thought, Lacey looked at me and asked, "Who will pet you?"

"October," I said. "Because I will find her. I refuse to allow her to be taken from me by whatever force this is. Until I can do that, I will take you to the Court of Cats, where you'll be safe and warm. None of my subjects will harm you, not unless you provoke them."

They exchanged a look. They were soft, domestic housecats, used to a pampered existence inside a private home. They weren't equipped to survive outside. And still they hesitated to consider my offer.

I didn't attempt to hurry them along, sitting down and beginning to groom my paw as I waited. Every nerve I had was screaming for me to continue my search, but my little fish would never forgive me if I left her cats to fend for themselves, and no one has ever successfully compelled a cat to make their mind up before they were prepared to do so.

Finally, the sisters looked back to me. "We will go," said Cagney.

"It is appreciated," I said, and looked around for signs of watching humans before I stood on two legs and stooped toward them. They leapt into my arms, nestling against my chest, Lacey already purring. "Hold your breath," I advised, and stepped into the shadows, holding them close.

I could feel their hearts beating fast as we ran along the Shadow Roads, until I emerged into the strangely soporific Court of Cats. I set them down, and called, "Let it be known that these cats are here under my protection, and any who troubles them does so at the risk of offending your King."

I didn't wait for a response, instead stepping back into the shadows to resume my search.

The panic that had taken root inside me the moment I found myself away from home was beginning to blossom and grow, putting out thorny branches that wrapped tight around my heart until I feared I might be strangled by them. I could die of terror, if it was given sufficient time to bloom. It had more than fertile soil on which to feed.

My wife—my pregnant wife, and there was a phrase that came draped in a terror entirely its own, one October bore no responsibility for but would have to navigate the length of—was missing. Our home was abandoned, our possessions vanished, our housemates as absent as October herself. My Court was strange, transformed in some way I didn't yet fully understand but would have to face soon enough, once I knew where my lady was.

Once I could breathe again.

When October needed aid, she went to one of two places to begin, and of late, had gone almost exclusively to the same one. So I turned my steps in that direction, and ran until the road told me I was near my destination. I slipped from the shadows into the mortal neighborhood where the Luidaeg kept the entrance to her home, and froze.

For as long as I had known her, the Luidaeg had kept her apartment anchored in the same mortal apartment building. For a creature as mercurial as she, her dislike of change was well established and broad. The neighborhood had molded itself to her presence. For all that it was in a rougher part of the city, it was perfectly safe, with fewer crimes and less public misery than similar areas. The humans living there were happy and healthy to a much greater degree than their kin who lived elsewhere. The domiciles looked like hovels from the outside, but I had never known a vacancy to last more than a few days.

Perhaps that was another thing about to change, for the alley I emerged into looked like any other where it would be considered unsafe for someone to walk alone by night, or even during the day. Trash was piled against the walls, some of the bags torn open to allow their contents to leak out onto the streets, and the air smelled of stale urine and decay. The buildings were crumbling in earnest, not only in the most superficial of appearances, and several of the windows I could see were broken.

Cautiously, I approached the door that had always led to the sea witch, pausing only to drape myself in the thinnest of human disguises. I knocked, and the crying of a child answered. I knocked again.

This time, the door opened, a mortal woman in a housedress and slippers glaring at me from under the tangled fringe of her hair. "Whatever you're selling, we don't want it," she snapped. "Go back to the Castro with your own kind."

Then she slammed the door, and I was alone.

My family was missing. The sea witch was missing. Everything was wrong.

I stiffened my spine, breathing through my nose until the urge to weep passed me by.

THREE

IF THE SEA WITCH was missing, I would need to locate my lady on my own. Perhaps Arden would know where October was. If something had happened to scatter us across the kingdom, surely October would have gone to the Queen who controlled her Court, seeking reassurance and alliance in my absence. There was a time when I would have expected her to seek her liege, Sylvester, but he was no longer the ally he had once been, having chosen his wife and her strange loathing of October over his obligation to one of his own sworn vassals.

The Divided Courts are a confusing place indeed. I was to set my crown aside because I could never have chosen a vassal over my lady: in that, Sylvester and I were aligned. But his insistence on holding his position when he knew he would always place Luna above those who put their lives in his hands was inexplicable to me. Almost as inexplicable, the fact that Queen Windermere allowed it.

Still, Arden was a reasonable enough woman, and her affection for October was well established, if often leavened with frustration—a mixture I understood quite well where my lady was concerned. I threw myself back into the shadows and raced for Muir Woods, forcing myself to keep moving even as my lungs began to ache and my legs began to protest the distances I had already traveled on this evening, the blood I had already shed. The battle with Titania felt very distant now, the sort of thing that had happened to another man in another lifetime. But in truth it had only been a few hours, and my body marked the time, even if my heart could not.

The mortal side of Muir Woods was open when I arrived, stepping out of the shadows in a far corner of the parking lot. Most of the spaces were full; none of the cars I saw were October's. I shook the shards of my brief, irrational hope away and walked toward the park entrance, where a human ticket-taker waited to admit me.

A quick expenditure of magic later, and he believed a slip of paper I had picked up from the gutter during my approach was a valid access pass. I walked on, not sparing any attention for the human tourists who had come to gawk at the natural wonders of the state around them. They had their lives; I had mine. There was no reason for us to intersect, not in this moment.

Muir Woods looked much as it always did, and that normalcy was like a balm for my frazzled nerves as I followed the pathway through the trees to the curving hillside walk that would allow me access to Arden's knowe. It took me three passes to find the trail worn into the briars, the roots of towering redwoods forming a natural staircase up. I wrapped a don't-look-here spell around myself and began the climb, safely sheltered from the eyes of any watching humans.

The air brightened and deepened around me, turning fresher and cleaner than anything remaining in the mortal world, and I breathed deeply as I stepped off the root stairway onto the level ground above.

And then I froze. The tree that should have housed the entrance to Arden's knowe was gone, leaving a rotten stump where it should have been. I approached slowly, staring at the moss-patched, spongy wood. The break was neither recent nor clean. The remains of the tree were still there, mounded over with growth and reclaimed by the forest, but from the appearance of everything around it, it had fallen decades before. Maybe as long ago as the Earthquake.

For October to disappear was a personal tragedy but well within the realm of the possible. For the Luidaeg to go missing at the same time was suspicious, and terrifying. For the Queen in the Mists and her entire knowe to vanish was something else altogether.

The world was broken. October was gone, everything was out of order, and none of this was ever going to make sense.

My legs were abruptly too weak to hold me up any longer. I shuffled to the nearest log and sat, my knees giving out halfway through the motion. Shock was very clearly setting in.

There were so many other places I could go looking, but what was the point? I had already visited the most likely and found them deserted. October would never have done this to me on purpose; whatever had happened, it must be outside her control, huge and terrible and inescapable. I put my hands over my face and my elbows on my knees, trying to concentrate on breathing through the panic. On anything other than the looming feeling that the sky was about to fall, and everything I knew and loved was going to be ripped away.

Or already had been. I was starting to remember more about the moments right before the light. Specifically, I remembered the smell of roses. Roses have always been a common element of magic, more common than most others. I'm not my little fish, to pick a person's magic apart and name the precise origins of its every aspect; tell her someone's magic smells of apples and she can tell you what type of apple, where it was grown, and whether it comes fresh from the tree or has been doctored in some way. Her line is uniquely sensitive to the markers of another's magic.

I can't do what she can do, but I can remember the smell of roses. October's mother smelled of roses, as did her sister. As did Evening, may she sleep forever in the shadows.

As did Titania.

That thought was like a key unlocking everything else. I sat suddenly upright, staring into nothingness as I remembered October screaming, and Titania's appearance in the doorway.

"*I can't hurt you,*" she had said. "*But I can make you someone else's problem.*"

And after that, to me: "*I don't think there's a place for you in what I'm doing.*"

That was when everything had gone red, then white, and I had been alone in the Court of Cats, disoriented, with no idea how I'd come to be there.

I stood. So this was Titania's doing, then. I felt a little foolish at having taken so long to put it together, but in my defense, I had been very deeply in shock, and could be forgiven for a little panic when faced with the First among us all.

The Luidaeg was missing, and with her, one presumed, Oberon, as the man had been in her keeping and company since his return. I wasn't sure how much help he would have been anyway: he'd shown very little inclination to be anything more than a silent presence, making things awkward without making them better. I had always assumed that Oberon's return, should I live to see it, would somehow improve Faerie, or at least try. Instead, what we had was an absent father figure who just happened to be in the room.

Perhaps the answer was in finding another among the Firstborn. They couldn't match Titania for power, but they might be able to see the traceries of her machinations. Whatever this was, they were the ones who stood a chance at unraveling it.

Still seated, I began running down a silent count of the Firstborn I knew, and who claimed them. There was the Luidaeg, of course, famously a daughter of Maeve and already eliminated through sheer virtue of her absence. For all that I knew, Hirsent still haunted the hills of Armorica, terrorizing the unwary and threatening the unwise. She wouldn't be pleased to see me again, and anyway, she was a daughter of Maeve as well.

Two of the daughters of Titania I knew of were entirely inaccessible to me, Eira because she was elf-shot and asleep on a road I could not reach, not even through my shadows, and Acacia because she dwelt in the skerry created by her late husband, separate from the Summerlands and all but exiled for most purposes.

Amphitrite, on the other hand . . .

Amphitrite was a daughter of Titania, named and claimed and honored as such, and she had danced at my wedding and given us a good and generous gift. She was well inclined toward me, or at least toward my lady, and might be able to tell me what was wrong, that I might set it right. I stood, the need to speak with her burning in my breast, and turned a slow circle as I recovered my bearings.

Muir Woods was originally chosen to serve as the royal seat of the Mists for many reasons, not least of which is its proximity to the water. Only three miles separate the state park from Muir Beach, which is popular with human tourists and fae alike. It's not the best place for meeting with Merrow or Selkies, as privacy can be difficult to come by. It is, however, home to several lovely, abrupt drop-offs, land giving way to water in gloriously sheer cliffsides.

I needed one of those now. I finished my turn and broke into a run, heading as swiftly as I could into the surrounding forest. As I ran, I shifted forms, trading bipedalism for the swiftness of four strong legs and the keenness of feline senses. When even that proved too slow for my hammering heart, I leapt into the shadows and let them carry me ever more quickly to my destination.

The next time I emerged from the shadows, it was onto the high overlook from which visitors might view great swaths of the Pacific Coast in a glance. Luck was with me: while the beach far below was spattered with people, the overlook was empty upon my arrival, none of the current visitors having chosen the dizzying heights and often strong winds of the overlook itself. I still stepped as far back from the edge as I could before shifting into two-legged form. Once that was done, I cast a notice-me-not around myself. The last thing I needed now was to accidentally activate the protective instincts of nearby humans.

While it was more than possible to fall from the overlook, it had been built with the expectation of curious children and careless tourists, and was thus set some distance back from the actual end of the coastal cliffs. I climbed up onto the overlook rail, the salt-tinted air slapping at my face and my hair blowing wild in the Pacific wind as I stepped down on the other side. The ground there was rocky and uneven, not intended for passage, barred to casual wanderers by the sternly-worded signs of the local park service.

Those signs were intended for humans, not for me. I ignored them as I picked my way closer and closer to the sea, choosing each step with absolute care, until I was standing where the land dropped away, replaced by the endless frothing expanse of the sea. It was so far away. It seemed as if anyone who fell from here would fall forever.

I took a deep breath. What I intended to do next was more a page from my lady's playbook than my own, and shared more of her foolish bravery than my own normally measured caution. Had I been less afraid for her, I would never even have been able to consider it.

But Amphitrite was a daughter of Titania. She was Firstborn, and the Luidaeg trusted her, which meant she was unlikely to have lied to me, or to October, without good cause.

And at our wedding, she had promised us that neither we nor any of our children would ever need to fear death by water.

The drop between me and the sea only seemed to grow greater the longer I hesitated. This wasn't going to kill me. It was, however, going to hurt: of that I had no doubt.

I could, I supposed, descend the more ordinary way and go wading, hoping Amphitrite was close enough that I would catch her attention when I inevitably began to drown. But the Firstborn I have known have always appreciated grand gestures, and my striking the water would doubtless activate whatever magic she had used to grant us her protection, calling her to my location. It was still a risk, but a calculated one, which would hopefully end in my reunion with the First among the Merrow, and not with my bones at the bottom of the sea.

And the longer I stood here trying to convince myself, the farther away Titania could be whisking my wife and unborn child. I tensed, closing my eyes against the view.

Cats, it is said, always land on our feet, which was part of the reason I leapt as a man, when the instinct to twist all four of my limbs downward to hit at the same time would be easier to fight. A Selkie I loved once, a very long time past, told me that the safest way for a man to strike the water is stiff and straight as a board, with toes pointed downward and arms flat against his sides. "Be an arrow," he'd said, laughing at my confusion. "Strike the water like a blade."

"Easy for you to say; when you jump in the water, you're a seal," I'd countered, and we had gone on in joy, under starlight, with no more thought of the fathoms below.

Well, now, the fathoms below were all that I could think of. "Amphitrite, may you be as honest as your sister," I muttered, and leapt before my mind could catch up with my body and interfere with the command.

I dropped like a stone, fighting to arrange myself as I had been instructed when every instinct I possessed told me to flail and fight, to search for purchase in the air. The wind whipped by so fast it stung my skin, all but guaranteeing my introduction to the saltwater waves would hurt even more than I had expected it to.

Such are the actions of a desperate man. I pulled in as much air as my lungs would hold, far too aware that it might be knocked out of me upon impact, and held myself like the arrow I had once been instructed to be.

Still rigid, I hit the water, the force of my impact driving me deep below the surface. My concerns about air were, it seemed, unfounded, as consciousness left me first, slapped away by the sensation of slamming into something akin to granite. From a great enough height, even water may turn into a weapon.

Insensate, I drifted. Up or down, I do not know. For how long, I do not know. Whether I broke any essential pieces of my body when I fell, I do not know. These are the very small mercies afforded to me by that first day, that first succession of panicked, painful hours.

When I woke, it was with the taste of blood and seawater lingering in my mouth, and with something hard and cold beneath me, and white light above, filtered through some pinkish substance. I blinked, several times, trying to get my eyes to adjust, and slowly the fixture above me became clear as some sort of dangling assortment of lights caught inside large conch shells, their translucent sides filtering it.

"Oh, good, the suicidal son of a chowder head is awake," drawled a bored, only half-familiar voice. "I suppose I can let the rest of you go back to screaming without worrying about what that's going to do for his recovery."

The speaker snapped their fingers as I was still trying to place why they sounded so familiar, and suddenly people were yelling. More familiar people, in both the sense of number and in my degree of familiarity.

"—out of here," snarled Dianda. "This has to be Titania! No one else could do something this large!"

"You're remarkably accepting of the idea that a Queen of Faerie is going out of her way to ruin our lives," said Patrick, his voice much more tightly controlled.

"Who else could cut us off completely?" demanded Dianda. "Who else could split us so summarily from our family?"

"Not just yours," said the first voice. "Now stop yelling before I shut you up again. And before you get any funny ideas about telling me, again, that I'm a guest in your knowe, allow me to remind you that you're all guests in my ocean." The voice got closer as it went on, until a shadow fell across me. "Hello, cat."

I turned my head to face the speaker, relieved when the motion didn't hurt. I had felt no pain since waking, but my brief memory of impact left me certain that I should be in incredible amounts of it, suffering every time I took a breath.

The woman who loomed over me smiled thinly, not offering her hand. "Glad to see you're back in the land of the living. You know, when I gave you a fancy wedding gift, it wasn't with the intention of you taking it for a test spin the first chance you get. A more polite response would have been to appreciate the gesture and try to avoid violent death, not to fling yourself off of a cliff."

"My most sincere apologies, my lady Captain," I said. "But I saw no other means of reaching you, and had dire need, which your companions seem in some part to understand."

Amphitrite—better known as Captain Pete—sighed. "Yeah," she said. "I get that."

The Firstborn seem to fall into one of two camps: either they do their best to blend in with the people around them, becoming unremarkable and unassuming, until they can pass through crowds unnoticed, or they stand up bright and blazing, like memorials to the Faerie that once was. Pete fell into the second category. She was tall and statuesque, with the build of a woman born to sail the open seas and wrestle sharks for her supper. Her thighs were monuments to the sailor's art, and her arms were so thick with muscle that I had no doubt she could have hoisted me over her head, had she cared to. Her skin was the eerie bone-white of a great white shark's belly, so pale it gleamed, and streaked with lines of tiny, glittering scales. Gleaming opal refractions filled her long black hair, which fell almost to her waist in heavy, easy curls. She was lovely, of course, but no one could ever have mistaken her for human, or for one of her own descendants.

Expression impassive, she watched as I pushed myself up onto my elbows, levering myself into a sitting position. I didn't hurt, and yet everything felt slightly numb, as if I had spent too much time submerged in icy water. Which perhaps I had. "Death by water" and "death by hypothermia" are not the same thing, after all.

"Why did you toss yourself off a cliff like so much chum?" asked Amphitrite. "Assume I know nothing, and don't worry too much about telling me things I've already heard. I want honest answers more than I want easy ones."

I took a deep breath. In the moment, honesty seemed like something very large to ask of me. "I was home," I said. "With my October, and our family around us. We had—"

"Was Simon there?" interrupted Dianda.

I kept my eyes on Amphitrite, who looked annoyed by the interjection, and answered, "No. We left him at Shadowed Hills. Sylvester indicated that August was on her way to bring him back to Saltmist."

"She left to fetch him after we received word that the fight was done, and he had been injured but healed by October's intervention," said Patrick, his voice still tightly controlled. I recognized the sound of a man who was struggling to keep himself from snapping. I heard it every time I spoke. "Before either of them could return, the—" Amphitrite shot him a warning look. He stopped mid-sentence.

She turned her attention back to me. "Continue."

I swallowed. "We had concluded our business at Shadowed Hills, and returned home to handle some more personal business of our own. At the time of our departure, everything seemed to be well. We had begun the process of settling in for the evening when October began to scream as if she were in extreme pain. I could see no source of her suffering. The rest of our household rushed to aid her, and we were gathered together when . . ." I slowed.

My memory was still fuzzy on this point, but the more I thought on it, the more I was sure of what I'd seen. I swallowed and continued. "When Titania appeared in the doorway. She said she knew 'the roads through riddle and restriction' and that while she couldn't hurt October, she could make her someone else's problem. Then she told me I had no place in her plan. Everything went red, and then white, and then I found myself alone in the Court of Cats, which was—wrong."

"Wrong how?" asked Amphitrite.

I shrugged helplessly. I like to think myself a reasonably articulate man, but the wrongness of the Court was so subtle and all-pervasive that its exact details yet escaped me. I focused instead on the parts I *could* identify: "It seemed seated in a place we haven't used extensively for years, and the cats were indolent at best, unsurprised by my arrival, which should have stunned them, given recent days. It was almost as if they had all . . . given up. And whatever it was, it was so expansive that none thought to speak of it, for any royal cat would know the situation, most of all their King."

I took a deep breath. "I left the Court for my home, thinking to reunite with October, but found an empty house instead, with no signs that we had ever dwelt there."

"What about the wards?" asked Patrick, tone unusually sharp.

"Those were gone as well," I said. "No magic remained, nothing of our time there, of our lives. I would have thought myself in the wrong place, had I not known that house so very well—and had I not found October's cats outside in the garden, locked out and confused. Their presence proves we lived there."

"Where are they now?" asked Amphitrite.

"I took them to the Court of Cats for their own safety before I continued my search," I said. "We welcome mortal cats who have need of the shelter we can offer them. It seems the very least that we can do for our smaller cousins."

"Good," said Amphitrite.

It warmed me, that she should care so well for cats she didn't know. The Firstborn are capable of compassion. I've seen it many times, most often from the Luidaeg, but from others as well. Some of them remember that the world moves more quickly than they do, and that they must be kind to those who are more temporary than they are.

"After that, I thought that October might have gone seeking help, so I went to the sea witch," I said. "Is she here?"

"My sister is yet banned from these waters," said Amphitrite—not without genuine regret in her tone. "She is not here."

"She's not where I normally find her, either. The city seems to have closed itself around the space she left behind. I'd say it was like the healing of a wound, but her absence seems more like an injury than her presence ever did."

"So you'd say it was like she never existed?"

Amphitrite's voice was sharp enough that it made me pause before I nodded, slowly.

"Yes. I would. I was dismayed by her absence, and proceeded to Muir Woods, thinking to ask Arden's assistance. October does tend to cling to the hierarchy of the Divided Courts when under pressure, and if she were looking for me, her queen would be a reasonable destination.

But I found the same in Muir Woods as I had in the city, and at the house. The entrance to the knowe was absent, and no signs of magic lingered. I don't understand. How is this even possible?"

"Mom," said Amphitrite, with utter disgust. "How does this end in your diving to your death?"

"I was . . . I *am* somewhat concerned by the disappearance of my wife, for reasons I prefer not to discuss at this time," I said. "We were in the middle of a rather sensitive conversation, which I know she would never have left voluntarily, and while I am normally willing to allow her sufficient autonomy that I don't panic the moment she leaves my sight, these are special circumstances."

"We understand," said Dianda.

"I remembered your very generous wedding gift, milady," I said, careful to keep my eyes on Amphitrite. "Truly, it was kind beyond all measure. I thought the counsel of one among the First might serve me better than any other, and because of that gift, I thought I might be able to catch your attention more quickly than I could complete a quest for one of your siblings."

"And so over the cliff you went," said Amphitrite. She sighed, pinching the bridge of her nose. "I sort of expected that one of you would jump off a bridge when I decided that was a better gift than a dinette set, but I really thought it was going to be Toby. If she's rubbing off on you, I'm going to be deeply irritated with you both."

The thought of irritating one of the Firstborn wasn't as terrifying as it should have been, considering everything else that was happening. I had managed to wind up in the path of Titania's anger, and that was worse than anything I could imagine Amphitrite throwing in my direction.

"As you say," I said, wearily.

"Well, you were looking for me, and now you've got me," she said, letting her hands fall to her sides. "I'd ask you what you were going to give me in exchange for answers, but since you've already plummeted to your certain death just so I'd pay attention to you, I guess I can answer a few questions."

"She showed up in the knowe dragging you by the arm and shouting about how her sister was going to kill her if she let you die," said Dianda. "It took our healers the better part of three hours to put you back together. Whatever it is you actually did, I would recommend not doing it again."

"I had no intention of it," I said, and finally stood, turning toward my hosts.

Patrick looked about as tense as I felt. His eyes were wild and his hair was disheveled, sticking out in all directions. Dianda was seated next to him on a rolling chair that had clearly been designed for her use; while her fins spilled over the bottom, they didn't dangle so close to the wheels as to be in any danger. She looked less tense and more like she was restraining her temper through sheer force of will. I had never seen her quite so visibly furious.

"Good," she said, voice gone flat. "We have other things to worry about right now."

"Based on how long it would have taken you to accomplish all the things you've described, I'm going to say that all this happened at the same time," said Amphitrite. "I was already on my way to Saltmist when you hit the water, which is why I was close enough to retrieve you before permanent damage could be done."

"Why?" I asked, only half-warily.

"Because right about when you were ripped from your home and lost track of your wife, this section of the Undersea was sealed off from the land kingdoms," she said flatly, snapping my attention back to her. "Not just that, but from itself. Leucothea and Cala Siochaint screamed when they were sundered from the rest of the Undersea, as did the Sunlit Seas. From what I can tell, the Undersea regions adjacent to the Mists, Silences, and the Golden Shore have all been severed from the greater Undersea. There's a wall between us and them. None of the channels that should allow passage to the surface are open. I can force my way through, but it hurts and exhausts me, much more than should be possible, unless . . ."

"Unless the line was drawn by your mother."

Amphitrite nodded. "If I'd been in any other part of the Undersea when the wall came down, I wouldn't have been able to reach you. You still wouldn't have drowned. But with none able to reach you, your injuries would have gone untreated, and there are lots of ways to die at sea."

She sounded unnervingly matter-of-fact about that, like she was telling me something I should have known all along. I managed, barely, not to shudder.

"As all this was happening, the palace shook in its foundations, I assume because walling us off from the rest of the Summerlands sent a shockwave through the duchy, and all the Roane and Selkies who should have been up on shore appeared in the air-breathing portions of my knowe," said Dianda.

I straightened. "All of them?"

"Yes, all of them."

"Gillian." October's first child had been born a thin-blooded changeling, more mortal than fae, and had been stripped of her Dóchas Sidhe heritage to save her life after she'd been elf-shot by her own cousin. That would have been the end of her involvement with Faerie, had she not been abducted for use as a pawn against her mother, and been elf-shot a second time, this time without the convenient presence of fae blood that could be manipulated to clear the venom from her veins.

Instead, she had been granted a precious Selkie skin and transformed for the sake of her own survival, a transformation that had become complete when she allowed herself to be bound to the skin as one of the reborn Roane. She was part of Faerie now, and had begun carefully considering the nature of her relationship with her birth mother: she'd even come to attend our wedding. I hadn't seen her since.

Dianda nodded. "She's in the dining hall with the rest of the seal-shifters. She doesn't know anything about October being missing, or if she does, she's surprisingly good at not letting on."

I shook my head. "There's no sense in worrying her. October is terrifyingly resilient. I'm sure she's fine."

"And I'm sure you're lying," said Dianda. "You're not the only one who's missing family. Simon and August were both topside when the walls came down, and if they're trying to get to us, it's not working. We tried to send a group up to find them. No luck."

I stared for a moment, then looked back to Amphitrite. "Am I *trapped* here?" I asked.

"The fact that you were able to get out of the Court of Cats means you probably aren't, although the passage may be difficult for you," said Amphitrite. "Mother always did think poorly of the fae with more animal attributes, your own line included. She considered you little more than performing beasts that could be trotted out to do tricks when necessary, but were better left ignored."

"Meaning she would have sealed the Shadow Roads if she'd cared enough about the Cait Sidhe to remember what we're capable of," I said, in grim conclusion.

Amphitrite nodded. "You aren't worth her notice, and so she didn't notice you."

"The Shadow Roads maintain their integrity through use," I said. "When neglected, they become more difficult to travel. I'm not sure why anyone would have pushed them this far down beneath the sea. I may not be able to access them from here."

"Well, you're gonna have to try," said Dianda. "Unless you want to be a widower locked in with the angriest widow you're ever likely to see."

"Don't discount my anger in this situation," said Patrick. "I'm going to kill her."

"You can't kill Titania," said Amphitrite, reasonably enough. "She's our First. She's more than our First. She's the *First* of the First. I'm pretty sure killing her is actually impossible."

"I'm innovative," said Patrick.

He sounded so calm as he said that that for a moment, I truly believed he could do what he was threatening. If Titania kept us away from the people we loved, he was going to find a way to kill the Queen of Faerie, and he wasn't going to be sorry about it, not in the slightest. He was protecting his family. I could respect that.

"A moment, please," I said, and turned my back on the group, focusing my attention on the place where shadows gathered at the very base of the wall. They were thin and questionable, battered on all sides by the warm light that flowed from the body of the room, but I could feel them, if I reached. I took a deep breath, straining to connect to the shadows firmly enough to make them open for me.

They twitched, and I stepped back, breaking the connection.

"I'll need better darkness," I said. "What's here is very weak."

"We live at the bottom of the sea," said Dianda. "We have the deepest darkness you've ever seen. We just prefer to keep it outside, since it's everywhere, and we keep things well lit inside the knowe. I can get you darkness, if that's what you want. Is the road there?"

"It is," I said. "I wouldn't want to risk running it with a passenger in tow—it's hard enough to carry October alone though the shadows in the lands above, where the roads have always been well used and remain open enough to know us well. It's going to be difficult to navigate these roads alone, much less burdened in any way."

There was a flicker of disappointment in Dianda's eyes. Patrick, who was less practiced at hiding his emotions, scowled and turned away, clearly crestfallen.

"Did you hope I could carry you both out of here?" I asked.

"What do *you* think?" asked Dianda. "You hurled yourself from a cliff rather than accept that your wife was missing. We're short a husband *and* a son *and* a daughter. There are very few things we wouldn't hope for right now. Including Titania's head on a platter."

"Peter doesn't know yet," said Patrick. "Helmi has been set to keeping him sheltered from the rest of the household, and he believes August and Simon have simply been delayed in their return from the surface. He'll be devastated when he realizes they *can't* come home. He adores August. He's fond of Simon, but it's going to be years before he accepts him as a second father. August, on the other hand, has been his sister since the wedding. And when he realizes we've also lost Dean—this is going to crush him. We need to fix it as quickly as possible."

"I think we're all agreed on that," said Amphitrite. "But the cat isn't going to kill himself trying to get us all out of here, and we're not going to figure out what Mother did by standing around and arguing about it. Tybalt, have you eaten?"

"Not recently," I admitted. "I've had other things on my mind."

"Understandable. And now you're going to eat."

I turned to scowl at her. "I'm sorry, who are you to order me about? I am a King of Cats. I haven't set my crown aside yet, and until I do—"

"Until you do, you're still a king, and even after you do, you'll still be a royal cat, and I'll still be among the Firstborn." She smiled, slow and languid and deeply menacing. "You know, all the Firstborn have honorifics. It's a way to avoid invoking us by name. Call the sea witch, don't attract my sister's attention. Speak of the Rose of Winter, you might still be left alone."

"Yes," I said. "They call you Captain Pete."

"These days, yes, they do," she agreed. "But they used to call me less flattering things. 'The Devouring Deep' was one of my favorites. 'Mother of Sharks' was also a pretty good one. Don't think that just because I choose harmlessness now, you can afford the cost of offending me. You may be our only way out of here, and you've just been through a massive healing. You need to eat. You need to sustain your body, or you'll never make it back to October."

That was the deciding command. I couldn't help my wife, or our child, if I was dead on the Shadow Roads, and when a Cait Sidhe falls in that darkness, the night-haunts never come for our remains. I had all faith that whatever was happening, October would eventually be able to resolve it on her own, but it would be faster if I was with her.

"Fine," I said. "We eat."

"Excellent," said Amphitrite, sounding smug. "Dianda?"

"I'll order lunch," said Dianda. "And Tybalt, I'm no happier about this than you are, but I can see the sense of it. Never go into a fight already weakened."

"Is this going to be a fight?" I asked.

She smiled, thin and sharp. "If I have anything to say about it, yes, it is."

FOUR

LUNCH WAS SOMEWHAT COMPLICATED by the fact that Helmi, who was watching over Peter, generally ran the household. Dianda didn't want to pull her off her duties, and so the four of us wound up seated at a large wooden table in the kitchen while anxious servants placed platter after platter of leftovers and staples in front of us.

After the third tray of mixed cheeses, Amphitrite laughed and waved them off. "Go, go," she said. "This would feed an army, and we're a detachment at best. We'll handle ourselves from here." She picked up a short loaf of bread, pointing it at me like a sword. "There's smoked fish, cat. You should be content."

"That's a stereotype," I said. My stomach was in knots. The thought of anything heavier than toast was almost painful.

"Yes, but it has a root in truth." She put the bread down, and sighed. "My mother has never been a very reasonable woman, and she's been absent for centuries. This isn't as much of a shock as I want it to be."

"You're certain it's her, then?" asked Patrick.

Amphitrite nodded. "Tybalt saw her, Toby offended her, Father betrayed her—she has every reason in the world to be furious, and she's never cared about collateral damage. Annie's absence, though, that's the telling thing. Me being locked in the water, I have siblings who could accomplish that, if they were really making an effort. Eat, cat, or I stop talking, and you're stuck here waiting to gather your strength, not learning anything at all that might help you."

I picked up a slice of bread, hurriedly. Patrick shot me a sympathetic look and offered me a jar of fish paste, which I took before smearing it liberally over my selection.

Amphitrite nodded again, this time looking satisfied. "As I was saying, me being locked in the Undersea falls within the power limits of several of my siblings, assuming they're awake and around and mad at me, which some of them always are. We're a temperamental bunch, and those of us who've survived mostly haven't done it by being sweethearts. Annie, though . . . she's another matter. As strong as I am, she's stronger."

Dianda looked appalled. "But you're my First."

"Don't be tiresome, little mermaid. There's a reason that when the humans stole that story, they set the sea witch above the daughter of the sea. Annie's always been more versatile and more powerful than I am. If she's missing, and there's no reason to think she'd have gone willingly, then it's because something she couldn't fight against hit her. That means Mom, her mom—who's still missing as far as I know—or Dad, and Dad didn't have any reason to put himself out like that. I'd been suspicious before Tybalt told us Annie was gone. Now that I know she is, I'm not suspicious anymore. I'm certain."

"Why were you here?" I asked, and took a bite of bread. The fish paste was excellent, thick and heavily salted. It coated my tongue in a way that would have been delightful, if I'd been in any mood to allow myself to enjoy food.

"Dad," said Amphitrite. "I saw him at your wedding, but not for long, and we didn't really have time to talk the way I wanted to. He was a lot more distant than I expected him to be after so long, and I was hoping . . . I know he's here, with Annie, and she's been looking after him. I sort of hoped that if I hung out in the coastal waters for a while, he'd come down below to see me. The Duchy of Ships gets by just fine without me most of the time, but it's also good for me to spend time at home when it works, and this has been a good excuse."

"And then you heard the seas screaming and came to see what was going on?"

"And then I heard the seas screaming and tried to go to the shore to find out what had happened. I hit a wall, which repelled me, and determined that it ran all along the coast of the Mists, and all the way down the coast to the border between Golden Shore and Angels, and up to the border between Silences and Evergreen. I beat myself against it for a while, decided that wasn't going to do me any good, and looked at the local demesnes to decide which one was most likely to be involved in fuckery. I was on my way to Saltmist to ask what the fuck when I felt a geas I had placed on myself activate and realized that if I didn't hurry, someone I'd promised would never need to fear death by water was going to drown, on account of tossing himself off a cliff and knocking his fuzzy ass unconscious when he hit the surface," she said, without rancor. "So I scooped you up and brought you here, and now we've reached the present day, and we can get on with things. This has been going on long enough."

I nodded. "My apologies. I don't know how much time passed between Titania's arrival in my home and my awakening in the Court of Cats. It felt immediate."

"Let's be realistic," said Amphitrite, glancing over at Dianda, who was scowling as she assembled a sandwich. She managed to slice cheese like she was cutting throats, every motion infused with violence. "Ten minutes of forced separation from our families would have been too long. But no. A full day between the sundering and reaching the borders of the wall; two more to throw myself against it; and we've spent two days on top of that trying to get you back to the lands of the living. I hate to repeat myself, and I'm not revoking my wedding gift over a moment of oddly understandable panic, but if you ever do that again, I will personally transform you into a nudibranch. Do we understand each other?"

I couldn't answer. I was too busy staring at her, once again feeling as if the air had been knocked out of me. My slice of bread slipped from my suddenly nerveless fingers, landing fish paste–side down on the table with a splat that would have been comic under almost any other circumstances. Patrick grimaced as he leaned over to pry it up, and one of the knowe's many ubiquitous Cephali appeared with a cloth clutched in his tentacle, quickly wiping away the mess.

"Not sure whether that's understanding or shock," said Amphitrite. "Tybalt?"

I didn't answer her. I was too busy shoving myself away from the table and turning in a frantic circle, scanning the kitchen for shadows I might be able to use for my escape. There were a few patches, mostly under things, deeper than the ones in the room where I'd awoken, but still not deep enough for my liking.

"Tybalt!" repeated Amphitrite, this time with a note of sharp command in her voice. "You will stop and look at me *right now*, or you'll wish you had when I gave you the chance and the choice."

Forcing myself to grab for what threads of rationality I could find, I turned to her. "Five *days*?" I demanded. "You didn't think I might want to know that it had been *days*?"

"Since no Firstborn has ever been who can control time, I didn't think it mattered," she said. "We're moving as fast as we can, given the circumstances, and while I'm sure you want to get back to October, all we'll do by letting you kill yourself in the process is piss her off, which isn't the best idea anyone's ever had. Five days is not that big a—"

"She's *pregnant*!" I blurted.

Amphitrite stopped. ". . . ah," she said, after a pause. "That explains a few things. I'm sorry, Tybalt. This must be very difficult for you."

"None of you knew me the first time I was married," I said. "Her name was Anne, she was a human, and she died because the Divided Courts refused to help her when the birth went badly. The child died with her. October isn't Anne, and she's *unlikely* to die of anything as ordinary as childbirth, but—I can't control what frightens me."

"You have every right to be afraid," said Amphitrite. "I still need you to eat before I can allow you to attempt the Shadow Roads. You're right about them being thin this deep. I remember when my Father gave them to the Cait Sidhe. It was your use that would keep them easily accessible, when so many other of the old roads have closed or fallen into disrepair. Even the Tidal Roads are difficult to use in this modern world, and I can't currently access them at all. I think Titania remembered to seal them off, because she understood the need to eliminate the Undersea."

"Well, I don't," said Dianda hotly. "I'm a descendant of hers as much as Patrick is, and I don't understand why her perfect Faerie would involve pretending I didn't exist."

"Maeve," said Patrick. We all looked at him. He shrugged. "Oberon and Titania were both hiding in the Bay Area, and they both seemed to be things they weren't, yes? Did Oberon give any indication that he'd known where Titania was before she was unmasked?"

"No," I said. "He seemed as surprised as the rest of us." Although no one would ever match October's sheer shock over the discovery that her childhood friend had been Titania all along. For her, the loss of Stacy had been and was always going to be devastating.

"So it's not unreasonable for Titania to assume Maeve might be hiding somewhere nearby," said Patrick. "More, that she might be hiding in the local Undersea, where she would be surrounded by the strongest aspect of her own magic and shielded from the bulk of her sister's. We have illusions here in the deeps, good, strong ones, but they aren't subject to the rising and setting of the sun. They don't anchor themselves the same way."

"Seal off the Undersea, potentially eliminate the threat of the missing Queen," I said. "It makes sense."

"If you're lashing out, sure," said Amphitrite. "Mom's pulled this sort of bullshit before, just on a smaller scale. She'd make entire Courts forget their liege, or mortal villages forget what year it was. It was usually a fit of pique, and Dad would always come along at Moving Day and set things straight again."

I stared at her. "Moving Day's not for four *months*," I said. "I'm not waiting four months to have my wife back!"

"And we're not waiting that long for our husband, or our children," said Dianda. "But breaking an enchantment woven by one of the Queens isn't going to be something easy, or that we do just because we want to. This is going to take planning and effort, and first, it's going to take getting you out of here."

"Which means getting him safe passage to the Shadow Roads," said Amphitrite. "We do have the Almere . . ."

"No," said Dianda.

"They have access to the Shadow Roads, where they cut through the abyss," said Amphitrite.

"No," said Dianda again.

"I thought you wanted your husband back," said Amphitrite. "Your daughter. Your son."

"You're talking about dealing with the devils in the deep," snapped Dianda. "You really think they're going to help us?"

"You, perhaps not," said Amphitrite. "Me? The Devouring Deep? Oh, me, they'll help, even if it's only to the extent of propping a door open."

"It's dangerous."

"So is going up against Titania. So is trying to access the Shadow Roads from the bottom of the sea. So is basically everything we've been talking about doing, and everything we're about to do. A little more danger is nothing after you've already signed up for this much." Amphitrite turned to me. "What do you say, cat? You ready to face something unpleasant on the chance that it gets you home that much faster?"

"I'm willing to face Titania at the end of all this," I said. "I can handle a little unpleasantness in getting there."

"I wouldn't call the Almere 'a little unpleasantness,'" said Dianda. "More like 'slavering monsters sensible people avoid.'"

"They're my brother's kids, I can handle them." Amphitrite stood.

"Come along, then. If we're going to do this, we should get it done with. I don't even know if it's going to work."

I was so relieved to be moving, to be *doing* something, that I nearly knocked my chair over in rising and hurrying to her side. Patrick followed more sedately, and Dianda gestured for him to take control of her wheelchair, leaving her hands free as he wheeled her after us.

"This is a *terrible* idea," she said. "At least let him rest and try on his own before we go deep."

"You don't have to come," said Amphitrite. "You could stay here, in the light, if you're afraid."

Dianda stiffened like that was the worst insult she could possibly have received. "No Merrow worth their fins has ever been born or lived a coward," she said.

"No, but many have died that way," said Amphitrite. "Patrick?"

"I'm not Merrow, and I'm already on the verge of breaking down due to the disappearance of half my family," he said, in an artificially calm tone. "I'll stay here and be ready to talk to Peter if he comes looking for something to eat. Maybe I can keep him from noticing that Simon and August are still gone. We'll have to tell him soon."

"Not if we can get them back," said Dianda.

"So get them back," he said, and let her chair go.

She stood, scales melting into the fabric of a long skirt as she turned to grab the front of his shirt and yank him into a fierce kiss. He went willingly, lingering in her arms until she finally broke away and turned to Amphitrite.

"You're my First, but they're my subjects, and while we're below, you listen to me."

Amphitrite nodded. "Whatever makes you feel better."

Patrick stayed behind as Dianda started moving again, storming down the hall with me and Amphitrite by her sides. Amphitrite looked faintly amused, like this was the best possible outcome. Dianda was furious; Patrick was no longer a potential weakness in our little group; whoever these Almere were, they were presumably something we could handle on our own.

Speaking of . . . "Who are the Almere?" I asked. "I'm feeling rather woefully uninformed at the moment."

"There are more secrets in the deep than we speak of to the fae of the land," said Dianda. "When we die, as happens when you go to war as often as we do, our bodies fall like they would anywhere else. And like all fae flesh, ours does not decay. But the night-haunts are creatures of the air. They can't fly beneath the waves. Faerie makes do.

When there's a gap, Faerie fills it. And as our bodies began to fill the abyss, Faerie sent us the Almere, born to a son of Oberon who dove too deep, seeking to recover the body of his fallen lover. They ripped their way out of him and claimed the deepest waters—and unlike your night-haunts, they were never bound."

"Never . . . ?"

"They can still attack the living," said Amphitrite. She sounded almost bored, like this wasn't something horrific and unthinkable. "Strip the flesh from their bones and leave what's left for the tide to take. Fae bones don't rot, either, but the waves will roll them along and break them down. What we offer, the water gladly claims."

"Ah."

"They technically belong to Saltmist, and hence answer to me," said Dianda. "Doesn't mean they're very interested in listening most of the time, but if this is what has to happen, this is what has to happen."

Our trajectory had brought us to a large, circular door in the wall. Clear panes set at eye level showed me the living sea outside, and I stopped, catching my breath.

"I know I can't drown, and I appreciate that, but have either of you stopped to consider the fact that I can't breathe below, either? I can still suffer, and I'll be easy prey for these Almere if I go below in no fit state to defend myself."

"Oh, that's easy," said Amphitrite. She snapped her fingers, and a stinging sensation lashed along the sides of my neck, like I had been raked at by a kitten's claws. I hissed in pained surprise, raising my hand to touch the raw area. Amphitrite caught my wrist and pushed my hand back down. "You're fine. Don't worry about it. Dianda?"

"Oh, I love being ordered around in my own knowe," said Dianda, and opened the door. The water didn't so much flood the hall as expand into it, cascading over us in a huge, frothy wave that somehow had no force behind it, despite the sheer volume involved. It should have hit like a hammer, or at the very least pushed us back against the wall. Instead, it merely entered like a dubiously invited guest.

Both Dianda and Amphitrite were abruptly finned and scaled from the waist down, their legs replaced by powerful flukes. I glanced down at my own body, suspicious, and found my legs where I normally kept them, apparently unchanged. That was something of a relief, especially given that I was still breathing. There was a strange pulsing in the sides of my neck, and I knew that if I succeeded in touching it, I'd find gills where no gills should have been.

Well, in a way, I *had* asked for them. "Come along, cat," said

Amphitrite, and dove out the opening. Dianda was close behind. I paddled after them, feeling slow and awkward, and Dianda doubled back to catch my hands and tow me along with her, which was only slightly embarrassing. There's no shame in being ill-suited to an environment where one doesn't naturally belong, but I disliked the feeling of helplessness.

Once she had a firm grip on my wrists, Dianda accelerated, tail pumping hard. She easily caught up with Amphitrite, who accelerated in turn, until they were both racing through the water at a horrifying speed. I glanced back to see the seashell spires of Saltmist fading into the distance, gleaming luminescent against the dark water.

Then that same darkness swallowed us, all light lost to the distance as we began to plunge rapidly down. Interestingly, the temperature didn't change, remaining clement and pleasant and clear. The lack of visibility was entirely due to the depth, and not to any sort of sediment or pollution. Amphitrite snapped again, the sound carrying clearly, and a globe of white light appeared in front of her, leading us farther down like a fisherman's lure guiding a hapless minnow into the net.

All I had to do was hold on, and so I held as tightly as I could, clinging like a limpet, glad that my current size would make it harder for the current to wash me away, but also somewhat sorry for my lack of proportionately sized claws. I could extend them while in man's form, but they would be longer, and it would be less like jabbing needles into Dianda's flesh and more like stabbing her with hands full of knives. Not precisely the way I wanted to thank her for carrying me down into the darkness.

Which wouldn't normally have been a good thing. I certainly didn't start my nights going "I certainly hope a mermaid will drag me fathoms below the sea to meet with a pit of murderous cannibals who apparently have access to the same secret network of passages through Faerie as my own people do." But right now, with Faerie in disarray and October missing, this was the best thing I could possibly have conceived.

Down and down and down we went, farther than I would have thought possible, down as if the sea had no bottom and was simply an endless pit into ever-deeper darkness, darkness so profound that even Amphitrite's light seemed to dim, unable to shine more than a few inches in any direction. She was only a partial shape in the pale light, and Dianda was much the same; when I looked back along the length of myself, I could no longer be sure I had legs, or feet, or anything beyond a foot or so of torso. I closed my eyes, unable to trust the fractured images they were feeding me.

They were still closed when I felt Dianda start to slow and heard Amphitrite snap again, three times in quick succession. I opened my eyes, and saw that three more globes of light had joined the first one, all of them bobbing in the water around her head like a loose crown of gleaming brightness.

It was enough to cast her sharkbelly-pale upper body into view, gleaming through the darkness like a ghost. She raised one hand, webbed fingers spread wide, palm facing away from her.

"My name is Amphitrite, daughter of Titania," she said, and her voice was clear and carrying, undistorted by the water. "The seas were given to me by my mother, although she had no authority to do so, and I patrol them in her name, for all that I would very much prefer not to. It is in her name that I ask you come and speak with me, who is your aunt, who is your blood, who has raised her legions to kill and be killed, thus filling your larders and nurturing your children. My name is Amphitrite, daughter of Oberon. I have authority in these waters. I am accompanied by my own descendant, who claims direct dominion over this abyss, whose authority here exceeds even my own. It is on her behalf that I ask you come and speak with me, who would not have come to vex you of my own accord. My name is Amphitrite, beloved of Maeve. I am aware of your hatreds, and share many of them in my own hidden heart. If you answer to my calling, you will upset and offend the one you hate most of all, will cause her shame and suffering beyond all measure. My name is Amphitrite."

Her other hand rose out of the darkness, clutching a coral dagger, and raked the blade across her palm in a single sharp gesture that left blood billowing into the clear, dark water. It was red when first it left the wound, but quickly turned to black as the current carried it farther from the light.

Through all of this, Dianda said nothing, and so neither did I. This was clearly a ritual, and one of which I had no experience, no way to contribute or contest, but all rituals can be disrupted, and the last thing I wanted to do right now was accidentally throw the whole thing off and make it harder for us to get what we needed. The taste of blood tickled my lips, carried by the water, and I fought the urge to turn my face away. October would have hated this.

Not as much as I hated being apart from her. That thought strengthened my resolve, and I remained perfectly still as the dark water began to pulse and shift, not visibly changing, but giving the strong appearance of moving all the same. The water around us grew heavy and oppressive. We were clearly being watched, even before the first flecks of luminous gold began to appear in that pulsing dark, uncounted tiny creatures opening their eyes. Then the susurration began.

Like Amphitrite's voice, it was clear and carrying, with no sign of distortion. It sounded like hundreds of tiny voices whispering to one another, like the sound shadows would make if they could speak. The whispering got louder, and individual voices began to make themselves known.

"Blood."

"She brings blood."

"Blood of the mother of sharks."

"Not of *our* mother, though. Never of *our* mother."

"We *had* no mother. Only our father, Harns, whose blood was silt and brackish water, who fell beneath our fangs when we tore our way from his body. We swallowed him whole, but we have never had a mother."

And then, in a wondering tone, closer to my ear than any of the others had been, "*I* wonder what a mother *tastes* like."

I jerked away instinctively, turning to scan the darkness with wide eyes. The dark water erupted into giggles, continuing to pulse, more and more golden specks appearing as our audience—one presumed the Almere—gathered for the show.

"What *is* that?" asked a voice.

"Not fin nor scale; not Merrow, not Siren, not descended of the deeps."

"Skin and sinew, bone and blood."

"We could take it."

"We could eat it."

"An offering?"

"A . . . sacrifice?"

The voices grew closer and closer. I hadn't felt so helpless since I was a kit. I could breathe, thanks to Amphitrite's magic, but I couldn't swim as well as anything with a tail, I couldn't change forms without being swept away, I couldn't defend myself or escape. I shrank against Dianda, hoping she would somehow defend me, hating everything about the situation in which I found myself marooned.

"Not a sacrifice or an offering," said Amphitrite. "He is under my protection, and I don't think, little niblings, that you're prepared to battle me for ownership."

"Not yet, perhaps, but soon," said a voice.

"Our time grows ever closer, for the deep is dark and the dark is deep and Maeve comes not near these waters."

"Why are you here, Auntie?"

"Why have you come, if not to offer?"

"I offered you blood," she said, mildly. "Isn't that enough?"

"It never has been before." A figure separated from the greater darkness, moving closer to Amphitrite's light. It looked like her in silhouette, sharing her shape and size. It swam toward us, stopping before the light could reveal any proper details of its form. "We're hungry, Auntie."

"No wars in these waters, no wars for ages."

"Would there be a war, do you think, if we gulped down the one who claims dominion? Would her holdings fall into chaos as her heirs fought to claim the throne? Nothing like a regicide to inspire a little healthy bloodshed."

"Delicious bloodshed . . ."

"War is coming," said Amphitrite. "Titania has seen to that. She can't turn away from what she's done, and the seas will soon enough run red, you have my word of that. We're here because we need your help."

"Help? Us?" The figure leaned closer, face moving into the sphere of Amphitrite's light. I fought back the urge to recoil.

It was made of eels. Dark gray, slick, limbless eels, their bodies pulsing as they writhed within the confines of their current shape. They leaned in until the face they had formed was only inches from Amphitrite's, then burst apart, scattering in all directions, back into the pulsing dark around us.

We were surrounded.

"We don't *help*."

"We harm. We do that very, very well."

"Shall we harm you, Auntie?"

"The shadows open for you," she said, as if they hadn't said anything, as if their words contained no threat. "Here where the dark of Faerie is deepest, where the remains of the Abyssal Road once fell, the Shadow Roads still open."

"We don't like them."

"No water there. No air."

"Passage is hard."

"But you use them all the same, when something falls in the waters of your kin. Because of the Shadow Roads, every abyss is the same abyss for you, and you can always find a morning meal. You can open and access them."

"So?"

"So?"

"So the visitor you noted, the one who is not a sacrifice, is a King among the Cait Sidhe of the land above. The cats run the shadows as well as you do, and their presence keeps those roads open even in the brighter places. He's here because Titania has ensnared the world again, making things wrong, and sundering him from his family. He's trying to get home. Can he use your entry to the Shadow Roads? Down here, where the connection is strong, and he can make the journey without being lost?"

"A King?"

"A King of Cats?"

"Which one?"

That last question carried a dangerous, familiar note. I straightened in the water, pulling myself up as if I were to face every noble of the land who had ever questioned my right to place or to title.

"Tybalt, King of Dreaming Cats," I said, and was pleased when my voice came out clear and steady. Water magic still wasn't familiar to me—might never be—but at least it was willing to work a little in my favor.

"Not always, though," said the whispers in the dark. "From far away, once."

"I was originally of the Court of Fogbound Cats," I said. "After, I served other places, but the farthest was fair Londinium, where I began my journeys."

"I remember you," whispered the dark.

I glanced at Dianda, at what I could see of her outline. She squeezed my hand, encouraging. "Do you?"

"They took me in the night; they threw my body to the sea. The Almere had me, for all that I had been of their jurisdiction for only a short time, and then only in a thief's weeds. They carried me below, and they kept me so."

I blinked. "Bradwr?"

"Rand."

Again, a shape moved out of the dark, this time toward me, and when it grew close enough the eels around it fell away and a more common form was revealed: a dark-haired Selkie man in a sailor's clothes that had been out of fashion for centuries, his throat a gaping wound that did not bleed, but leaked pure darkness into the surrounding sea.

"What is this witchcraft?" I whispered.

"The night-haunts of the world above were bound to forbid them living flesh, and to compel them to the dead, for they had no taste for it," he said. "The Almere were born of blood and biting, and had no need of such binding. We'll take the living, if they're careless enough to allow it, although we prefer the dreamless dead. As such, we have no need to wear out the faces we assume, and they live in the deeps forever. Your lover has remembered you since the day he died, and will always be here, remembering you, long after you have gone to the night-haunts, been worn to tatters, and rest forgotten."

It was a strange sort of secondary immortality. I stared at the man in front of me—the dead man, who had stolen from the Selkies and paid the price of his transgression, as thieves always have—until I could look no more, and turned my face away.

"It's good to see you, Rand," he said.

"It's been Tybalt for centuries now," I replied, not mentioning that it might be Rand again soon enough, once my crown was formally set aside. People react so oddly to the changing of names, as if anyone has ever been defined by a simple sound. We are complex creatures, land, sea, or sky, and what we call ourselves should matter not at all. But it does. Always and every time, it does.

"And it was Dylan when you knew me."

"Yes."

We'd had six weeks, he and I, and hundreds of years had passed since that dalliance; I looked at him and felt no longing, only the vague sorrow of remembering a life cut short too soon, and for no good reason beyond custom and tradition, two things I had become increasingly disillusioned with over the passing years. Whatever immortality the Almere offered, it wasn't the same as a life lived in the sun, as the life he should have been allowed to live.

"I admit, I never thought to see you lost at sea," he said, and smiled. "Not unless you decided to become a ship's cat and found yourself swept over the side in a gale. We've had a few Cait Sidhe who've come to us through that route, and while none of them have been delighted by the situation, they were well enough pleased once they realized they could still move in shadows, just in a new way."

"I never became a ship's cat," I said. "I did leave Londinium, however, and have since found my heart's true home in the Kingdom in the Mists. Her name is October, and Titania has taken her from me. I'm here seeking a way to return to her side. You say you remember me. I hope that means you remember that once you cared for me, at least in some degree, and that you'll help me now. Please. I need access to the Shadow Roads as they anchor here, so I may return to the Court of Cats, and from there unto my lady."

"What will you pay us, for the use of our door?"

The question was plainly asked, with no obvious hidden meanings. Still, I hesitated. If what Amphitrite and Dianda said was accurate, the Almere were very old, and had been a part of the Undersea almost since the beginning. Their words could conceal all manner of tricks and deceptions, intended to snare and drag me down.

I had been promised I would not die by water. Teeth, however aquatic their owners, are not the same as drowning.

"He will pay you nothing," said Amphitrite. "He is under my protection, and I will not let him deal in debts below the sea. All prices will be paid by my hand."

"Or by mine," said Dianda.

There was a general murmur through the pulsing dark. Bradwr's shade turned to the others, then smiled, a horrible expression that split his face literally from ear to ear, as his familiar visage transformed into something alien and cruel.

"Acceptable," he said, and lunged for Dianda.

A mighty sweep of her tail caught him in the midsection and shoved him back—or would have, had the blow not caused him to break into nearly countless eels, their lithe bodies streaking off into the blackness. Dianda let go of my wrists.

"Go!" she shouted. "Find your door, and go!"

I reached into the darkness all around us, into the shadows that were the world, and pulled until they parted for me, swinging open like the curtains of a stage. Sparing a glance back at my two allies, surrounded by biting, swarming eels, I dove through into the deeper dark, and I was gone.

FIVE

THE SHADOW ROADS AS they anchored at the bottom of the Undersea were not flooded, for which I was thankful. They were, however, freezing, as cold as October had always claimed the ones above to be, and they fought against me as I moved through them, slowing my progress from a run to a sluggish walk, like I was wading through molasses. Things cackled in the dark, the wild, mad laughter of birds or of spirits, and several times I thought I heard the slithering bodies of the Almere moving behind me, preparing to attack.

I forced myself to keep moving forward, taking note of every landmark I could detect, every point where the road itself told me I could exit if I felt the need. After I had been walking for no small time, I felt the presence of Saltmist on the other side of shadow, and knew I could step out here and arrive in Patrick and Dianda's knowe, back where I'd begun but safe from the depths.

I kept going.

The farther I got from the bottom of the sea, the easier my ascent became, until I was moving as easily as I ever did. The road was coming to accept me as I would have hoped, and I turned, backtracking a bit, to verify that it was behaving as the Shadow Roads were meant to do. The way back was as easy as the way forward had been. The road would remember me after this, and if I needed to return to the Undersea, I could do so on foot, without making a grand leap from the cliffside.

Good. I took the deepest breath the thin air would allow, set my shoulders, and broke into a run, racing for the safety of the familiar, moving through the dark as I had always done, a cat among the shadows.

The air was thin and the way was cold, but I knew this darkness well, and it knew me in turn, and it let me pass.

Soon enough I was stepping into the warmth of the Court of Cats, where the dim light was almost blinding after so long spent in total blackness. Bodies moved around me, the clean, honest sound of fur rubbing against fur, rather than the squamous wetness of eels slithering in the mud, and I heard claws clacking on the concrete train station platform. We were still here, then? Interesting.

I could understand why Titania would want to rid herself of the Court of Cats. But why relocate where we kept our gathering? It made little sense.

Then again, none of this made much sense, and as all of it seemed openly designed to piss me off, I wasn't that interested in her reasons anymore. I closed my eyes and stood where I was, listening to the Court around me, waiting for someone to demand my attention.

The demand, when it came, came in an unexpected form as a body slammed into my own, arms wrapping tightly around me. Their owner was slightly taller than I was, with a slender build and sufficient strength to crush my own arms against my sides in a firm embrace. It wasn't enough to hurt, but it was enough that extricating myself would have required some effort.

I knew who it was even before I smelled the black pepper and bonfire scent of his magic. As with many young things, his magic had shifted as he matured, going from the clean, uncomplicated paper of his childhood to something more akin to a backyard burn. The fire was a constant, and the smoke, but whether what burned was fallen leaves or crumpled paper was more difficult for me to tell.

October would have known. October would have known without even asking the question, pulling the knowledge out of the air like a gift from the universe. Since she wasn't here, I bent my head to the side enough to rub my cheek against his, and murmured, "Hello, Rajiv. Is there a reason you're behaving in such an uncouth manner?"

"Toby's cats are here and they said you brought them but you weren't here and I was afraid something had happened to you since you kept not coming back," he said, rapid-fire, his voice half-muffled by the fact that his cheek was pressed against my shoulder. "Are you okay where have you *been* have you seen October have you seen *Quentin*?"

"If you breathe and speak at the same time, you can take things called 'pauses,'" I said. "They'll make you easier to understand. Now let go of me, before I'm forced to scruff and shake you."

Raj obediently let me go. I opened my eyes and turned my head, following his movement.

I wasn't the only one. As before, every surface in sight was covered in cats, most of them sleeping snugly. The ones who weren't asleep had raised their heads to watch us with vague interest, as if we had become their afternoon's entertainment.

Raj looked about like I felt. There was a hollow cast to his cheeks that hadn't been there a week before, and dark circles around his eyes. His clothing was stained in several places, as if he had been wearing it for that entire time.

"Now," I said. "What's going on? Assume I know nothing, and tell me what you've been able to ascertain from the last five days."

"Something locked all the Cait Sidhe in the Court of Cats," he said, promptly. "*All* the Cait Sidhe. The thin-blooded feline changelings who can't transform are here too, and some of them spent the first three days crying to go back to their mortal companions."

"What happened after the first three days?"

"There was a . . . ripple, I guess. Like everything was adjusting itself again, like it hadn't finished the first time, and after that all the cats who'd been crying just went to sleep. They didn't ask to go home anymore. They didn't even seem to remember they had homes to go to. But they were all still here. I— Would I even have known if some of them were gone?"

"You would," I said, firmly. "You are a royal cat, and royal cats cannot be held long by illusions without focused effort on the part of the one who casts it."

"This is an illusion?" he asked, dubiously. "How is an illusion locking us in?"

"That's the second time you've mentioned being locked in," I said. "Can you not leave?"

"I can," he admitted. "And Gin can. But no one else can even open the Shadow Roads right now. It's like someone took away the doors when they try. How is that even possible?"

"Titania," I said. "Wait—if all the Cait Sidhe are here, and no one can leave, how are they being fed?"

Raj looked at me wearily, and his obvious exhaustion took on a whole new layer of meaning.

"Gin and I have been hunting and stealing food for them," he said. "Sometimes I can steal a human's wallet, and then we go and buy all the food at the nearest pet store and carry it through the shadows to rip open in the middle of the gathering room. But most humans don't carry that much cash, and we won't be able to keep going back to the same pet stores and using credit cards under different names for much longer before someone catches on."

"That's when you rob a bank, or spin a new human disguise and start over from the beginning," I suggested. "We can also target grocery stores, and warehouses. There are many ways this can be addressed, but we need to buy ourselves some time to come up with something more sustainable. If all the Cait Sidhe are here, how many cats are inside the Court?"

"I don't know exactly," said Raj. "Probably around three hundred, between the purebloods and the changelings who can shift and the ones who can't shift. And since that second ripple, none of them have known anything was wrong. They're all hungry, but they're almost resigned about it, like they think this is just the way things have always been, and are always supposed to be. But you didn't answer my question. October and Quentin. Have you seen them?"

"No," I said, and looked around until I spotted a wooden crate with no cats curled atop it. I walked over and sat down, resting my elbows on my knees. "I've been absent because I've been searching for them, or for anyone who might tell me where they are. I've been to the Undersea and back again, and there's been no sign of them, or of anyone else from our household." I was almost ashamed to realize that I hadn't spared a thought for May, or Jasmine, or Rayseline, since this all began. I wouldn't have questioned Simon or August's locations, either, if not for my time in Saltmist.

"I've tried to go looking," said Raj in a small voice, sitting down next to me. There was a time when we would both have been able to fit easily on the crate. Now it was a tight squeeze, and there was almost no one else I would have tolerated that kind of closeness from. "The house is empty."

"I know," I said. "I found the cats outside. They don't know what happened, either. They're not Cait Sidhe. They wouldn't have survived on their own."

"I thought that must have been what happened, when I found them and not you," he said, voice soft. "The Luidaeg . . . the Luidaeg isn't there, either."

"I know. And I know the knowe at Muir Woods is gone."

"Not gone—sealed."

When I turned to look at him quizzically, he shrugged.

"I asked the pixies, and they showed me the scraped-out hall that would be the door, if the door were open at all. But it's not, because Arden disappeared a hundred years ago and never came back."

I frowned. "Arden disappeared, yes, but we found her. October found her."

"Not here," said Raj. "It's like the world has completely rewritten itself. The old Queen is back on the throne, the one who held the Kingdom before Arden. The one without a name."

I stiffened. "That's not possible."

"But it's happening."

The false Queen had been put in place by Eira in her guise as Evening Winterrose, part of the Daoine Sidhe First's long plan to shape Faerie to her desires. I didn't know her before her ascension; I don't know who she was or why she wanted the throne. All those things ceased to matter when Evening put her in power, using the chaos that followed the Earthquake to cement her position before anyone could object. The existence of King Windermere's children had been an open secret in some circles, but it seemed those circles had never extended to include the High Kingdom. The presumptive new Queen had taken the throne with the support of a local noble of high station and higher reputation. What more could be expected?

Nameless and without a family to stand behind her, that new Queen had ushered in an age of suffering for the changelings and shapeshifters of the Mists. Under her, we had been treated as little better than beasts. I had attended her Courts solely to annoy her, seeing it as my duty to keep her uncomfortable if she was going to oppress my people so. The Cu Sidhe and Swanmays had all but left the Kingdom. The cats remained. The cats always remain. Without us, the Shadow Roads begin to crumble, and the balance of Faerie falls out of true.

The false Queen had always hated changelings in general, and had come to hate October in specific. October had been mouthy and insouciant, unwilling to accept her "place" in the social structure, or in Faerie as a whole.

In many ways, she has always been more feline than she realized.

October's reputation as a king-breaker had begun at home, when she'd been forced by the false Queen's own hand to put Arden on her father's throne and depose the pretender. That hadn't been the end of our problems, as the woman had come back again and again to try and reclaim her throne, until she had finally crossed the truly unforgivable line by arranging the abduction of October's daughter. It was because of her that Gillian had become a Selkie, bound to Faerie for a hundred years in defiance of her own Choice.

The false Queen had been taken into custody after that, and had been imprisoned in Arden's dungeon for the past year and a half while the slow wheels of pureblood justice ground toward a condemnation. Everyone knew she would be punished, but as elf-shot was no longer the sentence it had once been, and none of the people involved wanted to cross the lines of morality that she had so gleefully skipped over, things had been moving at a crawl.

I stared at Raj for a long moment, silence building between us, my motionlessness a challenge. He looked back, unblinking, until I was forced to look away, conceding the version of reality he described.

"So Arden is gone and the false Queen holds the throne," I said. "What other horrors wait in the world outside our walls?"

"There hasn't been a lot of time for us to go poking around, with the whole Court needing to be fed," he said. "I think this is the longest I've been able to sit still in about three days. And while we have the old station restrooms, they're not enough for everyone, and they can't help the people who can't change shapes at all. We've had to set up litter pans in the tunnel, and getting trash bags and more litter takes almost as much time as food collection does."

I grimaced. "How uncivilized."

"It's how mortal felines handle things," he said, with a shrug. "And just stop for a second and think about it. Normally when a member of the Court needs to relieve themselves, they use the shadows to reach a private location. Well, right now, they can't even get into the shadows. We have one public bathroom and one employee bathroom. Both of them work, although I'm not sure how, since it's not like the plumbing can *go* anywhere, but they have to be cleaned five times a day."

"I hope that's a duty you've been able to evade."

"Oak and ash, yes. I pulled rank when one of the older tabbies tried to force me to pick up a mop. But like you said, this isn't sustainable, and it hasn't left me a lot of time to explore."

I nodded. "Have you been to Shadowed Hills yet?"

"No. It's too far to go without knowing what I'll find when I get there, and Gin and I have both been hoping you'd come back from wherever it is you disappeared to. Why *did* you decide to go to the Undersea instead of coming back here?"

"After I failed to find October at our house, and discovered our closest allies missing, I needed to consult with another of the Firstborn, to determine whether Titania was truly behind this, as I had already started to suspect," I said. "The only one of her children I could think of who might be nearby was Amphitrite, who had promised at my wedding that neither I nor October nor any of our children would ever need to fear death by water. I decided to test the limits of her gift, and went to her in the water."

Raj looked at me with horror. "And did you die?"

"I am a King of Cats, but I am very short of lives anymore," I said. "I didn't die. I found Amphitrite, and she took me to Saltmist, where I learned that the Undersea has been cut off from Faerie even as we have. Dianda and Patrick are sick with worry over the missing members of their family—Simon, August, and Dean were all above the water when this began, whatever it is. According to Amphitrite, this is her mother's doing, no question, and is thus a very large and complicated illusion."

"If you get hungry inside of an illusion, you still need to eat," said Raj. "If October's cats had been trapped outside due to an illusion, they could still have been hit by a car or mauled by a dog. Whether this is an illusion or not, we're suffering, and you're still King here, even if it's not for that much longer."

I took the implied criticism with as much good grace as I could muster. He was correct. This was still my Court and these were still my people, and while I had agreed to step down out of the understanding that I could not be fully present for them and for my family, the transition was still ongoing.

"I won't apologize for worrying first for my wife, but I returned as soon as I was able," I said. "We'll find a better way."

"We have to," said Ginevra, stepping out of the shadows near the wall. Like Raj, she looked utterly exhausted, her normally rosy cheeks pale and wan, her eyes dull. "I don't know how much longer we can do this."

"There must be other royal cats we can reach out to," I said. "Shade, in Berkeley, or Barbara, in Tamed Lightning. Perhaps things are not so dire where they are. Has anyone attempted to reach the other Courts?"

Ginevra shook her head. "Both the people you've just named are Queens. I *can't* go to their territory without an invitation."

"What of your father?" I asked. "You could return to him."

"Running the shadows all the way to Silences will take me the better part of a day," she said. "I couldn't go until you returned, because I couldn't leave Raj alone."

"And I am sorry to have done exactly that," I said. "I wasn't thinking. I couldn't spare the time to think. When the world changed, October was ripped away from me, along with the rest of the occupants of our house, and while I will do my best to be here for you and for the

Court, she must remain my first priority. If that means I set my crown aside and we begin the challenge for succession right here and now, that can be arranged."

I didn't want to force Raj into a challenge before he was ready. If he lost, he'd be exiled, and if he won, Ginevra would have to leave, while I would abandon the Court immediately to seek my missing wife. Both of them looked alarmed at the idea, and Raj actively recoiled.

"If you need to fight me to satisfy your ideas of right and wrong, we can," I said. "You'll lose no face if defeated by the current King, as you cannot challenge me while you stand regent. But if you force me to choose between the Court and my family, I'll choose my family, every time."

"What about me?" asked Raj, voice gone small.

"You will always be my beloved nephew, but our time of being able to live freely in closeness is coming to an end," I said. "Once you're King, I will be banned from this Court. We both know that. The only way I can avoid leaving San Francisco entirely will be to renounce my place here, and find a new place for me to be. That means you'll only see me when your duties allow you the time to step away—and as this past near-week has demonstrated, the duties of a King are often overwhelming."

"It's not fair," he said.

"Now I know you've spent too much time with October," I said. "Her strange obsession with fairness has passed to you like fleas within a litter of kittens, and you may never be free of it. Regardless, if you've not yet been to Shadowed Hills, that seems a place I should go, and stop off to see Shade on my way. The rules regarding visiting monarchs during a regency are ill defined, for they rarely require use. Ginevra, would you be amenable to a visit from one of our local Queens, if she's able to get here?"

"I'm afraid she may be having the same problems we are, but if she can help with our food and hygiene situation, I'm down for anything," said Ginevra, sounding exhausted. "When this is over, I'm going to eat twelve cheeseburgers and sleep for a week."

"I look forward to seeing that," I said, and ruffled Raj's hair before I stood. "You have done excellently well, both of you, and I regret that I must now leave you to continue as you have been. It's a cruel repayment for a great service."

"You're coming back, right?" asked Ginevra.

"I am," I said. "I'll go first to Berkeley, and then onward to Shadowed Hills, to seek my lady in the halls of her liege. Whether I find her there or not, I'll return, and either way, Shade may well get here ahead of me."

"Please be safe," said Raj.

"I'm a King of Cats, Raj. I'm always safe. It's everything around me that's in danger," I said, and stepped backward into shadow. The road rose up to meet me, dark and cold and welcoming as it had always been. No traces of the depths remained, for which I was grateful, even as I oriented myself and broke into a run, heading for the distant beacon of the Berkeley Court.

Berkeley is an unaffiliated area within the Kingdom of the Mists. No one truly claims dominion there, aside from Shade, and even she would have left the place to its own devices, had she not been necessary to keep the Shadow Roads properly anchored to her side of the water. The university at the city's heart is often assumed to be the reason, a place of lore and learning that attracts young people of all stripes and species from around the country and even the world. Who wants to deal with the fealties and conflicting obligations of students from a hundred fiefdoms, each of them convinced that *their* liege knows the proper way of doing things?

It's an easy answer, but it may not be a true one, as many cities have large universities, but few are allowed to go entirely unaligned. The choice was made by the Divided Courts before I came to California; it has never been any of my concern.

I ran until I felt the point of decision open ahead of me. I could turn one way and exit into the mortal city, or turn the other and pass into the Court of Golden Cats, where Shade kept her company. It was rude to trespass upon another monarch's territory uninvited. Rude, but not an unforgivable insult, as I was a King and she a Queen; we're allowed a certain amount of visitation, something which I assume lingers from the days when we thought there might be some connection between the status of parents and the appearance of royal kittens. A King who mated with a Queen could surely expect to sire royalty!

Except that it didn't work that way, and never had. The chances were good that none of my children would be royal, and having them with Shade would only have resulted in us killing one another before the babes were weaned.

Normally, I would have gone to the mortal city, found a cat to carry a message for me, and asked Shade for her permission to visit. Under the circumstances, I had to hope that she'd forgive my presumption. I turned toward the Court, still running, until I reached the moment when I needed to step out of the shadows.

I emerged into warm air, and had a moment to see the Court of Golden Cats spread out before me, similar to my own in that every surface I could see was covered in furry bodies, all packed together in a way that bordered on unnatural for healthy felines—before a ball of claws and fury slammed into me, knocking me backward and to the ground.

SIX

MY ASSAILANT HISSED AND spat, clawing at me with the wild fervor of a beast pushed beyond the bounds of endurance. I changed forms, dropping away from the bipedal attacker as I fell to the ground and went bounding away into the Court, which resembled the storage space behind a school auditorium, hard plastic chairs stacked up in unsteady towers against corkboard walls. The stranger followed me, cats scattering as we ploughed through them, neither of us slowing down.

I reached a tall redwood post anchored to one wall and raced up it, using my claws for traction. The stranger grabbed for my tail, barely missing as I whisked it out of the way and made for the rafters. Once there, I stopped and looked back, hissing.

The stranger was clearly Cait Sidhe, wearing one of the forms we strove to hide from the rest of Faerie. For the most part, we present ourselves as either fully feline or fully fae, lingering as little as possible within the in-between stages, but even as we can extend our claws regardless of form, we can shift ourselves in other small ways.

This person was currently halfway between feline and humanoid, furred and tailed, with a muzzle in place of a flatter fae face. I couldn't tell their age or their gender, only that it wasn't Shade, who was a colorpoint cat when transformed. This person was a tabby, brown and orange and anger, tail lashing as they circled and snarled up at me. I adjusted my place on the rafter, making sure my balance was good, then transformed back into my two-legged shape, frowning down at the prowling stranger.

"I am Tybalt, King of Dreaming Cats," I said, sternly. "I have come to see your Queen, who knows me well, and did not think to be met with violence."

The stranger hissed. One of the other cats stirred to motion, rising and sauntering over to rub against the stranger's ankles before transforming into a two-legged form and looking up at me. She was a lithely built teenage girl whose golden hair still bore the ghosts of tabby stripes in this shape, betraying her feline heritage.

"We've seen no one pass here in years," she said. "How could our Queen know you well when you've never been here before?"

I hadn't interacted much with any of the ordinary Cait Sidhe of my own Court since this began, only with the other royal cats. An illusion cast by Titania would be powerful enough to ensnare them, and re-write their memories to suit whatever Titania needed them to be. What had she chosen to make the Cait Sidhe she had locked away believe about *why* they were thus confined?

"Pray believe me that I *have* been here before, and answer why an arrival was met by an attack."

"Maeve's creations took the Shadow Roads for their own these many years ago," she said, as if this were a reasonable and well-known fact. "The dark is filled with monsters, and none may pass there save the royal, whose duty it is to hunt and feed us, that the Court of Cats might endure until fair Titania has the time to cleanse the shadows."

I blinked, very slowly. Of course there would be a reason. Of course her illusion would have its own terrible internal logic. It was very tidy, in its own way, and readily explained why an entire community of fae would lock themselves away and no longer hunt or fend for themselves.

"Can you even *access* the shadows?" I asked.

She shook her head. "Not since they were sealed."

"If you know that royal cats can still pass, why would you attack a stranger with such immediacy and vigor?"

"Roland saw the shadows open, and knew you were not our Queen, and thought to protect the kittens from a monster," she said.

The one who had attacked me hissed a final time before melting into a grizzled tabby tomcat and stalking away, losing himself in the crowd.

"Will you come down?" she asked.

"Will you swear I'm not to be attacked again?"

"Not until our Queen returns and vouches for you."

"Then no, I think I'll remain where I am, and wait for her to come back from— Where did you say she'd gone?"

"Hunting for the Court, as is her duty, as you should know, if you're the King you claim to be." She looked at me with narrowed eyes. "I have my doubts about you."

"The feeling is most mutual."

She turned and followed her friend, still in humanoid form, and I remained where I was, balanced on the rafter, feeling a little bit of foolishness and a great deal of fury at the same time. For Titania to remake the lives and history of my people so casually was unforgivable, and all the more so because I had no doubt it would result in deaths. Shade was a single Queen, with no heirs that I was aware of, and her territory was twice the size of my own. Some of her older subjects would surely starve if we didn't end this quickly.

My own Court was in a much better position to survive Titania's reality, with myself, Raj, and Ginevra all able to hunt for our people— but that hunting would leave us with no time to do anything else. Titania had said there wasn't a place for me in what she was doing, and that I wouldn't ruin this for her. It seemed she was willing to use the lives of all the Cait Sidhe as a lever to make sure she got her way.

Every time I thought I couldn't think less of her, she found another way to dig the pit she was already standing in a little deeper. Maybe when she hit the center of the Earth, she'd plummet into burning lava and cease to be my problem.

It was a pleasant-enough thought to pass the time with while I waited. I didn't dare leave the Court to go seeking Shade; the chances that I'd be attacked again upon my return were too great. So I stayed where I was, and watched, waiting for her return.

Shade would have been within her rights to make me wait for days, as an uninvited intruder in her space. Instead, it was less than an hour before the shadows rippled and Shade emerged in her bipedal form, dragging a massive bag of dry cat food with one hand, an entire dead deer with the other. I dropped down from the rafters. She recoiled, still halfway in the shadows. I moved to grab the deer's other hind leg and pull it properly into the Court. She relaxed.

"Tybalt," she said, Taiwanese accent coloring the syllables of my name in a way I rarely heard from anyone else. "I was wondering where you had gotten off to in all this chaos."

"I've been looking for my wife," I said. "Raj and Ginevra have been keeping my Court."

"And have you come to offer the help I so obviously need?" She hoisted her bag of cat food onto her shoulder, shooting me a frustrated look. "Your Court has three sets of hands to protect it. Mine has one. I haven't slept in days."

"Unfortunately, no. I came hoping your Court was in better condition than my own, and that we might be able to ask for aid from you." A foolish thought, clearly enough.

Shade laughed, bitterly. "I wish it were so, but no. We fare poorly."

"So I've seen. One of your people attacked me upon my arrival. Another told me the shadows were filled with monsters and forbidden to all save the royal." A few cats were coming to sniff around, clearly interested in the food. I hissed, warning them off. "Is there someplace we can speak in private?"

"Yes, if you'll help me get another bag of food when this one mysteriously vanishes," she said.

"It's done."

"Then come this way." She dropped her burden and stepped into shadow. I released the deer's leg as I followed her, and together we emerged into a small, square room with mirrors on the walls and coats piled on the floor, like something out of an old-fashioned theater. Shade sighed and flopped into the coats, clear exhaustion on her face.

"I don't know how long I can do this, Tybalt," she said. "I spend every waking moment gathering food for them, and they try to eat reasonably, not glut themselves, but some of these cats were abused by humans before this happened, some would never have chosen to live within the Court, and their self-control is lacking. And then there are the kittens . . . oh, Tybalt, the *kittens*."

Her tone was bleak, and I wanted very badly not to ask. "How bad is it?"

"Their mothers have to fight to get enough food to keep their milk coming, and the children go hungry. They cry. I'm sure the same is happening in your Court, even with the three of you to keep them fed."

I nodded slowly. Asking Shade for help wasn't an option; the question had become how *we* might be able to help *her*. "I've been seeking answers as to what has happened," I said. "It appears Titania has returned, and announced her intention to become true Queen of all Faerie by revising the world to remove the elements she didn't care for. She couldn't remove us completely, so she simply put us where we wouldn't be a problem for her any longer."

"Our mother seeks to lock us away to die?" asked Shade, horrified.

I had forgotten she claimed descent from Erda's line. I grimaced. "I don't have all the answers yet, but what I have seen so far seems to indicate so, yes. I'm on my way to Shadowed Hills, where I hope to locate October. I'm sorry I wasn't able to come to see if you were in need of aid sooner than I have. There may be things I can do, once I return. I have allies in the Undersea, and it's possible to reach them via the Shadow Roads. I'm sure they have an excess of fish they might be able to donate to the cause of keeping our people alive for as long as it takes for us to end this."

Shade looked at me with utter weariness. "Anything would be welcome, Tybalt. I really don't know how much longer I can keep doing this."

She wouldn't be alone in that, not by a long shot. Even if only the Kingdoms Amphitrite had described as sundered from the Undersea were impacted, that was easily half a dozen Courts of Cats and quite possibly more, each of which had suddenly been filled to bursting and made the full responsibility of a very small number of royal cats. What good did it do for us to be able to see through Titania's illusions if we were so busy fighting to keep our people alive that we had no time to move against her?

Or maybe that had been her plan all along. If she'd been unable to outright kill us for whatever reason—Oberon's geas, or her own lingering traces of empathy for the world she had once helped to create—then locking us away to wither, forgotten and unable to escape—might have seemed like a way to be rid of us while keeping her own hands technically clean.

I growled under my breath, fingers flexing as my claws tried to extend of what felt like their own accord. Shade eyed me warily.

"Please, Tybalt, I'm too tired to fight with you, and if you want to challenge for my Court, only say, and I'll gladly walk away."

"I don't think you could," I said. "You care too deeply for your people. You would stay, no matter what, even as I'll return, despite everything I am screaming for me to run and keep running until I have my lady safe back in my arms. I'm bound for Shadowed Hills now. If you could warn your people that I'll be returning and ask them not to attack me when I do, I would very deeply appreciate it."

"I'm sorry about that," she said. "They have a whole different history from the one I remember, and in their minds, the only things that come out of the shadows are myself and monsters. They must have thought you were an attacker."

"Their willingness to defend your Court from the unknown speaks well of their loyalty," I said. "The scratches on my face speak to their ferocity. If you can only keep them fed, you'll be well served through this horror."

"I will indeed," she said, voice gone solemn. "Is there any chance you could bring me a bag of food when you come back? I've been reduced to kibble, for the bulk it represents, and to hunting the wild deer on campus."

"I may be able to do better than that," I said. "Make me a list of everything you need, everything you want, and everything you don't dare wish for, shy only of your freedom, which is outside my power to address, and I'll study it on my return."

"A fool's exercise," she said.

"Then allow me to be foolish for a time, and have what faith in me you can," I said. I bowed to her before stepping backward into the shadows and resuming my journey.

The Cait Sidhe are everywhere in Faerie—normally. We mingle more with the human world than most fae, because our feline kin refuse to be confined to the Summerlands, and we refuse to abandon them. Still, most of us are like Shade, living parallel but separate lives, holding our independence above all else. I had been like that, before October came along and dragged me into her strange hybrid of the fae and human worlds.

I preferred a Summerlands sky to a mortal one, no question. But I also appreciate Chinese food and pizza delivery and cable television, and in the moment, I was appreciating the existence of a wonder May had introduced me to the year before.

The Costco big box store, which was a warehouse in all but name.

They had pet food, they had freezers that held more meat and fish than a king's larder, and best of all, they had long aisles where shadows gathered. If Shade was willing and we called Raj and Ginevra to assist, the four of us could clear out a retail location in an evening, and even a horde of ravenous Cait Sidhe would have enough to eat for several months. Best of all, there were multiple such stores dotted around the Bay Area.

Such acts of larceny were beneath us, and risked revealing the existence of Faerie, as the people who controlled the security cameras would certainly question our impossible appearance, and the equally impossible disappearance of all their goods. But we couldn't be blamed for surviving, especially not when we were crushed under such conditions as Titania had created.

Shade had probably never been to a Costco, and almost certainly wouldn't have conceived of robbing one. She lived too deeply in Faerie for that. There are benefits to the places where the fae and mortal worlds rub against each other. That thought caused me to step out of the shadows at the edge of the Berkeley campus, turning toward the building where the chemistry classes were taught before dropping down onto four legs and bounding toward the stairs. A stray cat was unlikely to attract much attention. An unfamiliar man with scratches on his face probably would.

The ventilation within the chemistry building was insufficient for the needs of the various classes, and so the doors were almost always propped during the day—a nightmare for security, a great mercy for people who wanted to avoid suffocation. I slunk inside and continued on, passing classrooms and offices until I reached the one I wanted.

The door was closed. I backed up until I could see the glass window toward the top of the door, then hissed at nothing, expressing my displeasure to the empty air.

The classroom was dark and deserted, and the name plaque that should have been next to the door was gone. Another ally, absent. Wherever Walther was, it wasn't here. Looking for Bridget would likely be equally fruitless, and as a bespelled mortal, she was unlikely to be useful even if I found her; if not for Saltmist, I would have been afraid Titania had somehow wiped out all of Faerie, leaving the Cait Sidhe alone in the lost places with nothing we could be restored *to*.

I leapt back into the shadows, not particularly caring who saw me, and this time I ran full-out for Shadowed Hills. If the knowe was gone as Muir Woods had been, then we were dealing with an even larger problem than the one I already recognized. If it was present but unchanged, we might be able to begin resolving the situation. And if October was there . . .

If October was there, I would collapse into her arms and then curl into her lap, heedless of form, and remain with her until the subtle, ceaseless shaking I could feel in my bones came to an end. I could slow. I could speak. I could consider the safety of my people, and of Shade's Court. I could see the need to find all the other missing people.

What I couldn't do was *care*. None of that mattered, not really, not in any way that counted, because October was pregnant and October was missing, and I had never been this afraid in my life. I did my best to avoid love for a very long time to escape moments precisely like this one.

Love is a knife forever suspended an inch from your heart, and if it falls or you stumble into it, you can all too easily find yourself impaled and bleeding.

I ran, and the dark unspooled around me, until it was time for me to drop into the light, landing in the woods outside Shadowed Hills. I paused, then. The air smelled different. It wasn't until I'd resumed moving toward the manor proper that I realized what had changed.

I didn't smell roses. I smelled oak trees, grass, loam, even the distinct waxen scent of hedges, but I didn't smell roses. Or any kind of flowers, really, which made no sense. Shadowed Hills has always been famous for its gardens, and Luna planted them all herself, cultivating a floral paradise for her comfort even as she wore a stolen fox's skin draped over her true vegetable nature.

I slowed, continuing onward with caution. If this was all illusion, I might be able to see through it by focusing my attention on the elements that seemed out of true, but what would be the advantage in that? Everyone around me would still be enthralled, and the royal cat's ability to see through such twisted reflections doesn't give us the ability to dispel them. Better that I see and be able to interact with the world as they saw it.

Especially since Titania's wards were no illusion. If I disbelieved a wall hard enough to stop seeing it, I still might not be able to pass through the space it occupied. I needed to see this world as Titania had made it, as much as possible, anyway, even if I refused to believe it in any aspect.

The woods were denser than I remembered them being, less cultivated and more permitted to grow as they liked. I moved between feline and bipedal form as I walked, shifting according to the cover the trees allowed, keeping myself as inobtrusive as possible.

At last, the shape of the great manor of Shadowed Hills appeared ahead of me. The trees grew so close to the walls that a bad storm would have been enough to do substantial structural damage, their branches overhanging the roof and making the darkness of the Duchy's name far more literal than it had ever been before. I settled myself once more in bipedal form, suppressing the feline elements of my nature with as much force as I could muster, until the black stripes vanished from my hair and my field of vision changed, ever so slightly, to signal my pupils becoming entirely round.

In this guise, I could pass for Daoine Sidhe, albeit a very blandly colored example of the breed. I have sometimes wondered if Titania didn't set that line above all others in her regard because they came the closest to looking precisely like she did. The only thing about them that deviated in any way from a very simple and precise design was their coloring, which ran up one side of the rainbow and down the other. They were otherwise all but indistinguishable from half a dozen other descendant lines.

That train of thought led to the unsettling conclusion that her hatred of shapeshifters—the Cait Sidhe, the Cu Sidhe, the Reynardine—stemmed in part from the fact that many of us looked like Daoine Sidhe when we chose to have thumbs. How dare we pretend at being a part of her favorite creation!

In this instance, however, the pretense would suit me well. If I was found wandering outside the knowe, I would be assumed to be a stranger seeking hospitality or employment. My current appearance could easily suit either narrative. I was scruffy enough to need both a hot meal and a way to feed myself going forward.

I approached the wall, looking up to the rail around the high promenade that served as a gathering place during outdoor events. I had been to a few parties which took place on that very balcony, moving through crowds of people who mattered to me only in the sense that they mattered to October, trying to avoid letting my disdain for the man she called "liege" show. In the Divided Courts, titles are handed out like crackers at a dinner: far too many are hereditary rather than earned.

The Court of Cats doesn't always get things right, with people like my own father standing as stark illustration of that fact, but we title only those who have the power to support and protect our people, and we make every effort to be sure those who *are* titled understand their role and responsibilities. No King or Queen of Cats worthy of the name would ever treat one of their subjects as Sylvester had treated October.

October was his niece. Even before she had known that Faerie considered Simon her father, Sylvester had been aware; he had been the brother of her mother's husband, and he understood the custom as well as anyone. He should have treated her like family. Instead, he'd behaved as if she was an amusing pet, worthy of food and a bed and a small amount of favor but not the consideration she should have been granted from the beginning. She might forgive him for that; if I knew her as well as I believed I did, she was well on the way to forgiveness. I never would.

Something moved behind me. I turned, and saw a group of Sylvester's guards coming around the corner, dressed in proper ducal livery, Sir Etienne at their head. The sight of him caused me to relax, slightly. He had been responsible for October's education in the knightly arts, when she'd first been granted her own title, and had always been an ally, if occasionally a reluctant one. Speaking to him would help me determine precisely how deep Titania's—

"Halt, stranger," he said, giving me a quelling look that held no spark of recognition. "Identify yourself and your business here."

Well, question answered. "My name is Rand," I said, spreading my hands as I fully faced him, straightening my position as much as I could to be sure I wouldn't look like I was preparing for any sort of lunge or attack. "I was . . . My wife has disappeared, and I had some hope that I might find her here, as she has spoken of this household in the past."

"We've had no new arrivals in several weeks, and Moving Day is as yet months from now," he said. "Did you give her cause to flee you? My liege would ill appreciate it if I gave a man who abuses his wife any excuse to claim the hospitality of this house."

"Not that I'm aware of," I said. "We have been content since our marriage. Her cousin has recently come to live with us for a year's term, and we're expecting our first child. Her disappearance was not her choice, and I very much want to find her and bring her home."

"From where do you hail?"

It seemed simpler to avoid lying to him as much as possible. "I hail originally from Londinium," I said.

"That explains the accent. And more recently?"

"I live in the mortal city of San Francisco, within the protectorate of Goldengreen," I said, following the same principle: Goldengreen was the closest demesne to the home October and I shared, and one with which I was intimately familiar.

He frowned. "Why are you here, and not laying your concerns at the feet of Countess Winterrose?"

Oh. Oh, no. I should probably have expected that, if the false Queen was back; why shouldn't all the worst people we'd ever known have returned at the same time? Still, on some level, I suppose I *had* expected it. After all, I was running out of ways for this to get worse.

"The Countess has never been overly receptive to concerns she feels beneath her," I said, hoping this version of Evening would have at least that much in common with the woman I knew. If she didn't, this world had been remade to such a degree that I couldn't imagine how it was meant to function.

Etienne's expression softened. "It's true—she rarely wants to hear from people she doesn't feel have earned the honor of her presence. I suppose you haven't properly flattered or tithed to her?"

"Not so's I've ever noticed." I shrugged, trying to look hapless. "Her ways are beyond me. But my lady always spoke well of Shadowed Hills, and I suppose I hoped there might be a way to entreat audience with Duke Torquill and ask him for his aid."

"Did your lady have some ties here?" asked Etienne, innocently.

"Not as such," I said, telling my first true lie. "But she had heard of the duchy's nature, and the generosity of its regent."

Etienne nodded, mercifully accepting this as truth. "The Duke is always glad to help a traveler," he said. "But it's more customary to come around the front, via the gates, than to skulk around the back of the place. There's nothing beyond here but the swamp, the briars, and the Lady Amandine's tower. She'd not thank you for coming too close to her daughters, and the Duke would not soon forgive you for startling his nieces."

"Nieces?" I asked.

"Yes. His brother, Simon, dwells yonder with his wife and their two daughters, August and October." Etienne's softness died. "You must know him, as he's the right-hand man and dogsbody of the Countess Winterrose. It strains credulity to think that anyone could live within her lands and *not* know Simon Torquill."

October's name was ringing in my ears, making it difficult to concentrate. I wanted to step into the shadows and be immediately away. I also wanted to be able to return here if necessary, especially with October so nearby. If I was unable to retrieve her immediately, this would be my most likely sanctuary, and what I said next could easily sour it.

"I know him, although more by sight and reputation than personal acquaintance," I said, and was amazed at how steady my voice was. "And knowing what I do of him, it seemed unwise to inquire too deeply into the matter of his family. I'm sure you can see that I'm not the sort who spends a great deal of time around the High Courts—I've had few enough opportunities to meet the Lady Amandine, and fewer still to see her with her husband. I don't think I've ever seen their children."

"October is not often welcomed at Court," admitted Etienne, seeming to resume a bit of his lost relaxation. "She was born to fulfill the household's obligation to Titania's Law and, as such, is not considered fit for much polite company."

"I see." I didn't, not in the slightest, but as this was the first I had heard of obligations or of Titania making laws, I had to be careful not to give myself away. "Is there a way I might see your Duke?"

It no longer mattered, not really—I knew October wasn't here, and

I knew where I needed to go in order to find her—but if I wanted Shadowed Hills to remain a possible refuge, I needed to preserve the fiction that I was still looking for a missing woman, and I might learn more by meeting Sylvester.

Etienne hesitated. "The Duke is . . . not always prepared for unexpected audiences," he said. "If you'll follow me, we can see whether this is one of the occasions when he is, and if he's not . . ."

"If he's not, I can return later," I said, hoping not to seem too eager.

Etienne nodded and, gesturing for the other guards to turn, began to lead me out of the woods, toward the doors to Shadowed Hills.

Away, I now knew, from October.

SEVEN

THERE WERE NO FLOWERS inside the knowe, no garlands of greenery around the windows or hanging from the rafters. Apart from that, it seemed exactly as it had always been. I recognized some of the household staff who passed us in the halls, although others were new to me, and most of the courtiers who moved silently through, barely acknowledging Etienne and the guards. A few shot curious looks my way, clearly interested in the new face.

We were almost to the receiving room when a familiar voice called from a nearby doorway: "Sir Etienne! I *waited* for you!"

Familiar, excepting for a note of hectoring entitlement that I hadn't heard in years, not since we were strangers to each other. I turned, fighting to control my scowl, and frowned a little at the sight of a bronze-haired boy in ducal livery standing there, hands on his hips, clearly indignant. *He* was making no attempt to control his scowl. *He* looked at Etienne like the man was his inferior in all ways, and he had no shame in showing it.

"Was I meant to meet you?" asked Etienne, with deceptive mildness. He had been, and based on that tone, he knew it.

"You promised me a lesson in swordsmanship! If you're to stand as my knight, you should really show up when you say you're going to!"

Quentin expected Etienne to stand as his knight? That was fascinating, and confirmed some of what I already suspected about October's station in this rewritten world. I had no doubt she was untitled. What few changelings I had seen within the knowe had been wearing servant's clothing, and none of them had raised their heads or met our eyes.

My suspicions about this world were beginning to crystallize, and I didn't like them in the least.

"My apologies," said Etienne, less mildly, but with no actual apology in his tone. "I received word of a stranger on the grounds, and went to see what he needed."

"And?" Quentin's eyes flicked over me, taking my measure and dismissing me in the same moment. "He looks like a vagrant. Send him to bother someone else and give me my lessons."

"A stranger in traveling clothes who asks for hospitality is to be met with kindness and care, not turned away," said Etienne. "He could be a powerful wizard in disguise."

"Or he could be one of the Firstborn," taunted Quentin. "You know he's *not*. 'Could be' is just an excuse for not keeping your word when you didn't want to give it in the first place."

"That's no way to speak to a knight," snapped Etienne.

"I'm not a squire yet, I'll speak any way I want to," said Quentin. "You can't stop me unless you agree to take me, and that means keeping your word when you say you'll teach me."

Etienne sighed, starting to turn in my direction. "My apologies for the failure of my hospitality, but will you take deep offense if one of my men escorts you the remainder of the way? The Duke may still not be prepared to see you, but you can arrange a time to return, if so. It seems I have other obligations."

"Vital ones," I said, in a neutral tone. "I can finish this quest on my own, and hope that we will meet again under less . . . hurried circumstances."

"Very well. Garm." He turned to one of the guards. "See our guest to the Duke, and ask if he's up for an audience."

"If he's not, I can return another day," I said hurriedly. I was willing to see this pantomime to its natural conclusion, but had no wish to draw it out longer than absolutely necessary.

"Of course, sir," said Garm. He bowed to Etienne, then turned to beckon me along the hall, heading for the receiving room. I followed, watching him as we walked.

He was Gwragen, tall and thin, with gray skin and eyes the color of the full moon at midnight. I had seen him around the knowe before; he wasn't a creation of Titania's illusion, which didn't mean much when peoples' very selves had been rewritten. Then, as we approached the receiving room door, he stopped and turned to face me, a small frown tugging down the corners of his thin-lipped mouth.

"Everyone I've ever seen has walked in a thin haze of light, claimed by the illusions which define and delineate our world," he said, voice calm and steady. "Everyone but you. Why is that?"

I blinked before I settled, once again, on honesty. He was Gwragen; his magic was focused in illusion, spinning images so precise they could fool even the Firstborn. There was nothing he could do to me, not with Titania already wrapping the world in illusions like smothering cotton. "It's because I'm the first person you can remember meeting who wasn't part of the shared illusion that holds you all."

The small hope that had kindled in my chest, that October would have somehow been spared from this illusionary world, if only to make it hurt her more, guttered out and died. Garm would surely have seen her, and if he could see the spell his world was under, he'd have noticed its absence in a changeling as quickly as he'd noticed it in a stranger. Still, it was an interesting interaction between his magic and Titania's, and unlike her reasonably clever confinement of the Cait Sidhe, it felt likely to be a genuine loophole in her spell.

Meaning it might be something I could use.

To my profound relief, Garm didn't object to my statement or attempt to argue with me. He only blinked once, very slowly, as if I had stated something patently impossible, before he nodded. "That makes sense," he said.

"It does?"

"It does. The Gwragen know perfectly well that our world has been revised multiple times over the course of its history. It's why we depend so heavily upon the Libraries, which are outside the bounds of any such revisions. The books they contain will always tell true, even as the world is remade in necessary ways. But why are you exempt from the great remaking?"

"Why are you so unbothered by the idea that I might be?"

"We have tales of such as you, and they always begin the same way: 'One day came a stranger to the hall.'" Garm shrugged. "I suppose I'm not disturbed because I've always hoped to one day stumble into a story."

"You're very calm."

"A personal failing of mine." His eyes, for all his calm affect, were bright, and he was watching me intently. If I tried to move in a way he didn't care for, he'd set off the alarm immediately. "You've come to see our Duke. Are you about to undertake some great quest or act of heroism?"

"I'm not a hero, although I married one, and I had thought my questing days were long behind me," I said. My own mind was racing, trying to come up with every interaction I'd ever had with the other version of this man. In our world, Garm had been Etienne's squire after October, and had joined Sylvester's guard once he was knighted; he was known to be a dour, suspicious man, and while he had been uncertain of October's loyalties at times, he had always been willing to assist her on his liege's orders. He was loyal. That was what mattered more than anything else, and as I watched him with lasting wariness, I wondered who held that loyalty in this world.

"I have, however, come to see your Duke," I said. "There has been a recent 'remaking,' as you term it, and my wife and I have been separated. I am hoping to locate her and make certain of her safety."

"Why would the Fair Titania have separated you from your wife?" asked Garm, with some concern. But then, if the Gwragen were aware that Titania could occasionally remake the world to suit herself, they would naturally worry that those remakings might part them from their own loved ones.

"I'm not sure," I said, which was only partially true—hurting October had been much of the point of this spell, after all. "I believe in part it may be because neither of us is in fashion in this new iteration of Faerie. My lady is a changeling, fae-born but human-sired, and I am . . . not entirely as you may assume upon looking at me."

"You bear no illusions," said Garm. "I would see them if you did, even though I wouldn't be able to tell you exactly what they were. You are what you appear to be."

"Have shapeshifters been so thoroughly eliminated from Faerie that the obvious answer becomes unthinkable?" I asked.

Garm frowned. "A shapeshifter would have no cause to wander courtless, sir. You make jest of me."

"I assure you, I do not," I said, and loosened my control over my appearance, allowing my teeth to sharpen and my pupils to narrow to their more natural shape. Garm gasped, and I knew the stripes had come back to my hair. Such small things can seem so very dramatic when unexpected.

"How . . . ?"

"As I said, shapeshifting," I said. "My lady is a changeling, and I am Cait Sidhe, and my people have been swept away and locked in our own spaces, forbidden the rest of Faerie."

"But the Cait Sidhe . . . Oh, revisions," said Garm. "The Library would know—I'll get a pass as soon as I can, and go consult the books. You can't be here, sir. It's not safe."

"How is it unsafe?" I asked, pulling my feline attributes back beneath the surface, where they couldn't be easily seen. "Have we been made illegal?"

"Extinct, more like. The great purging was conducted centuries ago, after Maeve betrayed all of Faerie. The changing kinds were eliminated, for they couldn't be trusted. No cats have walked our Courts since then."

"What a lovely world Titania's made," I said, hot venom in my voice. "How delightful. How happy her people must be, to go about their days and know they've killed innocents for the peace that they enjoy. Only there's no blood on their hands, not yet, for my Faerie existed a week ago, and I lived happily with my family, and the Cait Sidhe came and went as they chose. Now they're locked in the Courts, and only the royal cats may pass, and our kittens risk starvation so Titania can play house with other people's lives."

Garm paled. "You seem angry."

"I'm furious."

"Good."

That gave me pause. "Good?"

"Good." He leaned forward, tone turning conspiratorial. "The Gwragen have always known that the world changes when we're not looking, but we can track those changes by consulting the Library. We know Titania remakes the world to suit her, and we know she doesn't realize we can see it, or she'd take that understanding away from us. We would vanish, as has every other descendant line to have crossed her. We don't want to vanish. Nefyn worked too hard to raise us from our cradles to vanish simply because we managed to offend Titania. Yet every time she changes the world, she changes us to suit her."

"How is it that you can have a tradition of knowing this if she remakes you when she changes the world?" I asked.

"Because a world has to make sense," he said, firmly. "It has to hang together, or it's nothing but a rough idea, worth pursuing, perhaps, but not capable of standing on its own. She puts us down in her new Faerie, and leaves us mostly as we are, because we exist and thus have our own internal logic, and then the illusion does the rest. It fills in all the places she didn't think of. I'm an only child. If she decided, the next time she changed things, that I should have a sister, she would tell the world to give me a sister, and then the illusion would weave our childhood and our relationship to one another entirely on its own. A weaker illusionist can't give their workings so much freedom. Titania can."

"I . . . see," I said, still somewhat baffled.

"So we know what she does, and we know how she does it, if not her reasons why, and we hate her for it, because we can't preserve our own past. When I get off shift tonight, I'll get a pass to the Library and write down as much as I can of what you've told me in one of the books we keep there, to keep each other aware of the revisions. Titania can't change the Libraries. We pass our notes through them. But be *careful*. Unless you think you can unmake this entire working, you need to stay unnoticed. She won't like this."

"No, I suppose she won't."

Garm stepped back. "Perhaps it's time to approach the Duke," he said. "Will you return here and speak with me?"

"If I can, but if I have that freedom to move, I think it best I go to the Library," I said.

He nodded. "Very good, sir. I hope to see you again." He turned, then, and took the last few steps to the receiving room door, where he knocked and glanced back at me. "Wait here," he said, and slipped inside.

I was left alone.

It was the perfect opportunity to slip into shadow and run. If October was at her mother's tower, she was safe—in body, if not in mind or heart—and I could reach her quickly. The thought of delaying even this little bit ached. Garm would understand.

The Duke, however, might not, and if I intended to steal October from the tower and flee with her into the Summerlands, I would need a place to go. I had found one unexpected ally in this hall. If I pushed my luck, I might yet find a second.

Several minutes passed. The door eased open again, and Garm appeared, peering somewhat anxiously out at me.

"He says it is his duty to receive a stranger, should one present themselves," he said. "Pray, enter. But be warned—our Duke is in a melancholy mood this day."

"Your Duke is yet Sylvester Torquill, is he not?"

"Yes, sir. He is."

"Then I find the idea of his melancholy difficult to believe." Sylvester had always been a violently passionate man, prone to rages and periods of irrational behavior rather than melancholic sulking.

Garm shrugged and pushed the door further open, gesturing me inside.

The receiving room of Shadowed Hills had both changed completely and not changed at all. The architecture remained as it had always been, overblown and grandiose, with a ceiling too high by half, and a floor wide enough to host a King's ball. Sylvester as I knew him was so fond of inviting the entire duchy to his celebrations that even that vast expanse of space was sometimes crowded, bodies covering the black-and-white checkered floor in bright festival attire as music filled the air.

The atmosphere of the room, however, was something I had never seen before. There were no people, the attending court entirely absent, and shrouds of cobweb silk covered the windows, pale, glittering gray and undyed as they billowed in the faint breeze. No tapestries or paintings softened the stark whiteness of the walls, and in the absence of milling bodies, the checkerboard of the floor seemed less whimsical and more sterile, designed to confuse the eye and disorient anyone who approached.

At the far end of the room, in front of the tall doors that would open to the exterior promenade, a dais sat, holding a single high-backed chair. There was a man seated there, positioned in the shadows so that even my feline eyesight wouldn't allow me to see his face. I hesitated. Perhaps claims of melancholy were truer than seemed possible. This was another world, after all. One where, near as I could tell, Luna had never entered Sylvester's life.

Both Torquill brothers had placed great stock in family for as long as I had known them. A Sylvester with no family to call his own would be, almost of necessity, a sorry soul, and it seemed Titania's ideas of creating a perfect world didn't extend to supplying new loves to people whose old loves she had removed.

That was almost reassuring. There was a violation in the idea of waking to find someone I had not chosen in my bed that I didn't want to contemplate. Garm approached the dais, and I followed, keeping my head high and my shoulders low, trying to avoid any sort of posture that could be interpreted as a threat.

The man on the chair shifted position and, in the movement, finally became clear. I stumbled, taken briefly aback by the picture he presented.

Etienne was someone I knew reasonably well, and Quentin someone I knew very well indeed, having lived with him for some time. Both of them had looked very much like themselves, save for the new arrogance in Quentin's expression. In rewriting their lives, Titania had clearly not gone out of her way to be intentionally cruel. Sylvester, on the other hand . . .

The essentials of his person were unchanged. He was tall and fair-skinned, with the unnecessarily vivid coloring favored by the Daoine Sidhe: hair the color of a fox's fur, and eyes the color of midsummer honey. The rest of him had been entirely remade. He looked as if he'd lost easily thirty pounds in the week since I'd last seen him, becoming almost gaunt. His hair was greasy and uncombed, his skin wan and waxen, his eyes shrouded by deep circles, as if he had abandoned even the idea of sleep. His clothing, while worn and threadbare, was at the very least clean. That was the best I could say for him.

He looked as if he hadn't shaved for several days. To be fair, I hadn't either, but I had been running and throwing myself off cliffs and fleeing from flesh-eating eel-people miles below the sea, while he had been safe in his duchy, surrounded by loyal courtiers and staff who would have been happy to assist him with the bare minimum in terms of hygiene and presentation. "I simply couldn't be bothered" was a poor impression to present to any who might come seeking audience.

Sylvester lifted his head and looked at me without a drop of recognition. "I am told you come to my lands seeking for your missing wife," he said. "I regret to inform you that no such woman has been sighted here."

"She's a great deal of trouble, my wife," I said. "Very headstrong, very opinionated. I assure you, you would have made note of her presence. I apologize for troubling you, and appreciate the honor of your attention."

Garm was looking at me, jerking his head very slightly toward Sylvester as he did.

Ah, yes. The etiquette of the Divided Courts has always been strange and frustrating, wasting time that needed not be wasted. I bowed, deeply—more deeply than the man as I knew him deserved, to be quite honest.

Sylvester waited until I straightened to speak again. "Have you a name, stranger?"

"Rand," I said.

"Not a name heard often in this time."

"No, but mine all the same."

"Do you require the hospitality of my house?"

It would be a gamble, to linger so close to Amandine's tower, if I failed to remove October on my first attempt. Still, it would also be a convenience, and give me more opportunity to speak with Garm about what the Gwragen knew, and what was kept within the Library. I would have to do my best to keep out of Etienne's way, and avoid Simon if he came to visit his brother while I was in residence.

"It would be a great honor, sir," I said.

"Then you have three full days from this moment, and should you please us, your time may be extended," he said. He slumped in the chair then, moving one hand in an odd gesture which I interpreted as dismissal. "May your quest be fruitful, and your bride to your bower be restored, even as the rose is brought back unto the thorn."

It was an old blessing, and not one I had heard in quite some time. I hesitated before turning away.

Titania was trying to return Faerie to an older state, and a time when we had been less joyfully entangled with the mortal world. That was no real surprise, and yet still it startled me, as did my revulsion toward the notion. I had been as opposed as any other to Faerie's entanglement at one point; it was dangerous, to yoke ourselves so closely to such a changeable world. My attitude had altered with time, and with exposure to October and her friends, all of whom had been very much a product of that collision between cultures. It was hard to hate something that had given me some of my favorite people.

Garm bowed as he moved to join me, escorting me from the receiving room. "Melly will prepare a room for you," he said, once we were back in the hall.

"There's no rush: I won't be using it for several hours," I replied. "I have lingered long enough, and must go to seek my lady. When does your time of duty end?"

"An hour past midnight."

"I'll return for you then," I said. "I wish to accompany you to the Library."

He nodded, and I had time to see his eyes widen as I stepped into shadow, vanishing from the knowe.

I was assembling quite the list of tasks. Feed my people. Assist Shade in feeding hers. Go to the Library. Learn what I could. Find October. Snap her out of this illusionary reality in which she was trapped. Return Simon and August to the Undersea. And, one assumed eventually, track down and murder Titania.

Really, it was a social calendar that would have exhausted a lesser man. I was tired just thinking about it. I ran through the darkness, covering the short distance between Shadowed Hills and Amandine's tower in a matter of seconds. I was preparing to drop back into the Summerlands when I slammed into a barrier that knocked me back a step, leaving me disoriented in the dark.

I frowned, moving carefully forward to the point where I had been knocked back, and sniffed at the thin air. Blood and roses, and a trace, distant but clear, of mulled apple cider. Amandine's tower wards. That was . . . interesting.

Before the divorce, they had always been set to admit family, while keeping everyone else locked out. It was reasonable that she wouldn't consider me family, but October did, and previously that had been sufficient to get me through doors locked in such a manner. Titania's spell might have changed October's mind, briefly, but it couldn't change the nature of our bond, or unmake the vows we had made to one another. She was carrying my child. Whatever she thought or felt in the moment, we were family.

. . . and unless Titania had thought through things in more detail than seemed to be her custom, October was *not* Amandine's family. Neither were August and Simon. The divorce had been as magically binding as our wedding. That style of ward would have left them all sealed outside and left her alone.

Oberon's protections had covered those of us whom October *considered* her family. What damage would Titania's careful revisions have done to that connection? Perhaps October and Amandine once more believed themselves to be family. I couldn't think about it in too much detail or I would drive myself to distraction, chasing my own tail with no chance for clarification. Better to worry about it later, and deal with the immediate issue to hand: either Titania's spell had changed things on a deeper level than I would have thought possible, or Amandine had changed her approach, whether she understood why her customary wards weren't working or not.

Backing up, I found the edge of those wards and stepped out into the Summerlands, finding myself in the tall grass easily twenty yards from the tower. This was untended heath, growing wild and uncultivated. That was little change; I was accustomed to the land around the tower being a bit more grassy and dense with wildflowers, but at least no major structures had appeared or disappeared. The tower itself looked as it always had, tall and white and implacable against the twilight sky, jutting up from Amandine's walled garden like a challenge to all disarray.

Cautious, and aware that I would be all too visible from the tower windows, I began to approach.

I hadn't gone but half the distance between myself and the garden wall before I was seized by a sudden wave of agonizing pain, like all my nerves were catching fire at once. I stepped back, and the pain faded.

Another layer of warding, then, this one geared specifically at people who might mean Amandine ill. I took a deep breath and tried to clear my thoughts, telling myself that for all her failings, this wasn't her fault; she wasn't the reason for Titania's return, or why October had been swept away from me. It was a difficult train of thought. Maybe this wasn't her fault, but so much else had been that it was hard to find any grace for her, however hard I searched.

Finally, sure that I no longer wished her ill—at least in the moment—I took another step forward, and stumbled back as the pain returned. The wards were not going to allow me passage. I was still too far away to stand and yell, if that would have even helped. Well.

One of the reasons some nobles of the Divided Courts hate the Cait Sidhe so much is our gift for getting in where we technically shouldn't be. A cat may look at a king, after all, and that means a cat must be able to *access* the king in question. I dropped to the ground, shifting into feline form, and began to trot forward. I passed the point where the pain had been lurking without any further troubles, and flicked my tail smugly before continuing on.

Half-familiar magic pressed oppressively down on me, and I knew changing back into a more humanoid shape would be impossible while inside the spell's border if it was actively engaged in protecting its people. The thought brought a jet of panic with it. Amandine had imprisoned me in feline form once before, to compel October's obedience, and the experience had left me traumatized, terrified to change forms, frightened of my own magic. It was no way to live. It had very nearly been enough to destroy me. The thought of it happening again . . .

For October, I would endure it. I prowled onward, belly low to the ground, wind bringing me all manner of information that a Sidhe nose would be incapable of collecting. I smelled flowers and herbs, both healthy and flourishing. I smelled blood and roses, and smoke and mulled cider, and the faint, distant traces of freshly cut grass. October had been here, and recently enough that her magic yet lingered in the air.

When I reached the wall, I leapt up onto it and sat, curling my tail around my legs as I stared into the garden. It was as lush and thriving as its scent implied, flowers in every possible color of the rainbow blooming everywhere I looked. At the center of it stood the tower, pristine, white, and smooth. Some of the windows might have been accessible through the trees, and as if in answer to that thought, one of those windows opened and August slid out, dropping into the waiting branches of a tall cherry tree. Her arrival sent pink petals cascading like confetti, and more fell as she descended.

A moment later, a second head poked out of the window, so familiar that my heart stopped beating and my breath caught in my throat.

"August, you walnut, what do you think you're doing?" October demanded. "You *know* Mother's due to return home today! She'll scold you silly if she finds you outside the tower, and strip me of all indulgences for a *month*!"

"You worry too much," scolded August, as she descended. "Mother will never know— Ah! What's *that*?"

She had spotted me on the wall. As her attention swung in my direction, I stood and stretched, arching my back in a way people have always found endearing. Finished with my display of adorable nonchalance, I began to saunter toward her along the wall, tail high and whiskers forward, projecting harmlessness and enticing softness with every stop.

The apple whizzed by a few inches over my head, landing with a *plop* in the grass. I froze. August was bending to grab another out of the grass.

"Shoo!" she yelled. "Shoo, terrible beast!"

October was still watching from the window, eyes wide and utterly devoid of recognition. She didn't know me. I froze for a moment, ears going flat, and stared at her. She didn't *know* me. My wife, the love of my life, had no idea who I was.

At least that meant she wasn't suffering my absence as I was suffering hers. But it also meant she wasn't struggling to find her way back to me as I was struggling to find my way back to her, and our reunion would be entirely upon my shoulders. Most of her was concealed by the wall beneath the window, but her pregnancy hadn't been apparent six days ago; I would have no outward way of confirming it now. I managed to open my mouth and meow, piteously, pleading with her to recognize me after all.

She recoiled, as if the meow of a cat were the most terrible thing she had ever heard, and still there was no recognition in her eyes, and still my heart felt as if it were broken. August threw another apple, once again missing me entirely, and I attempted to jump down into the grass by her feet, only for the tower wards to stop me. The ones which had refused passage to me in man's form had only been the outer circle; there was another around the garden proper, refusing to let me pass. Damn and blast.

"Go *away*, creature!" snapped August. She had another apple in her hand, and a sharp glimmer in her eye. I saw no malice in her, and suspected she had been missing at least partially on purpose, trying to scare me off rather than do me harm. Still, my refusal to be easily frightened away was beginning to unnerve her, and she wouldn't keep missing for much longer.

"What *is* it, Aug?" called October.

"A cat," said August. "They're mortal beasts. This one must have slipped through an unguarded door. It has no purpose here. It's probably come to beg for food. Moving Day isn't for months yet, creature! This isn't the time for begging!"

She pulled back her arm for another throw. I recognized my cue and jumped down from the wall, away from the garden, leaving the sight of her behind.

I could still see the window, however, and October leaning out, looking down at her sister with concern. She was as beautiful as she had ever been, and I could see the humanity in the angles of her face: whatever Titania had done to her, she hadn't forced the rebalancing of her blood. I had to believe that meant she hadn't interfered with the pregnancy in any way. I had to, for to believe anything else would have driven me mad.

I turned my back on the tower and slunk away into the tall grass, waiting until I was beyond the edge of the wards to slip back into shadows and leave behind the one woman I had believed would never break my heart.

EIGHT

THE RUN BACK TO San Francisco was made more difficult by the fact that I felt like I couldn't breathe even before I slipped into the thin air of the Shadow Roads. If Titania had been aiming her arrows specifically at me, she couldn't have hurt me more deeply than she already had. Knowing that October was well and physically unharmed didn't make me feel as much better as I would have hoped, because she was locked in a life not of her own making, designed by someone who sought only to destroy her.

The fact that October was not included in the family wards worried me even more. Oberon had bound Titania against harming Janet's direct descendants, but Titania had mentioned loopholes. If this version of Faerie acknowledged the divorce, was October even considered a descendant of Janet Carter? How far back along the line did the sundering go? Did Oberon's binding protect her at all?

Was my child safe?

The binding against harming Janet's line wasn't the only one Titania carried: she was ostensibly also forbidden to harm October, or anyone she considered family. If October didn't know the child existed, could she consider it her family? Would Oberon's bonds prevent either of them from being placed in the path of some other, greater monster, the way Eira had once used Simon and Oleander to do her dirty work, so that her hands could remain, technically, clean? The fear was all-consuming, and it was tempting to allow it to consume me, to take a moment to roar and snarl and behave the beast Titania believed me to be. Still I ran, because my duty was greater than my distress, and when I felt the pull of my destination loom nearby, I stepped out of shadow and into the Court of Cats. Ginevra was collapsed on a pile of furs, while Raj was throwing packs of grocery-store fried chicken into the teeming throng of cats.

Spotting me, he lit up with relief. "Tybalt!"

Ginevra raised her head, blinking blearily.

"I am here," I said, and picked up several packs of chicken he had yet to distribute. I waded into the sea of feline bodies, heading for the edge of the crowd, where the older and weaker Cait Sidhe had gathered. The aged and the invalid. Under normal circumstances, they would have been the first to feed when we needed to open the stores of the Court to our people; them, and the kittens, none of whom I saw here.

But with the entire population of the Court locked inside and begging like street dogs for the smallest scraps, the least among us were going to receive exactly that unless measures were taken. I crouched and ripped open the foul plastic covering the food, setting each packet in front of a different small cluster of cats. A few stronger-looking cats tried to interpose. I hissed at them, and they retreated.

Turning my attention back to the elders, I urged them forward. "Here," I said, voice soft. "This is for you. You need to keep your strength up."

Not that they would be keeping their strength up very well on this, which looked to have been fried within an inch of its life before sitting under heat lamps for hours, but as I hadn't been helping with the scavenging, I wasn't going to criticize. I was just going to help.

With my hands now empty, I straightened and waded back to Raj, who shot me a grateful look.

"Your aid is appreciated, Uncle," he said. "I know this isn't the best way to see everyone fed, but without any other way to manage it, we're doing what we can."

"I've been to see Shade," I said, solemnly. "Things are worse in her Court. She's alone."

"So is Ginevra's father," said Raj. "She slipped out to the mortal world and found a phone, called the comic book store. Her mother is working the counter."

"And?"

"And the King of Whispering Cats is the only royal cat in his domain. Her sisters are trapped inside the Court with the others, but at least his people respect them well enough that they can stand guard over the food as needed, when he goes to sleep or comfort their mother.

They don't remember her. She remembers them being born, taken into shadow, and growing up in the Court, without her seeing them again. What sort of world *is* this?"

"A terrible one," I said. "The kind of world Titania would make, if she were allowed the control she so desires. A cruel one, that sunders a mother from her daughters, men from their wives, and children from their parents."

"Did you find October?"

"I did." I turned my face away, unable to bear the thought of looking at him as I answered. Wanting something to do with my hands, I grabbed a few more packets of chicken from the pile and lobbed them into the crowd, watching them vanish in a flurry of claws and snarling. "She is in Amandine's tower with her sister, and by the reports I have from Shadowed Hills, with Simon as well."

"And Amandine?"

"And Amandine, of course. Titania has torn my family apart to restore one that never truly existed, one that collapsed entirely on its own."

"I don't . . ."

"You say Ginevra's mother remembers the world as it never was, a world where she has never known her daughters as we both know she did? Well, she's not alone. The minds of everyone I met today had been remade, and not all for the better." I honestly couldn't say that *any* of them had been remade for the better, although I didn't know Garm well enough to be confident of that. Perhaps this was the best possible version of a man I had never truly known. Someone had to thrive in this horrible perversion of Faerie.

"So why don't we remember things that way?"

"Royal cats have always been resistant to certain forms of illusion; we see through them, regardless of the power put into their construction. Titania must have known we would shake off her new history of the world, and thus created a situation where we would be needed to keep our people alive. As long as we're working to keep the Cait fed and stable, we can't be getting in her way." I looked at him, lips pressed into a hard, thin line. "Which means I want nothing more than to get in her way. We have to organize this better."

"We— You'll stay and help? Even with October in her mother's tower?"

"Yes." I said the word as if it pained me, because in truth, it did. "Simon will not harm her, nor allow harm to come to her if he might prevent it. The people I spoke to in Shadowed Hills described him as one of the better versions of himself, and given that all I have ever known him to want was a home, a family, and the respect of those above him, it seems likely their description was an accurate one. He serves as the Countess Winterrose's dogsbody, and it's a role he's filled before. He does it well. He'll protect October while I can't."

"Why can't you?"

"She's in the tower," I said. "I can't get past the wards. Oh, with time, I'm sure I'll be able to manage—wards that can keep a truly determined King of Cats out have never been invented, to my knowledge, and it seems that for the moment, all I have is time—but she doesn't know me. Should I appear in her bedroom, a wild stranger, and steal her away to a kingdom of ravenous cats, to be my prisoner? That is one human fairy tale that doesn't particularly appeal to me. She seems well, for the moment. She looked at her sister with fondness, and she is clearly being fed and properly cared for. I will set myself to improving the lot of the Courts, for I won't be able to be here consistently."

Not being able to go to her felt like it was killing me, but I could accept, for now, that I was doing what was necessary. And when I could no longer accept that, well. We would cross that bridge when we came to it.

Raj blinked. "No?"

"No. One of Sylvester's men, a Gwragen named Garm—"

"Oh, he's one of the knights," interrupted Raj. "Quentin says he's naturally suspicious, and sometimes a little too quick to think the worst of people. Etienne knighted him too soon, because he thought he was going to have to stand for Quentin, and he didn't want to have two squires at the same time."

"It seems history repeats itself, as Quentin appears convinced Etienne will stand knight for him in this new world, and Etienne seems less than enchanted by the idea."

"You saw Quentin? How is he?"

"At Shadowed Hills, and safe, if a bit spoilt and demanding. I think this is a version of him who was never given cause to question the superiority he had been told was his by right of birth. You probably wouldn't like him much."

Raj frowned. "Huh."

"Yes."

I passed out more chicken, waiting for him to catch on to the one part of my explanation that I had expected him to object to. When I heard him inhale sharply, I knew he'd done it.

"Yes?"

"Simon—he *can't* be working for *her*," said Raj. "She's asleep some-where out in the dark."

"Yes, and the false Queen is back upon the throne, and Arden ab-sent." I turned to look calmly at Raj. "Titania has remade the world. Who's to say how many people we think dead and gone she's resur-rected for her purposes? And I'm sure she *does* have a purpose to the people she's brought back. The Countess was never dead, more's the pity, but I'm sure Titania wanted the company of her favorite daughter and saw this as an opportunity to have her ideal version of it, a daugh-ter who never argued or went against her will—assuming she didn't simply walk into the dark and wake the woman for her own amuse-ment. I don't know all that she's capable of. None of us does. For the moment, we assume she can do anything Oberon hasn't specifically thought to forbid. If she wants *that woman* as a part of her Faerie, she'll have it."

Raj blanched. "You mean she could have brought back my father?"

"If it would ever have occurred to her to resurrect one of the Cait Sidhe, I'm quite sure she could have brought him back, in image if not in actuality," I said. "We have no evidence these people are real, and not just extensions of the illusion. I'm fresher than you are right now. Let Ginevra sleep. I'll distribute the rest of this chicken, assuming there's none meant for any other chamber, while you go and find some people for me."

"Who?" asked Raj, suddenly wary.

"I want Gabriel, Cal, and Emil," I said. Two of my largest enforcers, and Raj's frequent scout. In our version of reality, all of them had ex-perience in the human world, and Gabriel knew how to operate a motor vehicle. They might or might not be coaxed into entering the shadows, assuming they could access them with me to aid, but I trusted them to help us distribute or hide whatever we could steal.

"All right," he said, relaxing. "I didn't want to leave the Court. I'll be right back."

He dove into shadow rather than stepping, and the gathered cats surged forward, the ones who had yet to feed meowing in distress. It was an overwhelming scene, and not one I was eager to linger over. Still, they needed to be fed, and Ginevra needed to rest.

"We are working to alleviate the current situation," I said. "But begging like common street dogs won't make me feed you faster. Please, settle and be patient, and allow any who have not been fed today to move to the front."

They fell silent, and for a moment, I felt smug, sure that my kingly commands had fixed things. Then they began meowing again, even louder, and Ginevra opened an eye.

"Requests for civility might have worked before they were starving," she said. "I've had to add powdered milk for bottle-weaning kittens to the supply list, as their mothers aren't getting enough to keep them properly fed. This isn't sustainable."

"I know that," I snapped, and hurled three more packs of chicken into the crowd. Crude as this distribution method was, it at least kept them from mobbing me and tearing me apart in their eagerness to eat. It would be a deeply unpleasant way to die.

"You sent Raj away," she said, and yawned a massive, bone-cracking yawn. "Do you have some sort of a plan?"

"Shade is doing this all alone," I said. "She needs our help."

Ginevra started to object. I held up a hand, cutting her off.

"I understand we're needed here," I said. "Our people come first, always. But if we can get things settled sufficiently to no longer be in a state of constant crisis, we can possibly assist her, and send word to your father of what we've done to make things better."

"He's managing alone, but better than we are," said Ginevra. "He's been using the store's business account to buy cat food in bulk. Mail order and sending Mom to the wholesalers means he's been able to get a lot more supplies in, even without anyone to help him out. I'm pretty proud of him, honestly."

"I can see that," I said gravely. I had a decent quantity of mortal money but no credit cards, and with Titania's exile of the Cait Sidhe, there was no telling whether my accounts were currently accessible. It would have been nice to have an ally in the human world who could go and inquire for me, but I couldn't . . .

Janet.

Titania wasn't allowed to harm her, and she was living in the city with Cliff, when not ensconced in the hidden courtyard she had anchored to the Summerlands in Berkeley. Janet was strange and fey in the mortal sense, and not always an ally, but she was human, and was one of the people Titania was explicitly forbidden to harm. She might remember Faerie as it really was.

She was worth searching for, anyway.

I was spared from needing to continue my conversation with Ginevra by Raj's return, with Emil, Cal, and Gabriel in tow. Opal had also come along, her daughter, Alazne, in her arms. I knew the child could walk on her own—I'd seen it—but Opal was reluctant to allow her to do so, preferring to keep the girl close at all times. Given the circumstances of Alazne's birth, and the loss of her littermates, I couldn't fault her mother's protective streak.

"Hello," I said, tossing the last of the chicken to the cats in the crowd and turning to face the group I'd summoned. "I appreciate you coming,"

"Our King calls for us," said Gabriel solemnly, and bowed. "We are grateful for the chance to aid in any way you see fit."

"I wonder what version of the past you remember," I said, suddenly speculative. Gabriel looked at me, confused. I waved a hand. "No matter. We need to feed the Court."

Alazne perked up at the thought that food might be in the offing, then slumped again as she realized I wasn't offering a meal. Opal kissed the top of her head, then shot me a strained look.

"I don't mean to tease, child," I said. "But I may have a means by which we can access plenty. Are any of you strong enough to access the shadows?"

"I did, once," said Cal. "On a dare. I concentrated as hard as I could, and when I reached into the air, my whole hand vanished. It was still attached. I could feel it. It was just someplace I couldn't see, someplace very cold. But that was the most I could do."

"No matter; I only wondered," I said, soothingly. "My plan doesn't require you be able to move through shadow. Opal, do you think you could stay here and speak for the Court for a short while if Raj, Ginevra, and I all leave together?"

Looking flustered, she bit her lip and nodded.

"No one will give you any trouble, and I'll tell them before we go that you have the full authority to reduce anyone's rations if they try to abuse your position. It will be all right." I turned to Emil. "The Fell Street Garage remains a part of our domain, yes?"

A parking garage in the mortal world, it had been featured in many works of human cinema before its demolition, which had been enough for portions of it to become lost when the building came down, sinking into the strange sub-realm that was in our keeping. It would provide sufficient room for us to stage everything I intended to steal tonight.

"Yes, sire."

"Excellent. Is anyone currently dwelling there?"

"It is isolated and cold, with no access to plumbing or fresh water," he said. "No one lives there that I know of."

"Even better. Please go and clean out anyone who's gone looking for privacy and thought to find it in cold concrete, and we will be there shortly."

Emil nodded and turned, walking briskly away. I turned back to Gabriel and Cal. "The two of you will be helping us with acquisition and distribution tonight," I said. "Mortal sunset should come in three hours or so. Has the Court been fed well enough to wait that long for another meal, if I can promise this will be a plentiful one?"

"It has," said Ginevra.

"Then we will take these three hours to be sure no one has any merry ideas about following us to steal the choicest bits of whatever we obtain, and we will plan our approach once the garage is secure. Go with Gabriel and Cal to join Emil. You, also, Raj."

"What about you?" asked Raj.

"Shade seemed very concerned about the kittens of her Court," I said. "I know you and Ginevra have been doing your very best in my absence, but I worry, and will walk the Court before I join you, to be sure all is as well as it can be. I'll be with you inside of the hour."

Raj looked uncertain, glancing from me to the others with small motions of his head, clearly anxious.

"Costco," I said to him, like an incantation, and maybe it was, because his uncertainty faded, replaced by dawning amazement.

"I never thought of that," he said.

"This time of year, they close as the sun is setting," I said. "We'll arrive after the human staff has departed, and we'll do what must be done. But for now, I need to see my Court, and you need to see the space we'll be moving things into. After we finish this task, I have an appointment to keep, in Shadowed Hills."

Oh, I was going to be exhausted before this night's work was done. But then, Ginevra and Raj were already exhausted, and I was still intending to take them with me and then leave them once more in charge of the Court.

If Titania survived this horror, she belonged to the Court of Cats. Of that, I had no question in the slightest.

The others walked away, and I turned to head down the tunnel, toward the part of the abandoned station that had previously been used as living quarters, when we had been more inclined to denning down here, before we'd found proper anchors to the outside. The smell of too many bodies and the dreaded litter boxes addressed my nose not long after my journey began, telling me I was heading in the right direction, however unpleasant that direction chanced to be. I kept walking, and was soon rewarded with a door that didn't belong in a train station.

Opening it put me into one of the impossible, zigzag hallways that streak through the Court of Cats like threads through a tapestry. It's rare for an entire hall to be lost, and so our halls are made up of segments strung together, five feet from a manor here, ten feet from a shopping center there, until they form a contiguous whole. When the magic to make the Court of Cats was first pooled together, the working must have been a wonder such as had never been seen before in all of Faerie.

The hall led me to a series of large rooms, honeycombed together by open doorways, filled with beds and piles of cloth and fur, filled in turn with cats. Most were sleeping; in a few such nests, groups of kittens rolled and tumbled, one or both parents watching tolerantly. Not all of them were cats I recognized. Many were more mortal than fae, thin-blooded feline changelings swept off the streets by Titania's enchantment.

There were more of them than I had ever considered there might be, and while I hated the circumstances, I was glad they were finally here. This was their birthright, as much as anyone else's: they had the right to be here, to raise their children in safety, to be cared for, even if they didn't yearn for human keepers.

I sat on the corner of an unoccupied bed, extending my hand toward an unfamiliar mother cat for her to sniff. She did, gracefully, before knocking her head against my knuckles in acceptance and polite recognition.

"Hello, mother," I said. "Your children look well. Healthy and strong."

She meowed, making no attempt to hide her own hunger. I nodded.

"Yes. I understand that you would like a more substantial meal, and confidence of another coming after," I said. "We're working to arrange it. How old are your kits?"

A meow.

"A good age." They'd need soft foods soon, for the weaning. The unfamiliarity of the mother cat told me she was likely one of the mortal cats with a few drops of fae blood who had been confined by Titania's treachery. Her children would remain feline in form, and not be able to move on to human baby foods. An issue only in that food for human infants was somewhat easier to come by than food for weaning kits.

She meowed again, then settled deeper into her bed, closing her eyes.

It was rare for me to be so summarily dismissed, and I was charmed despite myself. She knew I was the King here. She simply didn't care.

"If you need anything, find a member of my Court," I said. "We will do our best to see it done."

I rose and continued on my prowl.

Every room I entered contained more of the same. Cats on every surface, listless, sleeping the days away.

The people who say a cat has a natural instinct to roam are projecting human attributes onto feline forms. True cats, whether purely mortal or changeling, have no need to roam. They want to eat and drink, to have warm places to sleep and clean places to eliminate themselves, to play and be engaged by their environment. They can be happy their entire lives in a single room, if the room is suited to their needs.

Fae cats are somewhat different. Not because of our instincts or "wild natures" or whatever justification humans are using for letting their pets roam wild *this* week, but because we're intelligent creatures, and we need more stimulation than a simple animal. We're also magical shapeshifters who can evade most urban threats that would destroy a domestic cat. For us, being sealed inside the Court—and having memories that implied this had been going on for years, if not decades—was a form of genuine torture.

My subjects were suffering. Hunger aside, confinement was hurting them, and it wasn't going to stop unless I stopped it.

And I was *going* to stop it. I was going to get my family and my life and my *world* back, and let them all run free, as they should have been from the beginning. This was unendurable.

Satisfied with what I'd seen, with the horror of it all, I turned and made my way toward the buried parking garage where my companions would be waiting. All were there, save for Opal, who had presumably remained behind to keep the cats of the Court calm. Ginevra, while yawning, looked much better than she had immediately upon my arrival. Not *well*, to be quite clear, but better.

"Tybalt," she said, seeing me enter.

"Ginevra," I replied mildly.

"Raj says we're going to Costco?" she said, in a disbelieving tone. I nodded, and was amused to see the way her eyes widened.

"We are indeed," I said. "The store will be closed upon our arrival, and they have those flat carts for people who want to buy more mustard than they have space in their homes. We'll load them with cat food and the contents of the butcher's shelves, and with anything else we might need, then tow them into shadow. If we can pull the handles through to where Gabriel and Emil can grab them, they can bring the carts fully into the Court, and Cal can handle the unloading."

The young Cait Sidhe I had requested for this task stood a little straighter, puffing their chest out in pride at being asked to do something of obvious importance.

"I requested this garage not only because of its size and isolation from the main Court, but because of its location," I said, looking at Ginevra. "Touch the Shadow Roads, and try to chart a course to the nearest Costco."

Costco is a chain, or I wouldn't have been nearly so cavalier about robbing them for everything that wasn't nailed down. There are locations all over the Bay Area and, according to May, the United States. But as distance is still a factor when navigating the Shadow Roads, it was only the closest location we were concerned with. Ginevra closed her eyes, brow briefly furrowing, before her expression cleared and a slow smile blossomed on her lips, making her more lovely than she had ever been.

"Tybalt, you're a genius," she said, opening her eyes and turning to face me again.

"I am a man who understands desperation," I corrected, politely. "The Court must be fed, and I must be free to seek my lady. I've found her body. Until I can free her mind, finding the physicality of her does me little good. This new world has some strange ideas about changelings that I have yet to fully comprehend. I need time to learn more, and the freedom to spend it as my quest makes necessary. So we go to the place with the most gathered resources, and we take what we need, and then the three of us will be able to go to Shade and help her do the same, thus keeping her Court from calamity, and I can go seeking a way to free my lady from her unfair predicament."

"That doesn't make you not a genius, it just makes you practical," said Ginevra.

I turned to Gabriel. "Will Opal be well?" I asked.

"She will," he said. "She's strong, and she understands the necessity of keeping things under control. I don't understand much of what you're saying, but the Lady Ginevra has explained to us that the world isn't meant to be the way it is right now, and I honestly believe her. There's no way we could have survived this long, sealed in and depending on only three people to keep us fed and comfortable. We would have starved in the dark decades ago. And there are too many mortal cats."

I blinked. "What does that have to do with anything?"

He looked uncomfortable. "A mortal cat, unaltered, will go into heat on a regular basis, and those of us who aren't royal find it much more difficult to refuse our instinctual response. If we'd been locked in for as long as I know we have been, there wouldn't be so many cats with mostly mortal heritage. They'd all have been bred to full changeling generations ago. That they haven't means the numbers don't add up."

I wouldn't have thought to use the kittens as proof that Titania's reality was a false one, but if it worked for Gabriel, I wasn't going to argue.

"I wish you could walk the shadows with us, old friend," I said.

"Believe me, so do I," he responded.

The Costco would close soon. I moved to stand with Raj and Ginevra.

"Once we have the supplies here, we'll leave Opal and the others to handle distribution and storage, and the three of us will repeat the action in Berkeley," I said. "It's best if it were all to happen on the same night, to keep them from bolstering their security, and in my company, Shade will allow your passage." Privately I thought that at this point, Shade would allow the passage of Faerie's greatest monsters, if it would just leave her able to feed her people.

Ginevra nodded. "And then you're off to find October."

"To bring her home," I said. "Yes. We may have allies, but it will take time to be sure, and my time will not be freed to that purpose until we have the food to keep our Court alive. Are we ready?"

Both nodded, and I gestured for them to follow as I stepped into shadow.

Even with the efforts we had made at proximity, we would have to pull the carts of stolen goods a short distance along the Shadow Roads. It wouldn't be easy, or pleasant, and yet it was the only way.

Just because the Shadow Roads are shorter than other means of travel, that doesn't make them instant. Still, we ran only perhaps twenty yards before we stepped out into the dim, cool air at the back of the warehouse store. Raj gasped. He had been to Costco before, but during the day and with a means of payment, not after hours and considering the whole place as a prize to be looted. Ginevra merely turned and embraced me, pressing her face against my upper arm.

"We can save them," she said. "Oak and ash, we can actually save them."

"Then let's get started."

We each grabbed the largest cart we could manage on our own and fanned out through the empty aisles, filling them from top to bottom with everything we could lift. The pet section was denuded in a matter of minutes, canned and dry food going into the carts with no concern for brand or quality: we were trying to fill stomachs, not preserve kidneys over the long stretch of time. If this went on long enough for feeding my subjects cheap cat food to become an issue, we were going to be doomed for other reasons. No veterinary care in the Court of Cats. No healer in my Court, although I had encountered them in others. No way out.

Raj filled a cart with treats, toys, and soft beds with fleece linings, shooting me a sharply challenging look when I seemed too curious. "We need to keep them happy as well as fed. Once their bellies are full, they'll have more energy," he said.

"There are toys for human children toward the front, and blankets. Be sure to grab some of those as well, for the kits that prefer to play in two-legged form, and for additional bedding."

Raj brightened and ran off, loading his cart further.

In short order, we had completely filled our carts and were ready to push them through the Shadow Roads. Exchanging a look, we filed into the dark, our ill-gotten gains slowing us enough that what had been a journey of some seconds became an almost ten-minute trudge through the cold. Still, it was balanced by the looks of surprise and delight when we emerged into the garage and handed off our burdens to be unloaded.

"We'll come through to collect these carts when we bring the next batch. Humans sometimes put tracking devices on things they own, and I don't know whether that includes shopping carts. Better not to find out the hard way," I advised.

Gabriel nodded, hoisting a massive bag of kibble onto each shoulder. "Of course, sire," he said. "Whatever you desire."

I flashed him a smile and dove back into the shadows.

We repeated this process half a dozen times, stripping the store of everything a cat might like, as well as every can of meat or fish, every pound of meat in the butcher's department, all the fish in the fishmonger's case, the cheese and preserved meats, the canned fruits and easy snacks for two-legged children, soft drinks and bread and so much else. Eggs and green things, fruit and pastries, toothpaste and brushes, diapers and cans of formula, until all three of us were exhausted and our willing helpers in the garage stood amidst towering piles of supplies.

Our last trip was just the three of us pushing the final set of empty carts through the shadows and out into the denuded store.

"They're going to be mad in the morning," said Ginevra.

"Let them be. They probably have cameras, but they'll show nothing but three strangers and what seems to be a strange glitch in the security. Now come. We must away."

"To Shade? Tonight?" She looked at me pleadingly. "With as much as we've just collected, we might actually be allowed to sleep. Please, Tybalt, I need to sleep."

"What you have done with Raj in my absence is what Shade has done by herself," I said. "Alone, with no one else who can exit the Court on her behalf. She needs this. Her *people* need this. She has been an ally to me and to our Court often enough in the past that if we can aid her now, we have a duty. Erda would ask no less of us."

Ginevra sighed. "All right. We go."

"Excellent. Come, Raj." The three of us threw ourselves into the dark, racing along the Shadow Roads toward Shade's Court. It was a brief-enough journey, sped by exhaustion spurring us to move as quickly as we could, and in what seemed like the blinking of an eye, we were emerging into Shade's Court.

None of her people attacked me this time, for which I was profoundly grateful. They lifted their heads and looked at us warily, and I seized the opportunity to beckon to one stripling a few years younger than Raj and ask, "Will you go and find your Queen for me? I have a proposal she will want to hear, and quickly."

The child bobbed a quick bow and scurried away, vanishing into the shadows of the Court, which were shallower and less consuming than the shadows we'd been moving through for the last hour. I moved closer to Raj and Ginevra, both of whom were looking with horror at the gathered cats.

"As I said, she's been doing this alone," I said. "She seemed particularly concerned for the kittens. The four of us together should be much better equipped to support two Courts, even if I am of necessity often absent."

"You are returned," said Shade, voice radiating relief. I turned and smiled as she walked up to me, her earlier exhaustion still present, etched into the bones of her, but no longer drawn quite so tightly around her lips and eyes. "I was afraid you might decide to run instead of dealing with my problems."

Her voice caught for a moment as she caught sight of Ginevra, and I had the distinct impression that the whiskers she didn't currently possess were flattening themselves against her cheeks in displeasure at the obvious intrusion of her territory.

Raj and I were male. I was a King, and he a Prince on the cusp of

Kingship. Ginevra, for all that her current position was difficult to define within our hierarchy, was a Princess at the absolute least, and radiated the power of a rival Queen thanks to her time in regency over my Court. For her to enter Shade's territory was on the absolute cusp of active challenge, and while Shade might say she'd be happy to hand the responsibility off to someone else, she wouldn't be able to resist the need to fight if she were pushed. I stepped in front of Ginevra, not blocking her, but breaking Shade's eyeline.

"This is my heir, Rajiv," I said. "He will be King of Dreaming Cats very soon. Until that time, as my lady needs me enough to make me unable to properly occupy my throne, Ginevra Field stands as his regent."

"I am honored by admission to your territory, Your Majesty," said Ginevra. "I have no interest in offering a challenge, as I have promised my father, the King of Whispering Cats, that I will return and stand as his heir when my time in the Mists is done. He understands the rituals necessary for passing a Kingdom from King to Queen, and is well prepared to perform them for my sake."

Shade relaxed slightly. "If not to challenge, why are the three of you here?" she asked, with a note of wariness in her voice.

I couldn't entirely blame her for that. Still, we needed to move, and quickly. October wasn't in active danger that I knew of, but my patience was not a construct without limits, and I had need to learn more about this remade world.

"We have a proposal," I said, and smiled at her, waiting for the moment when understanding lit her eyes and she gestured for us to follow her deeper into the Court.

It was going to be a long night.

NINE

THE SECOND COSTCO WAS even easier to rob than the first, being somewhat larger and less filled with twisting corridors of merchandise. Shade managed to rouse four of the larger members of her Court to unload our carts and stand guard over the goods, and by the time we finished emptying the store, she was all but weeping with the joy of knowing her people would be cared for.

"Whatever your Court requires of mine, always," she said, embracing me as we made to go. "We are allies evermore."

"We can come back," said Ginevra. "Raj and I, I mean. Tybalt needs to deal with some personal stuff, but there's two of us and only one of you. We can check in, and then we can do another run when necessary."

"I would like that very much," said Shade. "I grant you permission of passage in my lands for so long as this crisis continues. We will protect the Courts together, as the royal cats always have, even back to Malvic's day."

"And on that loving note, I must away," I said. "I'm meeting a knight of Sylvester's service, who says he can get me into the Library of Stars. According to him, the books don't change when the world is rewritten. I have cause to hope I might find more of what I'm seeking there."

"Best of luck, then," said Shade.

"Open roads and kind fires to you all," I said, and dove into shadow before anything else could require my aid, running hard in the direction of Shadowed Hills.

It would be a close thing: between explaining our plan to Shade and carrying out our raid of the Costco, I had been left with little under a quarter of an hour to get to Shadowed Hills and locate Garm, lest he go to the Library without me. I didn't have a card, never having sought to obtain one, and the only person I knew locally who did was Simon Torquill. I might not suspect him of harming October intentionally—if anything, he was likely to be as much a victim in the current situation as she was—but that didn't mean I trusted myself in a room with him when he was part of the group keeping her away from me.

Nor would he have any reason to do me a favor if I asked. No. I needed to play nicely with Garm for the time being, and that meant arriving when I'd said I would.

I ran as fast as I had ever run, and dropped out of the Shadows onto the promenade as the clock was striking the hour. I stopped there, breathing hard, before I moved toward the glass doors and peeked inside.

A small gathering was assembled in the ballroom. Not large enough to be considered a party, not properly so, but a dinner perhaps. Sylvester was not in evidence. Neither was his brother. Etienne was there, looking uncomfortable as he spoke with a noblewoman in a blue velvet gown. None of the other faces were familiar, save for a Candela in guard's livery who stood in one corner, her Merry Dancers circling her head and a bland scowl on her face. Grianne, another of Sylvester's knights with whom my relations had been cordial in the past.

I frowned. If I entered, Etienne might have questions; if I tried to go around, someone else might. I didn't know where, exactly, I was meant to meet with Garm, only that he was hopefully expecting me. I turned and walked away from the door, dropping down onto all fours and continuing onward in feline form. As Sylvester's guest, the wards here were already inclined to welcome me, and for all that I often told October I wasn't a bloodhound, being able to trace Garm by scent was an advantage I couldn't push away.

I didn't know Garm well enough to pick him out of a crowd, but there was only one fresh Gwragen trail on the promenade, scented with moss and stagnant water. I put my nose to the stone, sniffing, and followed it, taking the rail around the outside of the manor rather than trying to invade the ballroom. On the other side, I found a high, open corridor, the stars twinkling overhead, and dropped back down to the main trail, trotting faster as the scent grew stronger.

At the end of the corridor was an open door, and a stairway leading up to the guards' quarters. I followed the trail to another door, this one closed, and rose onto two legs to rap my knuckles against it.

"Coming!" called Garm, a bare moment before the door was opened and he was looking at me in mild confusion. He was half out of his livery, having removed his tunic but not yet his breeches, and his gray-ish cheeks were flushed. "Oh. You're quite timely."

"I try to be." I stepped into the room. It was small, simple, and well appointed. The furnishings had clearly been where they were for some time, acquiring a layer of clutter and sinking into their places like well-set tentpoles, each clearly set where it belonged.

The bed was unmade. He hadn't been expecting company.

I turned to watch as he pulled a fresh white under-tunic on over his head, rumpling his hair still further. "I didn't expect you to be on time. Royalty rarely is."

I blinked, briefly confused. "I never claimed a title."

"You didn't need to. You said only royal cats could pass after what had been done to the world, and I can read. I went by the ducal library on my lunch, and looked up what we had on Cait Sidhe. It said you kept your own Courts, granted by Oberon himself, and divided your-self into royal and common cats, based on power rather than birth. You'd have to be either a Prince or a King, to be considered royal. The book was unclear on what the difference is, from a power perspec-tive." He paused, clearly waiting for me to fill in what the book hadn't supplied.

"There isn't one, or if there is, it's more about experience and time than pure power. A Prince who's new to the area won't have deep ties to the local Shadow Roads, or know all the ways in and out of the Court. So the local King can easily defeat him, if it comes to a chal-lenge. Given time, the shadows begin to bend more and more to the individuals, to understand what they'll want, and the Court chooses its favorites, always. So a Prince and a King are likely to be comparable in power, but only the one who can defeat the other may claim the higher title."

"Fascinating. Which are you, then? Unless that's an unspeakably rude question, I'm just excited. I've never met a Cait Sidhe before."

"King," I said, with a small curl of my lip.

"Your Majesty," said Garm, and pulled a pair of trousers from a drawer. "We can head for the Library as soon as I finish getting dressed. I was able to get a pass, and it allows me to bring a guest, as long as we both promise not to start any trouble while we're there."

"I know the rules of the Libraries," I said. "If there's trouble, it will not begin with me."

"Excellent. Were you able to find your lady?"

I tried to control my face but must have schooled myself too slowly, for Garm winced as he looked at me. "It went that well?"

"I . . . found her," I said, gravely. "As I said before, she is a change-ling, and not Cait Sidhe. She knows me not. She doesn't even know *herself.* I had no way of approaching her without frightening her un-duly, and so I chose to retreat and help my own people while I seek more information on the situation."

"Hence the Library," said Garm. "Well, if you love the Maiden Oc-tober, then I wish you only well. She's a good, dutiful daughter to her household, and she deserves better than what Titania's Law intends for her."

"That is the second mention of that law I've heard," I said, tamping down my annoyance at his accurate guess. "It describes no decree I have ever been aware of."

"It is the duty of all noble households, and all Firstborn, to provide at least one changeling child to be pressed into service to Faerie," said Garm, with the vague detachment that meant he was reciting a proc-lamation, not giving an opinion. "In the occasion that a titled noble has not yet produced their own heir, the duty may be delayed to avoid possible questions of succession."

"Does that mean changelings can inherit?" Maybe Titania had cre-ated a fairer world than I would have expected of her.

Garm shook his head. "No."

Maybe not.

He wasn't finished, however: "After Maeve betrayed her sister, hus-band, and all of Faerie, and was lost to us, the hope chests were de-stroyed for our protection. There might yet be one remaining—there are always rumors. So I suppose it's possible a changeling could find a way to become purely fae and challenge for a crown, and that possibil-ity is best avoided. That avoidance is why our Duke is spared the per-formance of his duty for the time being, as he has yet to take a wife."

The confirmation of Luna's absence explained much about what I'd already seen of Shadowed Hills, but raised more questions that I had no idea how to answer. "What of his daughter?"

"The Duke has no children, lost or living," said Garm. Then his eyes widened. "Unless—are you saying the Fair Titania edited a *child* away?"

"I've already heard claim that two people I know to be sleeping off the sentences for their crimes are awake and active within the political structure of the Mists, while others are missing," I said grimly. "I wouldn't put anything past her at this point. But come. We must to the Library. How were you intending to travel there?"

Garm paused. "I wasn't sure you would make it back to accompany me," he said. "Even if you did, I wasn't sure you would actually want to."

"All right . . . ?"

"So I arranged a ride with my customary companion," he said. "I apologize if you wanted to keep your presence a secret. She's very good at discretion."

"She? She who?".

The shadows in one corner of the room rippled. I tensed, moving to place myself between them and Garm. The chances of a knight of Shadowed Hills being attacked in the Duke's own knowe were slim, but as he was one of the only allies I currently had, I didn't want to risk them, no matter how slim they were.

The ripples increased, and Grianne stepped out of the shadows in a flare of greenish-white light. Like Garm, she had set aside her livery; she was wearing a simple green sundress that complimented the striated gray of her skin and nearly matched her eyes. She stopped when she saw me, Merry Dancers bobbing next to her head as she tried to figure out who I was and what I was doing there.

Grianne was, in many ways, the platonic ideal of a Candela. She was lithe and compact, not tall enough to attract attention if she was trying to lurk in a bog or fen, with ash-colored skin and hair a few shades darker, like an exposed granite cliff face. Both were striped with bands of darker and lighter gray, making it even easier for her to blend in. Two globes of light wove and danced around her: the Merry Dancers she would once have used to lure human travelers to their deaths in sucking mud and quicksand, in the days when such action would have protected all of Faerie.

She looked at me with confusion, frowning, and turned to Garm, cocking an eyebrow in silent question.

"Grianne, this is Rand," he said. Then, in a tone that implied the sharing of a delicious secret, he added, "He's the Cait Sidhe I told you about. He'll be accompanying us to the Library."

"Can't," she said, brusquely.

I didn't take offense. The Candela are infamously terse, as a whole, and my past dealings with Grianne had clearly illustrated that she was short-winded even for one of her kind. "Why not?" I asked.

She shrugged. "Shadows won't allow."

Ah. Like the Cait Sidhe, the Candela are able to access the Shadow Roads. The desire to keep Candela in her Faerie—or at least the lack of desire to get rid of them—was probably what had caused Titania to assume she could leave the Shadow Roads connected without risking the escape of the royal cats. I wanted to believe she had done it so we could at least try to feed our people, and could then claim her hands were clean when we failed and starved, but even that cynical a position was beyond me. She didn't care about us enough to give us a lifeline. If she'd left the shadows open, it was because she thought there was some advantage in it.

Such as the movement of the Candela, who were often employed as messengers, despite their taciturn natures. But the Shadow Roads didn't belong to them as they belonged to the Cait Sidhe. Taking passengers was difficult, even for us. For the Candela, it was virtually impossible. Honestly, I was impressed that Grianne was strong enough to carry even Garm.

"Have no concern for me, Lady," I said. "The Cait Sidhe anchor the Shadow Roads. I can get myself to the Library, if only you tell me where we're going. When last I looked, the Library of Stars lay its anchor in San Francisco, on the mortal side, near a wholesale flower market."

"That place was abandoned some time ago," said Garm. "These days, the Library lays anchor in the city of Vallejo, near the water. Can you follow Grianne along the shadow paths she carries me through?"

"I can," I confirmed.

Vallejo? That was an interesting choice of anchor. It was a mortal city whose fae side belonged to two fiefdoms at the same time—since the bounds of Shadowed Hills were formally determined by "the shadow of Mount Diablo," the hillier portions of the area were part of Sylvester's domain, while most of the city belonged to Duke Carrig in Wild Strawberries. I had never heard of the Library moving that far from the seat of the Mists, not even during the false Queen's reign.

"The distance will be no trouble, and the light the Dancers cast carries even on the Shadow Roads; I'll be able to follow easily enough," I continued. "Lady Candela, when you're prepared to begin the journey, only go, and I'll be right behind."

Grianne nodded brusquely before taking Garm by the wrist and falling backward into shadow, pulling him with her. I shrugged and dove after them.

As I had promised, the light of Grianne's Dancers was more than sufficient to let me find them in the darkness. She began to run, hauling a gasping Garm along in her wake, neither of them moving as quickly as I would have considered safe. I hurried to catch and keep up, barely pushing myself above a walk, even as she clearly struggled. Finally, taking pity, I leaned over and said, in a mild, carrying tone, "I can take him if you would prefer, Lady."

Her Merry Dancers bobbed ready assent, and I caught his free wrist even as she let him go. She sped up as soon as she was unburdened, moving nearly twice as fast as she had been before, and I sped up to match her, towing Garm along with me.

I could still hear him choking, struggling to breathe in the shallow air of the Shadow Roads. "This goes better if you hold your breath before the journey begins," I said, as kindly as I could. I felt for our location, and decided we were near the mortal city of Martinez. Not too far from Pleasant Hill, then, and not over water.

"Grianne, a moment," I called, and pulled Garm with me out of shadow, onto a warm green hillside, the moon shining overhead and the air of the mortal world blowing around us. He sucked in several deep, greedy breaths before he began to cough, wiping the ice from his lashes at the same time. I let him go and took several steps back, folding my arms as I watched.

"Was this your first time on the Shadow Roads?" I inquired mildly.

Still coughing, Garm shook his head in the negative.

"No? How odd. I would have thought you'd know to hold your breath, then, before diving down into the darkness. The air there is very picky about who it allows to breathe it. Unless the Roads recognize your magic, they'll treat you as an intruder, and freeze you out."

There was a soft pop and a flare of light as Grianne emerged from the shadows and stood impassively back, watching Garm's recovery.

"He knows," she said, voice tight as always. "Doesn't care much."

"You haven't let me suffocate yet," said Garm.

"First times happen," she said.

"I think our Lady Candela has just made a joke," I said. "Truly, this is a remarkable night. Now, then: for the remainder of our journey, Sir Grianne, if you would lead, I will follow, bringing Sir Garm, who *will* be taking a deep breath before we depart. I have no desire to haul a corpse through the shadows, nor to deal with the possible consequences of killing a knight of Shadowed Hills while my own title holds even less authority among the Divided Courts than I am accustomed to."

"Of course," said Garm, looking chastened.

Grianne shot me a curious look. I waved her off.

"I'm quite sure the Librarian will demand a full accounting, which you can listen in on without the need to ask questions of your own accord," I said.

She nodded, seeming pleased by this response, and dove back into shadow. A woman of few words.

Turning back to Garm, I offered him my hand. "A deep breath, if you please," I said. "I've no interest in killing the only person I've found on land who understands the situation, even in part."

"On . . . Never mind." He shook his head and took a deep breath, taking my hand at the same time.

I pulled us both back onto the Shadow Roads, where there was no need to converse, only to run.

It was almost amusing. There had been a time when I viewed carrying October into the dark as a great transgression, a skirting of the bounds which governed my Court. Now I was acting as a taxi service for a knight I barely knew, all in the hopes that he would get me admission to the Library where I might learn more about the current situation.

How the world changes and complicates. How it stays the same.

Grianne turned in the dark ahead of me, the outline of her face limned in green by the glow coming from her Merry Dancers, and gestured for me to follow as she dove out of the shadows and back into the starlit world beyond. I followed, still pulling Garm, and found myself standing behind a house in one of Vallejo's residential neighborhoods, out of sight of the street. The house was dark, the curtains drawn; no one stirred.

Garm pulled his hand from mine and staggered a few feet away to cough the cold out of his lungs. I looked to Grianne, waiting for further instruction. Would we need human disguises? Did we have a long walk between us and the Library?

Instead, she shook the ice off of her own hands, turned to the house, and walked up onto the back porch, opening the screen door and gesturing for us to follow.

Lovely. I do so enjoy traveling with people who have an allergy to explaining themselves. I sighed and followed her, with Garm close behind me and still wheezing. The shadows don't care much for intruders.

Grianne waited for us to join her on the steps before she knocked. No lights came on, but I heard someone moving inside, and when Grianne knocked again, I heard the door unlock. She pushed it open, and stepped into the dark hallway beyond, leaving us to follow her.

Which, of course, we did, and as I stepped over the threshold, I felt the unsettling jerk low in my stomach that could mean a rarely used transition between the human world and the Summerlands. It was never the disorientation for me that October had occasionally described, but it was still noticeable, and made me pause long enough for the door to swing shut behind me with a bang. I glanced back at the sound, and when I faced front again, the hall had changed.

Instead of a dark, deserted mortal home, it was a long corridor lined with tall bookshelves and lit by glowing spheres suspended from the ceiling by thin silver chains. Not that I could see the ceiling; the shelves rose higher and higher until they vanished into a pale golden mist. The chains descended from the same mist, which threw back the light that shone upward, making it all the easier for us to see.

"Librarian?" called Garm, voice still rough from all the coughing. "I have a pass, for myself and a guest."

"I do not have a pass," I called, assuming he'd want Grianne for his plus-one. "But I am aware of Library rules, and may have information that would be of value to you."

There was a clatter, before a woman appeared at the end of the hall, moving into view with unseemly haste. She was short and petite, and even from this distance, I could see her long, pliant dragonfly wings, two to either side of her body, half-spread and shedding glitter into the air.

"Librarian," said Garm, with some relief.

The figure broke into a run, racing toward us, wings starting to beat as she ran, until she looked to be on the verge of taking off. Garm looked alarmed, taking a step back. Grianne tensed but didn't move. I simply watched. I knew this Librarian. Her name was Magdaleana, and she had been Librarian to the Library of Stars for a very long time. Even if she didn't know me, I didn't fear her.

And then she raced past my companions to fling her arms around me, wings snapping fully open as she wailed, "*Tybalt!* Oh, I thought she had actually killed you all!"

I blinked down at her. We had known each other for a long time, but we had never been what I would consider hugging friends, or even such close acquaintances as to excuse this level of familiarity.

"I thought you said your name was 'Rand,'" said Garm, sounding hurt.

"It is," I said. "Royal cats will customarily have two names. The one we bore as kittens, and the one we claim for ourselves after we take a throne."

"Librarian's crying," said Grianne.

That made me pause to look at Magdaleana again. She was, indeed, crying as she clung to me, wings fanning lazily and leaving trails in the air. "May I hazard a guess that you remember the world as it is meant to be?" I asked.

"You may," she said, finally letting me go and taking a step back to wipe her eyes. "Titania can change things outside as much as she likes, but she has no authority over the Library system. She never has. None of the Three do."

That was a fascinating wrinkle on the mystery that was the Libraries. No one really knew where they had come from, who had opened them, when, or why. They were independently mobile, politically neutral, and took steps to protect themselves.

"Then why did you relocate?" I asked.

"Somehow Titania's managed to dispose of Queen Windermere and put *that woman* back on the throne," said Magdaleana. "*That woman* was always fond of interfering with the Library, or trying anyway, when she was actually in charge. I didn't feel like being played with, and neither did the Library, so we moved a few towns over to weather things out. I didn't know what had happened until the Gwragen started showing up and asking questions about revisions."

"I wasn't the first," said Garm.

"No, you weren't," agreed Magdaleana. "It seems that while they're as susceptible to the changes as anyone outside of a Library, they can see that changes have been made. They can see that there's an illusion covering everything they know. And since they know it's there, they can try to figure out what's changed, mostly by coming here and checking the histories that haven't been modified."

"And how do you know that the Summer Queen is behind this?"

"She's done it before," said Magdaleana. "Never on this scale, that I can find, but it's one of her favorite tricks. When backed into a corner, Maeve transforms, Oberon conceals, Titania rewrites. This is her work. But you're here, and alive! Oh, I am *so* relieved to see you. And I won't be the only one, I'm sure. Come, come, all of you." She stepped back, adding, "Library rules are still in effect, although this is considered a time of emergency. While no open war has been declared, self-defense is temporarily allowed. Protecting yourself will not see you asked to leave, or the defenses of the Library activated against you. Do you understand?"

"This sounds like the sort of speech that normally comes right before turning a corner and finding someone who's all but guaranteed to attack," I said, warily. "Is Titania here?"

"No," said Magdaleana, sounding offended. "She doesn't have a Library card. Come on, then."

She walked on, and the rest of us followed, lacking any other choices in the matter.

TEN

THE HALLWAY ENDED IN a large, square space formed by book-shelves, at the center of which several couches and chairs had been positioned to form a reading and conversation nook. Only one of the couches was currently occupied, by a sleeping woman in a voluminous black taffeta skirt and a sequined vest bedazzled in several dozen eye-searing colors. Her hair, while brown at the roots, was streaked in pink, blue, and purple, like a cartoon idea of a sunset.

I stopped dead at the sight of her, staring. "How . . . ?"

"She can't leave," said Magdaleana. "When she tries, her body gets fuzzy around the edges, like it's folding inward on itself, and she screams and runs back inside. I think she's impossible in the world Titania's created, and so she has to remain outside it or be forced back into her original shape."

Which, for May, would be one of the night-haunts. She had this form and face only because she'd sampled October's blood, a long time ago, when my dear little fish had been trying to solve a murder through some of the most boneheaded methods possible.

Then again, I had just been speaking with the Almere. Maybe I didn't have as much room to talk about foolish heroics as I wanted to think I did.

"When did she—?"

"About a week ago. When the world changed, and the Library relo-cated for its own safety. Just appeared, right in the middle of the break room while I was trying to finish my salad. It was very rude, and I'd be furious if she hadn't been hysterical for most of the time she's been here."

"Then she's taken this change about as well as I have, and I cannot fault her for that." I walked over to the couch where she was stretched and sleeping, kneeling down behind her and reaching out to brush the hair away from her cheek. She made a small snorting noise, swatting at my hand, and otherwise didn't move.

I would never have thought to have a Fetch for a sister-in-law, nor to call a death omen a treasured member of my family, but then, I've done many things I would never have thought to do in the years since I began my close association with October, and there are few of them that I would trade away. May is nowhere near to making it onto that list.

"That woman looks like October, if she were more mortal," said Garm. "Why?"

"Oh, that's May," said Magdaleana. "She's October's Fetch."

"Right, right, of course she is," said Garm. "That makes perfect sense. Why wouldn't she be October's Fetch? Why wouldn't the changeling daughter of our Duke's brother have a Fetch? Yes, this is all very normal and not strange or messed-up at all."

"You're the one who told me you'd found a Cait Sidhe," said Grianne.

The shock of her speaking in a complete sentence was apparently enough to silence Garm, however briefly.

I shook May's shoulder this time, trying my best to stay gentle. She grunted, eyes still closed.

"May," I said, wearily. "I don't have as much patience right now as I'm sure we both wish I did, but things are very difficult at the moment, and I could use another ally."

Her eyes snapped open immediately, and she rolled onto her back, staring at me. "Tybalt?" she squeaked, after a moment's stunned silence.

"To my occasional deep regret and frequent relief, yes," I said. "May?"

"As long as I stay inside the Library, yeah," she said. "When I try to go outside, I start becoming Mai again, and she doesn't have any of May's memories, not even the ones I got from Toby."

"Does this make any sense to you?" asked Garm.

"Strangely, yes," said Magdaleana. "Now shush, and let them talk. If you have research to do, I can direct you to the stacks."

"No, that's fine," said Garm. "This is way more interesting."

I was sure it was, but my attention was far too focused on May to spare any for him. She was still staring at me, gray eyes wide and wounded in her half-familiar face. She looked like October had before she'd been forced to burn quite so much of her mortality away. Not like the woman I'd married, but very like the woman I'd fallen in love with.

"Do you know what happened?" she asked.

"According to Amphitrite, and supported by the Librarian and Sir Garm, Titania has rewritten the world to remove the pesky little parts outside her control," I said. "This is Faerie as written in her image. The Cait Sidhe are considered extinct, locked in our Courts with only the royal cats able to come or go. Changelings are intentionally bred to serve noble houses. October lives with August in Amandine's tower. Simon has been swept into this grand delusion as well. The Lordens are beside themselves with worry and rage."

"But Toby's okay," asked May. "I mean, except for the abusive, narcissistic mother situation she's been thrown back into. That part's not great. Have you seen Jazz at all? Or the boys?"

"Raj is in the Court of Cats. Quentin is at Shadowed Hills. Rayseline is nowhere to be seen and, as Sylvester apparently never married her mother, may be, like you, impossible and exiled to some out-of-the-way place where Titania can forget about her."

"And no Jazz?"

Silent, I shook my head.

May swallowed hard. "Okay. Okay. She's fine, I'm sure she's fine. She's a big girl, can take care of herself, and from what I understand, Titania hasn't been *hurting* anyone—not by pureblood standards, anyway. She's just pushing us around like pieces on a game board."

"That matches with what I've seen."

"Then we need to figure out how to win." She laughed, just a little, sounding unmoored. "That's normally Toby's job. But here we are, both of us on our own."

I tilted my head. "Should I go seeking your lady?"

"*No*," she said, with surprising fierceness. I blinked. She sighed. "She won't know me. You can't bring her here, and I can't go to her. Knowing where she is would only make it worse for me."

"Ah," I said. "And for me, the uncertainty would be the worst thing of all."

"I may be able to help with the figuring out how to win," said Magdaleana, stepping forward again. She was holding a large, cloth-bound book that she must have picked up when I wasn't looking. "After I found May in the stacks and the Gwragen of the region began showing up to read old history books, I started doing some of my own research. Puca aren't common anymore, and haven't been for a long time; we've historically been one of the first targets when Faerie's existence has become too blatant for the humans to ignore, thanks to our inability to conceal ourselves. If something was going truly awry, I needed to know about it."

I frowned. "And?"

"And Titania *has* done this, several times in the past, usually when she didn't get her way about something she felt was important. It takes a lot out of her, and she can't sustain it forever, as it effectively has to be recast every day, when the sun comes up and starts punching holes in the edges of her spell. The people who've been put on record after one of these enchantments ended have reported odd dreams followed by waking with memories of things that never happened cluttering their minds, only to fade as the night went on. If you're going to try approaching someone under the illusion's control, I'd suggest doing it as close to dawn as possible, for a better chance of success. It wears on her. The longer and larger the spell, the heavier it becomes, until eventually she *has* to try putting it down."

"When does that happen?"

"If this is meant to be a short-term punishment, any moment. It's already got to be draining her reserves. Given May, however, and the confinement of the Cait Sidhe, and the fact that apparently people believe the Undersea was destroyed in the 1906 Earthquake? As if that makes any sense at all, it's an entire realm, and it's very large, one earthquake isn't going to be enough to wipe it out—"

"Mags," said May, tone sharp as she nudged the other woman back toward the point.

"What? Oh. Sorry. As I was saying, this doesn't feel temporary. This feels like Titania aiming for a permanent revision. Which means she needs a way to fuel it, to keep it from collapsing in on itself."

"That would make sense," I agreed, tersely.

"I think she's intending to anchor it to the Heart of Faerie on Moving Day. Samhain is the next stop on the wheel of the year, and if Titania can Ride, as the Queens used to, before Maeve was lost . . . if she makes her sacrifice to the Heart as the old ritual intended, she'll be able to pull enough power to anchor her spell into the Heart itself. It'll be powered by the raw force of Faerie, and it'll spread like a virus, until it covers the entirety of our world."

"No pressure," said May cheerfully.

I stared at Magdaleana. "Moving Day."

"Yes."

"In four months."

"Yes," she said again, and offered me the book she still held. "This should help us figure out the structure of Titania's spell, and what she's hoping to achieve."

"We know what she's hoping to achieve," I said. "She wants to rule our world."

"She's always wanted that," said Magdaleana.

"So now we get to stop her," said May.

Garm and Grianne were watching us, her with bafflement, him with growing excitement. "You can count us in," he said. "I don't have anything specifically against Titania, but the Gwragen who takes down the Mother of Illusions—he'll be a legend. No one will ever try to challenge him."

"You're not getting a title out of this, you know," said Magdaleana, sounding mildly amused.

"Happier Duke, though," said Grianne. We all looked at her. She shrugged. "I listen. Man wants a family. Simon's not enough. Had a wife? Doesn't know. Get her back."

"I don't think there was a single complete sentence in there, and that still felt like a speech," said May.

"She's right," I said. "We'll all be happier if we make this go away. Some people may prefer this world, but those are people I'd rather not know. Dianda is going to raise an army in the Undersea if we don't resolve this quickly, you know she is. They won't be able to get through the barrier, but they'll be standing by, armed and angry, for when it drops."

"Fun times," said Magdaleana.

"Who's Dianda?" asked Garm.

"Duchess of Saltmist, the neighboring Undersea demesne," I said. "She's a very nice woman, as long as you don't annoy her in some way, and she's married to Simon Torquill."

Garm blinked. "What does Amandine think of that?"

"Not much, as the marriage happened following his divorce from her. She's never been what I would term a very good spouse. The Amandine I know is alone, left by her husband and both her daughters. Simon and August chose life in the Undersea over the risk of coming back into contact with her. October stayed on land, for me."

"I've done some interviews with people who've come to visit the Library since the change, to document the differences," said Magdaleana. "I don't dare go outside, for fear the illusion will catch me as well; it can't get past the Library doors as currently cast, but that's a dubious sort of safety, and I don't want to risk it."

"And?" I asked.

"You mentioned the role of changelings in this world," she said, a little more hesitantly, watching me with the suddenly wary air of someone who had remembered that they were in the presence of a predator. "Titania can't unseal deeper Faerie without Oberon's aid, and those doors are still locked, which makes me suspect that when she cast her spell, she knew she couldn't wrap him up as tightly as she needed, and so she shoved him away somewhere to keep him from interfering. She's still smart enough to know that with the fae confined to the Summerlands and Earth, contact with humans is unavoidable."

"There are also many changelings she's actively forbidden to harm," I said. "Even with her tendency to tuck people away and keep them out of her path, she couldn't put them all in safe places and expect them to stay there. She had to integrate the changelings somehow."

"Yes, and she's historically been resistant to doing her own labor. Half her descendant lines are rumored to have come about because she wanted children who could serve in her household. Most of them chose Oberon when they came of age, to escape the mother who'd treated them like servants since they were born. Having a class of people who are inherently seen as 'lesser' and could be exploited that way without an easy escape would have seemed like a benefit to her."

"Not only that, but it feeds into Oberon's Law's loophole about murder," I said grimly. When I'd been younger, the fact that Oberon's Law prevented purebloods from killing one another but treated changelings as if they were humans, with no protection and no punishment if one should die, had made perfect sense to me. They were temporary creatures, here to go, and the Divided Courts had based so much of their culture upon the Changeling's Choice, which forced discretion by ensuring that every fae parent knew they might be required to kill their own child. Changelings were expendable.

Then I'd gotten to know some of them properly, as people, even before October, and I had seen the Law for the cruel joke it really was. The Divided Courts called *us* beasts, while they sanctioned murder in their homes for the sake of convenience.

"How so?" asked Garm.

"Someone you're allowed to kill without consequence must be considered less than yourself, or else how could that ever be permitted?" I looked back to Magdaleana. "I have the feeling you're about to tell me something I will truly dislike about this world."

"I am. Titania's Law, as you call it, requires the households of all titled purebloods to sire or bear changeling children, to maintain the population and keep 'proper' fae from dirtying their hands. Some of the less-ethical nobles get around this by focusing on the word 'household.' They say, 'Oh, it's not me who has to do it, it's any member of my house,' and they push the task off on their courtiers—or their knights. Anyone they can convince to take the burden on their behalf. But regardless of who their fae parent is, those changelings aren't allowed to marry or to start households of their own. They're expected to serve from birth to death, and if they reach their majority without a place—if the house where they were born doesn't need them, or there's no other household looking to take them in—they can be given to anyone who'll have them. As of right now, this world has been moving forward for little enough time that I don't think anyone's been seriously hurt, but that's going to change."

"And it's a loophole Titania can use to avoid her bindings," said May. "She's not allowed to hurt a member of our family or a descendant of Maeve. I never heard anyone mention her being required to intervene if someone else was about to do harm to someone in those categories."

"Create a world that puts the majority of changelings into harm's way, then sit back and let it unfold the way it would naturally," I said, bleakly. "She's put the nameless Queen back on her throne, and that woman hates changelings. Always has. I doubt any changes to her history would have changed her mind on *that*. With Devin gone, there's nowhere for them to go."

"Wait," said Garm, suddenly alert. "What happened to Devin?"

I turned to blink at him, trying to make that question make sense. I couldn't do it. "What do you mean?" I asked, finally.

"Devin? Kinda slimy, lives in San Francisco, runs a flophouse for changeling runaways, fences stolen goods?" Garm shrugged when he saw the way we were all looking at him. "My cousin's kid ran away when he turned fifteen. He wound up at Devin's place. Stayed there for about five years, then moved down the coast to Golden Shore. Most changelings do, eventually. Things are better for them there."

"Fascinating," I said. I could understand why Titania's world wouldn't function with Arden on the throne, and why she'd want her favorite daughter awake to rule by her side. What she could want with Devin was harder to see. He was a nuisance, always had been, a pesky reminder of a time when Faerie had been more lawless and people had all but belonged to the houses where they'd been born . . .

And just like that, it made sense. Parents often loved their children. I won't say that as an absolute; between my father and October's mother, I knew better than to assume parenthood was enough to guarantee affection. But more often than not, parents loved the people they created, and changeling or pureblood didn't matter when they were your own flesh and blood. Some of *them* had to rebel against the system, even if their changeling children had been too ground-down by trying to survive it to dream of doing so on their own.

Devin provided a necessary safety valve for Titania's system, and as Stacy, she'd been one of his kids, just like October had. She knew how his organization functioned, how he conducted his business, and how those things would need to be changed if she wanted to control him. He'd even had an alliance with Evening, before his death. That could no doubt be repurposed to better serve Titania's needs. He was useful, and so she'd brought him back.

I stood abruptly.

"I need some air," I said. "Madame Librarian, is it safe to go outside?"

"Put on a human disguise before you do; your stripes are showing," she said. "But yeah, it should be fine. Wild Strawberries is a reasonably relaxed fiefdom, and the fact that we're anchored here means the locals are used to seeing strangers pop in and out without much warning. Just try not to attract any attention if you can avoid it, and for the love of Maeve, don't go telling anyone you're Cait Sidhe. I'd rather avoid Titania's notice for as long as I can."

"Of course," I said, and stalked away, back to the hall where we'd entered. I paused to throw a human illusion over myself, stripping away the feline aspects of my nature, blunting the fae elements under a veil of mortality, then stepped outside into the cool night air.

The stars were very bright, even this close to the city. I turned my face toward them, closing my eyes, and took several deep, anxious breaths. I hated this. I hated everything about it, and even more, I hated the fact that I was old and experienced enough to know that I couldn't just charge back to Amandine's tower, grab October, drag her onto the Shadow Roads, and confine her in the Court of Cats until this was all over.

Even if she would have eventually forgiven me—of which there was no guarantee—it would bring the wrath of Shadowed Hills, Simon Torquill, and a minimum of two of the Firstborn down upon my head. Amandine, I might have been able to survive. Her greatest weapons are in the manipulation of blood, and I am entirely Cait Sidhe, from one end of my descent to the other. But Evening . . .

The woman who commanded Simon might be a construct of Titania's magic, designed to mimic her daughter. It didn't matter. Construct or not, if she had a fragment of the Winterrose's power, she would end me.

No, we had to approach this like sensible people, slowly and with care, and that was the last thing in the world I currently wanted to do.

Something rustled at the edge of the yard. I tensed, opening my eyes and lowering my head as I scanned for some sign that I was being watched. I didn't see anyone.

The fence on the far side of the yard was partially obscured by a small cluster of ash trees, spaced widely enough for their roots to thrive but closely enough that they would eventually undermine the fence as they grew. I frowned and moved toward it. It was probably a raccoon, or a stray cat. If the former, I could startle it away. If the latter, they might know something that would benefit us.

Instead, as I approached, a man stepped out of one of the trees, looking at me with anxious eyes.

"My apologies, sire," he said, words coming out rapid-fire, one atop the next. "I was told the Library was open for visitors, and did not intend to disturb anyone. I'll come back tomorrow night. I sincerely regret disturbing you, and hope only that you won't see the need to report me to the Duke."

I blinked. "Report you? For what?"

"For being away from my station without leave," he said, sounding as bewildered as I felt.

I glanced down at myself. I had, as was my custom, clad myself in leather trousers and a well-fitted shirt. The clothing was illusion anchored over my true traveling clothes, and cast out of habit; it always pleased October to see me so. At some point, that pleasure had become enough to dictate the appearance of my wardrobe, such as it was. But I could understand how he would have mistaken me for a visiting noble, seeing me come out of the Library so attired.

Sometimes I think the open hissing and snarling of the Court of Cats is infinitely cleaner and healthier than the intricate manners of the Divided Courts, which treat no one kindly, not even those they claim to serve.

"I am a visitor here, but not one who intends to make report to anyone," I said, aiming to reassure. "My name is Rand, and I hail originally from Londinium. You are . . . ?"

"My name is Eion," he said. "I, and my family, serve in the Court of Duke Carrig of Wild Strawberries."

"Not entirely of your own free will?" I guessed. He shied back, eyes going wide. "Peace. It's only that someone who serves a household voluntarily rarely fears being reported for being away from their station."

I didn't know Duke Carrig as he was in the real world, but I had never heard anything negative about the man. Certainly nothing that would leave a Hamadryad courtier flinching like a whipped dog over having been seen away from his post.

"I am . . . My family and I, we are . . ."

"Hamadryads?"

"Yes," said Eion. "The Duke, in his mercy and grandeur, tends to our trees and keeps them in good health."

Hamadryads are not like true Dryads; they can leave their trees for extended periods of time and, when necessary, can even break the bond between themselves and the trees, tying their life forces into a new vessel. Some call them the weaker strain of treefolk. I say they approach the matter differently but with no less honest connection to the soil of the Summerlands.

I frowned. "You say he tends to your trees. Does that mean he holds the land they grow on?"

Eion nodded, and said nothing.

"Your service is compelled, then."

"He has always been good to us, up until this past year," said Eion. "Our daughters, Ashla and Gable, were born at his request. He had been called upon to hold to Titania's Law, and wished to wait for the moment when love came to him before he went seeking solace in mortal bowers. So he asked us, and we were glad to serve. They were lovely seedlings, and well beloved of all the Court, but as they grew into saplings, he began to withhold his favor, and now, as they strain toward full growth, he begins to speak of the fullness of his household, how it can't be expected to stretch to feel unnecessary mouths forever. I . . . I sought the Library in hopes of finding some book of custom that would compel him to let us remain, at least long enough for both of them to be of age. Once they reach their majority, we can leave as a family if we have the need, but while Ashla is underage, to remove her from the Duke's halls would be considered theft of property, and they would be within their rights to hunt us down."

"I know of no such book of custom," I said, as gently as I could manage. The man's pain was evident, and the other side of the coin I was carrying for myself. He only feared for his family. "But if you have the time before your daughter's birthday, if you have the spine to stand up against the long nights between here and there . . . Moving Day approaches. Surely there's somewhere safe that you could go?"

I wouldn't recommend Devin's. Not to a man with concern for his young daughters foremost in his thoughts. The city wouldn't suit them, anyway. They'd be unable to find new trees to bond to before the Duke could lay axe to the roots of the ones they already had, and they would be lost.

"Golden Shore is known to accept changelings who find themselves without a patron," he said. "They have good, fertile land there, and the trees they do grow high."

"So bide your time, and when Moving Day arrives, you can leave for the Golden Shore," I said, well aware of the irony of telling him to wait for the same term I had refused to wait myself. "I regret that I have no better path to offer you. The Library *is* open, if you want to look for better answers."

"I hope you'll take no insult when I do," he said, shifting as if to move past me to the door.

"None at all. Children are precious, and you're doing the right thing by taking care of yours."

He paused, glancing back at me. "You're a father?"

"I am." Raj was son enough to me for my answer to be an honest one, even with my pregnant wife far away from me and under an enchantment I couldn't touch.

"Is there anything that would be too much to do, for your children?"

"No."

And that, at the end of everything else, was why I could leave October where she was—why I *would* leave her where she was, much as it pained me to do so. She was safe. She was fed. She was within the bounds of Titania's enchantment, and while she had few rights there, she had Simon and August to protect her. Simon Torquill was a man inclined to make poor choices, absolutely, but always in service of his family.

I couldn't protect her. If I pulled her out of the dreamworld she'd been cast into, I would be doing nothing but subjecting her to the risks of a reality where she had few rights, I didn't exist, and my people couldn't do anything to aid either one of us. Worse yet, if I ripped her from the life she thought she knew, I would be subjecting her to the stresses of abduction by a stranger, frightening her, and leaving her with cause to hate me. I couldn't do that. Not to her, and not to me.

Leaving her where she was was the right thing to do. It was the only thing to do. And I hated it as I had hated very little else in my life.

I stayed outside in the starlight, waiting for the world to change again. Maybe this time, for once, it would change into something I could live with.

Maybe this time it would change into something kinder.

ELEVEN

AFTER THAT FIRST TRIP to the Library, I fell into an uneasy dance of waiting and gathering information. Garm and Grianne returned to their duties at Shadowed Hills, the one excited to be part of a conspiracy, even if he didn't fully understand what we were hoping to achieve, the other willing to help both her friend and me, for reasons she had been characteristically silent about, but for whose aid I was deeply grateful all the same. Between the two of them, I would know everything that happened in the duchy, and be able to react if things seemed to be going badly.

May and Magdaleana were still confined to the Library of Stars, as trapped in their own way as my people were in the Court of Cats. If they left, they risked being absorbed by Titania's illusions—or unmade, in the case of May, since we were still unsure what would happen if the memories she'd taken from October were stripped entirely away. Mai had been a very pleasant person, as night-haunts went, but that didn't mean May wanted to go back to being her. Simon was a frequent patron, forcing me to keep away and May to conceal herself in the deepest stacks lest he ask why she had stolen his daughter's face.

Eion proved to be a stroke of luck, in his own anxious way. He was a courtier in the service of the Duke of Wild Strawberries, mostly serving as a messenger and scribe, and as such was allowed in almost any room he chose to occupy, so long as he seemed busy while there. His wife and sister served with him, and all three were intending to take their children and leave for Golden Shore at the very start of Moving Day.

The holiday, for all that it was confined to a single night in proper measure, extended over the course of an entire week, and during that time, even changelings were allowed to move freely, seeking a new demesne in which to dwell. If they were quick, they could make Golden Shore before the time ran out. I would have offered to aid them, but Hamadryads are uniquely ill-suited to the Shadow Roads. Their roots freeze in the cold, and the shock can be fatal.

Until then, we had a source of information from that Court as well, and once Moving Day arrived, things, which were presently happening with an unpleasantly glacial slowness, would begin to happen very quickly indeed.

There were still things to be accomplished in the meantime, of course. May remained firm on not wanting me to search for Jasmine, preferring to believe that her love was safe when there was nothing she could do to bring them back together any more quickly. The Courts were stable, for now, although Rajiv and Ginevra were occupied at all hours of the day and night seeing to their needs; I felt somewhat guilty at staying away as much as I was, but told myself it would be good practice for the day when I stepped down entirely. There was too much to be done for me to return for any true length of time.

The next few days and nights slipped by in a haze of work and study, slipping into the Courts to aid with food distribution and trash removal and any matters that needed my personal attention, then heading for the Library to dig deeper into the history of Titania's past transgressions. The previous times when she had done something of this sort had been geographically restricted, at least according to the Library records, limited by her power and petulance. How long was she willing to punish a swath of Faerie over what would almost always prove to be the actions of one, maybe two people?

In the past, she hadn't been looking to make her changes permanent, or maybe she'd just been aware she'd never succeed, not with Oberon and Maeve both set against her. Now Oberon was missing once more, and Maeve was as yet unfound—not only unfound, but near-erased from Titania's rewritten history. According to Garm and Eion, Maeve had knowingly invited the breaking of her Ride, betraying all of Faerie and confining us to the Summerlands when we should have been free to travel as we would across the Realms. Oberon's actions in locking the doors had been omitted, and all the blame placed on Maeve.

The summary execution of the shapeshifting fae had been justified by claiming that we couldn't help siding with Maeve if Faerie went to war; it was in our nature. And so a Wild Hunt had been called, and the fae with more than one form to their names had been hunted down, executed for the crime of deviating from Titania's perfection. I'd been forced to take a walk after Garm told me that slice of their history, and only the fact that it had supposedly happened so long ago that I knew it hadn't happened at all had been enough to keep me from attacking him in misplaced rage. The Court of Cats and May's placement proved that Titania's spell had simply picked up anyone whose existence it denied, shuffling them out of the way so they wouldn't be a problem.

If she managed to anchor her illusions into the Heart of Faerie, that would change. Once the spell was connected to a better battery, it would be able to spread, and none of us knew what that would mean. The kindest interpretation was that all the impossible people would find themselves locked away like the Cait Sidhe were, trapped in skerries and shallowings, unable to reach the Summerlands. They might also remain free but turn imperceptible, masked by illusions so strong that they might as well not exist. None of the possibilities were good ones. None of them were things I wanted to see.

That was why I was standing in Ginevra's chambers at the Court of Cats, trying not to fuss as I watched her collect herself.

"You fidget like a kitten, Tybalt," she said, shooting me a weary, half-amused look.

"Yes, because it's well past time I inform our allies of what we've learned since last I saw them," I said, impatience getting the best of me. "Are you ready to go *yet*?"

"I've never been to the Undersea before. I'm allowed to be a little anxious. Does this count as visiting royalty?"

The thought of Captain Pete as "royalty" was comic enough to draw a snort of laughter out of me, despite the seriousness of the situation. Ginevra shot me a wounded look.

"Gin," I said, as gently as I could manage, "we're visiting Patrick and Dianda. You've met them, if only in passing. They're nobles, yes, but they're also worried parents and partners who just want news of their missing family. You don't have to come with me if you'd prefer not to. Rajiv is close to their older son, as Dean is romantically involved with his best friend, and might be better suited to soothe them."

"Raj needs to stay here in case something goes catastrophically wrong," she countered. "This is a King's Court, not a Queen's. Without him, the Court is essentially undefended."

"And that's why I would prefer you be the one to accompany me. If this is done quickly, however, I could take either one of you."

That gave her a moment's pause. Only a brief moment, however: in what felt like no time at all, she was rising from the dresser where she'd been seated, shaking back her hair, and saying, "Then we'd best be quick about it."

"Yes," I agreed, as if I hadn't been trying to make the same point for the past twenty minutes, and offered her my hand.

She took it, her posture as perfect as any princess of the Divided Courts, and together, we stepped into shadow.

The journey to Goldengreen was swift and easy, although Ginevra looked at me oddly when we stepped off the Shadow Roads and into the field behind the museum which housed the knowe's mortal entrance.

"Tybalt," she said, voice low and tight, "this is *Goldengreen*."

"Yes. I've noticed."

"You-know-who is in charge here. If she sees us . . ."

"As long as we don't attempt to enter the knowe or violate her wards, we'll be gone again before she has a chance to notice us, and this is one of the easier points from which to enter the pathway down to Saltmist."

"Are we really going to take the Shadow Roads *under* the water?"

"Yes. I know the way now, having walked it once. We daren't descend too deep, or we'll enter the point where the Roads pass from our possession into the realm of the Almere, but as long as we exit when appropriate, we'll be fine." I was trying to sound more confident than I entirely felt. It seemed to be working reasonably well, which was a pleasant change. "Getting back may be slightly more difficult. There are surprisingly few shadows at the bottom of the sea. But I have faith in Dianda's ability to make them if I tell her it's necessary."

"So why didn't you do that the first time?"

"We needed to be sure the shadows would open for me, and that they were safe to travel that deep down. Now that we know they will, and they are, we can descend. Trust me, Ginevra. Even if I had decided you were my enemy, I wouldn't want to leave Rajiv alone."

"And killing me off would mean abandoning him every time you went to stalker-stare at Toby," said Ginevra. "Okay. Let's go."

I took a deep breath. She did the same. And together, we stepped into shadow.

The Roads were colder this close to the sea, the air thinner and more difficult to breathe. There was no physical change to mark the moment when our route took us beneath the water, but there was a change in the atmosphere, a thickening that slowed our steps, as if we were running through watered-down molasses instead of open space. Still, we kept on going, forcing our way forward through the dark.

The whispers and slithering sounds I had heard before resumed, distant but audible, and entirely out of place here in a world that had never been inclined to anything but silence. Ginevra stumbled, and for a moment, I thought her hand was going to be wrenched out of mine. I fumbled for a better grip, and pulled her with me as I ran on, until the air changed again, still thick and cold, but now with that subtle, undefinable quality that told me we were approaching our destination. I adjusted my grasp on Ginevra's wrist and leapt, throwing myself at the opening I could feel off to the side.

Not every departure from the Shadow Roads can be as graceful and elegant as we might like. My heels hit a wet patch on the floor as I landed in the knowe, and I went sprawling, sliding a few feet before I hit the wall. Ginevra, who had been given a moment's warning when she felt me start to fall, had shifted to cat form in that instant, which would have been a good idea if she'd been aware of the open pool of water at the center of the room. There was a splash, followed by an indignant yowl.

I pushed myself to my feet, moving to retrieve the wet, furious Ginevra from the water. I had just scooped her into my arms when I heard footsteps running down the hall toward us.

"You might want to shift back," I murmured, setting her on the floor. "We're about to have company."

"You already do," said a low, dangerous female voice, from directly behind me. "Best explain yourselves, and quickly, unless you're a type of fae who doesn't need their kidneys to function."

Slowly, I turned. One of the octopus people, the Cephali, was clinging to the wall, her tentacles still a creamy shell-white along half their length. She had a wicked-looking knife in one hand.

"It's been almost two weeks since I've seen my wife; I was starting to miss the experience of having people point knives at me," I said.

"So you break into our knowe?"

"I believe, unless things went much, much worse than anticipated after I left here, that I remain an invited guest," I said.

The Cephali looked as if she wanted to argue this point, eyes narrowed and knife unwavering. The portion of her tentacles that didn't match the wall was a vivid red, matching her hair instead, and the skin on the human-seeming part of her body was a creamy white speckled with generous freckles. Her hair was a wild cloud of corkscrew curls, and her only attire was a simple wrap top that matched the wall almost as well as her tentacles did. If she turned the rest of her body that color, she would effectively vanish.

Camouflage is the greatest tool of the Cephali. They can't turn invisible without invoking illusion spells, but they can change their color as easily as they breathe, which is an innate form of transformation, and—most usefully of all—doesn't call upon their magic in any measurable way. Helmi could blend in to anything she wanted without the scent of the spell giving her away.

It would make them fine assassins on the land, if they had any interest in leaving the sea. Fortunately, they have never seemed so inclined, and prefer to gather in the knowes created and cared for by Merrow, attaching themselves to noble households and serving in relative safety.

"Helmi, stand down," said Patrick. I looked over my shoulder. He was standing in the doorway, near a doused, dripping Ginevra. She was back on two legs, wringing the water from her hair.

"A towel might be welcome," I said dryly.

"I'll have Helmi get right on that," said Patrick.

The Cephali woman lowered her knife, looking unhappy about the whole situation as she slipped it into a sheath attached to the top of one tentacle, like a particularly dangerous garter. "A towel for our uninvited guests?"

"Please. And if you could let Dianda know that King Tybalt has returned, with a guest, I would appreciate it immensely."

"Tybalt?" Helmi looked at me with new interest. "The one you said might be bringing the rest of our family home?" There was a note of unfeigned longing in her question.

"Yes," said Patrick.

"Right away, sir," said Helmi, and dropped off the wall, landing with a *plop* before ambulating out of the room with remarkably impressive speed. I couldn't call her means of locomotion "walking," as it involved her tentacles moving in a strange synchronized dance, grasping the floor and pulling her forward with vast muscular flexion. It was definitely enthralling; I had trouble taking my eyes away.

"It used to distract me, too, watching the Cephali move around the knowe," said Patrick. "It gets worse when they forget that air-filled rooms normally have gravity. They'll just go straight up the walls. Who's your dampened friend?"

"My apologies: my manners aren't presently what I'd like them to be." I gestured to Ginevra, who paused in wringing out her hair to bob a quick, awkward curtsey. "May I present Princess Ginevra of the

Court of Whispering Cats, currently standing formal regent for Prince Rajiv of the Court of Dreaming Cats. Ginevra, this is Duke Patrick Lorden of Saltmist."

"Ducal Consort," corrected Patrick. "Technically, I'm still a Count, or would be, if I went up to the surface. Gilad never got around to revoking my title, and I've had no formal reason to repudiate it."

"Oh." Ginevra shot me a look, clearly mystified.

"The Divided Courts enjoy overcomplicating simple things," I said, in a soothing tone. To Patrick, I added, "We only have six formal ranks. King, Queen, Prince, Princess, Monarch, and Prime. The latter two are rarely used but do occasionally come into play. Regent is a position, not a rank, and relevant only in a situation such as my own. Forgive me if this is rude, but you look like hell."

Patrick, who did, in fact, look like hell, chuckled dryly. "I could say the same to you, you know."

"I am a cat, sir. I always look my very best, even when I don't, and to so much as imply otherwise is to run the risk of treason."

Ginevra looked back and forth between us. "Okay, boys, chill. You're both pretty, you're both very important, and you're both the most special boy in the whole room."

We shot her matching looks of wounded offense, and she laughed.

She was still laughing a moment later, when Helmi returned, pulling Dianda Lorden by the wrist. Dianda was in her own two-legged form and had a towel slung over one shoulder.

And, much like Patrick, she looked like hell.

Neither of them appeared to have slept since the last time I'd been in the knowe. Patrick definitely hadn't brushed his hair since then, and it stuck out in all directions, somehow managing to be dry and greasy at the same time. Both had dark circles under their eyes, and Dianda's cheeks were hollow; she wasn't eating. Half-healed bruises marred her shoulders and neck, and I realized with a pang of guilt that I was so accustomed to October's swift, impossible recoveries that I'd never considered whether she might be genuinely hurt when the Almere attacked.

She saw me looking and waved her free hand, dismissing my concern. "Amphitrite took the worse of it," she said. "I just had some bruises, and a few little divots taken out of my tail. Nothing major. Helmi patched me right up, and I'll be fully recovered any tide now."

"Yes, because having your wife dragged home bleeding and delirious by her own equally injured Firstborn is always easy on the nerves," muttered Patrick. "Especially when your husband and two of your children are missing. That's the *best* time for something like that. I can't recommend it highly enough."

"Will you *stop*?" Dianda glared at him. "Tybalt wouldn't be here if he didn't have something to tell us. Maybe there's been a change in the spell."

"No change, milady." I stepped forward to take the towel, passing it solemnly to Ginevra, who promptly began drying her hair. "We've been researching it within the Library of Stars, and attempting to chart its boundaries. Has there been any more word on the isolated portions of the Undersea?"

"A wall runs around the sundered oceans, clear as glass and thin as a whisper, but entirely impermeable," said Dianda. "Yell, scream, attack it with all the force that you can muster, it doesn't budge or crack. We've had the Asrai attempt to unweave it, sent the Naiads to try to pass through to the water on the other side, nothing. We're well and truly cut off."

"Merrow sing storms, do they not?"

Dianda nodded.

"Have you any contacts within the Air Kingdoms?" When she looked at me in bewilderment, I shrugged. "It seems that storms would be part of their domain as well as part of your own. If the barrier extends to the bottom of the sea, perhaps the Air Kingdoms could tell us how high it goes."

"Even if we had a way to communicate with them, would knowing even make a difference?" demanded Patrick. "We're bugs in a jar. Being able to determine exactly how big the jar is doesn't change that we can't get out, or that some of our people are outside where we can't get to them."

"Titania's power is not infinite," I said. "We think we've figured out her plan, and Moving Day is when she'll put the next phase of it into action. She can't push the borders of this spell any farther until we reach that point—can't, or won't. Perhaps she could, but at the cost of some fidelity."

Patrick's face screwed up like he was going to start yelling at me. Then he stopped and sagged, resignation wiping the fury away. "You've seen them."

Dianda looked sharply over at him, then back to me. "What?" she asked, a dangerous note in her voice.

Upsetting her wasn't something to be done lightly, or, if possible, at all. I stood my ground, refusing the sensible urge to retreat.

Patrick did not refuse the less-sensible urge to advance. He moved toward me, managing to seem menacing in a way I had never previously seen from the man. It didn't suit him. He was not a figure made for menace. "He's seen them. There's no way he'd be standing here calmly talking about phases and limits if he didn't know where they were."

Ginevra lowered the towel, clearly prepared to jump into the fray if it came to that. I raised a hand, motioning for patience.

"Patrick is right," I said, and watched as Dianda's eyes narrowed and the helpful readiness drained out of her face, replaced by stony chill. It was like watching a storm roll in over a previously calm and clement sea, and a good reminder that the undertow was always present, if not always in evidence.

"I haven't seen all of them," I continued. "But October . . . I found her, and she's well. Titania has put her in Amandine's tower."

"With Amandine?" asked Dianda.

I nodded. "It seems Titania couldn't imagine a better way to torture my wife than placing her back in the company of the mother she despises."

"And Simon?"

This was going to be the tricky part. I took a careful breath, delaying for a few precious seconds, before I said, "There as well, as is August, and returned by Titania's whims to the service of the Countess Winterrose, who once more has dominion over Goldengreen. As the Cait Sidhe were sealed into our Courts, May was sealed into the Library of Stars; it seems Titania has removed the impossible people from her reality, placing them in safe, secluded locations. Dean would be one of those. I don't believe she'll have harmed him, physically. I don't know where he is."

"But we know Simon is back in the company of two of the women who tortured him for decades," said Patrick, voice low and dangerous. "Is Oleander . . . ?"

"Of Oleander, there has thankfully been no sign," I said, grateful to have at least that much good news to give them. "I think even Titania saw that Faerie was better off without her."

"Not only that," said an unfamiliar voice from behind me. The speaker had an Irish accent, several centuries removed from what the modern island sounded like, mixed with something unfamiliar, something sharp-edged and brisk. It was an odd blend, like one of October's sandwiches, two things that shouldn't have worked together and yet somehow did.

I turned. A Roane woman had emerged from the pool at the center of the room and was standing behind me, water sheeting from her clothes and a distant, dreamy expression on her face. Her hair was gold and her eyes were blue, deep and drowning and inhuman, even though the color could just as easily have belonged to a mortal swimmer. Something about the way her irises were shaped shifted her slightly outside of what humanity considered possible.

"The Lady of Flowers cloaks herself in lies because she cannot endure what *is*," she said. "She hates and fears those who see what yet may come to pass, and hates us all the more because she's never once been able to find the precise pattern to dance between the raindrops. She always winds up getting wet. It's why she nudged and implied and hinted until her children, who only wanted to please her, agreed to close our eyes eternally. It's why she allowed so many cruelties. The Peri, for all that it's not what they're best remembered as in this world of now and nothing, saw as clearly as any did, when they turned their eyes to the future. She would never have considered calling one of their kind back from beyond the border of death, not even to make those who've stood against her suffer."

"Mary," said Patrick. "You know you don't have to be here. We can handle—"

"The ebb and flow of ordinary tides, my Pat, but not the aching undertow of the ones we swim through now. I think you take too much after your source, sometimes; you don't want the prophet present when she might speak prophecy that you'll dislike." Her words were not unkindly said, but they had a quiet accusation to them that even I could hear.

Patrick heard it much more clearly than I did. He shied back, seeming almost ashamed.

The Roane woman—Mary—fixed her attention on me, and began to approach, steps as slow and measured as her voice. "You won't like them either, King of Cats. So many crowns, stretching back so far, and not a single one of them won out of wanting. You are a king of necessity and service. You don't know what it is to sit idle. But it seems you'll need to learn."

"Mary, what are you saying?" asked Dianda.

"There's no guarantee you sail this ship safe to harbor. Once the Three get involved, the future refuses to clarify, stays as cloudy as a mariner's morning. But this I can tell you: nothing changes from here to Moving Day. Not for them. You can throw yourselves against the cliffs of their isolation, but they remain where and who they are. They're not your loved ones, not right now; the Summer Queen has made them over in other images, and they won't know you. Move too soon and you might lose them."

"If it were only October, I might be able to wait; she's a hero, after all," I said, forcing my voice to stay level. "But she doesn't walk alone."

"Oh, the baby?"

"Yes, the baby." We hadn't told anyone. There hadn't been time to tell them. But it wasn't really a surprise that this strange Roane woman would look at me and know.

"I wouldn't worry," she said, and walked past me to Dianda, taking her hands and looking her square in the eye as she continued. "So long as she can eat and sleep and care for herself, the babe will be more than hale."

I frowned, no longer sure that I was the one being addressed. "They don't seem to be starving her. From what little I've seen, August would never allow it." I had been to watch from outside the tower walls more times than was advisable, sitting in the tall grass at a reasonable distance and staring at the girls as they went about their business. While August was more likely to sniff at flowers as October gathered herbs or pulled weeds, she was also likely to braid flowers into her sister's hair, or bring October fruits gathered from the other side of the garden. There seemed to be true affection there. Whether created by the illusion or no, they both believed it, and that made it real enough for the moment.

"But only if you wait," she continued. "Test the bounds too much, press Titania too far before the time is right to take your chance, and she may modify the illusion. She may recast the roles she's prepared for them to play. For now, she sets your lost ones within a loving family, showing them what their lives could have been if they'd been spared the undercurrent of destiny and heroics that has always pulled them in its wake. Give her reason, and they could be thrown like jewels into the sea, for the current to take where it will. There are other places the inconvenient may be deposited."

"Is that a threat?" asked Patrick.

"Oh, Pat, my Pat, you know I would never threaten you." Mary dropped Dianda's hands and turned to face him. "I don't speak for Titania. I can only speak for what the water shows me, and it says she's done away with the Seers, made them a forbidden shadow of Maeve's hand, washed them from the foundations of her Faerie. No Roane, no Peri, no one who might cast their eye ahead and say what yet might be. She'd make a world with no destinies, and while I can see the kindness in that—too many die cold deaths on the road to what's been destined, never realizing that the words they heard were not for them, but for another who fit the bill of fate as cleanly—she does it not out of mercy, but out of meanness. She thinks she can prevent what she feels is near, can stop the old bills coming due. Oberon bound her not to harm the children of Amandine's line, and so she's harmed them not, even the ones who claim that place upon a technicality—the Fetch shines in the Library of Stars, the disowned, beloved, re-adopted daughter swims with the rookery deep below the waters, and the child without a name grows in safety, existence concealed by the same illusion that denies any knowledge of conception. She harms them not."

"She's harming *Simon*," said Patrick, staunchly. "Handing him back to a woman who hurt him so badly that he came to us terrified of the touch of a friendly hand, unable to believe that he was worthy of love, or care, or anything but paying for what he'd done—"

"Not the real woman. A shadow of same. Even Titania cannot wake her sleeping child, nor reach her where she presently sleeps, on the Road of Thorns," said Mary. "Amandine's crime was neglect, and while those wounds also run deep and grow infected, they were inflicted far less intentionally. If we interfere too soon, we lose them all."

There was a finality in that statement that I didn't care for, and my breath caught like a stone in my throat, impossible to swallow around. Ginevra moved closer to my side, offering comfort through her presence. There was nothing she could say. Here we were, leagues and leagues below the sea, being lectured on patience by a Roane woman who seemed to weave in and out of lucidity with every other word, and there were no easy answers. Moving Day was yet almost four months distant.

Could we keep the Court alive for four months? Could I retain my sanity for four months? Could Eion protect his children for four months? Such were the questions we suddenly had to grapple with, and not a one of them was pleasant to consider.

Dianda took a very deep breath, visibly steadying herself. "The Roane have always advised the Undersea well, when they have cause. We listen."

"My first crown came about because a Roane maiden by the name of Naia came before the Court of Londinium and warned us of the coming plague," I said, and was proud when my voice failed to shake. "It pained her to stand before the Court, and she did it anyway, and I listened. For her word, I killed my father and made myself a King. For her word, my life was set on the path it has followed ever since. If the Roane caution patience now, I will listen. I have no real choice."

"You always have a choice. A future Seen is not a future set, or nothing could ever change." Mary looked at me kindly. "I know this hurts you. I know how much you want to run to her, and I wish I could promise you the happy ending you deserve. But there are miles to go, and you'll be back to Babylon before it's finished, down to the bottom of the sea and out to Miles' Cross. Everything repeats."

"We just came here to tell you what we'd learned so far," said Ginevra, sounding anxious. "And so I could meet the Lordens properly, since I'm working with Tybalt on the land side of things."

"Will you be patient, Pat?" asked Mary, with more fierceness than I'd heard from her yet.

He startled a bit, taking a half-step back. "I don't want to be. But as I've found no way out of the water yet, I suppose I don't have a choice."

"If you're persistent, you'll find a way to dry land," said Mary. "Disaster will follow. You improve nothing by rushing in. You endanger everything you hope to save. You have to be a patient fisherman, my Pat. You have to hold the line to set the hook properly. Moving Day is when things come to fruition. Can you survive so long as that?"

"Our son . . ." said Pat, pleadingly.

"I cannot see him, nor know where now he stands, but he *is* safe," said Mary. "He may be hungry or afraid, but he *is* safe."

"You really want to count on *my* patience?" asked Dianda. "Our son. Our husband. Our stepdaughter. They're all missing. Even if we know where their bodies are, they're not really there."

"No, and you have no way to free them." Mary cocked her head. "Even Amphitrite can't unmake a working of Titania's own hands. Even my own First, wherever she is now, can't release them. You'll need to find her, of course."

"Titania?" I asked.

"No, my First. She can guide you through stopping her stepmother, once she's free to do so." She waved a hand, like she was suggesting something simple. "She's a keyhole yearning for a key. Find the key and you'll find your way to her. She can't break the spell, but she has other uses. To unbind the world, you must find an oathbreaker, an unmaker. She'll be the one to undo what's been done."

"October," I said.

Mary looked at me, a brief smile playing on her lips.

"Yes," she said. "If you can stay your hand long enough for her to come to herself, she might come back to you. Moving Day is the time to move, in more ways than one. On Moving Day, she'll leave the safety of the nest, and you may enter in her absence, to see the things I know your heart yearns to see. After that, if you're clever and careful and don't frighten her away, you'll have a chance to bring her home. Speak to those she calls family if you see the chance, but not until then, or events begin too soon, and you will fail. On Moving Day, it all comes together, or it all falls apart. Will you wait?"

I knew the answer I wanted to give. It burned in my breast and clouded my senses, leaving no room for anything else. And yet somehow, miraculously, when I opened my mouth, it was another word that fell out.

"Yes," I said, and the course was set.

TWELVE

GINEVRA WAITED UNTIL WE got back to the Court of Cats to comment on what she'd seen.

"Does that happen often?" she asked.

"The prophetess of the deep surfacing to spill pearls of perplexity across the floor?" I shook my head. "No. I haven't heard a Roane Seer speak so much of the future in centuries. I never thought to hear it again."

"But we have to wait."

"Yes." The admission pained me.

"Why?"

"Seers are . . ." I paused, sorting through my thoughts. "They're not guarantees. A Seer glimpses a possible future, or several, and tells you how to claim or avoid them. The big prophecies, the ones that tend to slide into story and be remembered, happen when so many futures align that the Seers can't focus on anything else. If you lose in nineteen out of twenty possible endings, they don't see the one where you win. That's why we tend to listen. If Mary says patience gets us what we need, then we have to be . . ." Bile rose in my throat. I swallowed it back, and forced out the final word, resenting every syllable: "Patient."

"You're really going to stay away from October until *Moving Day*?"

"It seems I must, for the sake of never leaving her alone again. I'll keep my peace, and watch from a distance. Come Moving Day, I'll enter the tower to set the next phase into motion, and then speak to any member of her family who happens to cross my path. Until then, they say patience is a virtue. It seems I am to be a virtuous man."

"But there's things we can do in the meanwhile," said Ginevra. "She mentioned her First—that's the Luidaeg, right? The sea witch? You said she was missing . . ."

"Eira hates her. Titania was the one who bound her into what she is today. It makes sense that Titania wouldn't want her around, with or without her memories intact."

"All right. Where could she have gone?"

"Not to the Undersea. Pete hasn't seen her either." Talking about the location of Firstborn in such a casual manner was still strange and unsettling.

Ginevra didn't seem to find it so. She frowned, tapping her fingers against her chin. "So she's probably somewhere like the Court or the Library, that can't be accessed through most normal means."

"A skerry or a sealed shallowing would seem to make the most sense, yes," I agreed. "She could be anywhere."

"Good thing we apparently have almost four whole months to find her, then," said Ginevra.

I didn't throw anything at her. Sadly, there was no one else present to admire my restraint, as we had arrived in my private quarters. Only semi-private; she and Raj could both come and go freely. So could Julie, the changeling girl I all but raised after her mother died, but she seemed to have forgotten our relationship in the transition to this new world. According to Gabriel, she had been taken in fosterage by another, a Cait Sidhe woman who had lost her own child, and grown up happy, surrounded by love. There was no point in ripping her away from that before it became necessary.

"There are other locked realms where she could be hidden," I said, slowly.

"Do lost people ever wind up in the Court, or just lost things?" asked Ginevra.

I stared at her. "*Things*," I said, firmly. "Never living, either. This is not a lost and found for pets and children who've wandered away from their keepers!"

"Or for sea witches, I guess." She sighed. "That would have been too easy."

"I would suggest Blind Michael's skerry, as I know it survived his death, and rumor says he's still alive in this version of our world, but people have always accessed that by claiming a Babylon candle from the Luidaeg herself—or when he abducted them. We'll find no answers there."

"Maybe I could find one of those candles, though. It seems worth checking. Come on." Ginevra beckoned me to follow her as she made for the door, energized by the thought of a task she might actually be able to perform.

I, in opposition, was exhausted and dispirited, the weight of the situation descending on me with a new, crushing finality. Four months. We had been married for such a short time, and October was already denied to me, and I to her. Did she even know she missed me? Or was I just a shadow in her dreams, something to regret without comprehension?

It would almost be better if she had forgotten me entirely—I didn't want her to suffer—but I couldn't wish for that, no matter how merciful it might be.

Ginevra led me out of the room and down the hall, to a stairway that wound sharply, unsteadily upward. I eyed it warily. Stairs in the Court of Cats are not trustworthy things, as a general rule; everything we have is lost, after all, and lost staircases are often better described as "death traps."

Still, she seemed to know where she was going, and as she charged up the stairs, I followed close behind. After ten steps, she shifted to her feline form, and I did the same, trying to leap where she leapt, step where she stepped, and match her move for move. Her tail was a flame-colored comma, leading me ever onward, and it was surprisingly like playing with my sisters, back in long-gone Londinium, when we had been careless and young and unaware of how terribly wonderful the world was going to be.

I missed them still. I expected I always would, even to the very end of time.

The stairs ended not at a landing but at an open doorway looking out on a vast warehouse-like room filled with junk. Ginevra leapt through the doorway, landing lightly on a rafter, and began to pace along it. I followed, allowing her to lead me.

Rooms like this formed all across the Court of Cats like cysts in wounded flesh, filling with the debris and detritus of the Summerlands and mortal world alike. If a thing was lost and not destroyed, it wound up here, at least until it was found again. If one of us found an object in the jumble, it would no longer be lost, and wouldn't become a relic for some human archaeologist or curious child to stumble over.

Many famous treasure-hunters have been Cait Sidhe. This isn't always something to be proud of, but it's something that has purchased a remarkable amount of tuna over the years.

Ginevra began descending, using shelves and chests as steps to the floor. Again, I followed, and we both shifted back to bipedal form when we reached the ground.

"Babylon candles are made using people's blood," I said. "I doubt anyone's lost one. We probably couldn't use it even if they had."

"Everything is already terrible, focus on finding something that can help." Ginevra stalked off into the shelves, poking at things as she passed them. I watched her go and sighed, feeling momentarily helpless. This situation needed magic other than my own. It needed solutions I couldn't access. It needed October.

But then, there had been situations before that would have been *easier* with a gifted blood-worker at my side, but hadn't been impossible, mostly because I'd been willing to *try*. This had begun with me making an effort, and now I was just standing around as my nephew's Regent at least tried to find an answer. That couldn't be allowed. My magic might not be enough to help me here, but I was a cat, and cats have other gifts. I straightened, then transformed, hitting the ground on all fours.

As I have often told October, I am not a bloodhound. Neither am I Dóchas Sidhe. October can trace a person by the faintest hint of their magic, finding someone's trail days or even weeks after they've passed through. Magic is a function of the blood, after all, and she takes it to its furthest extreme.

I can't do that. But my nose, in feline form, is far more sensitive than a human's, and I *can* find things that aren't visible to the naked eye. If we were looking for a Babylon candle, we were looking for something that had been crafted by the Luidaeg. It would still smell of her, assuming it had been in her presence any time recently. I pressed my nose to the floor and sniffed, beginning to walk.

The room was very large, and filled with scents. No mice or rats, sadly—if prey animals could enter the Court of Cats, our current struggles would have been substantially leavened—but traces of all the people who'd lost these things. I continued to walk and sniff, looking for any hint of the familiar.

We weren't being entirely unreasonable. There *is* a logic to the way lost things tumble into the Court. While architecture tends to come from all over the world, objects will normally fall into the Court of Cats closest to where they were lost. It aids with finding them, on the rare occasions when we care enough to assist. Stolen things don't come to us. A thing that has been stolen may be lost to its original owner, but it's not lost to the new one, and our strange magic over misplaced things does not extend that far.

I had paced along two of the aisles, focusing more on scent than surroundings, before I caught a hint of something as familiar as my own breath. I stopped, whiskers fanning forward in surprise, before I began following the scent with more dedication. There was no trail as such; October had never walked here, in the depths of my Court, although she had seen far more than should have been allowed to one who was not feline. Still, something of hers was nearby, and I was going to find it.

The scent led me to a pile of discarded clothing. I stood on two legs, seeking the convenience of thumbs, and began digging into the heap, continuing downward until my fingertips brushed against leather and I knew that I had managed to find my objective. Holding it like a sacred relic, I pulled it from the pile and sat back, simply staring at it.

Not every scrap and bit of refuse winds up in the Court of Cats. We wouldn't have the room. What's loved enough to look for comes to us, and perhaps that was how I could be here, alone, with October's leather jacket—once my own—in my hands.

Ginevra came around a corner and stopped at the sight of me, blinking for a moment before she asked, "That Toby's jacket?"

"Yes," I managed.

"Take it with you next time you go to Shadowed Hills."

I looked sharply up at her. She shrugged.

"Call it intuition. She'll need a change of clothes eventually, and you know it's her size. Maybe the smell of your magic will call her. So take it and slip it into their lost and found. She lost it, you found it. Maybe she can find it too."

It wasn't the worst idea I'd ever heard. I allowed Ginevra to take the jacket from my hands. The scent of it would just distract me, and we still had a candle to find.

I transformed again. Ginevra has been capable of changing forms for less time than the average Cait Sidhe, having spent the bulk of her life as a changeling, and sniffing out a trail was as yet outside her experience. So I continued to take the lead while she followed, jacket draped over her arm, watching where I paused.

Two aisles over, I finally found a trace of the Luidaeg. I stopped and meowed, loudly, before beginning to follow it with new focus, stopping at a closed credenza that seemed far too large to have been lost in a manner that would bring it here. I meowed again, and Ginevra, using her convenient thumbs, opened the credenza door.

A cascade of flatware poured out, forcing me to skitter backward to avoid being hit by falling silver. Ginevra laughed. I glared at her, then began pawing through it, sniffing for traces of the Luidaeg's scent. I was following the smell of who she was as a person as much as her magic—anything she'd handled frequently would stand out. Even if I just found her favorite teaspoon, it would give us something Ginevra could use for her own search.

Forks, knives, and spoons tangled together on the floor and on the half-filled shelves. I knocked them out of my way until I found the source of the scent: a key. It was surprisingly heavy, for all that it seemed to have been made from a single piece of silver, accented with strips of other metals. I paused a moment, paw on the teeth of it, before I shifted back to human form and closed my hand around the key, standing.

"We need to go back to the Library," I said. "I believe I know what this is."

Ginevra looked surprised. "What?"

"I want to be sure before I start making promises. But if I'm correct, it's a key that can unlock the door we need to find. Can the Court spare you?"

"I'll go ask Raj," she said. "Wait here?"

Then she stepped into shadow and was gone, leaving me without the time to answer. That was fine. I stared at the key in my hand, willing it to be what I required. If I was right—if my memory served me correctly—I had seen this key before. The Luidaeg had shown it to me once, while Quentin and October were picking up burritos for eating during what he called a "found family game night."

"This is the Summer Roads Key," she'd said, inexplicably solemn as she held out the little piece of twisted precious metals for my study. Study only—I wasn't allowed to touch it. "It's very old. My father made it as a courting gift for my mother, back when the world was much younger and courtship still seemed like a good idea. My sister"—*and the disgust in her voice had been enough to tell me that she spoke of Eira: no other could invoke that mixture of resentment and loathing in her tone, not even Titania—"thought it belonged to her, because it was old and pretty. She couldn't use it, but she took it anyway. Your weird girlfriend gave it back to me."*

"Is that why you like her?"

"It's one of the reasons I tolerate her." She had closed her hand around the key then, making it vanish, and I hadn't quite dared ask her why she'd chosen to show me. She was the sea witch. If she occasionally wanted to brag about the treasures she'd accumulated, that was her right.

The night had gone on as normal from there, and she had never mentioned the key again. But this key smelled of her, and I recognized it. It had to be the same one.

The shadows parted, Ginevra stepping into the room. She no longer had the jacket, and I felt a pang of loss at its absence.

No matter. I would have it back again when it came time to carry it to Shadowed Hills.

"Raj says we can go," she said, and I nodded, sharply, before stepping into shadow, Ginevra close behind.

Together we ran, all but side by side, through the darkness, emerging in the streets of Vallejo. By this point, we knew the way well, and had no trouble walking the short remaining distance to the Library.

Magdaleana was already in the doorway, looking bemusedly out as we approached. "Tybalt, Ginevra," she greeted. "I didn't expect you. I thought you were going to the Undersea."

"We did," I said, and held up the key. "We need to know what this is."

Her eyes widened as she gestured frantically for us to get inside. She shut the door behind Ginevra. May appeared in the hall behind us, blinking blearily. "What's going on?"

"Tybalt appears to have found a prize at the bottom of his cereal box," said Magdaleana, sounding more irritated than I had ever heard her before.

I held up the key for May to see. She blinked again.

"Huh. Would have expected Titania to give that back to Eira, if she was passing toys around."

"I found it in the Court of Cats," I said, lowering the key. "We went to the Undersea. A Roane Seer informed us that we would need to be patient until Moving Day, but said resolving this would require finding the Luidaeg. What did she call her, Ginevra?"

"A keyhole waiting for a key," supplied Ginevra.

"A keyhole waiting for a key," I repeated. "Ginevra suggested we search one of the rooms at Court where lost things go, and we found this. It smells of the Luidaeg. I remember her showing it to me once . . ."

"May I?" Magdaleana extended her hand expectantly.

I dropped the key into her palm. She pulled it closer to her eyes, wings vibrating with what could have been either excitement or fear, and studied it for a moment before offering it back to me.

"I'll have to look it up to be sure, but yes, I'd say this is a Summer Roads Key. It should grant access to whichever road or roads it's been connected to. Given that the Luidaeg had it, I'd be willing to wager on it opening the Thorn Road, which belongs to the children of Maeve. The Luidaeg is rumored to have a key for that one. Perhaps more importantly, October was with her the last time the key to the Thorn Road was used."

"Why does that matter?"

"A lot of the items made with old magic remember who they belong to, but can be coaxed into allowing their most recent user's name to be added to the list of people who can use them," said Magdaleana. "The keys tend to operate that way. It belongs to the Luidaeg. October should be able to use it, when the time comes."

"We have the key," I said. "But we need October to use it, and we need the Luidaeg to finish this. What do we do now?"

Ginevra grimaced sympathetically. "What we were told to do, I guess. We wait until it's time to take a key and find a keyhole—and when that time comes, you won't be coming with us."

I stared at her for a moment, eyes going wide as I felt my claws pushing against the tips of my fingers, desperate to be freed. "Excuse me?"

"You heard me." She looked at me levelly. "She's going to be confused, no matter what's going on, and probably afraid. Titania hasn't left her equipped to understand who she is or what she can do, and you can be a little . . ."

"Intense as shit," supplied May.

"Yes, that," said Ginevra. "You can help us find her, and convince her, but when the time comes for us to use this key, you're going to be somewhere else."

"I don't . . ."

"I'm sure you can find something to keep yourself occupied. If you're there, our chances of success go down. We could lose her."

Those were the magic words that were intended to make me agree. I looked away, clenching my hands into fists I had no intention of using. I wasn't going to be manipulated by a Princess less than a quarter of my age. I wasn't going to be sidelined, not in this fight. Not when it mattered.

"I am not having this conversation with you," I said, through gritted teeth. "I am not going to agree to stay behind and allow you to gallivant off with my wife to seek the sea witch on a locked, forbidden road."

Ginevra had obviously expected my resistance, and refused to be put off. "Please, Tybalt. You remember what Mary said—"

"Do not think to interpret Roane prophecy to me, child. I heard the speech of Seers centuries before you first drew breath. Mary said I was to stay away until Moving Day, and not a moment longer. I pray you will consider the matter closed with this refusal. Now I'm going outside before I lose my temper and this becomes physical."

"You do that, kitty-cat," said May. As I stalked away, I heard her ask: "Since you're all here, anyone want pizza?"

THIRTEEN

THE NEW PATTERN OF our lives was a cold, terrible one. I was no longer accustomed to sleeping alone, nor to rising in the Court of Cats, surrounded by my people and their many demands. It may seem petty, to complain of the duties of kingship, but as I had been weaning myself away from those duties for some time, it was a shock to resume them so abruptly.

Still, we fared well enough, especially compared to the Courts with fewer royals to serve them. Raj became a frequent visitor at Shade's Court, spending as much time as he could helping her keep the nursing cats fed and the kittens healthy. Considering the fate that had befallen his own mother after Oleander poisoned the Court's supply of food, it was understandable that he would take this personally.

Ginevra worried about her father, who had thus far refused her offers to come and visit, saying he would have trouble letting her go again if she did, and wanted to avoid throwing us all off-balance. "Royal cats have always been precious," he'd informed her. "Now, however, we are the key to survival, not just of the Shadow Roads, but of our entire species. Continue to do whatever it is you say you're doing to change this reality, and I'll hold the fort up here. Fix it, Gin. If anyone can, I know it's you."

He'd asked her to stop calling after that. When she called anyway, he refused to discuss anything of any import, or to answer any specific questions about his Court. She was, politely and with the absolute greatest regard, cut off.

All three of us were frequent visitors at the Library of Stars, now that we knew the situation. Technically, we had no Library cards.

Magdaleana was unable to issue them without the Library's approval, and as the Library was opening its doors without objection, she assumed that meant we were allowed. The rules had, after all, changed during this effective assault upon us all.

Visitors came and went as normal, doing their own research, working on their own projects. Really, that was in some ways the worst of it; Titania's Faerie was so *normal*. It continued as if it had always been this way, as if this were a perfectly reasonable interpretation of the world. As if Maeve were a traitor, fae with animal qualities were "beasts"—a fact that never seemed to account for the fact that humans, like cats, dogs, and seals, were animals born of the mortal world, and yet had somehow shared their qualities with many among the fae—and changelings existed to serve.

Garm brought several other Gwragen to meet us at the Library, proud and smug over his ownership of the mystery we represented. All of them were surprised to see us, not having realized how deep the revisions went, but all also agreed, after checking the histories describing the Shadow Roads, that we must have existed all along, or else the Candela would have lost the power of passage.

Grianne was more of a surprise. She also came to visit with us in the Library, over and over again, and when I made use of my room at Shadowed Hills, she was frequently there, not speaking, just sitting in a shadowy corner and watching me. I would have thought I was being spied upon, were I not a cat, and well aware of the feline means of showing interest and fondness. Perhaps that was why we shared the Shadow Roads with the Candela; they were, in many ways, a very feline type of fae.

I came periodically to Shadowed Hills to see if anything had changed, and to try for a glimpse of my October—after meeting with Mary in Saltmist, I had stopped going to the tower more than once a week, not wanting to allow my own impatience to risk a bad outcome to our situation. August chased me away whenever she saw me, and as October never exited the tower unescorted, August always saw me first.

It was difficult not to take that behavior personally, even as I knew August had no idea that I was anything other than a stray that had somehow managed to enter the Summerlands. She seemed to truly care about October's wellbeing, and keeping wild animals away from the garden was just a part of that concern.

I had seen Simon at the tower twice, both times from a great distance, and once at Shadowed Hills, exiting the receiving room. He seemed to be in good spirits, and was closer to the man I'd known when August was young than the man that he'd become in Evening's service; well-fed, clean, with properly tended clothes and a tendency to easy laughter.

Of Amandine, there had been no direct sign. Apparently, one of the things Titania had done in creating her "perfect world" was dispose of the hope chests while simultaneously making Amandine's nature known. Amandine was thus living the life she had once feared, constantly in demand by outlying fiefdoms who wanted her to adjust their changelings, making some more fae to serve in the homes of higher nobles, and some more mortal to work in the places where Faerie and the human world collided.

It was barbaric. I had seen October offer that precise choice to others, but she had always been exceedingly clear that it was a *choice*, a way of giving power back to people who had all too frequently been powerless. Ginevra had elected to become fully Cait Sidhe even without knowing that she would be a royal cat when the process was done; she'd wanted better control over her powers, and to be able to fully embrace her father's world. Neither of her parents had pressured her in one direction over the other, and no one had *ordered* her to accept the transformation.

Cait Sidhe are natural shapeshifters. Perhaps that's why we have such a natural loathing for people being changed against their will. Still, Amandine had little rest. She had position and respect and awe, all things I knew she would enjoy, but they came with a lack of privacy and a constant stream of demands upon her time. I found that somewhat charming. It galled me to admit that I took pleasure in any part of Titania's workings, but I did. I enjoyed knowing that Amandine was still suffering, even in a world where she thought she had everything she wanted.

Eion worried for his daughters. I couldn't blame him. The more I learned about the treatment of changelings in Titania's world, the happier I became that all the changelings of the Cait Sidhe were safely locked up with the rest of my Court, well out of the reach of any of these people who thought themselves better than us as they behaved more like beasts than we had ever done. His daughters were good girls, young, sheltered enough to see nothing wrong with the lives they had lived or the society they had lived them in; they would do well on the Golden Shore, if he could only get them there. I had advised that he take a route through Shadowed Hills, where Sylvester's general air of ennui and failure to enforce any truly draconian controls would mean their journey was more likely to succeed.

As Moving Day approached, we all grew restless and uneasy. Amphitrite had returned from her mapping of the barrier around the isolated Kingdoms, having determined that it was in truth unbreachable, and had been in Saltmist ever since, the additional anxiety of having her First in residence driving Dianda to climb the walls.

I would have liked to have my own First in residence. Or the Luidaeg, if I could have been allowed the luxury of choice. Even Hirsent, with whom I had a rather checkered past, would have been welcome. Anything to feel as if we were preparing for a fight while actually armed, and not swinging wildly in the dark.

Attempts at finding Janet had been fruitless. If she existed in this world at all, she wasn't any place where I could find her, and there simply wasn't time to continue focusing on it once it became apparent that it wasn't going to be a quick, or easy process. The doorway to her courtyard was gone as if it had never been, and I had no mechanism for determining where it might have been relocated to. All I achieved by continuing that search was splitting my focus and increasing my frustration. We had more important things to worry about.

At least I knew our Undersea allies were working diligently to breach the surface. According to Amphitrite, they could swim higher every day, until the sunlight through the sea touched their skins. It was unclear whether this was the daily process of sunrise eroding one of the barriers of Titania's spell, or whether her focus was simply slipping as her denouement approached, but she thought they might be able to touch land soon, to come out of the sea and touch the transformed world.

We had been below twice more, to keep them updated, and once—as we reached the last month before Moving Day itself—for a planning session that had been unpleasant for all of us. It began as usual, with Ginevra and me descending to discuss the rapid approach of Moving Day, while Amphitrite stood in for the absent Mary, providing what context she could for the Roane Seer's words. Dianda was frazzled and furious, as always seemed to be the case in this remade world, while Patrick had visibly lost weight, and haunted the back of the meeting room like a wraith, clearly consumed by his fears for their missing husband. I felt a kinship with the both of them that I had never known before. We were united in our misery and our fear.

I would have preferred a less-unhappy bonding activity, but I suppose we don't get to dictate the world—and if Titania's example was anything to go by, that was entirely for the best.

"On Moving Day, October will 'leave the safety of the nest,'" I said.

"I presume that means her mother's tower, as Mary said I would be able to enter once she was outside. I'm also interpreting that to mean I *should* enter, that it will influence events in some way that helps us."

"That seems fair enough," said Patrick. "Otherwise, Mary would presumably have told you to stay out of the tower if you'd make things worse by going inside." This was a familiar refrain. We had engaged in several miserable debates about interpreting the Roane Seer's words, and they were beginning to drive me almost as mad as my lady's absence.

"I hate prophecy," muttered Ginevra. "It's never a clear set of steps. It's like trying to assemble an IKEA bookshelf using an instruction booklet that's been translated from Swedish to Japanese to English without a human double-checking the translations."

"I have no idea what any of that meant," I said. "But. On Moving Day, October will come out, and if we've done things correctly to this point—"

"Hard, when you don't know what that means," said Ginevra.

I shot her a quelling look. "—she'll come to us," I finished. "At that point, I can give her the key to the Thorn Roads, and we can go to find the Luidaeg."

"Sorry, that's not going to happen," said Ginevra.

I turned, slowly, to blink at her. "I beg your pardon?"

"You're not going to be the one who approaches her with the key and the quest," she said. "I am. I adore you, Your Majesty, but there's no way you'll be able to control your emotions well enough to keep yourself from scaring her. Even on your very best behavior, you're a little too intense for the person October thinks she is right now."

"As I have told you before, the matter is not up for discussion," I said, in my iciest tone. I could feel my teeth sharpen in response to this challenge to my authority—this betrayal. How dare she? How dare she deny me the right to go to my own wife, the woman I had promised to protect above all others? And how dare she try to force the matter in front of our allies, people who were not Cait Sidhe and would think less of me if I answered as she deserved?

Ginevra didn't look away, only met my eyes with a challenge of her own, and I could no longer hold myself back. She didn't flinch as I flung myself into motion, slamming her back against the wall. She hissed at that, lips drawing back and nose wrinkling, and I heard Dianda start to rise from her wheelchair.

"No," said Pete. "This is how the Cait Sidhe settle things. My father gave them his consent when he granted them their own Court."

"If you scare her away, we lose," spat Ginevra. "If you treat her like the woman you know, we lose. This task is *mine*."

I snarled at her, pressing her harder to the wall. She continued to glare at me, not yielding.

"You'll see her, and you'll tell yourself that you'll resist, you'll swear you can follow the plan, and then someone will insult her as a changeling or order her to do some menial task, and you'll take them apart, and scare the life out of her in the process," she said. "This can't fall to you."

"How long have you been planning to betray me?" I demanded. She was silent. I shook her. "How *long*?!"

"She's right, Tybalt," said Dianda. "That's why I can't go either. Even if we'd been able to get abovewater by now, there's no way I could look at Amandine and not break her nose. Right before I lost my grasp on my legs and fell into fins in the middle of some Court that thinks we all died a long, long time ago. We're both sidelined for this one."

"Ah." I released Ginevra, who dropped to her knees and clutched her throat, still glaring at me. As long as she didn't look away, she hadn't lost her challenge. "So you've been planning to betray me together."

"No one's betraying anyone," said Patrick. "This is the best way to bring our people home. To bring back our *world*."

I stared at him, a thread of surprise penetrating my anger, as I had expected that he and his wife would side with me in this matter. He looked back, and sighed.

"You've been doing the right thing for this long," he said. "Can't you make it just a little longer?"

Patience is at times a necessity of kingship. I sagged, the fight going out of me. So much was riding on this, for everyone. Ginevra was unquestionably invested in the situation, but she stood a better chance of keeping a level head and handling things in a rational manner.

"Fine," I said, sullenly. "But if it seems in any way that things aren't proceeding as we hoped, I will intercede at once."

"If that's what has to happen," said Pete, voice soothing, as if she were trying to quell an irrational child. Which I suppose we all were, to her.

The thought took some of the sting out of the situation, and I returned my attention to the others. I offered Ginevra no apology. That's not how we do things among the Court of Cats. She had won; she would be the one to take our case to October. That was better than an apology, as we measure things.

Beyond that, once I had accepted the necessity, I could even see some advantage in it: Titania had known me when she was Stacy, known me too well for me to take many risks where she was concerned, but she had never had much knowledge of Ginevra. That, combined with her distraction, might be what we needed to succeed—and Titania *was* distracted. We had determined that she spent most of her time traveling, but when she was in the Mists, she stayed with her beloved daughter at Goldengreen.

And she had been preparing for a Ride.

On that final night of our wait for Moving Day, I came back to my room at Shadowed Hills after leaving my leather jacket among the knowe's repository of cast-off human clothing—October would have laughed at the amount of time I spent arranging it to catch the eye while still appearing innocently haphazard—to find Grianne once again keeping silent watch from her habitual corner. I stopped in the doorway, frowning at her. "Why do you help us?" I asked. "You're loyal to Duke Torquill, in this reality as much as in the one I remember, and we've never been particularly close."

She shrugged. "Candles," she said.

"I realize the rest of us have far more of a tendency toward verbosity than you do, but I do need more than a single word if I'm going to understand."

Grianne sighed like I'd just asked her to do something entirely unreasonable. She held out her hand, and one of her Merry Dancers came to nestle in her palm. "Candles exist to light the way," she said. "We used to have all the roads, a long time ago, before Maeve's Ride was broken. If a path could pass through Faerie, we could pass there. Shadows and thorns, blood and children, we led you all to your destinations. Candela exist to light the way."

"And you're helping me because . . . ?"

"The Shadow Roads are anchored by the Cait Sidhe. We've been trying for years to figure out how they hadn't collapsed in your absence. Then Garm started saying the world was an illusion, and that the real history was something else that Candela couldn't see. He didn't know the real history, but he knew this one was a lie. That made so much sense. The Roads were still there because the Cait Sidhe were still there. We don't have many paths left to us, and more and more, our purpose is forgotten. Do you know what happens to a candle no one needs?"

"Not in specific."

"It gets blown out." She put her hand over the Merry Dancer in her hand, blocking its light, and looked at me gravely. "I help you because if you're telling the truth, you can help the Candela keep our purpose. And if you're not, who cares? You're not hurting anyone. Nothing you've said or done has threatened my duke, or asked me to go against my oaths. Either you're going to save us, or you're harmless and deserve to have someone looking after you so you don't hurt yourself."

I blinked at her. "That is . . . very practical. You have my respect."

She nodded, mouth tightly closed once more as she released her Merry Dancer into the air.

"You also have my apologies for making you talk so much when I know it discomforts you," I said. "I needed to understand, especially with Moving Day approaching."

The festivities would begin at midnight. Eion would start his journey toward Golden Shore, and the period in which changelings could move freely would begin. I had entertained a few quiet fantasies of October realizing her situation and running away the moment Moving Day made it acceptable, but had dismissed them as it became more and more clear that she had no idea anything was wrong with her life. She wouldn't run.

According to Mary, however, on Moving Day October would "leave the safety of the nest," and I would be able to intercede. I could enter the tower once she was gone. I could verify for myself that her life there was as kind as it looked from the outside, that she wasn't being bled behind closed doors, that she faced no dangers. I might attract Amandine's attention if I had to push through the wards, but October wouldn't be there for me to endanger. No more waiting. No more staying so close and yet so far away.

An echoing blast from outside signaled the fireworks, and the beginning of the night's celebration. Grianne rose, gesturing for me to follow her.

"Come," she said.

"I would prefer not to."

She looked annoyed and gestured more emphatically. "*Come.*"

Cats are well known for our stubbornness, and continuing to argue was a tempting idea. But then, she had explained herself when I asked her to, even as it caused her obvious discomfort. I didn't want to aggravate her when she was helping me, and so I straightened my shirt and followed her out the door to the hall.

Any illicit thrill of being a guest in Sylvester's home when he didn't remember the true nature of our relationship had long since faded. Etienne had been easily convinced to keep extending the hospitality of the house, as I had proven myself to be a respectful and reserved house guest. Every week, he asked me for updates on my search for my missing wife, and every week, I answered honestly, with increasingly reduced details as I worked to conceal the fact that she was no longer missing, simply unavailable in any meaningful way.

The rest of the denizens of Shadowed Hills were polite if a bit distant from the stranger with no known noble house or affiliations who had taken up residence in one of the guest rooms and kept a low profile, mostly keeping company with two of the less-popular knights. I offered no advantage in the games they played—and those games, which had always been present, had turned more vicious under Titania's lead. Everything was a challenge for position. Everything was an opportunity to gain or lose face.

Eira was the only Firstborn I knew of to have openly ordered her descendants to fight for power, but it seemed she had learned that form of love well at the feet of her mother.

There were still people missing, even beyond Janet. All my inquiries and attempts to search had failed to locate Dean or Rayseline, or Arden and her brother. Chelsea Ames and the Brown children were likewise unaccounted for. Walther was in Silences, serving as Court alchemist to his parents, well out of the way of Titania's plans. It seemed she had done her best to split us all up, scattering us across the land she had claimed within her illusion.

Grianne led me down the hall to the great ballroom I had seen on the day of my arrival. It was full of people, or seemed so, from a distance; looking more closely made it quite clear that this party was sparsely attended, a celebration for the socially outcast and unfashionable. If every body in that room took to the dance floor at once, there would still be room to move easily through the crowd.

Sylvester was seated at one end of the room, looking as if he would rather be almost anywhere else. Simon was standing next to him, a goblet in one hand and the other resting on his brother's shoulder, speaking to him quietly.

"Amandine went to Silences," said Grianne, voice low. "Work."

So she'd be away from the tower for several days, given the distance involved. It also explained Etienne's current absence; he was usually the one tapped to transport people around the duchy when they were important enough to occupy such a key resource. As far as I knew, he couldn't make the jump to Silences all at once. I could probably expect Amandine to be gone for most of the week.

Grianne watched my face, nodding with satisfaction when she saw me finish puzzling through the implications of Amandine's absence.

"Guest," she said, and gestured toward the ballroom doors.

I scowled at her. "Brat."

She smiled, tapping two fingers to her temple in a mock salute before she somersaulted backward into the shadows and was gone.

She was, however, correct that I was a guest in these halls, and guests are generally expected to meet a certain standard of presence. I ran my tongue over my teeth to be sure the more feline aspects of my nature were properly suppressed, then strode into the ballroom, pulling my very best mask of disdainful detachment over myself.

The assembled revelers glanced my way, then away again as they recognized me as Sylvester's vagrant houseguest. I had nothing to offer them, and so they offered me nothing in return.

Easily, I moved through the crowd, plucking a wineglass from the tray of a passing server and smiling at everyone in ducal livery. They were the ones most likely to be punished for having harbored me if things went poorly. I worked my way toward the Duke and his brother, pausing at a respectful distance to bow and wait to be acknowledged.

"Ah, my hopeless houseguest," said Sylvester. "Rise, rise. Have you met my brother?"

Thanks to my own efforts, not in this reality, but I couldn't say that, and I had no civil way to avoid the introduction at a celebration such as this one. Surely, the start of the Moving Day festivities was close enough to Mary's command that I could speak to the man. I straightened. "I do not believe we've yet been introduced, Your Grace. Twin?"

"To the hour," said Sylvester, radiating boredom. "Simon followed me into the world by a matter of minutes, and has never since shown patience."

"A poor introduction, brother," said Simon, and turned to fully face me, a practiced smile on his aristocratic face. "I am Simon Torquill, Baron of Kettled Time. It is a pleasure to make your acquaintance."

"And yours as well," I said, keeping my own face impassive. "I am Rand, once of Londinium, of no notable family name, although I've been known to use 'Stratford' when necessity forced me out among the mortals. I've been enjoying the hospitality of your brother's halls."

"So I've heard," said Simon. "The questing houseguest. You've managed to mislay your wife?"

"Not intentionally, sire, and not because I gave her cause to flee from me or anything of the like," I said. "We are the targets of an unkind magic."

Simon's face clouded. "How wicked!" he said, and I heard no insincerity in his tone. "How could anyone be so cruel as to part a family in such a manner? I hope your quest is brief, Rand, and that she is back with you in short order."

"May the root and branch hear your words and lift me up to meet them," I said.

"Sylvester tells me you've been keeping company with his knights?"

"When I can," I said "They are pleasant people, by and large, clever and interesting to speak with. Well, to, in the case of Sir Grianne—she doesn't speak much *with* anyone."

Simon laughed. "No, I suppose she wouldn't."

"Candela never do," said Sylvester.

Simon turned then, setting his half-empty goblet on the tray of a passing server. "It seems that time, in passing, has left me at a disadvantage. Rand, it was a pleasure to meet you. Brother, I shall see you upon my return."

"Your master calls?" Sylvester asked, with a slight sneer.

"My liege and patron desires me to attend her celebrations, and how can I deny her?" Simon's smile was dazzling. "I am fortunate to be called to serve the Countess Winterrose. I would never think to disrespect that calling by refusing to attend on her. I will see you both quite soon, I'm sure."

With that, he stepped down from the dais and vanished into the crowd, moving toward the door. I looked to Sylvester.

"Is he always so quick to go?"

"Since we were children," said Sylvester, and sighed heavily. "He means well. He just doesn't handle idleness gracefully, and his wife's duties leave him with too many idle hours. So he hurries about when he's free to do so, and that contents him."

"Well, it was a pleasure to meet him at last, after so many years of seeing him only as a face in the crowds of Goldengreen. But I think you wear that face better, sire."

"You already have the hospitality of my house through the end of the holiday, Rand; there's no need to flatter for further," said Sylvester. "Go, and enjoy the night, and if you move on with the rest come the end of Moving Day, I won't blame you. Surely, you've near to exhausted the local possibilities in your search."

"I have good reason to believe it will soon be drawing to a close," I said politely. "Still, I have appreciated your patience and your kindness to a stranger. I won't forget it."

I wouldn't, either. As I turned and made my way toward the balcony, I considered the irony of it all: for the first time in our adult lives, Sylvester and I were getting along, and all it had taken was erasing the whole of our shared history from his mind. Perhaps we could have been on good terms all along, if he'd just taken a strong enough blow to the head.

The balcony was populated with celebrants seeking a respite from the noise indoors. There might not be as many dancers as there would have been at a truly fashionable party, but the string quartet played as loudly as they would have for twice the crowd or more, and the sound had a way of swelling to fill the space available. A few of the courtiers I knew from the knowe nodded in polite recognition, while others looked at me with calm assessment, trying to take my measure.

The temptation to let my control slip, just a little, and flash them a hint of fang or a shadow of my stripes was strong. How would they react, these defanged pets of Titania's, if I reminded them of the real Faerie?

But no. No, I wouldn't. It was almost Moving Day—three days more, and everything would be over. I would have my life back, or I would be in the horrible aftermath of this frozen period of unwanted patience. Either way, antagonizing people who had no idea what had been done to them was unkind.

Fireworks exploded across the sky, briefly blotting out the stars. Unlike their counterparts in the mortal world, they left no falling embers or smell of gunpowder in their wake, only scintillating brilliance that obscured, however briefly, the fact that the clouds moving overhead weren't clouds at all, but vast swarms of pixies heading south, away from the Mists.

Pixies almost always relocate on Moving Day. I've known only a few colonies to put down roots so deep that they refused to move when the opportunity arose; something in the old rhythms of Faerie lives on in their blood, calling them to follow. Those who don't can provide stable havens for their kin but are all too often shunned because of their refusal of tradition. The political lives of pixies can be surprisingly complicated.

I watched the fireworks burst in the sky above, and watched the pixies fly between the flashes, and wondered how many rhythms we moved to that we didn't even register any longer, tides that were baked into our blood and our bones, immutable. The party went on around me, and the clock ticked down toward midnight, and the Moving Day festivities had begun.

FOURTEEN

THE PARTY LASTED UNTIL the small hours of the morning. Several times, my guilt led me to wander into a dark corner, beginning to reach for the shadows, only to pull myself back. Ginevra and Raj knew where I was. They had known even before I left that I wouldn't be back until well into the next day, assuming I came back at all. This might be the day they lost me. So much hinged on Amandine's wards, and any other protections the tower might have, because I was going in. Oberon himself couldn't have held me back any longer.

As the revelers began to make their apologies and slip away, I joined their crowd, letting them sweep me toward the gates. Grianne saw me amongst them and nodded, bidding me a silent farewell, and otherwise did nothing to attract attention to me. I smiled over at her as I continued onward, not pausing. The time for pausing was well and truly finished.

And then I was outside the bounds of the knowe, the nobles either stepping out of the Summerlands to return to their cars or taking the arms of Tuatha courtiers who would be able to portal them to their destination. A few Tylwyth Teg who had attended the celebration mounted yarrow branches they had brought for precisely this moment—although none of the ones who'd worn a dress or gown to the party, I noted. In the end, I was the only one who chose to walk.

Of course, I walked because my destination was so near. Heading through the woods and across the fields, toward the white spire of Amandine's tower. I was near the edge of the wards when I saw a small group of people shuffling away from the garden gate, shoulders slumped and postures weary.

They seemed oddly familiar. I hurried in their direction, pausing when I recognized the man at the head of their group. Eion and his family, the rest of whom I had not been given the opportunity to meet during my visits to the Library.

"Eion!" I called.

He looked up, and motioned the others to a halt as I trotted the rest of the distance over to meet them on the road.

"My friend," he said.

"What happened?"

"We walked here, as we had planned," he said. "But the woman who answered the door offered only the barest hospitality, and had clearly been well coached to avoid implying the offer of more. She left us no openings to ask. We were given food, and direction to a place where we might take root for the night, but when I saw that she was a change-ling, I admit, I hoped for more."

My heart sank. "Was she so cold to you, then?" I asked, with careful gentleness.

"No. Not cold. Just . . . trained?" He looked at me, frustration clear in his eyes. "She knew what was expected of her, and she didn't slip from the script she'd been given. I doubt she knows how."

"They crush the questions out of changelings one 'know your place' at a time," said one of the women, her arm around the shoulders of a clearly exhausted changeling girl.

"Where did she tell you to root yourselves?"

"In the briars beyond a pixie-infested swamp. She said no one claimed them as their land, and so we wouldn't be troubled if we slept there."

"She spoke the truth, in that that land belongs only to the duke, and he doesn't stir himself enough to care," I said. "I can help you there. The pixies should be preoccupied with Moving Day, and we'll likely reach our destination without issue. But you look dead on your feet. How far did you walk tonight?"

"Only about fifteen miles overland," said Eion.

"And is this something you do often?"

"No! Never!"

"Then I'll thank you to omit the 'only,'" I said crisply, and the girls, neither of whom had reached their majority, giggled at my choice of words. "Come along, before I have to carry you."

I started to walk, and they followed, slow and listless after their long journey. Fifteen miles wasn't much in a motor vehicle, or via the Shadow Roads, but on foot at night, with two teenage girls unaccustomed to such exertion? It was all but impossible. Asking them to go farther before dawn was a cruelty.

Especially when the ground began to shift and soften underfoot, earth giving way to mud at swamp's edge. I gritted my teeth and kept going, until I was wading through muck to my ankles. The Hamadryads, who fed their vegetable sides through the soles of their feet, looked far happier to be wading through what was effectively a nourishing soup than I was, and I tried to focus on their pleasure, not the amount of washing I would need to do when this was over.

The ground began to harden again as we approached the mounded shape of a blackberry tangle. There, surrounded on all sides by thorny briars, was a circular clearing of the type that could easily be made by two enterprising young women with a heavy board to stand on, over the course of many years. The bushes were still fruiting, heavy berries hanging low for easy collection, and the girls fell upon them with a cry of gladness. Eion met my eyes and nodded, expression grave.

"We'll get to Golden Shore, and I'll see you there, my friend," he said. "With your lady beside you."

"I appreciate your faith," I said, and bowed to the girls, who looked at me with mouths full of blackberries and hands dripping purple juice, and were lovely. They were all lovely, this family of five fleeing for their lives from the system Titania had created.

This had to stop.

The sky was getting lighter overhead as the Summerlands' excuse for dawn approached, sun cusping higher behind the clouds. It would never fully appear, of course; twilight was the best this realm would do. But it marked the passage of time, and I had no more cause to hide. Turning, I leapt for the shadows caught among the berry briars, shifting to feline form as I did. I heard one of the girls gasp.

Then all was darkness, and the dark held me close as I ran the short distance back to the tower. I stopped when I felt the wards press back against me, dropping back into the field, and approached with caution.

Voices on the road to the manor caught my attention. I turned, and saw August and October walking away from me, heading toward Shadowed Hills. August appeared to be teasing her sister, who was arguing toothlessly. It would have seemed a dear, domestic scene if I hadn't been fully aware of just how false it was.

It was also a good thing. With Amandine in Silences and Simon off attending whatever fete Evening had organized for the occasion, them being out meant the tower was well deserted, and I wouldn't need to worry about unfortunate encounters. I could search for signs that October was truly being treated well to my heart's content. Heart hammering, I approached the ward line.

As every time before, it ignored the feline where it would not ignore the man, and I was able to approach the wall. This time, however, no one appeared to throw fallen apples or wave a broom at me as I hopped up, and after a moment of steadying my thoughts to clear away any thought of hostility or harm, I was able to jump down into the rear garden.

The scent of herbs engulfed me, underscored on every side by the more delicate, more-welcome scent of October. It seemed she had touched every leaf, every inch of ground, and for a moment, it was as if I could have rolled in the essence of her. I took several greedy, steadying breaths, then padded onward to the door.

The wards here were still strong. I looked around, finally spotting a small, high window into the kitchen. It was made of the sort of thick glass that fell out of favor in the human world several hundred years ago, the kind that could be wiped spotless and yet never seem quite clean. The frame was rowan wood, which meant it was mildly magic-repellent, and would probably represent a hole in the wards.

Perfect wards may seem like an aspirational goal, but they're actually a terrible idea. Much like the dome Titania had used to seal off the Undersea, they let nothing in or out, and people have died because their knowes caught fire and the wards were too complete to recognize that a person who was actively burning wasn't attacking them. Small holes are a necessity. They're just most often left with an eye to also evading any intruder larger than a pixie.

Quick and cautious, I jumped onto the water barrel against the wall, and from there to the windowsill, rubbing myself against the glass. It didn't budge, but I felt the absence of the wards like a breath of fresh air in a crowded room. Fine, then; there were other ways to do this, and I wasn't worried about being caught. Adjusting my position to keep myself from falling, I shifted back into human form and pressed harder against the window, nearly overbalancing in the process. Not my most dignified moment.

I put one foot down on the water barrel and pushed harder still. The window didn't budge. Either it opened outward, or it was locked. I looked around. This was a garden. There would have to be something I could . . .

Ah-ha. A large rock by the side of the garden path would do me quite nicely. I picked it up, testing the heft of it with a careful bounce before I whipped it at the window as hard as I possibly could. Neither Amandine nor Simon had any particular material tilt to their magic; the glass was unlikely to be reinforced, and just the fear of what would happen to someone who threw rocks at a Firstborn's home would likely keep it unbroken.

The rock flew straight and true and smashed clear through with a loud shattering sound followed by a clatter as it continued onward to the kitchen floor. I shifted back to feline form and repeated my leap from water barrel to windowsill, this time picking my way through the broken glass to the interior of the tower.

Moving with caution, for all that I knew myself alone, I slunk through the darkened kitchen to the front room, then up the stairs toward the bedchambers. If they were abusing October in any way, this was where I would find the evidence. There would be no legal consequences if they were, but it would determine how I treated August and Simon in the days ahead of us.

October's room was on the second floor, one level below her sister's, and was every bit as large. The linens were clean, and the urge to curl up on the bed and sleep in the scent of her was even stronger than the urge to roll in the garden had been. I searched the whole place but found no sign that she had been bleeding, or that harm had come to her, or to our child. There was nothing to indicate that she was anything but a well-cared-for second daughter of the house—or that she had any idea of who she truly was. They might intend for her to serve her sister's household someday, but they hadn't turned her into Cinderella for the sake of that ideal.

Time was passing. It was obvious that I had been here, that someone had entered the tower by force. I needed to give them an easy explanation why. I returned to the kitchen and to my two-legged form, gathering cheese, butter, preserves, three loaves of bread, a bowl of eggs, and a whole hanging joint of cured meat into a potato sack before diving into the shadows.

I dropped the sack before I reached the manor. Much as I wanted to give it to Eion and his family, if I was staging a robbery, I couldn't risk pinning the blame on them. They were free to move until the stroke of midnight on Halloween, but they were still unranked, and the girls were changelings. All it would take was a few days of detention and they'd never see the Golden Shore. No. I wouldn't do that to them.

I emerged onto the balcony. The party was well over by that point. The garlands and ribbons that had been tied around the columns were slumping toward the ground, which was littered with debris from the buffet and fallen flower petals from the décor. Servants moved through the mess, collecting what could be saved and sweeping up what couldn't be.

The air smelled of spilled wine, slightly stale buttercream frosting, and— I stopped dead, unable to keep myself from sniffing the air.

And blood.

October's blood.

The smell was almost as familiar as her magic, coppery, bright, and achingly present. I hated that it made my heart glad to smell it, because it meant she had been here, and recently. Been here, and been bled, while she was trapped under Titania's spell and hence defenseless. In all the time I'd observed the tower, I had never seen her pick up so much as a pair of garden shears, nor pluck a single rose. Whatever else this world allowed her to do, it didn't let her bleed.

A solidly built Brownie changeling was mopping up the point on the balcony where the smell of blood was strongest, using far more water than I would have thought strictly necessary. I strolled over to her.

"What happened here?" I asked.

"The Lady August and her sister come to visit," said the girl. "Lady went inside, sister stayed to help with cleaning up. Squire Quentin came over to talk to her, when she talked back, gave her a shove, and some chips of plate caught and cut her. Naughty girl, talking back to the gentry like that. Deserves the punishment she'll likely get when her father finds out."

"Indeed," I said, stiffly.

I turned away from her, stopping when I spotted Grianne on the other side of the balcony. She was back in her uniform, meaning she had started a guard shift right after party's end; she'd be exhausted and useless by nightfall. I walked quickly toward her.

"October," I hissed, once I was close enough, keeping my voice too low to be easily overheard.

If anyone could understand the meaning in a single word, it was Grianne. She nodded.

"Inside," she replied. Then, apparently realizing that wasn't going to be enough, she added, "Shaken, but fine."

"I'd gut him for touching her, but she'd be furious with me once this was over, for laying a hand on him." I scowled. "I don't like needing to forgive people for behaving badly based on the behavior of their other selves."

Grianne nodded, looking halfway sympathetic, which was really all I could expect. October and I were in the same place for the first time in four months, the same knowe. It felt like my skin was suddenly too tight, like every one of my nerves was on the verge of bursting out of my body and rolling away as their own composite entities, leaving the rest of me behind. I felt like a stripling waiting for the girl he'd been courting to walk around a corner.

It was exhilarating and exhausting at the same time, and I was trying to push the feeling aside when Garm ran into the doorway to the inside, out of breath, tabard askew. "Rand!" he exclaimed. "Baron Torquill is approaching!"

August and October were both in the knowe, and I had just broken into Simon's home. If he didn't know they were planning to come to Shadowed Hills . . .

"Does he seem angry?" I asked, trying to quickly decide how I was to handle this new complication. Simon might suspect me, as a stranger in his brother's halls, but surely he would have no place to anchor his suspicions. More, as my time here was nearly done and Moving Day had now officially begun, this might be my opportunity to speak to a member of October's family as Mary's prophecy had suggested.

There is little harm in learning, and sometimes there can be great benefit. I watched Garm intently, waiting for his answer.

"Furious," Garm replied.

"Then the warning is appreciated," I said, and stepped into shadow, following the Shadow Roads from the balcony to the gloom under the trees at forest's edge. There I stopped, and listened.

Simon's anger would make him less focused, less likely to wonder at why I was seeking his company after so many nights of managing to avoid his presence. It would seem less suspicious, also, if I wasn't hiding from him now. And Mary had said I should speak to those October called family. What family closer than her father, even if he played the role against his will? So I held my place, and waited.

It wasn't long before I heard Simon's approach, leaves crackling underfoot as he stormed toward the manor. I stepped onto the path, turning to face him.

"Baron Torquill! I didn't expect to have the pleasure of seeing you again so soon. How was the celebration you left us to attend?"

"Fine," he said, waving the question away as if it were nothing. Which, to be fair, it was. "I need to see my brother."

"I can escort you, if you'd like."

"That would be . . ." He paused, rubbing his face. "That would be unnecessary, but pleasant. I returned home to find a window broken and my daughters missing. Under the circumstances, I would appreciate the company."

I fell in beside him as we continued toward the manor, and he walked more sedately now that there was someone who could judge him for losing his composure. So the thought of a threat to the girls had been enough to upset him, and he'd said "my daughters," not "August and the other one." He really did seem to care for them equally in this world Titania had created.

But what benefit could that have? If she wanted October to be miserable—which she did, of that I was sure—then making Simon treat his changeling child poorly would have been a way to make things worse. Instead, he had created a warm and loving home, one from which Amandine was absent more often than not.

It didn't make sense.

We reached the manor and passed through the main gate, heading for the receiving room without pause. I knew my way around the knowe in its current configuration better than I had ever known its previous design, and Simon needed no direction. The few members of the staff who glanced our way as we walked looked quickly back to whatever they'd been doing once they saw the expression on his face.

When we reached the receiving room doors, Simon paused and looked at me. "I hate to ask something of a relative stranger, but I would appreciate it if you'd wait out here while I speak to my brother," he said. "This is family business. I'd like to speak to you when I'm done, however."

"Of course, sir," I said.

Simon nodded sharply, and slipped into the room, leaving me outside to consider the situation. I had been back in my little fish's near presence for only a short while, and already everything had devolved into chaos. Maybe this was going to turn out the way I had been hoping after all. Maybe I was going to get my family back.

Minutes ticked by, and there was no shouting from inside, only silence. The smell of river lupine and limoncello announced Ginevra's arrival before I heard her footsteps behind me, intentionally exaggerated to keep me from thinking that she was trying to sneak up. I turned.

"What?"

"You didn't come back," she said. "You were supposed to come back after you saw October leave the tower, so we could discuss our next steps. When you didn't, we were . . . worried." Meaning she was concerned that I had stumbled upon an opportunity to grab October and decided to take it. "Raj is holding the Court, and we did a small supply run last night; he'll be fine for the rest of the day, if not longer. I needed to know that you were all right."

I sighed, running a hand through my hair to buy myself a moment to think. Finally, I looked at Ginevra and said, in a hushed tone, "She's here."

She didn't ask who I meant. Instead, she stood a little straighter, rounded pupils turning oval and going narrow in surprise. "Where?"

"In the manor," I said. "Inside the knowe. Her own squire caused her harm—assaulted her while she was cleaning up after last night's party, and drew blood. It was odd, actually. I broke into the tower . . ."

"You did *what*?"

"You knew I was planning to enter as soon as she came out. No one was home at the time, I wasn't in any danger of being seen." I waved off her concern. "Amandine is in Silences, Simon was in Goldengreen, and both girls were on their way here. So I broke in to be sure they'd been treating her as well as it seemed they had. And there was no blood trail. Not from October. I smelled blood, yes, but all from other sources."

"Do you think they just haven't been letting her do blood magic?"

"Would you, if you were trying to keep her under control?"

Ginevra scoffed. "I wouldn't try to keep that woman under control. Even if you wouldn't kill me for even thinking about it, it would be like trying to wrestle a blizzard into compliance. Not the sort of thing you do when you want to keep all your fingers attached to your body."

"Raj and Helen were watching a program about human hospital services right before the world revised itself. It seems they could put your fingers back on, if you wanted to cross my lady."

She smacked me in the arm, and I laughed, pleased to have relaxed her so, before I continued: "As I was saying . . . she bled, and the staff removed her for reasons I don't understand as yet. I was speaking to Grianne when I was notified of Simon's approach, and now he's inside, speaking with his brother. But he's asked me to wait until they're finished, as he'd like to speak with me."

Ginevra's eyes widened. "Do you know why?"

"No idea. But as making nice with her father figure might create the opportunity for us to speak with October, I have to wait." Belatedly, it occurred to me that if Mary's prophecy hadn't encouraged me to take the chance to speak with Simon, I might be in October's presence by now. Such is the danger of depending on Seers. Prophecy will always cut both ways.

"Then I'll wait with you."

She leaned against the wall, folding her arms. I blinked at her, raising an eyebrow, and she looked calmly back, so I settled against her, and we waited.

People passed, going about their duties. Several members of the household staff bustled by, as did some of the courtiers who had chosen to spend the day at the knowe. It was pleasant, domestic, and mind-numbingly dull, and I was beginning to reconsider my patience when the door creaked open and August was there, so close I could have reached out and touched her.

"Oh," she said. "There's two of you. Father didn't say anything about *that*. Well, I suppose you'd best come inside."

She turned her back on us, door still open, and vanished into the depths of the receiving room.

Ginevra and I exchanged a look and followed her inside.

The door slammed shut behind us.

FIFTEEN

SYLVESTER WAS SEATED IN the high chair on the dais, and Simon was standing beside him, matching expressions on their shadowed, solemn faces. August continued across the room until she reached the dais, where she sat on the edge, boosting herself back until her legs were dangling, childlike, feet a few inches above the checkerboard floor.

Ginevra, who had never been to the knowe at Shadowed Hills before, was looking around with open curiosity as we approached, clearly trusting that I would catch her if she tripped. If not for Titania's spell, that trust might have been misplaced—a cat who trips and falls is a cat who deserves to be reminded that things which fall will hit the floor. I kept my eyes on my destination—on Simon, who was the reason we were here.

"My brother has never had much skill at blood magic," said Simon, as we approached. Sylvester shrugged, looking unbothered and unsurprised by this mild critique. "It's odd, given that we're twins and all, but he's always been the better illusionist, when he reaches for magic at all—he much prefers a sword."

"Better suited to a career in heroism," said Sylvester. "You can't slay a monster with an illusion, although you can sometimes trick them into running off the side of a cliff or something equally ridiculous. I was never the cleverness-and-trickery sort of hero. Brute force and stubbornness is much more my speed."

"Whereas I studied the alchemical arts and the science of potionmaking," said Simon, taking up the conversation with smooth ease. It was a bit like falling backward through time, to when we had all been children in Londinium and the boys had been inclined to present a united front—when they weren't trying to murder each other in the innocently malicious manner of young boys allowed to run half-wild around their parents' estate, that was. "I can borrow someone else's magic in a drop of their blood, and I can pick up the shape of someone's descendant line from the smell off their skin."

"Fascinating, although I'm not quite sure what that has to do with my presence," I said.

"Who is your friend, Lord Rand?" asked Sylvester, leaning back in his chair. "I don't recall seeing her in my halls before. Is this your missing lady wife, returned to us at last?"

It would have been a convenient falsehood. Sadly, Ginevra recoiled at the thought, a look of revulsion flashing across her face so quickly that she didn't have a chance to compose herself, and I didn't have a chance to claim the lie.

"Alas, no," I said. "I have a ward, a boy, whose father has stopped his dancing, and whose education I am thus responsible for, but the search for my lady makes me unable to do my duty. This is Ginevra, the eldest daughter of one of my oldest friends, who stands as my ward's teacher while I am unfit to guide him."

Ginevra recovered her expression of neutrality and curtseyed, quickly. Her form could have been better, and she never lowered her eyes to the floor as was considered proper in the Divided Courts, but still, I was impressed.

"I was surprised to finally meet you last night at the celebration," said Simon. "I had heard so much about this recurring guest in my brother's halls, the tragic figure whose wife had vanished and who now dedicated himself to the search for her. Everyone was so sure you would wear out your welcome in no time at all, and then, somehow, half the knights seemed to find joy in your company, and encouraged Sir Etienne to continue extending your period of hospitality. Even that might not have worked, had he not been so occupied with the taking and training of a new squire."

"The boy is *rotten*, Father," said August, her voice petulant and shrill and every bit the spoiled child I would have expected from Amandine. Then she continued. "October was helping the staff while I searched for cake—for the *both* of us, I wasn't being greedy, but you know they won't let me help out of fear for what Mother will say—and he *pushed* her, for no good reason at all! She wasn't antagonizing or taunting him, only trying to help, and he put his hands on her, and he *pushed* her!"

"Sir Etienne's new squire?" asked Sylvester, voice taking on a dangerous growl.

Simon shot him a look. "Unfortunately, there's not much we can do about that, poppet. The boy is here on blind fosterage—"

"So unseal it and send him home," she snapped.

"—at the request of my patron," concluded Simon. "She was the one who brought him to my brother's hall. It's a great honor to harbor a foster for the Countess Winterrose, and a greater honor to have been chosen as teacher for one she's taken a close interest in. She wanted him to grow up in a proper noble household, and wanted me close enough to watch over his education. He can't be removed."

"Then you tell him never to touch her again." August slid off the dais and whirled to face her father, unflatteringly pale skirts swirling out around her legs. I had never liked her more than I did in that moment. "You tell him he'll answer to me if he lays a finger on her. She's *my* sister, and not for him to harm!"

"Until you leave to found your own household, she's my daughter before she's your sister," said Simon. "And I say that my patron would object if we tried to dictate the behavior of her foundling."

Sylvester, who had been looking increasingly uncomfortable throughout this exchange, sat up and cleared his throat. "What of my objections?" he asked. "The boy torments *my* niece in *my* knowe, in the Duchy I command, and I'm to sit back because the Countess Winterrose would prefer he not be disciplined? How does that make me a strong ruler? How does that leave me worthy of my place?"

"Brother—"

"No, Simon. I swallow enough crow for the sake of that woman. Five times I've courted to the cusp of marriage, and five times she's stepped in and told the lady we're not a fit match. Her interference in my life is an ink stain upon its pages, obscuring what was written there. I'll speak to Sir Etienne. He'll remind his squire that manners and civility to those below him are an essential part of knightly valor, and the boy will mend his ways."

A silent "or else" hung in the air at the end of his sentence.

"And we've departed from the point," said Simon, focusing on me once more. "My brother is very dear to me. I have surprisingly little living family, outside of my wife and daughters. My niece January chooses to remain in Briarholme, where the memory of her parents keeps her company. So I'm sure you understand why I was curious about a guest in my brother's knowe who gave only the barest of explanations for his presence, and was frequently seen at the Library of Stars in the company of two of my brother's knights."

"We were allowed admittance," I said. "The Library keeps its own rules, and we broke none of them."

"I'm aware," said Simon. "I asked the Librarian about you, and she said I didn't have the secrets left to barter for yours. She's never refused me before."

I wondered privately what Mags would think of being told that this world's revised history had her answering to Simon Torquill's every whim. It was an almost-amusing image, if only for the amount of shouting that would surely follow.

"Still, I was unaware that it was unseemly for a man to visit a Library while on a quest."

"It's not, once," said Simon. "Repeatedly, and with several knights sworn loyal to my brother, starts to seem odd. And then, when I finally met you, I couldn't place your descendant line. You looked Daoine Sidhe, or perhaps Tuatha de Dannan—an odd example of either, to be sure, but within the bounds of possibility, especially if your parents had some long-concealed mortal ancestor whose appearance had managed to hold on throughout the generations. Some things will crop up, no matter how far removed from their origins."

He glanced at August, with her pale red hair, and I knew he was thinking of the fact that she wasn't technically related to him. August Torquill had been born purely Dóchas Sidhe, transformed by her mother while she was being carried. And despite that, the Torquill colors had held on, red hair and golden eyes, even if they'd been diluted by Amandine's actions. August was his daughter in every way that mattered, and her hair remembered that.

"Then I found you in the forest," Simon continued. "I thought it odd, at first, that the light should paint such perfect stripes upon your hair, and then we reached the manor and they remained, as if you'd forgotten to put them away. Now your friend is here, and carries the tinge of the same descendant line. Whatever type of fae you are, the two of you share it."

I glanced at Ginevra, at her cream-colored hair that slowly darkened to orange near the tip, each strand ticked in a way that was uncommon outside of feline lineages, at her wide blue eyes, a shade not found even among the Roane but remarkably present in certain breeds of cat.

"My *hair*?" I looked back to Simon, summoning every ounce of haughty disdain I could find. I had quite a bit. "My *hair* is reason to pull me in here and interrogate me in front of your daughter and the man who has shown me nothing but charity and kindness? Your Grace, I sincerely hope you will not take this as reason to have me expelled from your home. I am still trying to find—".

"The longer I've spent with you, the more time I've had to puzzle my way through the fascinating mystery of your lineage," said Simon. "I was very young when the purges were conducted, but my father recognized a gift for blood magic in me, and I was already keeping company with Amandine, who was going to need someone by her side who could help her sniff out things that should have been uprooted, in case they survived in changelings and in servant's halls. You're Cait Sidhe, the both of you."

August stiffened, standing up as straight as she could as she turned to stare at me with bewilderment and awe.

Sylvester merely sank deeper into his chair.

"That makes everything make sense," said Simon. "The loyalty of a Candela, once given, is absolute, but they don't *share*. Ask them a direct question, get an honest answer. Leave the question unasked, and they'll never volunteer anything they don't have to. Shadows and secrets, that's their game. And once upon a time, they shared the Shadow Roads with the Cait Sidhe. They have loyalty to your kind. Sir Grianne was clearly called upon to observe that bond."

"I didn't know about it until she told me," I said. "Which was only this past evening. I had no idea I was calling on some ancient obligation."

"So you admit what you are?" demanded Simon.

"I am a child of Faerie, chosen by Oberon to stand aside and observe, that the Courts may not collapse in on themselves from the weight of all the ritual and tradition they collect, like a child filling their pockets with pretty stones until they burst. Malvic was claimed a son of Oberon, as well beloved as any other, and Erda a daughter of Titania." It seemed wise not to invoke Jibvel in this moment, when things were already tense.

"The Cait Sidhe were exterminated years ago," said August, sounding horrified.

"Murdered, more like," muttered Sylvester, looking at his hands, and I had a sudden horrible flash of understanding as to what the nature of heroism had become under Titania's control. Heroes existed to right wrongs, overthrow wicked monarchs, and slay monsters. With Titania declaring everything to be correct as it was, and every crown rightly given, all that they had left were the monsters.

And the monsters had become anyone she said they were.

I knew, looking at Sylvester, that the man in front of me hadn't actually broken the Law, hadn't really put any Cait Sidhe to the sword. And yet he believed with all his heart that he had. No wonder he spent his nights sitting alone in a dark room and failed at every courtship he'd supposedly attempted; no wonder he drank too much and did the barest minimum to keep his duchy running while he allowed his household to manage itself.

He was carrying more guilt than I could understand, and Titania had put it all upon his shoulders for no good reason I could see. Simon got to have a charmed life with the family he'd once wanted above all others, even if he couldn't remember the family who truly loved and adored him, and Sylvester got . . . this.

"Can we agree on 'slain'?" asked Simon. "I'd rather not argue semantics all night. Not with my youngest daughter in someone else's charge."

My head snapped up. "What did you say?"

"I proposed 'slain' as a viable compromise."

"No. The other part."

"Duchess Zhou of Dreamer's Glass requested a member of my family attend on her to assist with a small matter," said Sylvester. "As neither Simon nor I was available, October volunteered."

"And you *let* her?"

"It's almost Moving Day. Custom says she can move freely until the stroke of midnight on Samhain."

"Why do you care so much?" asked August.

I glanced to her. "Come again?"

"You've never met my sister. You've never met either of us. So why do *you* care where October does or doesn't go?" She frowned, deeply, not taking her eyes off me. I had the sudden feeling that I knew who the most dangerous Torquill in the room was, and it wasn't either of the ones I would have expected. "She offered, and she went. She wanted to see more than just the tower. She's a grownup. She's allowed."

"Are you trying to convince me, or to convince yourself?" I asked. August scoffed.

I switched my attention back to Simon. "Your younger daughter is a changeling. This is well known throughout the fiefdom. Forgive me for being surprised that you'd let her leave so easily."

"Young things desire freedom. It's in their nature," he said. "If October wants to have a flash of adventure before she returns to the everyday pattern of her life, that's her concern, not anyone else's."

"I still can't believe you'd let her go," I said.

"I still can't believe you're this calm about being found out," said Simon. "How many of your kind escaped? Have you been spying on proper fae this whole time, preparing some sort of revenge? Did Maeve put you up to this?"

"Don't be tiresome," I said. "And we're calm because we can leave any time we like. You've learned nothing. You've found a fairy tale to chase, and may it keep you well occupied until your child comes home." *And may your child come home,* I added, silently. If something happened to October . . .

Nothing was going to happen to October, because Ginevra and I were going to head for Dreamer's Glass, and see to it that whatever task Li Qin had summoned her to complete was done well and properly and without putting her into any danger. She didn't know who she was. She didn't know what she could do. She was going to get herself hurt, and given her current condition, I couldn't allow that to happen.

"How do you think you're going to achieve that?" asked Sylvester wearily.

I frowned at him. "As your brother said, the Cait Sidhe and Candela walk the same roads."

"Yes, and this is my knowe." He leaned forward, watching me. "The only roads that open here are those I allow. So tell me, how were you intending to leave?"

Automatically, I reached for the shadows, and nearly recoiled as the knowe's wards flared and forced me away from them. We were cut off. Sylvester's memories of hunting and killing our kind might be false, but he'd been a hero in both realities, and his skills were real ones. I wasn't October, to sweet-talk his knowe around to doing things my way. We were far enough into the room that even changing forms wouldn't guarantee an escape, and Sylvester had no doubt taken our conversation as an opportunity to move his guards into position outside the doors.

I saw the moment Ginevra realized how neatly we had been trapped. Her shoulders drooped, only a fraction of an inch, and fear flickered across her face, hot and fast and honest. That was all. Her composure otherwise remained perfect, and in that moment, I was so proud of her I could have wept. She was still coming into her power. She already had the heart of a lion.

"Sir, you're making a grave mistake," I said.

"The Cait Sidhe were killed for good reason," said Sylvester.

"Sneaks and spies and liars all, and you've been spying in my halls for *months*. Do you even have a wife to search for? Could a beast like you truly love, much less marry?"

"Leave her out of this," I spat. "My lady is none of your concern."

"Nor yours, it seems, given how long you've searched in vain."

The receiving room doors swung open, and a group of Sylvester's guards marched into the room. Garm and Grianne were not among them. Neither was Etienne, I noted; he must not have returned from Dreamer's Glass yet.

"I find that a little isolation makes everyone more communicative," said Sylvester. "Don't worry, *Rand*. We're not the animals here. You won't be tortured."

"You're making a mistake," I said again. I could attack, could prove myself to be the beast Titania had convinced them I was, but all three of the people in front of me were precious in some way to people I cared about. October would never forgive me for assaulting Sylvester or Simon, and Patrick and Dianda seemed truly fond of August for her own sake as well as Simon's. Without the option of seriously wounding any of them, standing and allowing myself to be taken was the best of options.

So I stood, and they grasped my arms and tied them behind my back, and did the same to Ginevra, and neither of us spoke as they marched us away, out into the halls, and onward, to the dungeons.

SIXTEEN

SYLVESTER HAD NEVER BEEN much of one for taking prisoners. In the world I knew, the dungeons at Shadowed Hills were mostly used for storage. Lots of gardening supplies, lots of tools, lots of outdated statuary that Luna had stripped from the grounds but not yet managed to regift or dispose of. It only took a few minutes in these reimagined confines for me to decide that I liked them far better when they were used for pruning shears and not for people.

The guards had been sensible enough to put Ginevra and me in cells with solid doors instead of bars a cat could easily slip through. There was no iron or rowan in the makeup of the cell; we would be perfectly comfortable captives, for as long as Sylvester chose to keep us here.

At least until Titania's false Eira ordered Simon to ask his brother to slit our throats. How many steps did a command have to travel before the one who gave it was absolved? Titania wasn't allowed to harm me. Was she allowed to create a facsimile of her daughter who wouldn't hesitate to do precisely that, then stand back and just . . . let it all happen?

"I understand now," said Ginevra, voice muffled by the wood and distance between us.

"Understand what?" I asked.

"Why you had to stand aside for Raj. Why you can't be King any longer."

"Why, pray tell, did I have to do those things? Because at the moment, it seems like a futile sacrifice."

"Because you could have killed them all. They were all unarmed, and if you'd attacked, you could have incapacitated them at the very least. I'm not the fighter you are. I held back to let you act." She sounded frustrated but not surprised.

"And?"

"And you didn't, because they're October's family, and hurting them would hurt her. I knew you'd put her first. I knew it before Titania put us into this impossible situation with the Court and trying to keep everyone fed. But knowing something and seeing it aren't the same thing, and I *saw* it in that receiving room. You're standing aside because you can't put yourself ahead of her." She sighed, the sound heavy enough to cross the hall between us. "You haven't stepped down yet, but you've already left us."

"Your father intends to do the same for your mother, one day."

"Is it worth it?"

The question made me pause. There were times—so many times—when I could have answered yes without hesitation or thought. Here and now, confined to a small stone cell with no obvious means of escape, that answer was more difficult to give, and so I didn't even try.

Silence spun out between us, like a miller's daughter spinning seconds into gold, or perhaps lead, to belabor the metaphor beyond all recognition. I let my head rest against the wall and closed my eyes, trying to force down my fear. It was Moving Day. Things were finally starting to happen. I just had no idea what those things would actually mean, and Mary's enjoinder to be patient hadn't come with any actual guarantee of success. We could still lose. We could still lose everything.

October had been here. We had been here at the same time, together, and I had allowed her to slip away, vanishing into another fiefdom, while Ginevra and I had both been taken prisoner, caught by two men I'd all but dismissed as possible threats.

I struggled to keep my breath level, trying to keep panic from overwhelming me. This was all going wrong. This was all going so wrong, and—

The sound of footsteps snapped me out of my miserable contemplation of the situation, and I sat up straight, opening my eyes. There was no way to see who was approaching, but still, I clambered to my feet, straightening my clothing, and turned to the cell door, waiting to see what would happen next. After another minute or so, the door opened, and Garm was pushed roughly inside by a large Bridge Troll whom I had seen among the guard.

"Brought you a friend, *cat*," rumbled the troll, voice muffled by the wall, before the door slammed shut. I heard the door to Ginevra's cell open a beat later, and the exchange repeated itself.

"Grianne?" I asked.

Garm nodded.

"My apologies to you both. It wasn't my intention that you should be captured, or implicated in any sort of scheme against the duchy."

"You weren't scheming against the duchy, though, and *you'd know that, Tavis, if you listened.*" He raised his voice on the back half of his statement, not quite shouting, but definitely projecting for the benefit of an unseen audience. This done, he sagged, looking suddenly very small and very frightened. "What *happened*?"

"The Duke's brother recognized me as Cait Sidhe, and decided we must have been conspiring in some way," I said. "My being overly concerned for October, who has been sent out of the duchy on an errand for Duchess Zhou, didn't help."

"Of course it didn't. Baron Torquill doesn't like it when people take an interest in his children, especially *her*. He's protective of August, but she's a Firstborn's daughter who will always have her mother's protection. Everyone knows October was born out of obligation. Amandine doesn't care about her the way she cares about August. So Simon has to care for both of them."

"I said nothing improper. I crossed no lines."

"You didn't *have* to." Garm looked at me with near-desperation. "For Baron Torquill, just saying her name while hiding something, however small and inconsequential, would be seen as sufficient proof that you were plotting something improper. He's not the most trusting of men."

"Clearly not."

"Did you not know him well enough in your reality to know that?"

"I know him quite well. We were children together, he and I and Sylvester and September and Amandine. He escorted my wife to the altar at our wedding, and he's both ruined and transformed my life on various occasions. He's been a good man and a bad man, but he's never been inclined to trust quickly, or trust the word of any other above those he loves. I didn't mean to speak so vehemently. I was just . . . surprised."

"Well, now we get to be surprised together." Garm crossed the cell to drop onto the low bunk attached to the wall, making himself as comfortable as he reasonably could. Then he waved his hand, and the illusion of a well-appointed lounge swept across the room, coating surfaces in layers of plush fabric and softening the walls. I looked at him curiously. He shrugged.

"We're captives either way. May as well be captives in comfort. Unless your resistance to illusions means this isn't helpful?"

"I know the padding *is* an illusion, and if I try, I can see through it, but since seeing through it serves nothing but to make me more uncomfortable, why should I bother?" I sat on one of the cushions he had provided. "I can enjoy the comforts of a lie without believing it to be a truth."

"Self-serving."

"Cat," I said, as if that explained everything, and perhaps it did. After a moment to consider, I suited form to fact, shifting into feline shape and stretching.

Garm watched, clearly amazed. "You've never done that in front of me before," he said.

What a strange new world, where a simple shapeshifter could be a wonder in Faerie, when we had always been among the most common things of all! I turned a circle on the cushion, pushing at it with my paws, then curled up, tail over my nose, and closed my eyes.

Sleeping when things are stressful is a very feline response, and I freely admit that. But I would no longer be a cat if I lost the knack for it, and as long as I was confined here without access to the Shadow Roads, I couldn't do much else to help. I might as well keep myself in condition to run if I received the opportunity.

I don't know how long I dozed before the door opened again, faster this time—so fast that it swung all the way inward and slammed against the wall. I raised my head, blinking blearily, as Garm jerked upright from where he'd been dozing on the bunk.

There in the doorway, looking like he was on the brink of losing his composure entirely, was Simon Torquill. His face was pinched and pale, his lips tight, and he was trembling. August was close behind him, her body half-blocked from view by his, and looked as if she'd been crying. I sprang to my feet, transforming as I did.

"Where's October?" I demanded. "What's happened?"

"Why do you care so much?" Simon countered, coming fully into the cell. August followed him, and was inside when he closed the door, leaning back against it so that his weight would keep it from swinging open. It was clear that neither of them understood how afraid of me they should be, or how dangerous an uncontrolled Cait Sidhe could quickly become.

I forced myself to calm, pulling back the more bestial aspects of my appearance. When I spoke again, my teeth were blunter, less obviously designed to rend and tear.

"I know this will make no sense to you at all, but your daughter is very dear to me, and I'm worried for her safety."

"But *why*?" asked Simon.

Was there any way out of this situation—or out of this cell—without explaining the truth? If there was, I couldn't see it. So I stood up a little straighter, looked Simon dead in the eye, and said, "Because none of this is real."

He frowned. "I don't understand what you mean."

"This world, the world you believe in, doesn't exist. Titania has enchanted the entire kingdom to create a false reality in which she rules over everything, unchallenged and without equal, and in so doing, has removed certain 'undesirable' aspects from her creation. Including the Cait Sidhe. You asked how many of my kind escaped, when you spoke to me before. Well, the answer is an easy one. All of us, because there was never any massacre, never any purge of the shapeshifting lines. I don't know where the others are, but the Cait Sidhe are safe and well in the Court of Cats, and we had free run of the world until four months ago, when Titania wove her spell."

Simon stared at me.

"You must have noticed something, starting four months ago," I said, trying to play on the bemusement I saw in his eyes, where I could so easily have seen nothing more than enraged denial. "A change to the way magic works, perhaps, or a new linearity to your days. You have to know, on some level, that this isn't really the way things are meant to be."

"Do you really have a wife?" asked August, pushing herself in front of her father.

"I do."

"And did you really lose her?"

"Four months ago," I said. "Cait Sidhe can see through illusions, given time, and those intended to modify our minds have trouble taking hold for any length of time unless the caster is focusing very specifically on their target. In this case, the Cait Sidhe were all herded up and swept aside, and so some of us were able to shrug off the changes. I lost my wife and remembered her in almost the same moment, and I'll have her back, or Faerie will burn."

August shied back, clearly unsettled. I focused on Simon.

"Now," I said. "Why are you here? You've caught us. I'm sure your mistress hasn't demanded our heads this quickly." If she had, I would need to fight them, despite the pain it would cause October. I couldn't sit idly by and allow myself to be killed to avoid upsetting her.

"Etienne lost October," blurted August.

I went still as I blinked, very slowly. If they had retained any memory of the Cait Sidhe, they would have recognized that expression for a dangerous thing.

"What?" I asked.

"After she did the favor for Duchess Zhou in Dreamer's Glass, he took her to do an errand for him," said Simon, scowling. "I'll be having words with my brother about the way he trains his knights. Three acts of disloyalty in a single day is three too many to disregard."

"Hey!" protested Garm. "Grianne and I did nothing wrong. There's no rule saying Cait Sidhe have to be reported to the duke. I checked."

"There's no rule only because their escape and existence were unthinkable," said Simon. "Regardless. Etienne took October into the mortal world, and in the process of completing the task he set for her, she managed to get knocked through an open transport window. He doesn't know where she ended up."

I crossed the room at a speed he couldn't possibly have matched, grabbing the front of his shirt and jerking him toward me. "You mean he really *lost* her?" I demanded.

Simon didn't get angry, only looked at me, expression infinitely weary. "I should never have let her go," he said.

I released him, pushing him back against the door as I stalked back to where I'd been standing. "No, you shouldn't," I said. "She's defenseless out there. This world Titania's created made sure of that. You got everything you ever used to want, and October lost it all. If she's been hurt, if anything has happened to her, I won't forgive you."

"There have been rumors recently," said Simon. "Mutterings that perhaps the Summer Queen was too hasty when she decided we should require changelings to serve the noble households, that having them around ties us too closely to the mortal world."

"Living in the Summerlands ties us too closely to the mortal world," I snapped. "If we want to be untethered from humanity, we need to return to deeper Faerie."

"My mistress has hinted that we might be looking at precisely that, after Moving Day is past," said Simon. "Once we're free to go back to where we belong, we won't . . . we won't need the changelings anymore."

He sounded utterly miserable. August looked at him as if he'd just grown a second head, or revealed himself to secretly be an evil wizard, slinging spells from an impenetrable tower.

"Only hinted, never outright stated," said Simon hurriedly. "She never *said* anything was going to happen to the changelings, she never *said* we'd be leaving them behind—"

"But it's a possibility," I said. Titania was sure she'd be able to complete the ritual and make her spell eternal on Moving Day, at which point she, not Oberon, would command power over all of Faerie. She'd be able to open the doors he'd locked, and take the fae away from the human world forever, into a Faerie she alone controlled. One where her version of history overwrote all others.

The best way that ended for the changelings was being left behind, cut off from Faerie and losing all hope of access to anything beyond the Summerlands. The worst . . .

Intentional or not, Titania had created a world built on blood. The slaughters her loyal followers remembered carrying out would have been brutal, violent conflicts. Compared to pruning entire descendant lines from the Tree, what was the killing of a few thousand changelings, who were always destined to die?

I looked at Simon. The man looked all but sick with worry, and I knew that he had taken the more-charitable interpretation of the false Eira's words, hearing abandonment where I heard murder. From the horror on August's face, she heard the same threats I did, and took them just as seriously.

"You let her go to Dreamer's Glass because you wanted to see if she knew how to handle herself outside of your immediate custody," I said, slowly. "You wanted to know if she'd be able to survive without you."

"We've always sheltered her," he said. "Amandine did her duty, and I was glad of it, because I wanted the chance to be a father again, and August doted on her from the moment she was born, so it was easy to keep her close and safe. This knowe and our tower have been her world, and my brother would never allow any real harm to come to her. I'm not sure we've given October a realistic view of her position. She knows how dangerous the world is for changelings. I've never been entirely sure she understood."

"So you sent her away, with no one she knew to stand beside her, to test her ability to survive. Just her, alone, in an unfamiliar place."

"I meant no harm."

Oddly enough, I believed him. No version of Simon I had ever known would intentionally and avoidably allow harm to come to his children.

If he said he'd been sending October on a small, manageable adventure for her own sake, then that was exactly what he'd been doing. Whether it had worked out that way or not.

If he'd truly known October—the real one, not the polite house pet Titania had tried to mold her into—he would have understood that there was no chance a "small, manageable" adventure would stay that way. Once she got involved, the chaos would spiral out of anyone's control, and she would be left standing there, holding a brick from the foundation, utterly baffled as to how everything had fallen apart.

But he didn't know her. He knew four months of sharing the tower with her, and a lifetime of false memories—memories that didn't seem to have been enough to change who anyone else essentially was, so couldn't actually have transformed her on any essential level.

Or so I had to tell myself, to stay calm. To stay sane.

"I know," I said, and watched as he sagged with relief. "But now you're here. Why?"

"Etienne is . . . He's not here," said Simon. "He's gone looking for October, but there's no telling how long that might take. I need to be out there. I need to be looking for my little girl. Please."

"I don't understand."

"If I tell my brother to reopen the Shadow Roads, can you find her? Can you take me to October?"

"Us," said August.

Simon and I both turned to look at her.

"Take *us* to October," she clarified.

"August, darling, you must understand—"

"That you sent my sister away as some sort of trial run for taking her away from me forever? That you thought I'd be okay with leaving her behind and heading into deeper Faerie because Titania said so? She's *mine*." She glared at him. "She's *my* sister, and *my* best friend, and one day when I start a household, she's going to be there with me, because that's how this is supposed to work. You don't put her in danger. You don't have the right. So yes, take *us* to October, because I'm not leaving you alone with her. Maybe not ever again."

"Yes," I said. "But I'll need Ginevra."

"Yes?" echoed Simon.

"Yes, if you reopen the Shadow Roads, I'll take you to find October. Both of you. But as I can only carry one passenger at a time, I'll need assistance to do so."

"Not like we could have kept her confined once the Roads were open," said Simon, with a strangled sound that could have been a laugh. He turned to the door, hitting his fist against it four times. Then he looked back to me. "It will be done."

"Then we'll go," I said.

"Why are you so interested in my daughter?"

I looked at him coolly. "I've just told you the world you know is an illusion and a lie, built atop a messier, less-convenient reality. I told you that none of this was real. Do you truly need to ask me why I'm so interested in October? I've never known you to be anything other than clever, Simon. To refuse to see what I'm not saying smacks of foolishness, and I won't play along."

"I would never have approved—"

"What? Her union with a 'beast'? In my world, your approval was neither sought nor required, although she did choose the path you protected during the ceremony, and you led her to meet me at the altar. We were wed by the sea witch, in sight of Oberon himself, and you approved of me then. You knew I would protect her to the ends of the world and back again, and I intend to do precisely that." I smiled at him, allowing my incisors to sharpen and show. "There is nothing I won't do to protect her."

August scowled at me, unintimidated. "You married my sister? Did I give you permission to do that? I feel like I would remember, even if it was in another world."

I raised an eyebrow, looking at her. Contradicting her seemed unwise, as did lying to her, but if her relationship with October was as close as she claimed, I couldn't afford to alienate her. "I did, in fact, marry your sister. And as I have not divorced her, and Oberon did not appear to dissolve our union, I am still married to your sister, whether she remembers me or no."

The air shivered around me then, and I felt the Shadow Roads re-open all around me a bare second before a skinny teenager came barreling out of them and into the cell, nearly slamming into August in the process. She yelped in surprise, flinching away. I leaned over, catching Raj by the collar before he could run himself into a wall.

He hung in my hand like a startled kitten, eyes searching my face for signs that I was in trouble. "Uncle, I'm sorry to leave the Court, but you didn't come back, and I felt the Roads shift, but they wouldn't let me into Shadowed Hills. I was afraid something might have happened after you—something might have happened."

"After I what?"

Raj went still in that way unique to young things who think they may have said too much and gotten themselves into trouble. Glancing back and forth like he was looking for a rescue from the situation, he said, "Nothing."

"Raj . . ."

"Nothing," he said again, and shifted to feline form, the sudden change in size causing him to drop from my hand to the floor. He ran then, hiding behind August's skirts.

I sighed. "Raj, this is not the time. Sir Etienne took October out of the knowe to perform a task for Duchess Zhou, and he has since misplaced her. I was just about to take Simon and begin looking for her."

"And me," added August stubbornly.

". . . and August," I amended. "I understand that you were worried, but the Court is now unprotected, and I don't have time to stand here playing games with you."

Raj shifted back to his two-legged form, peeping out from behind August. He was still unaccountably jumpy. "But that's what I thought might have set you off," he said. "I know exactly where October is."

He was my adopted nephew, my all-but-son, and my heir. So I didn't grab and shake him until he explained himself, only went very still, watching him through narrowed eyes.

"Where, pray tell, would that be?"

Raj took a deep breath and stood up straighter, gathering his courage. Then, in a low voice, he said, "She's been arrested by the Queen's guard. For murder."

"Another frame job?"

"Oh, no," he said, sounding almost offended by the suggestion. "She did it."

I blinked. "She what?"

"I'm sorry, what did you just say?" asked Simon.

"I was ducking in and out of the Court to look for you, and all the pixies were in an uproar, so I asked a mortal cat who told me that one of the fair folk had been taken away for killing another of their number," said Raj. "It was kinda confusing, so I went looking for more information, and I found the Queen's guard in an alley, cleaning up a night-haunt mannikin that had been left in place of a pureblood. They were talking about the changeling girl they'd found covered in his blood. Said it was going to cause problems, because the Rose of Winter's servant was her father. I think Toby really killed somebody this time, and now the Queen has her, and when Shadowed Hills was sealed, I thought you'd lost your temper when you heard."

He paused then, wincing at my expression. "Or maybe you're about to."

"Do you see what you've done?" I demanded, turning to Simon. "October has been arrested. The Queen's dungeons are ripe with iron. The first time she was held there, I was only able to get her back by taking a Selkie without his skin to open the doors. Unless you have a magic trick for evading iron poisoning, we're going to have to fight the entirety of the Queen's guard to have her back, and all because you were a coward who sent her on an 'adventure' to see if you could abandon her safely."

Simon swallowed hard, skin waxen and eyes glossy. "I do, as you say, have a magic trick for evading iron poisoning," he said.

"I can tell by the look on your face that I won't like it," I said, tightly.

"Well, no," he said. "Because it doesn't begin with us going to the Queen's Court to retrieve my daughter."

"Where *does* it begin?"

SEVENTEEN

WE STEPPED OUT OF the Shadows and onto the promenade outside the royal knowe of Golden Shore. The sky was the color of a bruise, purple and yellow around the edges, deepening as night approached. We had spent almost a whole day locked in the cell at Shadowed Hills.

Raj was no longer with us, having returned to the Court of Cats after passing his message along. I set a half-frozen Simon to his feet, managing not to sneer as he wiped the ice from his eyes. Beside me, Ginevra was doing the same with August. A few seconds later, Grianne stepped out of nowhere, one arm slung around Garm, keeping him upright.

All our passengers were wheezing, ill-suited to the conditions of the Shadow Roads, and I spared a moment to wonder when we had become a taxi service. Simon coughed, clearing the ice from his throat, then strode toward the doors, limping a little from the chill in his joints. August leaned against Ginevra, who looked unsettled by this show of trust from someone she'd just met.

I followed Simon, unwilling to let him out of my sight. "We've come to Golden Shore at your request, moving *away* from October," I said, voice tight. "You had best explain yourself, and quickly."

He knocked before he turned to face me. "I know you can suppress your stripes," he said. "Don't bother."

I took a step back, blinking at him. "What?"

"This goes easier with some proof."

I frowned, and was still frowning when the door opened and possibly the last person I would ever have expected to see here looked out at us.

She was tall, with a reasonably average build, wearing a patchwork jacket that appeared to have been made from stitched-together pieces of tapestries and pennants, fabric pieced with no concern for pattern or color or whether or not it clashed with itself. Beneath the jacket she had a plain black shirt of mortal make, and a pair of black denim trousers. Her hair was a black so deep and glossy, it crossed over into appearing almost purple, and her eyes were mismatched, pyrite and mercury, sharp and wary. Her ears were sharply pointed, her skin a warm shade of light olive-brown, and she shouldn't have been here.

She blinked. I blinked. She focused on Simon.

"Baron Torquill," she said. "To what do we owe the pleasure? And where is your lady wife?"

"Amandine is aware that her services are not required on the Golden Shore," said Simon. "I wouldn't bring her here. I know how uncomfortable that would make many of the residents."

"But you brought the girl," said Arden, glancing past us to August. "Can she not do as her mother does?"

"She can," said Simon. "But she never has, and she won't be offering. Please. You know I wouldn't be here if it weren't an emergency."

"You're a traitor and a liar, and you'd do anything you thought you could get away with if it suited you," said Arden. "Why are you here, Simon?"

"I need your help," he said. "Yours and your brother's. I'm sorry, Arden. I know I promised to leave you alone, but it's October."

"The month?"

"My younger daughter." Simon managed to make the statement without raising his voice, although I saw his fingers flex, hands tensing as he tried to suppress his anger. "As you well know."

"Oh, right, the changeling." Arden shook her head. "She's not with you—why?"

"She's been arrested by the Queen of the Mists. For murder."

"You mean the lady who took my father's throne took your kid, too? Wow, that's terrible. I'm so sorry you've chosen to remain part of a corrupt and toxic system, and now you're finding out that sometimes, the hand that feeds you also starts beating the ever-loving crap out of you. For fun, even!" Her eyes took on an almost-manic gleam. "You didn't have any issues with the Queen when your owner decided to put her in charge of things."

"Arden, please. You were nowhere to be found. There were rumors that you'd killed the woman responsible for your parents' deaths. The Rose of Winter only put forth an alternative, to keep the throne for you until you could be found to claim it—"

"And when we did come back, huh? When my brother and I washed the blood from our hands and the dust from our hair and came back to *our* Kingdom, to *our* birthright? Did she stand aside? Hmm, no. I seem to recall she didn't. Instead, she tried to have *us* arrested, me for murder, Nolan for treason, even though the most treasonous thing he'd done was tell her guards to get away from his sister. So you'll excuse me if I don't really give a *shit* about your little problem."

"She's my sister!" shouted August, pulling away from Ginevra and rushing up to her father's side. She stopped there, vibrating with rage as she glared at Arden. "She's not a 'little problem,' she's my sister. Would you want someone talking about your brother like that? Huh? Is he just 'a little problem,' or is he someone who matters?"

"You were the ones who decided it was just fine to treat changelings like they weren't people who *could* matter," said Arden, composure only flickering for a second.

"I wasn't." August stood up straight, glaring at her. "I didn't have any part in that decision. She's my sister. She's trapped. She needs help. Father says you can help her."

"Me, or Golden Shore?" asked Arden.

"Both," said Simon. Arden turned to glower at him again. "I need to ask Their Majesties for permission to borrow you, and your brother, both. I know what you do for them—"

"You don't know anything, old man."

"—and I know iron has been a barrier for you in the past. If I can be allowed the use of one of your alchemical labs, and a few base materials that I know exist within the Kingdom, I can remove that barrier."

Arden frowned, wary. "And in exchange?"

"I want you to go to the Queen's dungeons and retrieve my daughter."

"Your daughter, who's been arrested for murder."

"Yes."

"Is this some sort of trap? We'll step into the Mists and find ourselves surrounded? And who the hell are these people?" Arden waved a hand, encompassing the rest of us.

I bowed to her, deep and respectful. "Tybalt, King of Dreaming Cats."

Ginevra, taking my cue, curtseyed and said, "Ginevra, Regent of Prince Raj of Dreaming Cats."

"Sir Garm of Shadowed Hills," said Garm.

"Grianne," said Grianne. "Knight."

Arden didn't look offended by the Candela's terseness. Instead, she focused on me, frown taking on a more confused edge. "But there are no more Cait Sidhe."

"Yet here we stand." I eyed her. "Are you another of the tiresome nobles who consider shapeshifters to be little better than beasts?"

"My best friend's a Cu Sidhe, so no," she said. "Madden will be delighted to meet you."

"Golden Shore shelters shapeshifters?"

"As many as we could. Theron and Chrysanthe will be thrilled to see you. They've always felt bad about not being able to save any of the cats when they were setting up their sanctuary." She glanced back to Simon. "You brought Cait Sidhe."

"Technically, they brought us."

"You realize this means I have to get you an audience, if only so that Their Majesties can see some proof the descendant line survived."

"The thought did cross my mind," he said.

Arden scoffed and stepped back, finally waving for the rest of us to enter. An uneven, unwilling troupe, we pressed on through the doorway, naturally falling into our cohesive pairs. Two Torquills, two cats, two knights sworn to a man who couldn't know what we were doing without facing treason charges of his own.

And one Queen in the Mists who resented the usurpation of her throne as the Arden I knew never had, who didn't know that she'd been deposed this time by Titania herself, who led us through the knowe with long, easy steps, clearly and entirely at home here. The first hall was plain, with gold-tinted wooden walls accented by gold-and-cream molding, each piece carved with fruits and flowers grown within the Kingdom itself. It was a constant, subtle reminder that we were in an agrarian holding, a place where things like Moving Day still mattered due to their connection to the seasons and not because people were courting Titania's favor.

That, at least, was true of Golden Shore in both the world I knew and this one. Titania had apparently put enough thought into designing her new reality to understand that people would still need to eat, would still crave their little luxuries to remind them of the lands we'd left behind. Goblin fruit and Avalonian apples, wine made with Elf-hame grapes, those were the things that could keep the oldest pure-bloods anchored and calm, not protesting their isolation from the lands of their birth. Golden Shore wasn't the only Kingdom dedicated to preserving fae plants and animals, but it was the only one within the scope of Titania's enchantment.

Unfortunately for her, and for the way she'd apparently wound the spell up and let it go, making the large changes while it handled the smaller ones itself, the farming communities have always had a tendency to attract changelings and those who feel Faerie should be more equitable, less focused on the counting of crowns. Theron and Chrysanthe were the monarchs I knew, and they were Ceryneian Hinds, as bestial as fae can be without changing forms entirely.

I wondered how they'd been able to escape execution as a descendant line, and more, how Titania could craft a world with such aggressive prejudices and still allow them to keep their titles. But then, Ioulia was a daughter of Titania; perhaps her descendants were granted a small amount of grace for that fact.

Arden was moving quickly, which was the only reason I didn't lose my temper with this delay. I was so tired of being patient. I was ready to rip this world down, and the fact that I couldn't was like fleas running across my skin, biting at me and draining my blood.

We turned a corner, into another hall. This one was larger and far grander, more in line with what I expected from the Divided Courts. The walls were abstract stained-glass mosaics, filling the air with light despite the darkness outside, and the windows were surrounded by gold filigree that matched the molding from the previous hall. The floor was softened by a long rug the color of harvest-ready wheat, and chandeliers hung from the ceiling, heavy with globes of glowing light.

At the end of the hall a pair of Daoine Sidhe wearing the royal livery flanked a tall pair of double doors. Arden nodded toward them.

"They'll let you in as soon as they get the sign," she said, and sketched a circle in the air with one hand, stepping through and vanishing.

I scowled at the place where she had been, then at Simon.

"This is *your* daughter we need to rescue," I hissed. "I hope you have a good reason to fuss and dawdle, because if you don't—"

"You'll what? Kill your father-in-law? Whether you're deluded or sincere about your memories of another world, you'll worry about upsetting October if you do that, and you've already shown yourself capable of restraint for her sake. We're fussing and dawdling, as you say, because the Queen's dungeons are full of iron, and we can't take on the entire royal guard. We need help. We need the Windermeres."

"Can't open a door through iron," said Grianne.

"Not normally, but I know how to make it possible," said Simon.

I shot him a suspicious look, and we continued onward to the doors.

The two Daoine Sidhe looked at our ragged little group without saying a word, expressions not changing in the least. We stopped.

"We're here to see the King and Queen," announced Simon.

They didn't react.

"Arden said they'd get a sign," said August.

I was so accustomed to being let in when I approached the leadership of the Divided Courts that I wasn't sure how to continue. Knocking seemed unwise, with two armed guards between us and the door; stepping into the Shadow Roads could be construed as an attack, if they were even open here. Warding a knowe against the Shadow Roads has always been possible, and unless they had a Candela in their guard, there would be no reason to leave them accessible. So I stood with the rest, seething and quietly panicked.

Then the door creaked open, and Arden poked her head out.

"Let 'em in," she said, to the guards. "Their Majesties are down for company."

The two guards turned, and opened the doors the remainder of the way, allowing us into the receiving room. It was possibly the gaudiest thing I had seen in a very long time. Every surface that *could* be gilded *had* been gilded, until it was like walking into a fairytale idea of a bee's hive, everything gleaming, everything gold. The roof was very high, and the ceiling rafters were exposed, lending a rustic element to the architecture that I wouldn't have expected, based on everything else around us. Two of the walls were made almost entirely of windows, and through them I could see the rolling hills and verdant orchards of Golden Shore. It was a beautiful Kingdom, a perfect, magical countryside that went on for what seemed like forever.

As was usually the case in such rooms, a dais sat at one end, occupied in this instance by two golden thrones. Despite the precious metal that had been used to make them, they were more functional than ostentatious, with no jewels set into the carvings and no effort made to make them loom larger than their actual size. In each of them sat a crowned Ceryneian Hind.

In form, they were much like Satyrs or Silene, but with the lower bodies of golden deer instead of goats or horses. Theron had antlers, small but pronounced, while Chrysanthe's brow was smooth below the circle of her crown. It was a simple thing, matching her husband's, both crowns crafted to look like they had been woven from stalks of flawless golden wheat.

The monarchs' skin was golden tan, and their fur was simply golden, matching the hair on their heads—golden as wheat, in his case, and gold as cornsilk in hers. Their eyes were a matching burnished gold, the same color as their hooves. Really, it was unrelentingly gilded.

Arden was seated on the edge of the dais, having been joined by her male counterpart. Nolan looked as comfortable in his surroundings as she did, and neither of them seemed aware that this wasn't where they belonged.

Theron rose as we approached, staring at me, then at Ginevra.

"The Cait Sidhe live," he said, in a low voice that shook with wonder. "The culling was a failure, and the Cait Sidhe *live*. But why have you hidden from us for so very long?"

Simon shot me a quelling look, clearly signaling that he didn't want me to start in on my wild story of other worlds and sealed-off memories. "Your Majesties," he said. "Forgive me for speaking out of turn, but time is of the essence. I am Simon Torquill, Baron of Kettled Time, and my youngest daughter, October, has been arrested by the nameless Queen to the north, placed in prison for the crime of murder. Whether she committed the crime is a matter for discussion, with her, and before a trained adjudicator. We both know she won't have any justice in the Mists."

"Why not?" asked Chrysanthe, looking to him with sharp, canny eyes. I suspected she already knew the answer. She just wanted to make him say it out loud, to make him own the culture he was part of.

"My daughter is a changeling born," said Simon. "The man she stands accused of killing was a pureblood. She may have acted out of self-defense. It may have been an accident. The Queen of the Mists will make no allowances for either possibility. October will stand, and October will be sentenced, and October will die. Please. I need to save her."

August made a small sound of dismay. I suppose she hadn't considered that execution would be the end of any changeling who broke the Law. That hadn't changed between my world and this one.

"How would you propose to do that?" asked Theron.

Simon gestured toward the Windermeres. "They know the Queen's dungeons. If they were to go and retrieve my daughter, they could enter and exit quickly, without being seen by any of the guard. There is no extradition agreement between the Mists and Golden Shore. She would be unable to return to our home, but a life in exile is better than execution. I doubt the Queen of the Mists is going to challenge a longstanding diplomatic relationship over a single changeling."

"Mmmm, problem, Captain Ginger," said Nolan. "Those dungeons are laced with iron. We won't be able to get inside."

"If I can have access to an alchemical lab for a short period, I can solve that problem," said Simon. He dipped a hand into his pocket, coming out with a small crystal vial of blood, which he held up for the room to see. "This was given to me by a Gremlin acquaintance of my patron, in payment for some services I had rendered to her. If I blend it properly with my own blood, and quicken it with the blood of the one intending to use it, it will allow their magic to cut through iron even as a Gremlin's could."

"Tuatha de Dannan are not able to borrow the power of others through potionry," said Chrysanthe.

"Hence the inclusion of my own blood, to bridge the gap," said Simon. "I've done this for others. It will work."

"It has to be their choice," said Theron. "They work for us. They don't serve us."

Arden and Nolan exchanged a complicated look. I saw part of their rewritten history in that exchange: this was a world where he had never been elf-shot, where they had never been apart, where they had grown up and to adulthood in and out of each other's pockets, unable to distinguish between one life and the other—not truly needing to. Arden turned to face Simon and the King.

"We'll do it," she said. "On one condition."

"What is it?" asked Simon.

"We want a second dose of the stuff that lets us access the dungeons. October isn't the first changeling to have been seized by the false Queen's guard, and she probably won't be the last. They won't be expecting us to get her out, and they'll probably try to blame it on her having some sort of special magic they didn't know to ward against, since she's a Firstborn's daughter. We'll be able to get in the next time someone needs to be rescued. No more bodies burning on the Tree."

Simon looked faintly ill at the reminder of the fate that awaited October if we didn't hurry, but nodded. "I should have enough blood to manufacture a second dose."

"Then a lab shall be made available for your use," said Theron. "Arden, take him to the Lady Yui's laboratory. She won't object to his borrowing her space for a time, and she's out on harvesting duty tonight anyway."

Arden nodded and bounced to her feet, bustling over to grab Simon by the arm and pull him through the portal that opened in the air in front of her. He didn't have time to say anything before he was gone, the portal winking shut and leaving us alone.

Theron turned his attention back to me. "Forgive me, but we thought you lost forever, all of you. We have grieved for you, who stopped your dancing."

"The world is not precisely as it seems, nor ever has been," I said. "Four months ago, Titania returned."

Chrysanthe frowned. "Returned from where?"

"Returned from her long exile," I said. "She vanished shortly after Maeve did, sealed away by Oberon to maintain the balance of Faerie. Four months ago, she came back, and she remade the world in her own image, to suit her own desires. The aspects she didn't care for were removed, but she couldn't kill us, due to Oberon's injunction, so she simply sealed us away. The Cait Sidhe and the Court of Cats remain where we have always been, and if I have my way, this false world will be vanishing soon."

"And who are we, in the 'real' world you would restore?" asked Theron.

"Monarchs on the Golden Shore," I said. "The last time I saw you was at the convocation to decide whether the cure to elf-shot that had been discovered could be distributed. You argued against it, to the shock of much of the room, on the basis of the fact that if elf-shot could be cured, purebloods would be more careless with it, and more changelings would die."

"That does sound like us, dear," said Chrysanthe.

"I suppose this is where you claim to be our closest friend and confidante," said Theron.

I shook my head. "I barely know you. Either one of you, to my shame, given how long we've been near neighbors, and given that it seems you have managed to remain decent people in the face of Titania's enchantments. I would never have thought to come to you when I heard October was in trouble."

"Your interest in the changeling girl arises from this 'other world'?" asked Chrysanthe.

"She is my wife." I looked levelly at the monarchs on the Golden Shore. "We were married in the seat of the Westlands, in sight of the High King and Queen. No authority in this world or any other has the right to separate us. We have been bound and blessed, and I will have her home, safe and well, or I will burn this twisted mockery of Faerie to the ground."

Chrysanthe blinked. "You wed a changeling?"

"Yes."

"But . . ."

"We act as if mortality and death were always the same thing in the same instant," I said, allowing my frustration to spill over. "She's mortal, yes, and one day, she'll die, unless we do something to change that—unless *she* chooses to make that change. But an hour in her company is worth a decade with another, or a century without her. I would rather face eternity as a widower than have gone without pledging my devotion to her before our friends and family."

August watched me silently as I spoke. When I was done, she turned away, saying nothing. I remained focused on Theron and Chrysanthe, waiting for one of them to say something—anything—to tell me whether they understood, or whether I was about to emulate my wife and start attacking monarchs of the Divided Courts.

"What about me?" asked Nolan, defusing the growing tension. I looked toward him. He was leaning against the edge of the dais, lounging and unconcerned, but there was a tension in him that spoke to a life lived running, to knives in the dark and blood on his hands. He was a hard man who looked like a soft one. It was a masquerade I knew quite well. "And my sister, of course. She's a nonsense creature, but I can't imagine we're not together in your version of reality. Not that I'm saying I believe you—it's quite a lot to credit, you must admit— just that I'm curious as to whether you're going to brush us all off as strangers to keep us from poking holes in your fantasy world."

"I don't know you so well as I might like," I began, and Nolan scoffed, apparently having expected that answer. He sobered as I continued: "I'm much better acquainted with your sister, October having helped to put her back upon your father's throne, deposing that dreadful pretender in the process. In my reality, your parents never publicly announced their union, and so Gilad, may his dreams rest easy in the wind, stopped his dancing without a known heir. The Countess Winterrose was able to put her own figurehead in place while the Kingdom was in chaos. That woman might have held her position forever, had she not decided to banish October from the Mists for the crime of arguing with her, and forced her to find a way to stay. Arden was in hiding. The sea witch confirmed her survival, and October found her and restored her to her proper place. We're not precisely friends, but we're well acquainted, and I enjoy her company."

"And me?"

"You were elf-shot by the false Queen to intimidate your sister into silence, and waking you was part of the purpose of the convocation where I last saw Their Majesties." I gestured toward Theron and Chrysanthe. "Since then, you have been a loyal part of your sister's Court, and named as her heir, should she ever step aside. You have always seemed an honorable man, to me, and well inclined to the protection and enrichment of the Mists. Pray, how did you come to the Golden Shore?"

He glanced to Theron, as if asking permission. Theron nodded, and Nolan looked back to me.

"As Baron Torquill was so quick to note, there is no extradition between the Mists and Golden Shore. A crime committed in one Kingdom is not enough to lever a perpetrator from the embrace of the other."

I nodded slowly, not sure what that had to do with anything.

Nolan continued: "When our parents were killed, the woman responsible came after me, and Arden. She would have done the same to us, but Arden intervened, and killed her. My sister had to flee, or face persecution under the Law. I fled with her, rather than be left entirely alone. We've been here ever since. We collect changelings from up and down the coast when they flee from the homes they've been kept in."

August gasped. It was a small sound, but still enough to snap my head around, staring at her.

"You're the snatchers," she said, almost accusingly.

Nolan laughed. "Very well reasoned, little monthling. Yes, my sister and I, we're the infamous and terrifying snatchers. Our range is quite extensive—a gift from our mother's side of the family—and we know the Mists very well, for obvious reasons. We can be in and out like the wind blowing through a keyhole, and we have our ways of finding out when people need help. We've been bouncing all over the place since the bell rang on Moving Day, finding the ones who were ready to run and getting them safely away."

"It's Moving Day," said August. "They shouldn't need any help. They're allowed to leave."

"Spoken like a true pureblood," said Nolan. "Tell me, do you believe everything the nobles tell you, or do you just like swallowing shit?"

"Nolan," said Chrysanthe mildly.

"Sorry, Your Majesty," he said. "Swallowing manure, how's that?"

"It's not— They wouldn't— Changelings are treated well! They get to live in Faerie, they get to be taken care of, they get to have everything they need provided for them!"

"How old was your sister when your parents started teaching her how to take care of the household?" asked Nolan, idly. "Does she do the laundry? The cooking? Sweep the floors and wash the windows? Do you do any of those things? If she wants to leave, is she allowed? If your parents order her to go work in someone else's house, can she say no, or does she have to go?"

August looked more and more uncomfortable as he went on. "It's not like that for her."

"Not for her? Good for you. How about for every other changeling in your Kingdom? Your sister's been arrested for murder, but if the tables were turned, you wouldn't be. You'd walk away without even a slap on the wrist, because changelings are possessions, and breaking a piece of property isn't half the crime that murder is."

August paled.

"So yes, my sister and I are the snatchers. We're the bogeymen in your closet, and we're glad, because we keep a few people from hitting their kids. 'Beat your changeling and the snatchers will take them away in the middle of the day.' We're terrifying because they never see us coming."

"And half the time they blame the children you snatch on Blind Michael," said Chrysanthe. "If that man ever spoke to adults, he'd find himself responsible for twice the abductions he's actually performed."

"Possibly so," said Nolan.

"But Blind Michael is a *monster*," said August. "Why would you be happy to be compared to a *monster*?"

"Because we're doing something that needs to be done," said Nolan. "I only wish we could do it more often."

Silence fell then, heavy and oppressive. I looked back to Ginevra, who had been silent through this whole exchange. She was watching me wearily, and it struck me again how much the people who depended on me had paid to see my quest advanced this far. With my distraction over October leaving me unable to fully devote my time to the Court, she and Raj had both been wearing themselves thin, and all for the sake of my family. She could have run back to her father and left me to do my job, which had been too long settled on her shoulders, and instead, she had stayed.

I moved toward her, saying quietly once close, "You can return to the Court for now if you like. Simon is a talented brewer. If he says he can get the Windermeres past the iron, he means it, and with the level of exposure she's likely had, October will be unconscious for some time."

"What, and miss the denouement of all this nonsense?" She kept her tone soft, almost teasing, and smiled a little as she said it, making it clear that she was trying to lighten the mood. "We've come this far, Tybalt. I'm not leaving you now. Not when she's almost back—and won't be back at all."

My face fell. "What do you mean?"

"Iron alone isn't going to destroy a spell cast by Titania, and you know that, but I can still *see* the hope in your eyes. You hope she's going to leave that dungeon as herself, and she's not." Ginevra sobered, attempts at levity dying. "She's still going to be the person Titania turned her into."

"You don't know that."

"I've read many of the same books you have. I do." She turned to Garm. "You're Gwragen. You know illusions. Will iron erase this one?"

"The Lady of Flowers can cast illusions that overpower even iron," said Garm, uncertainly. "She's been known to do so when under duress, such as when Faerie and the human world went to war."

"That wasn't the only time," called Nolan. "Be honest. We're all friends here." Then he laughed, a high, cackling sound.

Garm looked down. "Or when she wanted to lure the children of Maeve into an ambush," he admitted. "She can conceal iron under veils of light and shadow, so that you're almost upon it before you feel its presence. Even when she doesn't go to such lengths, her truly deep works won't collapse when iron is involved. Not like a normal person's might."

"You see?" Ginevra turned back to me. "I can't go back to the Court. Not when you're preparing to break your own heart, and not when I need to be here to talk to Toby as soon as she wakes up."

A portal opened in the air then, sparing me from the need to reply, and Arden stepped through, Simon close behind. She waved a hand. The portal closed.

"C'mon, Nolan," she called. "We're off to perform a jailbreak."

"You have the potions, then?" asked Chrysanthe.

Arden turned, bowing to the Queen on the Golden Shore. "As promised. Four doses. One each to get there and back today, despite the interference of the iron, and one each to repeat the trick when it's going to cause the most possible chaos. We would have been back sooner, but he also whipped up a bunch of sludge that's supposed to bind to any iron that gets into our system and pull it out before it can do real damage. Awful nice of him, or it would be, if I didn't have strict instructions to save the majority of it for this changeling chick we're picking up."

"No side trips," said Theron sternly. "I know you have many opportunities to help during this period, but our guests are worried for their friend, and she needs to come first in this instance."

"Sure, *Dad*," said Arden, rolling her eyes. She crossed to Nolan, handing him a small bottle from inside her jacket before hooking her arm through his. She sketched a portal in the air, and both of them vanished through it, and we were alone.

EIGHTEEN

SIMON WAS THE FIRST to break the awkward silence. "They'll be resistant to the iron blocking access to the Queen's dungeons for at least an hour. As long as they're reasonably quick about things, it should be more than enough to get them in and out without issue."

"The Windermeres are immature in self-defense, as exiles with no hope of ever returning to their family holdings, but they conduct their duties responsibly and with remarkable skill," said Chrysanthe. "I have never known them to fail once they set their minds to something, unless there's outside intervention."

"Outside intervention is exactly what I'm concerned about," said Simon darkly.

"Will this potion you've brewed work for me, and the Shadow Roads?" I asked. I should have asked before, should have provided an alternate plan, but he had seemed so sure, and I hadn't had a full night's sleep in so long—

"I have no way of knowing," said Simon. "Not without a sample of your blood, which would grant me a sample of your memory. That might be a swift way to verify whether your wild stories are true. No one can rewrite the secrets stored in blood."

I flinched at the thought of bleeding for the man, but . . . "If I bleed for you, if you see the truth of what I've told you, will you help me?"

"I thought I was already helping you." He gestured to the room around us, golden walls and watching monarchs, people who were still more strangers than allies—all save Ginevra, who watched him with the wary unease of a feral cat trapped in a room full of humans. I had come to know Garm and Grianne reasonably well in the past few months, but without the ability to read my blood and know I was telling them the truth, there was only so far they could believe me, after all. I was a stranger walking into their lives and announcing that everything they knew had been a lie. That wasn't an easy rock to swallow, no matter how I turned it.

"You're helping *October*," I said.

"You say she's your wife. Doesn't that make it the same thing?"

"You know better than that," I said, voice low.

Simon looked at me, refusing to flinch away. "If you bleed for me," he said, after a long and dreadful silence, "then yes. I will believe you believe the things you're saying."

"Not good enough. You can tell the difference between memory and delusion when it's witnessed in the blood."

Cait Sidhe don't share that particular gift, but I've known enough Daoine Sidhe in my day to understand more about their magic than most. Simon frowned.

"Blood can't lie. But blood can reflect lies."

"You're a smart man. I'm sure you can tell the difference between truth and fiction."

"You're both very impressive and awesome and smart and cool," said Ginevra, stepping between us. "Stop flexing at each other and do something useful. Simon, if you're willing to ride Tybalt's blood, and he's willing to let you, you should be able to say whether you're going to at least try to believe whatever you see there. And Tybalt, you need to agree to focus on a memory that won't upset the man."

Simon thought of his daughter as a sheltered changeling who'd never been outside the tower or away from home. He would be equally horrified by seeing her image covered in blood or in the throes of passion.

The humans have a saying: "*Don't think about the white elephant.*" It applies to the fae as well. Simon wouldn't be able to pull my entire life story out of a single spoonful of blood, but he'd be most likely to see what I didn't want him to, because those would be the things I couldn't help thinking about. I didn't want to show him sex or violence, and I didn't want him to see October's pregnancy. He'd learned of it before I did in the real world, when she'd used her blood to save his life and spilled her secret in the process. On some level, I took a small, smug satisfaction at knowing he'd forgotten immediately thereafter.

"I'll do my best," I said.

Simon exhaled, slowly, through his nose. "All right," he said at last. "If you bleed, I'll believe."

"Father," said August.

"What?" He turned to her. "The more we know, the better off we'll be."

She looked at him, uneasily, as he focused once more on me. "It is an insult to draw a weapon in the presence of a monarch you don't serve," he said.

"I'm well aware. I've been insulted by the Divided Courts more times than I can count. Fortunately, my weapons don't need drawing." I turned my left wrist toward the ceiling, laying the fingers of my right hand across it and flexing them, extending my claws in the process. The pain of them punching through my skin was almost grounding, making it easier to breathe.

I withdrew my claws as soon as I smelled blood. It was hard not to smile as I did, considering that October would have ripped her wrist open to get as much blood as possible, even before she'd learned how quickly and completely she could heal. My little fish always had been inclined toward the dramatic, even though I knew she'd deny it if asked.

I thrust my hand toward Simon, trying to focus on a memory I knew he'd find minimal fault with: October in her red-and-white gown, dropping rose petals like raindrops as she walked out of the wood on his arm, ready to be wed. Oh, there had been blood that day, and some of it my own, but that had come after Simon brought her to me.

"You're sure?" he asked.

"I'm bleeding," I said, and he nodded, understanding my assent. Carefully, he took my hand and lowered his mouth to the wound, the gesture so like October doing the same that it ached to see. Still, I didn't pull away, but thought of the way my heart had leapt at the sight of her, the feeling of my blood turned electric and effervescent at the same time, like it was going to come boiling out of my veins and leave me dead on the floor. She had been so beautiful, walking toward me— toward *me*—with that look on her face, like she had never seen anything finer in her life.

I could live another dozen centuries and never see anything as beautiful as she'd been in that moment. If I were trying to decide whether a strange man claiming to act in the best interests of my daughter was telling the truth, I would have liked to see a memory like that.

Simon swallowed once, twice, and then broke away, staggering several steps back and going still. His throat worked as his eyes went glassy and his eyelids drooped, making him look half-asleep.

I pulled my arm back, wrapping my hand around the punctures in my wrist. Ginevra was already moving toward me, producing a roll of gauze from inside her shirt and sighing.

"Here I thought that maybe Toby not being around would keep me from needing to use the first aid kit I carry for a change," she said.

"Come now, you never use it on her anyway." I smiled. "She heals too quickly."

"Yeah, and she'd never let me if I tried." She wrapped my wrist.

August, meanwhile, was moving to where Simon had caught himself against the wall, still staring off into nothingness. "Father?" she said, voice small and somehow meek. "Father, are you all right? Did he hurt you somehow?"

"He . . ." Simon sighed, voice faltering and failing him. Then he turned to look back at me. "He's not lying to us."

August recoiled. "What?"

"I saw your sister, August. I saw her dressed in bridal attire, moving to his side. The sea witch stood before them as officiant. More than that, though, I saw my parents. I saw *all* my parents." He glanced at me, and there was terror in his face.

Simon had never been one to speak freely of his origins, of the fact that while both Septimius Torquill and his legal wife, Glynis, had been Daoine Sidhe, the woman who actually gave birth to him had been mortal. Opening their marriage to include another had been nothing strange, and wouldn't have excluded the Torquills from polite company, if not for the fact that their third, Celaeno, had been human-born.

The boys hadn't been changelings for long, and in a world where changelings were less powerful but not an inherent servant class, it hadn't mattered in the slightest. Here, it must be the secret he most feared having escape into the world.

August frowned, not seeming to understand the significance of his last statement. "And? They died, didn't they?"

"A very long time ago," said Simon. He straightened, finally turning to fully face me, and bowed at the waist, deep and solemn. "I apologize for doubting you, and for forgetting our clearly long acquaintance."

Theron sat up a little straighter. "He's telling the truth?"

"Either we are currently wrapped in the largest illusion I've ever seen—"

"We are," interjected Garm.

"—which seems likely, given the cooperation of the Gwragen and the fact that the man, who belongs to a supposedly extinct descendant line, has been allowed free access to the Library for *months*, or his memories have been rewritten with such precision that it spills over into the blood, and I don't think that's possible." Simon glanced to me again. "Blood memory, once set, is locked in place, and the blood remembers everything, forever."

"Ah, so," said Chrysanthe, settling deeper in her throne. "Then it seems we're to set ourselves against Titania. Won't this be fun? Won't this be a delightful way to find out what it feels like to fly with the night-haunts? We'll do it, we just need to remember what it costs to go against the Summer Queen. She defeated Maeve. And I would wager none of us is anywhere near that level of power."

I was about to answer when the air opened and Nolan Windermere stepped through. He was slightly rumpled, hair askew, but didn't appear to have been in a fight.

"Got the girl," he said. "Gave her the anti-iron agent. What the hell do you put in that stuff, pure bottled gross? It tastes like every nasty thing in the universe, all mixed together."

"That means it's working," said Simon, unruffled. "Where is my daughter?"

"She's iron-sick and exhausted, and has been running for hours," said Nolan. "Arden took her to our room and put her to bed. She really needs a nap. I figured you'd be getting antsy, so came to tell you what's up before I go nap with her, and Arden takes off."

"'Take off'?" asked Chrysanthe. "Where is she 'taking off' to?"

"Don't worry, Mom, she'll be back by curfew, and she's not doing any snatching solo, we both know I'd kill her myself if she got herself caught. She's just going to pop over to Dreamer's Glass and see if she can get this Duchess Zhou to confirm a few things October said while she was lucid. Either she has a concussion or something *really* weird is going on here."

"Weird," said Grianne.

The rest of us nodded, supporting her decree.

Nolan shrugged. "Okay, so it's the weird one. Arden still needs to talk to Duchess Zhou—we're trying to figure out exactly how a changeling house pet wound up committing murder in the streets of San Francisco. One or both of us will be back."

He waved his hand and was gone again before any of us could object. Ginevra placed a hand on my arm, and I glanced at her, startled.

"You're growling," she said. "Maybe work on that?"

I glared at her. "Why would I want to do that?"

"Because these people aren't used to Cait Sidhe, and if we want them to take us seriously, we need to make it hard to dismiss us as animals." She shrugged as she took her hand away. "Just a thought."

I took a deep breath, trying to steady myself. "Yes. Of course."

Once again, October was so close and still so far away. This entire ridiculous situation seemed to have been designed to test my patience—or to make me learn more of it, which was as unnecessary as it was cruel. I have plenty of patience. I just choose, for the most part, not to exercise it.

Still, if the Windermeres wished to do some basic reconnaissance while my little fish was sleeping off her recent adventures, at least that meant she was sleeping, and hadn't been left entirely alone. I didn't know these versions of them very well, but I knew the real ones well enough to trust in their ethics and their honesty. They would keep her safe, and soon enough, *I* would be able to resume keeping her safe, the way I should have been doing all along.

The way I was going to do from now on.

Chrysanthe rose. "It seems we'll all be here for a while," she said. "I'm going to arrange for a dinner to be held after she wakes and you settle what needs to be worked out between the lot of you—food is important, even in the middle of a crisis, and I won't have anyone questioning the hospitality on the Golden Shore. Can I call for anything to be brought in for you? I have rosehip tea made with a varietal originally cultivated on Tír Tairngire that's quite popular with visitors, if any of you are thirsty . . ."

I wanted to refuse. I wanted to say that until October knew comfort, I would be fine as I was. Before I could, Grianne said, "Tea's nice," and a small outbreak of agreement and murmuring followed, everyone chiming in one by one until I was the last one standing silent. At that point, there seemed little reason to say anything beyond:

"Yes. Tea would be lovely."

"Then I'll be right back." Chrysanthe paused to press a kiss to Theron's temple, and then was away, her cervine lower body making her stride a fascinating thing to watch. It's not polite to stare at queens. I wrenched my eyes away, turning to Theron.

"You have been remarkably accommodating through all of this, Sire," I said. As a King of Cats, I am under no obligation to use titles or honorifics for monarchs of the Divided Courts, but under the circumstances, politeness seemed like the best possible approach.

"You tell me the Golden Shore stands in your other world, and while you haven't told us everything, the fact that you're willing to fight to have that world restored—the fact that you married a *changeling*, and see nothing wrong with her mortality, tells me your version of Faerie is likely to be kinder to my subjects than this one," he said. "We have the fewest purebloods of any Kingdom on the western coast, did you know that?"

"I suspected, but wasn't entirely sure."

"Very few purebloods choose to settle here. Not much chance for power, and having the best farmer's market in the Westlands doesn't make up for limited opportunities to put themselves above others. So they don't come, and those that do come don't often stay. More and more every year, we're a kingdom of changelings hoping no one notices how easy we'd be to conquer. It helps that people who yearn for power rarely want to spend their time picking apples or planting rhubarb, and like everyone else who's been eating mostly food grown in the mortal world for the last few centuries, our noble courts wouldn't know what to do without peppers and potatoes and tomatoes. They're addicted to the fruits of the human world."

"And?"

"Have the Cait Sidhe ever been inclined to farming?"

I shook my head. Theron smiled.

"I thought not. Some things have origins in Faerie. Goblin fruit, for example, or starberries. They grew first in the deeper realms, and when we had to leave those lands behind, people carried seeds or cuttings with them. Others, it's hard to say. Where did the first apple tree sprout, Avalon or Earth? Again, we don't know. We know where the first Earth apples were cultivated, and we know that the people who tended them did so in ways Faerie would never have considered, but we don't know if they originated there."

I frowned. "All very interesting, I'm sure, but I'm afraid I don't understand what that has to do with you being so calm about everything."

"The potato, on the other hand, well. We know where the potato came from. The people native to the continent we call Aztalan developed them over the course of centuries, without magic. Just hard work and the understanding that they needed the land to feed them, so they would convince it to do precisely that. They understood farming. They knew what it was to speak gently to the ground."

I looked at him, more confused than ever, and said nothing.

"Whenever a new noble has come here from Titania's Court, full of ideas about power for the taking and gaps in the leadership here on the

Golden Shore, they've wanted to plant their gardens of nothing but fairy fruit, and there are no fae potatoes," said Theron. "They want to feast the way they've become accustomed to, but also to sunder the food on their table and the food in their fields from one another. Tell them a potato came from mortal soil, they recoil and ask if you think them a changeling, to be fed on human scraps. They demand things that don't exist, fae peppers and potatoes. They'd collapse our Kingdom inside of a week."

"I won't pretend such attitudes don't exist in our Faerie, but I'll say that they're less common, and less . . . acceptable? I think that's the correct word. People who want to behave as if nothing good has ever come from humanity find it difficult to make much headway in modern society. We have our prejudices and our bigotry. We're trying to be better. October and I were wed in the knowe of the High King of the Westlands, our marriage officiated by the eldest of the Firstborn yet living. A Cait Sidhe monarch and a changeling, wed in sight of the greatest powers our world has to offer. And while our path has not been smooth . . ." There was a literal attempted coup *during* our wedding, but it had nothing to do, oddly enough, with the realities of our union. It had been politically expedient and conveniently timed, nothing more. ". . . while our path has not been smooth, no one has objected on the basis of what either one of us is. We're allowed to exist, with the possibility of happiness, which is more than Faerie would have offered us two hundred years ago. Who knows what it might offer us two hundred years from now?"

"And that, more than anything, is why I'm willing to accept your story," said Theron. "You don't threaten my Kingdom or my crown, or my lovely lady wife. You threaten the monarch to the north, who has never been an ally of ours, and whose exiled children would make much better neighbors. I admit, I don't like the thought of losing them. They're pests and problems, but they're *our* pests and problems, and the service they've provided to the Golden Shore is beyond measure. Which is, I suppose, where your story gets muddled for me. If Titania designed every aspect of the world, why are Arden and Nolan allowed to steal changelings on my behalf? Why aren't they good little nobles, sitting quietly in someone else's Court, free of all complicated thoughts and actions? You're outside the narrative you say she's made. They're not."

"Oddly, I think I can answer that," said Simon.

I turned to him, eyebrows raised. "Can you? Then, by all means. I'm ever so interested to hear what you might have to say."

Simon exhaled. "Titania is a gardener."

"Forgive me if I can't picture her getting her hands dirty."

"Not in that sense, not like you or I might garden. She's never needed to dig. Flowers blossom at her touch. Instead, she plants ideas, not seeds. She tells her children what will please her and walks away, trusting them to grow in the direction she desires. She sets her stage and doesn't bother to direct it."

"That's not a good way to grow a healthy crop," said Theron.

"Since when has Titania cared about healthy crops?" asked Garm. Everyone turned to look at him. He shrugged. "What? It's true. She doesn't care if Faerie's healthy, as long as it looks healthy enough that she gets praised for it. My liege before Duke Torquill wanted his guard to match, no matter what. Well, we had a Baobhan Sith join our company. She was real skinny, but had these huge feet. You'd never have guessed it to look at her. The chatelaine couldn't find uniform boots in her size. We had to order out to another fiefdom. It took them more than a month to arrive. And the whole time, she was doing her rounds in boots two sizes too small. Rubbed her feet raw, she did, blisters and bleeding, and all because our Count wouldn't allow her to wear shoes that weren't 'in uniform,' or go barefoot and have me cast illusionary boots for her."

He scowled as he stopped, apparently gripped by the unpleasant memory of his former comrade. In a softer voice, he added, "She left as soon as her feet healed. Wore her new boots until then, and took them with her when she walked away. I didn't get to say goodbye. The more I learn about the way Titania likes to handle things, the more she reminds me of that Count. She wants us to look perfect more than she wants us to *be* perfect."

"So the Windermeres aren't cultivated seeds that she planted with care and nurtured. They're like mint plants, or blackberries," said Simon. "Something hardy and good at holding on, that she uprooted and threw aside without checking to see whether it was going to land in healthy soil."

"Letting them have their father's throne would mean taking away one of her favorite daughter's best tools," I said. "She needed to remove them. From what we've been able to determine, she didn't kill anyone, only shunted them out of her way. Friends of ours have been scattered across multiple Kingdoms. For all that I know, some of them may be here, on the Golden Shore." This would be a logical place for her to have placed Jasmine, at the very least, and for a moment I entertained the thought of looking for her.

But no. May had made her wishes very clear, and I would be going against them if I were to put her into the situation I had been living in for the past four months, confronted with a functional stranger wearing her lover's face, unable to be close or offer comfort, unable to do anything but stand helplessly off to the side. It had been a kind of torture I'd never experienced before, nor ever wished to experience again.

I collected myself, and continued. "So she changed their circumstances enough to make them flee the kingdom while young enough to be tucked safely away in someone else's fiefdom. They were still themselves."

"Illusions can change your memories, but they can't modify the core of who a person is," said Garm. "A brave man will still be a brave man; a coward will still be a coward. If they were always going to be stubborn and overly ethically rigid, that was going to happen no matter what."

That raised some horrifying concerns about Quentin. I paused for a moment to stare at Garm, not quite ready to voice them, and Arden made her reappearance in that pause, stepping out of the air in front of the dais.

"Okay, shit's fucked," she announced. "I think we should all do quiet time until October wakes up and is ready to talk, because nothing's getting done until that happens."

NINETEEN

THE FALLOUT FROM ARDEN'S announcement was precisely what I would have predicted: everyone started talking at once, and was still talking when the door opened and Chrysanthe returned, followed by two servers with refreshment trays. She paused for a moment, taking in the scene in front of her with wide, puzzled eyes and then, when no one stopped their frantic requests for clarification, clapped her hands loudly, and yelled, "Everyone *shut the hell up!*"

Divided Courts or Court of Cats, it doesn't matter: when a Queen yells, you stop talking. The room went silent, everyone turning toward her like flowers turning toward the sun. Chrysanthe scowled as she stomped toward the dais, the effect somewhat spoilt by the dainty tapping of her hooves against the floor.

"Arden," she said, voice icy. She settled herself back onto her throne, resting her joined hands between her knees. "Care to explain why I came back from the kitchen to find a riot in my receiving room?"

"I didn't—" Arden began.

Chrysanthe silenced her with a look.

Arden looked down at the floor, twisting a toe against the stone like a child being scolded. It occurred to me that she was in some ways precisely that: she'd been young enough when she and her brother fled to Golden Shore that Chrysanthe and Theron must have functionally raised them.

"I went to Dreamer's Glass to ask what happened," she said, not looking up. "Duchess Zhou was pretty much the way she's been every time I've met her, but she had two other people with her. This blonde kid who kept appearing and disappearing—even more than Nolan and I do, it was like she thought taking more than a step was asking something unreasonable of her—and this lady with red-and-brown hair who kept *touching* her, like they were close, even though I've never seen her before. I asked the Duchess who they were, and she said they were her wife and daughter from another world, and that before Etienne took off with October, she 'removed the veils from January's eyes' so she could remember the way the world's supposed to be."

"Did they see this as a good thing?" asked Chrysanthe.

"They seemed to. Duchess Zhou said she would have asked October to do the same for her, but that doing it once was almost incapacitating, and Sir Etienne needed her for something. They all seemed to see unlocking January's memories as something that needed to be done, and that they'd do again." Arden finally glanced up, frowning. "January said she'd put the little girl—whose name was April, and are people just *trying* to use up the whole calendar or something? Because I'm starting to feel like I'm in one of those mortal camp groups where everyone's named 'Taylor' or 'Tyler,' only it's all months. Anyway, she said she'd put the little girl inside a computer before the change happened, because she was sure Titania was about to do something, and either these people were telling me some of the biggest, most ridiculous lies I've ever heard in my life or shit's completely fucked. I didn't want these people to be telling the truth."

"I know, dear," said Chrysanthe.

Arden shot one last furious glance toward the rest of us, then opened another circle in the air and vanished again.

"Ironic, given she was just complaining about April's tendency to flit about as if space were no concern worth attending to," I said. I glanced to Ginevra. "If she's back online, do you think Raj's phone will be working? I'm sure he would like to have someone to exchange test messages with."

"Text," said Ginevra. "Do you want to nip over and check on him?"

"We may be here for quite some time. If you wouldn't mind, I would appreciate the opportunity to clear my head."

"I'll hold the fort," she said, reassuringly. "And if anything changes, you know I'll come and find you."

"I do." I bowed to the dais before taking several steps back and diving into shadow. The cold air was like a slap to my face, stinging and snapping me back into the shape of my own skin. October could break Titania's enchantment. Of course she could—she'd been able to free me, after all, when Titania had seized me as a weapon against her. She could free them all, if only we had time enough.

Which we wouldn't. As soon as the work started in earnest, Titania would realize something was wrong and come looking for us. Even if she didn't, time was not on our side. Why, *why* had Mary insisted that we had to wait this long? If it had just been a matter of finding an excuse for October to leave Shadowed Hills, surely we could have fabricated something before now . . .

Unless there were other reasons this had to happen close to Moving Day.

I ran through the dark, letting the cold, thin air comfort and settle me, until I reached the border of my own Court and stepped out, into the dim glow of oil lanterns burning on every surface. Raj was crouched in the middle of the room, spooning some sort of fish puree into shallow dishes. The kittens he was trying to feed sat and watched him with a patience they would never have extended to any other keeper, feline or fae. They knew their Prince when they beheld him.

He lifted his head as I left the shadows, feeling them shift. After a slow blink, he smiled, hopefully. "Is it done?" he asked. "Is she back?"

"Not yet," I said.

"Oh." He sagged.

In many ways, this had been as hard on him as it was on me. All his friends were sealed away, locked in other lives; he was trapped in the Court, caught in a constant cycle of service, watching as I, his only real remaining family, sank deeper and deeper into despair. Guilt gripped me. He should never have been asked to shoulder so much.

"But I should see her soon," I added. "And Arden went to Dreamer's Glass in an attempt to retrace October's steps. She saw April. Check your phone. If you still have service, you should be able to text her now."

Raj blinked again, then scrambled frantically to get the phone from his pocket, nearly dropping the slim metal rectangle several times before he got it out and held it up to check the screen. Then he drooped.

"No texts."

"She may not realize you'd be receptive," I offered. "According to Arden, she was reasonably aware of the situation, and could be holding back so as not to confuse people."

Raj nodded and began tapping away, thumbs moving fast as he composed a message and tossed it off into the ether.

"Ginevra and I will be some time, I'm afraid," I said. "I need to be there when October wakes up, and once she's actively participating in her own rescue, I expect things will get fairly chaotic."

"I have things under control here," he said, just as his phone made a chiming sound and his whole face lit up, making him seem, briefly, much younger than he actually was. He looked at me and beamed. "April's responding! So's Chelsea! Nothing from Quentin or Dean, but two is better than none, right?"

"Right," I said. I smiled, quickly, and moved to ruffle his hair with one hand. He ducked away, already typing again. "Stay here and stay safe, and remember that I love you."

He glanced away from the screen at that, blinking at me. "Uncle? Is everything all right?"

Possibly not, depending on how the next few hours went, but really, nothing had been all right for months now. I sighed, trying to keep my smile from slipping. "I'll be back when I can," I said, and stepped back into shadow once again.

The journey back to Golden Shore seemed substantially longer than the one away from it had been, every step weighted by the knowledge of what was coming and how much we still didn't know. Knowing how much you need to learn is very rarely a comforting thing. So I ran away from my own discontent, racing back toward where my answers would hopefully be found.

I emerged into the throne room to find the refreshments cleared away and my party gathered near the dais, talking quietly. Their collective voices overlapped, erasing one another.

Ginevra looked up as I entered, then turned and hurried toward me, reaching for my hand. "I need you to stay calm," she said. "It's very important. Can you do that for me?"

I took a deep breath. "I can try."

"October's awake and on her way," she said, pulling me back toward the others.

I stared at her, struggling against the feeling that I could no longer draw a proper breath. The room spun, suddenly smaller and much less welcoming. She was coming? She was finally *coming*?

I could have missed her?

The door eased open, and almost as one, we all turned to watch as a woman slipped into the room. She wore an unfamiliar green dress and a familiar black leather jacket, and she looked surprisingly small, like she was afraid to take up space. Like she was afraid of what would happen to her if she dared.

I had never wanted so badly to see Titania downed and bleeding before me, but in that moment, I thought I could have killed her with the force of my anger alone.

October glanced around, pausing when she caught sight of our group. Then, with a shuddering sigh, she broke into a run, heading for us with such determination that my heart lifted and for a moment—a moment— I hoped. August broke away, running toward her, and October adjusted her path, ever so slightly, to intercept her sister. My spark of hope guttered and died, blown out by reality.

They slammed into one another, both shaking and crying as October clung to her sister and buried her face in August's hair. Simon shot me a sympathetic look before he started toward his daughters, putting one hand on each of their shoulders. October lifted her head, not letting go of August, and let it rest against his arm.

She whispered something I didn't hear.

"No, the apologies are mine to make," said Simon. "I should have seen that the timing was too convenient, the request too specific; this was an engineered attempt to get you away from us. Duchess Zhou confirmed it when I confronted her."

"She told me, too." October's voice was a balm and a knife to the heart at the very same moment. She lifted her head, looking up at Simon. "She . . . she . . ."

She started to cry again.

I decided I was absolutely going to murder Titania. It would be a pleasure.

Simon embraced them both, lowering his voice and saying something too soft for me to hear.

October sniffled and pulled away, wiping her eyes as she tried to compose herself. August let go of her, slowly, reaching back at the last moment, swift as a striking snake, to pinch October on the side of the hand.

"Ow!"

"That's what you *get*," snapped August. "Blood magic? Letting yourself be taken somewhere other than Dreamer's Glass? Getting *arrested*?"

"Yeah, it was lousy. Too bad you missed it," said October, sounding almost like herself for a moment.

"Never do that again," said August, hooking her arm through October's. "Now come on. There are people who want to talk to you."

"What? Why would anyone want to talk to *me*?" October glanced back at Simon as August began guiding her across the floor. He nodded, expression revealing nothing, and followed them at a reasonable distance.

August released her as they approached the thrones, stepping off to the side and letting her finish the journey on her own. October grasped the sides of her dress and curtsied. I turned my face away. My little fish had always insisted on bowing, ever since she'd received her title. To do anything else would be to allow them to think she didn't deserve the respect inherent to her rank. And she simply couldn't allow that. Turning her face to the floor, she held her position.

"May I present my daughter, October Torquill," said Simon.

October tensed, but didn't turn her face from the floor.

"Not your child born, I assume, Simon?" asked Theron.

Ginevra elbowed me, and I realized I'd been growling again. Theron knew full well that October was a changeling: all he accomplished by asking the question was making her feel small and unwanted here, and I didn't like it. Still, I composed myself. Regicide is more my wife's speed than my own, and killing him might have upset her.

"To my honorable wife, after a trip to the human world to fulfill her obligation to Fair Titania," said Simon. "Legally, she's as much my child as August has ever been. If you ask my heart, it will answer you the same. She's mine, and I claim her in all regards."

"So you don't regret your wife's decision to follow Titania's command?" asked Theron.

Simon paused, and when he answered, his voice was slow and deliberate. "I was sorry when Amandine was ordered to lie with someone she didn't love. Commanding the creation of children is cruel, commanding the creation of children solely for their service is worse, but it seems to me that commanding a conception out of obligation rather than love is also cruel, if not as strongly so. How could it be anything other than wrong, when every step is couched in cruelty?"

"Let the girl stand," said Chrysanthe, glancing at me and clearly seeing how close I was to losing what little control I had remaining over my temper. "She's still recovering from everything she's been through. You may rise, October."

October straightened, eyes still downcast, and Chrysanthe took the opportunity to look at her closely, taking her measure.

"Mmm, 'girl' is a bit dismissive, I think, upon seeing her better," said Chrysanthe. "Woman, then, but still allowed to stand up straight in our presence. You may look at us, October. We don't demand that you avert your eyes."

October glanced up, and I saw the startled confusion in her eyes before she managed to compose herself. "Forgive me, Majesty, but how is it that my father and sister are here?"

"Ah. That *is* a tale, and not theirs alone; they came with companions, who we have ignored for too long already." Chrysanthe waved a hand, airily indicating the rest of us.

And October turned and looked directly at me for the first time in months, and there wasn't a single scrap of recognition in her eyes until she got to her uncle's knights. Them, she clearly knew, while Ginevra and I were strangers to her. I had already known that we would be. Why, then, was that expression so painful to behold?

"October," said Garm, dryly amused.

October hesitated, then turned to study the rest of us. She looked at me so intently that I started to step toward her, summoned by her regard. Ginevra put her hand on my arm, reminding me of our situation. I stopped, but I didn't take my eyes from my wife. I felt like I had been starving, and seeing her, so close I could smell the cut-grass and copper scent of her skin, was like putting me in front of a feast and commanding me not to eat.

Then Ginevra moved forward, and I matched her. Garm and Grianne did the same, all four of us stepping slowly toward October, saying nothing, only closing the distance between us. It may not have been the best decision we could have made; October looked alarmed, like she didn't know what to do with the situation.

August stepped in front of her sister, glaring with a force I would never have expected from her. She looked ready to fight me with her bare hands. I almost believed, in that moment, that she could hold her own.

"We came here with you," she said. "We listened to your wild stories and we let you convince us to come, even though it really, really sucked. Now you're looking at my sister like you want to hurt her. You're going to stop that *right now*, or we're leaving."

"How were you intending to do that?" I asked. My voice came out rougher than I expected, vocal cords caught halfway between feline and human, warping the shape of my words. "It took both of us to bring you here. Garm would never have been able to make the journey if not for Grianne. How do you plan to escape our company?"

"Their Majesties have their snatchers," said August. "There have been rumors about them for as long as I can remember, and now we know those rumors are true. I'm sure they would be happy to take us back to Shadowed Hills, in exchange for a pledge of silence. The Golden Shore needs to keep its secrets."

"Charming as it is to sit here and listen to you coordinate a somewhat ill-considered blackmail plan against us, I'm afraid we need to be seeing to the banquet now that our guests of honor have arrived," said Theron. "I'll send one of those 'snatchers,' as you so quaintly put it, to collect you when it's time to eat. Please try not to get any blood on the floor." He rose, offering his arm to Chrysanthe. She took it, and together they walked out of the room, not looking back.

"August," said October, warningly.

"We'll leave if we want to leave," said August, eyes remaining fixed on me. "And if you don't stop looking at my sister like that, we *will* want to leave."

"August!" snapped October. August turned to look at her. October glared. "I can't go back with you."

"But . . . We came here to . . . Of course you can," said August. She sounded genuinely lost. "Mother doesn't know what's happened, but she won't be angry. None of it was your fault. It's still Moving Day, and we'd be traveling by Tuatha, so there's no chance we'd be stopped. Of course you can come home. Where else would you go?"

October turned to Simon, expression pleading.

He sighed. "August," he said gently. "What your sister has been accused of is a serious crime."

"But she didn't *do* it!" she said. "She can't have *done* it! She doesn't know how to fight, much less how to kill someone! They're—they're confused, and they're pointing fingers because she was an unclaimed changeling in the wrong place at the right time, and they want it to be her. But she didn't *do* it."

"Stupid girl," I growled, before consciously deciding to speak. I wanted to shake her. I wanted to *rage*. "She disappeared from a sealed holding cell belonging to the Queen of the Mists. You really think it matters whether she committed the crime they've accused her of? They'll have her tied to the Tree in the blinking of an eye. Escaping was disrespectful to their precious pureblood authority."

"Tybalt," chided Ginevra.

That was the last straw. I shrugged her hand off of my arm and stalked away from them, turning my back on the argumentative August and the woman who looked so much like my wife, who would hopefully be my wife again in the near future, but was currently a stranger dressed in her face. I had known it would be unsettling to see her so. I hadn't realized it would be quite so *enraging*. None of the anger I was feeling was for her, and yet. I didn't want to frighten her.

My little fish is very dear, and quite clever, but she has never been good at understanding the emotions of others—myself especially. She thought I hated her for years, long past the point where animosity had faded into affection. She was already upset. I didn't want to make matters worse.

I walked until I reached the far side of the room and stopped there, leaning against the wall, shadow falling halfway over my face. It was tempting to allow myself to tumble into it, slipping away and leaving them to their discussion. I was tired of talking. I wanted us to act.

October seemed to feel the same. She argued with August, shying away from the other woman when she reached out, until August finally grabbed October in a tight embrace, shouting, "They're *not* taking my sister away from me!" so loudly that I heard every word.

Ginevra raised her hands, clearly trying to placate August. The argument continued, August not letting go of October, and I stayed where I was, away from this drama whose only relation to me was its replacement of the family I knew and loved.

Simon said something. August looked at him, silently pleading, before slowly, reluctantly, letting go of October and stepping away. Ginevra stepped forward, and appeared to be speaking to them. I wished I could hear what she was saying, even as I understood, perfectly, that I needed to keep my distance. I didn't have the self-control to be any closer.

Their voices were a pleasant, distant blend of sounds, until two words in October's voice broke through the rest: ". . . Cait Sidhe?"

There are many things I could ignore. That wasn't among them.

Ginevra looked momentarily surprised, then answered, her own voice softer and less gripping to my ear.

Then, with utter, brutal clarity, October said, "I don't. I mean, I've never met a Cait Sidhe before. But I saw something, recently, that made me think you might be one."

Fury welled up in my gut. Titania had erased not just my marriage, but my entire species, in an effort to leave October without the allies she needed. I couldn't be angry at October for what had been done to her, nor at anyone else in this room, even August—her self-interested upset was almost comforting, in a way, as it meant that October had never been alone, despite what Titania had tried to do. Let her break people down to their essentials, they would still find ways to come together and to comfort one another. That was a consolation.

Not enough of one. The fury was still building up inside me, making it difficult to catch my breath. I spun around and punched the wall which, true, had never done anything to me, but also wouldn't complain at the assault. The pain was centering. It made it easier for me to get myself back under control, pulling my anger and dismay down into my gut and turning once more to observe the group.

I didn't want to overhear anything else they might have to say. I tried to focus on looking rather than listening, observing the way they stood, the way they interacted with each other. Simon was hovering uneasily behind his daughters, allowing them to approach the problem in their own way, but not removing his protection. August, on the other hand, was staying aggressively close to October, ready to fight anyone who got too close.

Grianne was just observing. Garm, interestingly enough, looked ready to join in with August on the fighting. He'd never been particularly close to October in our world, yet it appeared he would be happy to protect her here. Interesting.

There was so much about this world I didn't, and couldn't, know, so many things buried in a history I didn't have the time to learn. I punched the wall again, this time out of frustration with myself as much as anything else. From across the room, Ginevra shot me a quelling glance. She clearly wanted me to calm myself.

I was doing my best. I really didn't see what more she could ask. I was staying away so that she could talk to the woman I loved without the risk of my clear distress interfering; I was punching the wall, not shredding the tapestries or turning into a cat and hiding under the nearest piece of furniture. Really, by any reasonable standard, I was behaving myself fantastically well.

Ginevra said something to October, who went pale and stared at her blankly for a moment before shaking it off and draping herself in a veil of resignation. So she knew. At long last, she knew the world wasn't real.

What was she going to do from here?

TWENTY

THE CONVERSATION CONTINUED AFTER that, August defensive, October resigned, Ginevra trying to thread the impossible needle of telling the truth without antagonizing the people who desperately wanted her to be lying. It was a masterwork of diplomacy, even when viewed purely through pantomime, and I couldn't help but be impressed. She was going to be an incredible Queen someday, when she took a throne of her own and held it. She was going to be among the best of us.

She had been a gift from my lady to the Court of Cats, because none of us would ever have thought to go hunting a hope chest to allow Ginevra this opportunity to thrive. Really, all of Faerie was better when we came together, when we didn't split ourselves with artificial boundaries and pretend that we weren't meant to be connected.

October extended her hand toward Ginevra, and I thought, for a moment, that she was reaching for her, ready to take hold and connect.

Then Ginevra unsheathed her claws.

October yelped, the sound high and pained and electric, going straight to the base of my spine and burning there. The smell of blood came immediately after, covering the distance between us in a matter of seconds, bright and red and underscored with the ever-present trace of grass. I snarled, breaking into an immediate run. The distance between us was nothing. Even without the shadows, it was nothing.

I wasn't sure what I was intending to do. I wasn't *intending* anything. This was pure animal instinct, all my fear and frustration boiling up at the threat to my mate's safety.

Fear carried me across the room to Ginevra. Fear raised my hand, and slammed it into her cheek, knocking her back. She yelped, then hissed at me, eyes narrowing in clear challenge. I grabbed her throat with one hand and her hair with the other, jerking her head back and preventing her from getting away. Blood welled up from the scratches on her cheek as she reached up with both hands, trying to pry my hand from her throat.

No. I was still King. I was *still* King, and she had drawn my wife's blood intentionally and without asking my consent before she did it. The challenge to my authority couldn't stand. It couldn't be allowed, no matter how good her reasons may have been. It couldn't.

Garm and Grianne were staring at me. I suppose being able to identify one of the Cait Sidhe, and spending time with us in our guise as civilized members of Faerie, didn't prepare them for the reality of us. Simon and August looked horrified. August, especially, looked as if she couldn't decide between throwing herself at me in her sister's defense or running away as fast as her legs could carry her.

Either response would have been valid, really.

"Stop it!" shouted October, sounding so perfectly like herself that I turned to stare at her, my hold on Ginevra's throat briefly loosening. She was glaring at me, incandescent in her outrage, furiously angry and more beautiful than she had been since our wedding day.

For a moment, she looked like my little fish, and I wanted to go to her and take her in my arms and never let her go. Then the moment passed, and she was a stranger with a familiar face, glaring at me like she wished to do me harm. I felt my own face harden, years of practiced self-protection sliding back into play.

"She *hurt* you," I said. I didn't snarl. Every syllable was as crisp and perfect as any prince of the Divided Courts would have spoken it.

October didn't appear to appreciate the effort. "I asked her to!"

"I did not give her consent to *hurt* you." I shook Ginevra. She scrabbled frantically at my hand one more time, then went limp as a kitten, submitting. It was the best way to avoid me escalating this to a full dominance fight.

"You don't get to give people consent to hurt me," said October. "No one gets to give people consent to hurt me except for me. Not you, not my family, not the damned Queen of the Mists, not even Fair Titania. *No one*."

"Yet here you stand, willing to remain wrapped up in an enchantment that denies you your identity, your history, your true family—everything you've worked so hard to build." I shook Ginevra one more time, harder, before letting go, releasing her hair at the same time. She fell to the floor, clutching her throat and gasping. "I knew the spell was wrapped tight around you. I still expected you to fight."

"I'm not a fighter," said October. "It's not fair to ask me to be."

"No, I suppose it's not," I snarled.

I glanced dismissively down at Ginevra, then at October, and muttered, "But I still hoped you would," before I turned and stalked away, heading back to the wall. This time, I didn't stop when I got there, but kept on walking into shadow, letting the throne room and its complicated, conflicting emotions drop away, replaced by the familiar cold darkness of the Shadow Roads.

Then I stopped. Where was I going? Where did I have *left* to go? Back to the Court, to tell Raj I'd failed—or down to the Undersea, to face Patrick and Dianda and tell them the same? We had the Summer Roads key. We had October. We hadn't failed at anything yet, even if she wanted to be stubborn and impossible and—

And herself. The same woman she had always been. How long did we fight before she could allow herself to believe that I might love her? How long after that did we delay, trading honesty for familiar hostility?

Too long.

Still, I needed to talk to *someone*, and I was running out of places to go. Shadowed Hills was no longer an option. May ached even more than I did to have things put back to normal—something I would have thought impossible had she not been my October's Fetch and hence tied to her in ways we might never understand. Who . . .

I stopped, standing straighter and staring out into the blackness. Of course.

Dreamer's Glass.

My run was lumbering and unsure at first, feet having trouble finding purchase in the shadows. As I settled more confidently into my choice of direction, it got easier, until I was racing as fast as I ever had toward my unseen destination.

The shadows let me off in an unfamiliar hall, the furniture all old, heavily carved and upholstered, and out of sync with what I would have expected from either Li Qin or January. I stepped out of the dark and took a vast breath of air, wiping the chill from my eyes as I looked for any sign that I was not alone.

There weren't any. I was utterly and completely by myself, at least for the first few seconds. Then, without so much as a pop of displaced air, April appeared at my right elbow.

"Hello," she said.

I flinched away, barely restraining the urge to take a swing. It probably wouldn't have mattered if I'd done so; April's "body" was an assortment of wood chips worked into the internal workings of a piece of computer equipment. The form I could see was made of light, a complex sort of illusion in its own right. I had never tried too hard to disbelieve her—it seemed rude—but I had no doubt that if I tried to strike her, my hand would simply pass right through the space where she appeared to be.

That was all well and good, but her mothers were the regents of this demesne, and wouldn't take it well if I started hitting their daughter. She looked up at me with grave golden eyes, as solemn as she almost always seemed to be, and a ripple of static flowed across her image, distorting and briefly pixelating it.

"Tybalt," she said, with neutral pleasure. "I was not expecting to see you today. Raj has been texting me about everything that has happened while I was offline. He is very anxious. I am attempting to calm him."

"That's all very good to hear, April, and I'm glad he can text you now," I said. "He's been lonely."

"Yes," said April. She frowned briefly. "He and Chelsea are both themselves. Dean and Quentin do not respond to messages. Neither does Helen, although Raj has asked me not to tell him that. He is very concerned about her, and would prefer not to know."

Helen was Raj's girlfriend, a Hob changeling. They met in Blind Michael's lands after they were both abducted, and had been dating ever since. It was a casual arrangement, for so many reasons, not the least of which was my own relationship with October showing him what happened to Kings who loved too deeply outside the Court. Still, she was a pleasant girl, and good for him in her own way. Not being able to talk to her must have been deeply distressing for him.

"Excellent," I said. "Will you pass a message to him, for me?"

April cocked her head, waiting.

"Tell him I know he has a number for Peter. Dean isn't responding, but the Undersea is unaffected by Titania's enchantments apart from the barrier keeping them below. Tell him to tell Peter I will be on Muir Beach at sunrise, if Captain Pete has found a way to reach the surface."

April nodded. Then, switching focus in an instant, she asked, "Is that why you are here?"

I blinked at her, then bowed my head, looking down as I replied, "I had hoped to speak to your mothers. Arden indicated that both were present."

"I am sure they will be very glad to see you," said April. "Wait here, and I will verify."

She vanished then, blinking out like an extinguished candle, but leaving no scent of smoke behind. April had been integrated into the computer to save her life after human developers felled her tree. Since then, she had found purpose in part by serving as a sort of message network for her mother's demesne, making it easier for the residents of Tamed Lightning to communicate.

Or Dreamer's Glass, I supposed. I couldn't guess at why Titania would have chosen to do away with a relatively politically unimportant County as a part of her revisions, but apparently she had, as January and Li Qin were now based out of Duchess Riordan's former holding, and not their usual home.

Li Qin had been standing regent of Dreamer's Glass for some time, of course, but, to the best of my knowledge, had never chosen to live there.

April reappeared in front of me. "They are in the library, and would greatly welcome your attendance," she said. "Do you know the way?"

"I'm afraid I'm not very familiar with the knowe," I said, apologetically.

"No matter." She waved a hand. "I can walk. Slow and inefficient as it is, I have learned to appreciate the conversation a walk makes possible."

"That's very generous of you," I said, suppressing a smile.

"Is it?" April looked at me quizzically as she started walking. I followed. "I thought it was showing a willingness to forgive the limitations of others. If nothing else, people are more forgiving of *my* limitations when I have already forgiven their own."

"That, too," I agreed. "People like it when you try to meet them in the middle. Can you tell me what happened here?"

"Oh. Mother was concerned that October's actions would have infuriated Titania, and requested I withdraw into my server, with a blood lock in place to prevent me from emerging unless she, or October, pressed the button. I agreed, as her concerns had an eighty percent chance of being justified, and it seems they *were* justified, as when October finally pushed the button, the whole world had been transformed—and not for the better, might I add. Our allies outside the afflicted area are furious and in a panic. Their emails are bouncing back, unable to reach us, which must be an unintended side effect, as

I cannot imagine Titania thought to implement curse-based network security when she created this reality. If she did, she is more clever than I thought, and might be more interesting to talk to."

"I hope you don't take this the wrong way, but I hope you don't get the chance to talk to her," I said.

April shot me a look that was equal parts aggravated and amused. "She took my mother away from me. If I had the opportunity to talk with her, I fear I might make an error in judgement."

"April, Titania would take you apart."

"Hence it being an error, and not a correction to the local census." She sounded utterly serene as she talked about assaulting one of the Three Pillars of Faerie. We had passed down several halls as we walked, and come to a wide, rectangular doorway. The room on the other side was filled with floor-to-ceiling bookshelves. April motioned for me to go in.

I nodded to her, politely, and went.

Once I was inside, the door swung closed behind me, revealing itself as yet another bookshelf, and leaving the room with no visible exits. If I hadn't known I was among friends, I would have been direly concerned. Instead, I looked around to get my bearings, and frowned when I saw no one else there. If Li Qin and January weren't here, why did April bring me?

"Yoo-hoo!" January's voice was as bright and irreverent as ever. I looked up. The room was taller than I had first assumed, with a whole second story above me. From what I could tell, the rooms combined to form an inverted L, and I was standing in the short arm.

January and Li Qin were at the rail, looking down from the second floor. January was waving wildly, like she thought my vision was somehow based on motion, and I wouldn't be able to see her if she showed any restraint at all.

"What are you doing here?" she called down.

"Catching my breath and hopefully speaking to an ally who understands why it hurts to see October still wrapped in the skein of this spell," I called back.

Li Qin grimaced, glancing away.

"What are *you* doing?" I continued.

"Looking for books on unmaking illusions," said Li Qin. "We have a few, but I find that even though this is my library, parts of it are woefully unfamiliar to me. It doesn't make sense, really."

"You didn't assemble much of this library on your own," I said.

"Duchess Riordan did, before she was lost to Annwn. It's not surprising that it would be unfamiliar."

Li Qin's expression hardened. "Maybe not to *you*, but I've spent the whole day being told that things I remember never happened, and that things I don't remember *did*. So I'm getting a little tired of it, all things considered."

January patted her awkwardly on the shoulder. Li Qin bristled but didn't pull away.

"Being the only person not in on a joke is a horrible feeling," she said, looking at me rather than at January. "Everyone else knows what's going on, and I get to be the one two steps behind the rest of the conversation, trying to pretend I'm keeping up."

"A moment," I said, and walked under the overhang where they were standing. January leaned out to watch me go, but didn't yell after me. I think she understood what I was about to do.

Stepping into the shadows around the bookshelves, I took a few quick steps and emerged one level up, now standing some ten feet behind the pair. I cleared my throat. They turned, Li Qin throwing up her hands when she saw me there. "Does no one believe in linear distance anymore?" she demanded. "April bounces around like a photon, we just had that girl from Golden Shore stepping in and out of portals like doors don't exist, and now you're what, exactly?"

"Walking through shadows," I said. "You have my apologies, Duchess Zhou, if you would prefer a more standard form of travel. This just seemed quicker than searching for the stairs, and as I will need to return to Golden Shore shortly, I didn't want to waste the time."

"But you'll waste it with twenty words where two would do," she said. Her mood was uncharacteristically negative, and I blinked at her, trying to figure out where this was coming from.

"I apologize," I said. "I talk when I'm anxious."

"Why are you here, Tybalt?" asked January. "I know you've got to be worried about October—I would be, if I were you—and can't imagine you'd rather be here than wherever she is right now."

"Golden Shore," I said.

"That explains why you're in a hurry to get back there. What did you need?"

"Arden told us that you had been released from the enchantment which grips most of our world," I said. "That you remembered things as I do."

"Yes," said January. "October was able to break the threads around me. That makes what, three times she's saved me? I swear, if she counted debts the way the sea witch does, I'd never be out of hers."

"Thankfully, my lady has rather more leeway when it comes to matters of mercy," I said. I took a deep breath, then. "August is . . . concerned . . . that if she assists October in her own release, October will forget everything she knows of the enchanted world, and fall entirely back into our own."

"And those two have always been thick as thieves, unhappy as that makes Amy, so I'm guessing she's afraid of losing her sister," said January.

I nodded.

"I remember it all." January stood straighter, eyes locked on mine. "I remember staying in Briarholme as Silences turned more and hostile to outsiders, and wishing I could go anywhere else. I remember growing up there, alone, isolated from any sort of court or community that might have comforted me. I remember the night my father went out and didn't come back, and the notice that told me he'd stopped his dancing. I remember years in empty halls, and wondering how long I could stand it before I shattered under the weight of all that silence. And I remember my uncle Simon and his daughters, who came to visit sometimes, when his liege allowed him the grace to travel. He said family was important, and so he came to me, and he offered me what comfort he could in the spaces where the silence wasn't. But it's all a little distant, like a book I lost myself in for a while, except for the last four months or so."

"Those are the ones that were actually lived," I said.

January nodded. "I was figuring something like that. It's like building an MMO. You know lots of stuff had to happen for the world to exist, but you only flesh out the parts the players will actually encounter. Titania gave us a believable scaffold, and then we spent four months climbing it."

"Forgive me if this is rude," blurted Li Qin. "But who *are* you?"

I blinked. "I beg your forgiveness, Duchess Zhou. I'm so used to you knowing me that I never considered the need for introductions. I am Tybalt, King of Dreaming Cats, husband to October, and about as frustrated by this whole situation as you appear to be."

"Remembering an entirely different version of reality than your spouse does turn out to be somewhat unnerving," she said. "Although in your case, at least you remember that you *have* a spouse. I'm still trying to adjust to the fact that I am apparently happily married to and co-parenting an adopted child with a complete stranger."

"We'll find a way to fix this, Li," said January.

"I hope so, because if we don't, I'm going to have a nervous breakdown."

It was odd, seeing them so tense with each other, so far from the domestic harmony they normally displayed. Their lack of shared experience had to be feeding into that, and it made my heart ache from the familiarity of it all, the desperate little glances January kept giving to her wife, as if she couldn't understand the gulf between them, the tension in Li Qin, who clearly wanted this to be real, but couldn't quite accept it yet. And even as strained as they were, it was nothing compared to the gulf between myself and October. Hopefully, we'd be able to bridge it soon. Hopefully, I could handle things with as much grace as January was managing to display.

I bowed to the both of them, deep and sincere. "You have my gratitude, and my hope that knowing the memory of this world is not lost will enable me to convince August to agree to let us awaken her sister and help end this for all of us."

"I hope so too," said January. "This can't go on."

"No," I agreed. "It can't." And with that, I stepped into shadow, running back toward the dubious comforts of the Golden Shore. I didn't aim for the throne room, where the rest of my party was assembled. It hadn't been long enough for them to come to any sort of resolution, and I wasn't sure I could take another round of frustration and denial. Instead, I aimed for the promenade where we had first arrived, intending to both put myself someplace visible and catch my breath for a moment.

I've never been a fan of running to and fro, dealing with large groups of people. I much prefer the company of the people I consider my own, where I don't have to worry as much about subtle lines of etiquette and offense. It seemed I wasn't alone in that, as when I stepped out of the shadows onto the promenade, I surprised the Windermeres. They were standing near the rail, Arden resting against Nolan's side, his arm protectively around her shoulders.

I had observed them together before, but only ever in a world where she was called upon to be a queen and he was a man out of time, isolated from the people around him by decades spent in an enchanted sleep. They were normally reserved, even with each other, friendly but very aware of their positions and their personal dignity. Here, now, they were both relaxed, leaning on each other for the support they so clearly needed.

Not for the first time, I thought they might be some of the only people to have been well served by this twisted mirror of my Faerie. They could be happy here, if they didn't know any differently. Arden had never been defined by her title, nor Nolan by his position in her Court. It almost hurt, to know that we would be taking this away from them.

Not enough to stay my hand or shift my course, but still, I was aware that not everyone's situation was as straightforward as my own. Nolan lifted his head and turned to squint in my direction.

"You can come out," he said. "I know you're there."

I stepped into the open, leaving the shadows behind, and offered him a shallow bow. He looked at me mildly, neither pleased nor displeased by my arrival.

"What are you doing out here all alone?" he asked.

"I just went to Dreamer's Glass to ask January whether she retained her memories of this world in addition to her restored memories of the true one," I said. "It seemed important, if I were going to reassure August that we didn't seek to take her sister away from her."

"And did she?"

"She did."

"And why is August's comfort with losing her sister more important than anyone else's?" The question was reasonably calm, no anger or malice in his words.

I blinked. "It isn't. I don't—"

"What if not everyone thinks your version of the world sounds like the better one?" He cocked his head, watching me. "Everything I've heard so far makes me think Arden and I got the better deal in this version of things. We didn't get crowns or thrones, but we got to stay together. I didn't sleep away decades while she struggled on her own, no family, no support, no one to grieve our parents with her. We have a job we're good at, lieges who care for us and make sure our needs are met, a community that appreciates us for who we are, and not the titles we wear—this is a good life. Why would we want to trade it for the life you say we're 'supposed' to have?"

"Because it's a lie," I said. "And the Nolan Windermere I know is an honest man. Because people are missing. The inconvenient ones, the ones Titania couldn't wave a hand and explain away. Where I come from, a woman named May is October's sister in every way that counts. Blood if not birth, shared memory, shared history, and so much love between them that no one who sees them together would ever question their familial relationship. In *this* world, she can't leave the Library of Stars, or she begins to dissolve. Among the Cait Sidhe, only the royal cats like myself and Ginevra can leave the Court—the Shadows are closed against all others. Well, if we stop hunting for the rest of our people, stop bringing them what they need to survive, they'll starve, sealed away from the rest of the world. I'm not sure even the night-haunts will be able to reach them. Our allies in the Undersea aren't captivated by Titania's illusions, but they're trapped behind a barrier keeping them from reaching the friends and family members who had the poor fortune to be on land when this all began. Why would you want to trade this life for one you like less when you only have a thin description of it? Because people are *suffering*. Because changelings are suffering. You ask why you'd want to go back to the life I know you from? It's because you're still a good person, no matter what elements of your past have been changed."

"He's right, Nolan," said Arden. She sounded utterly miserable. "I mean, he's a little self-interested here—his wife's one of the people under the spell—but he's right. Too many people are too much worse off in this world, and you know Titania doesn't do anything that doesn't benefit her in some way. If there's a way to break this, we pretty much have to. Even if we have to turn back into people we don't know and don't necessarily want to be, we have to put things back the way they're supposed to be."

"That kind of self-sacrificing bullshit is going to turn you into the Queen in the Mists," said Nolan.

"Mom would be proud of me," said Arden. She looked at me, then, mismatched eyes sharp. "You should get inside, cat-man. They're about to call us all to dinner."

I frowned. "How do you know?"

The promenade door opened, and a servant in the royal livery appeared. "Dinner is prepared," he called, before turning to go.

I raised an eyebrow. Arden smirked.

"I saw him coming through the window," she said. Both of them stepped into portals then, vanishing.

After a beat to laugh at the simplicity of her answer, I followed.

TWENTY-ONE

WE EMERGED INTO A vast ballroom that clung stubbornly to the gold-on-gold color scheme of the rest of the knowe. The lack of variation stole the luster from the precious metal, making it all seem a little dull and undifferentiated. Not that I was here to critique the décor, but the temptation was strong.

The center of the room was occupied by round tables, each large enough to seat ten people without crowding, allowing for a dinner party of roughly a hundred and fifty people. That would be quite an assembly, and made me suspect that they allowed their changelings to dine with the rest of the Kingdom. I had never spent much time in Golden Shore. Everything I'd seen tonight made me think that might need to change in the years to come. I wasn't considering a permanent relocation, but agrarian amusements have always been popular with children. Perhaps October and I could bring our child here for berry-picking and pumpkin selection and all the other little harvest rituals of the modern year.

It was a pleasant thought.

Two of the walls were occupied by banquet stations, laden with food and drink and guarded by casually watchful servers who seemed quite prepared to smack anyone who approached too early with a ladle. I quite approved. A third wall was dominated by a long, shallow stage, of the sort I would have expected to present pantomimes or other small entertainments. Perhaps a band. Instead, the high table had been established there, already occupied by Theron and Chrysanthe, who nodded to me and gestured toward an open table near their seats.

Arden and Nolan appeared on the stage and settled to Chrysanthe's left, Arden pausing first to kiss the Queen on the Golden Shore's cheek. All four of them began a conversation, absorbed in each other.

It was nice, to see a family so united. It was too bad I was here to make sure they wouldn't be a family anymore. Once this was over, Arden and Nolan would go back to the Mists, and this sort of domestic moment would become a diplomatic event between two Kingdoms, not a casual meal.

Or as casual as the Divided Courts ever got, anyway. People began entering through doors arrayed around the edges of the room, nodding politely to the servers as they made for their tables with a minimum of fuss. It seemed tonight's banquet was not an unusual occurrence in this area. I moved to the table Theron had indicated, and issued my own polite nod to the server who came over with a basket of bread and a pitcher of water, leaving them both at the table's center.

This small nicety accomplished, I turned my focus to the crowd.

The people around me were an eclectic mix, purebloods and changelings, even a few merlins with rings of fairy ointment around their eyes. Their clothing was equally varied, ranging from formal gowns and velvet suits to jeans and overalls accented with mud and flecks of straw, as if the people who wore them had just come in from the field.

The main door opened. I looked automatically toward it, and felt the scowl which had only recently left my face reform as the rest of my party stepped into the room, October gawking like a country bumpkin at everything around her. Had she ever been that unpolished, or that incapable of controlling her reactions? Was this some cruel fabrication of Titania's, or was this how Stacy had always seen her childhood friend? Ideas about people that form when we're young are often slow to change.

It was a question for another time. I watched them approach through the crowd, not rising from my seat to pull back their chairs or filling their glasses with water. Ginevra settled beside me, putting a hand gently on my forearm. I resisted the urge to hiss at her, although I did transfer the focus of my glare briefly in her direction, and paused at the sight of the scratch marks on her cheek, red and angry. They had stopped bleeding, but had not yet scabbed over, and were a cruel reminder of my temper.

The others settled, Simon looking anywhere but at October. I had known him more than long enough to recognize the shame in his expression. Something had happened while I was off gathering information. Something that might yet prove important.

I returned my attention to October, staring at her like I thought I could force her to tell me everything I needed to know.

Instead, August elbowed her and gestured to a Satyr in servant's clothing pushing a silver serving cart between the tables. "I think that's the food," said August, a bit too loudly for propriety, but loudly enough to make October crack a small smile and look around.

A second server approached, this one carrying a mug of spiced tea. She began filling the glasses I had neglected. October leaned toward her, asking, "Is it like this every night?"

"Oh, no, miss," said the server. "This is a fancy night, as we've fancy people visiting. A King and Queen of another demesne, our Lord and Lady say. So while we're not full formal, we are a bit nicer than we might otherwise be."

She filled the rest of the glasses at our table and moved on, leaving October to stare after her in clear confusion. Something about that answer had been unexpected enough to be unsettling.

I didn't have time to dwell on what that might have been, as the Satyr had reached us, silver cart heavy with offerings. "What would everyone like tonight?" he asked.

One by one, the others selected their entrees. I received a plate of spaghetti in a rich meat sauce, green peas on the side. Ginevra took a serving of what looked like butternut lasagna. October's selection of salmon and risotto with asparagus pleased me, not only because it showed her taste in food remained the same, but because it meant she was *eating*, something which she was historically inclined to neglect when under any meaningful degree of stress.

"Your story is an interesting one, and has elements to recommend it," said Simon politely, looking across the table at me. "And I do appreciate the aid you've given us thus far in resolving the current unpleasantness. What were you hoping our October could do to help you?"

"I can't dispel the whole world," said October, stabbing her salmon with her fork and not looking up. "It's exhausting, and it *hurts*."

"It wouldn't be if you had access to stronger blood," said Ginevra. "We didn't come here to ask October to remove the enchantment from every person in Faerie one at a time."

"Good," said August sharply.

"We came here to ask her to help us remove it at the source."

October dropped her fork, head snapping up as she stared at Ginevra, and for just a moment, there was a flicker of frustration in her eyes that I recognized, that look she always got when she was being asked to do more than she thought herself capable of. What she had never figured out, although the rest of us knew it well, was that she was capable of nearly anything.

"According to everyone I've spoken to about it, this spell was probably cast by *Titania*," she said, voice low and tight with terrified frustration. "The Mother of Us All."

"In name only," said Ginevra, voice serene, even as she kicked me under the table to keep me silent. I shot her a wounded look. "Not every descendant line springs from her. Your own doesn't."

"She's still the Queen of All Faerie!"

"And that gives her the right to remake us in her image? To destroy our lives and change our memories? She excised entire *lines* from Faerie. She exiled the Cait Sidhe to the Court of Cats and the Roane to the Undersea. What happened to the other shifters? What happened to the other fae she deemed 'bestial' and thus unworthy of a place in her Faerie? Where are *they*? The Cu Sidhe, the Swanmays, the Reynardine, they don't have anything like the Court of Cats that can protect them, but she must have put them *somewhere*."

October sounded almost desperate as she looked back down at her plate and said, "I'm just a changeling. I'm not setting myself against Titania."

I couldn't listen to any more of her putting herself down. If I stayed here any longer, I was going to make things worse by saying things she'd hear as unutterably cruel, even if they were nothing more than honest. I dropped my cutlery and stood, shoving my chair away from the table. "I can't sit here and listen to this," I snapped, and stalked away, heading for the far corner of the room, where the shadows were deepest.

If I took the Shadow Roads, Ginevra would be able to follow me. At the last moment I veered and went out the nearest door instead, heart beating like a drum, so hard I could feel every pulse through my entire body.

The door opened easily and I stepped through, only to find Arden already waiting for me on the other side. I stopped for a moment, taken aback, then continued stalking down the hall.

"It's *rude* to follow people," I said.

"Yeah, well, it's ruder to walk out on a royal banquet without acknowledging your hosts, so I think we're about even here," said Arden, jogging a little to keep up with me. "You really sure you want to go this way? It's going to dump us out in the chicken yard, and there's only so much clucking a person can take before they start developing a real personal aversion to poultry."

I stopped walking, turning to glare at her. "I want to go anywhere that isn't back *there*," I said, doing my best to keep my voice tightly controlled. I wanted to yowl and caterwaul like the cat I was, to protest the loss of my wife and child once again, when this time the only thing keeping us apart was my temper meeting her lack of memory, and the promise I had unwisely allowed Ginevra to extort from me.

Arden looked at me closely. "That's not the full story. What am I missing?"

"We came here to free October from the false Queen of the Mists," I said. "Golden Shore was not our planned destination this night. The intention was that once we were reunited with October and I could confirm for myself that she was well, Ginevra would convince her to go on a quest to find the missing sea witch. I was never going to accompany them."

"Why not? You seem pretty possessive, and that's me being nice about it. I could be a lot nastier if you wanted me to be."

I took a deep breath. "If it were up to me, October wouldn't be going on any quests or taking any risks until this was all over. Unfortunately, it has never been up to me. She's a hero of the realm, named such by the Queen in the Mists, and some things are hers to shoulder, no matter what her loved ones wish."

Arden looked dubious. "There is no Queen in the Mists."

"There is when you sit your father's throne. October restored you to your proper place, and you rewarded her with a position that offers some small protection when her nature attracts trouble like cream attracts cats. Titania can change what's outside as much as she likes. She can't change the fact that October's a hero."

"So why wouldn't you want her to go?" Arden sounded more confused than anything.

"I have reason to be more concerned for her safety than normal, at the moment," I said. January had confirmed that memories from this reality carried over when someone was restored to the proper one, and I didn't want October to get mad at me for telling Arden she was pregnant. "Heroes can still be harmed. It's why we're constantly losing them."

"Guess that's true. You know, where I come from, girls generally don't like it when you glare and yell at them." She shrugged, opening the door to the outside. "You could try being nice to her."

"I *am* trying. It *kills* me to look into her eyes and see no understanding there, no memory of what we are to one another. She will go with Ginevra to retrieve the sea witch, and we will be able to unmake this twisted reflection of the world as it ought to be. We'll be able to go *home*."

"Home," said Arden, more softly. "I don't even know where that is anymore."

"Muir Woods," I said. "You have a beautiful knowe. The carvings reflect the history of your Kingdom, and the halls are filled with light."

"Last time I was there, they were full of dust and screaming," said Arden. "Did the Earthquake happen in your world?"

"Yes," I said. "King Gilad was killed, as was the woman we all widely believed to be his lover."

"She wasn't queen?"

"Not in our reality. He wanted to protect her, so he never took her as his wife. But Sebille was Queen of his household, no question, and those of us who haunted his halls knew that you and your brother were special. You have your father's eyes, and while he didn't claim you, he allowed you far more freedom than the children of a chatelaine would be expected to have."

"I see." Arden hesitated. "Do you know who killed them?"

"We always suspected Oleander de Merelands, but she escaped both capture and punishment in the chaos which followed. She was being controlled by the woman you call the Rose of Winter, which may explain how she so easily evaded consequences for her actions. Regardless, she died before you retook your throne."

"How?" There was a hungry desperation in Arden's voice, like she needed to know there was a world where she hadn't broken Oberon's Law before she reached adulthood.

"In our version of Faerie, Sylvester Torquill has a daughter, Rayseline. She's one of the missing in this world. We hope to find her soon. Oleander convinced her to form an alliance, and when Raysel turned on her, it caught her by surprise. Raysel used one of her own poisoned blades to end her life." It was a dramatically simplified accounting of what had happened, and that made it as accurate as it could be.

"Was Raysel executed?"

"No. She was elf-shot in the aftermath, and was found innocent due to extenuating circumstances. She was awoken right before this all began, and is to spend a year in our household, paying off the offense my lady claimed against her."

"Your world is complicated," said Arden, wrinkling her nose.

"I suppose so. To us, it's just the world we live in. And the complexity is part of how you know it's real."

"I guess I can see that." Arden sighed.

The yard behind the knowe was large, fenced in around the edges with chicken coops. It was late enough that none of the birds were stirring. I could easily see spending a pleasant afternoon here, playing tag with the roosters and prowling the grass for mice. But that was something for the future, when the world was back to normal.

"I will *try* to be kinder to her, if we come back into the same space. I will do my very best not to let my own pain translate into lashing out. But as I cannot guarantee my good behavior, I will remain here, away from her, until I know that she has gone."

"You're staying outside, then?"

I looked around.

"This seems a pleasant-enough space to sit alone with my thoughts. Yes. I'll stay here, for now."

"Gotcha. Well, I'll let you know when they're off, and if Their Majesties want you to come back. That *was* rude, you know."

"They have my apologies," I said, and watched as Arden opened a gate in the air and vanished, gone as quickly as this Arden always was. Was this version of the woman I knew flightier because she wasn't a queen, or because she hadn't gone through a lengthy period of isolation from Faerie, during which she'd been forced to conceal her magic? If anything carried over from this Faerie, I rather hoped it would be the ease with which she moved through our world. She was a good Queen, as monarchs of the Divided Courts went. It would be nice to see her comfortable with herself.

I walked deeper into the yard, listening to the sleepy clucks of the few chickens who were still awake. Most of them were sensible enough to be well asleep. The smell was strong but not overwhelming as I drew closer to their coops; they were clearly well tended, which matched with everything I knew about the fae farming techniques in Golden Shore. If these were Alectryon—fae chickens, for lack of a better term, although that was something like calling Daoine Sidhe "fae humans," which would be a quick way to enrage them—then they were each worth their own weight in gold, even before taking their eggs into account.

Some people said Golden Shore was the wealthiest Kingdom on the West Coast, and I suspected those people were speaking more truth than they realized. It was easy to take the excessive display of gold inside the knowe as the desperate flaunting of scraped-together wealth, and not see it for perhaps inadvisable commitment to a decorating scheme.

I found a bench between two hutches and sat, closing my eyes. The smell and sound of healthy chickens was reminiscent of my youth, when I'd gone often to the Torquill estate to pass my time with children near my own age. Father had allowed it because he saw it as a means for me to form bonds within the future nobility of the Divided Courts, believing it would advance the interests of the Court of Cats.

He would have been so ashamed of me, if he had survived my ascension to the throne. And knowing how badly I would disappoint him only reinforced my conviction that my choices had been good ones. Living my life to disappoint my father had been something to aspire to.

The quiet of the evening was pleasant, as was the wind blowing in from the fields, carrying more interesting scents to tickle my nose and keep me company. Inside, I knew, Ginevra would be attempting to convince October to accompany her on a quest to find the Luidaeg; Simon would, doubtless, be objecting. How I wished I had the right to object along with him! Never mind that in the *real* world, I had the right and he did not. We weren't living by real-world rules right now.

We were living by Titania's rules, and she said it was my place to sit and suffer in silence while my wife ran headlong into certain danger, all unaware of the possible consequences. I tried to think back to the earliest versions of October I had known, young, untested, burning to prove herself. She'd been chaos incarnate in those days, tripping over her own feet and falling on her own knife more often than not. Trouble had been a talent of hers, all the way back to the beginning, and if Magdaleana and May's suppositions about the structure of this spell were correct . . .

The two of them had never forgotten themselves, because Titania's casting had picked them up and shunted them into a place where they'd be harmless. If either of them left the Library, they lost the protection it offered, and they began to be absorbed into the illusion. Whatever hidden place that key unlocked was likely to be very similar to the Library, in that there would have been no point to wiping the memories of its occupants. They would know themselves, and some of them might know October as their enemy.

And here I was, unable to protect her, unable to even tell her what she needed to be afraid of. I had never felt so helpless in my life.

The sweet October air no longer seemed quite so sweet. I opened my eyes and lurched to my feet, graceless and tense. I couldn't go with them. I could, however, remind Ginevra of just how precious her companions were, of how much care she needed to take with them.

I could do that, and she could laugh at me, because I had already stressed that point more times than either one of us could count. I'd just slow her down. I'd just make everything harder than it had to be.

I was already moving, walking stiffly toward the door back into the knowe. Maybe I couldn't do anything to prepare them, but I could at least be there when they left. I could know that this step had been completed successfully. I could *try*.

The door swung open when I was almost there, Garm stepping out into the night. He was alone, no tall, silent Candela loping along behind him, and his motions were tense as he looked around, relaxing only when he caught sight of me and changed his angle so that he was moving directly toward me. I stopped, letting him come.

He stopped a few feet away. "They're gone," he said.

I closed my eyes involuntarily, taking a short, sharp breath. "Did the key work?"

"It did."

I opened my eyes again, looking at him gravely. "Then we have to hope that prophecy and justice will combine, and we'll have them back again. Where is Grianne?"

"She went with them, to help."

"Good. Ginevra is still new enough to her powers that I worry she'll be overwhelmed. If the Luidaeg's memories are muddled . . ."

"If you really thought that was a possibility, there's no way you'd have let this happen. You would have grabbed October and repeated your little 'jumping off a cliff' trick before you allowed her to go into the dark without you."

"Don't think I wasn't tempted," I said, softly.

"Anyway, Arden told me where to find you, and while I know this isn't going to be the best thing you've heard today, Simon and August are waiting inside."

I blinked slowly. "To what end?"

"They want to help." Garm shrugged. "They couldn't go into the dark with October, but they know she might be in danger, and they love her. Not the same way you do, I guess, and maybe their love was fabricated for them by Titania, but it's still love. I guess you could run if you don't feel like being the bigger person and letting them do something to feel like they're being useful. It's not like you can hurry things up."

I looked at him, briefly considering how easily his flesh would rip beneath my claws, but shook the impulse away. He was my ally, and I was not a beast, no matter how Titania would cast me if given the power to do so. Simon and August had done nothing to hurt October. They were victims here as much as she was, and they had done much to make her time under Titania's spell more pleasant than it could have been. They deserved what grace I could extend in their direction.

"I asked April to pass a message to Raj, while I was in Dreamer's Glass," I said. "It's a bit of a stretch, but if this works as I had hoped, our allies from Saltmist may be intending to meet me near Muir Woods, at a beach where we have sometimes come together after an adventure. I have hope that they'll be there. No certainty, but . . . hope."

"You really think they can get out?"

"I think we were told that Moving Day would be the time to move, and while people move in and out of the light—few fae are fond of sunbathing—the barriers on the divide between land and sea are in steady sun from dawn until dusk every day. The spell is eroding in those areas. We know that to be true. I think there's every chance a determined Firstborn and a furious Merrow will be able to batter their way through, even if they can't break much more than a crack in the wall that's been constructed. I think . . ."

I sighed, heavily.

"I think it's worth trying."

"At this point, everything seems worth trying, and if it lets them feel useful, we may as well give it a go." Garm shrugged. "Only thing to worry about is how many of us there are. I don't think you can take everyone through the shadows that distance, and it's not like the Windermeres are going to play shuttle service."

I grimaced. "I have a solution. I doubt any of us are going to like it, but it's worth trying. Have you ever heard of muscle memory?"

Garm looked at me blankly.

TWENTY-TWO

CONVINCING THERON TO LOAN us a vehicle turned out to be the easy part. Golden Shore maintained a small fleet of mortal cars and trucks, modified to strip out as much iron as possible and muffle what was absolutely integral to the engines with rowan and with marshwater mixes.

Convincing Simon to get behind the wheel of a car, well. That was harder.

"I swear, in my world, you know how to operate one of these things," I said, gesturing to the boxy black sedan that had been provided for our use. "You're quite skilled behind the wheel, at least according to October, and as she drives more than anyone else I've ever met, I believe her. We know that memory lives in blood. Even if you don't automatically know how to drive, you should be able to bleed yourself and access the information."

Simon looked unsure. "My lady would *never* . . ."

"Your lady did, in the true Faerie," I said briskly, cutting him off. "Your lady encouraged it, because it made you a more useful tool if you could move among the humans without standing out. This version of October has never learned to fight, but when pressed, her body remembered enough to defend itself. You can drive the car."

Simon frowned, then stuck his arm out toward me, fingers curled and heel of his hand pushed forward.

"Cut me," he said, and it was somewhere between a command and a plea. "If the memories of this 'driving' are in my blood, I need them at the surface."

I extended one claw, carefully nicking the meaty part of his thumb and withdrawing as blood bubbled to the surface. Simon pressed his hand to his mouth, a strangely intimate gesture that reminded me far too deeply of October. I turned my face away as he swallowed.

Then he paled and staggered, catching himself against the car. August cried out, wordless and alarmed, rushing to support her father before he could fall.

"It's all right, poppet," he said, looking at her, a trace of blood still on his lips. "It seems that in the interests of simplicity, some parts of the story were omitted. But he's right. I should know how to operate this contraption. It's a bit more practical than the variety I was inclined to favor."

"Overjoyed as I am to hear you describe driving my car as something you 'should' be able to do, I think this is where I leave you to it," said Theron, tossing Simon the keys. "I'd say to bring it back in one piece, but if everything goes well, this reality may never have existed, and who's to say whether it's a real car or not?"

"Please don't start the philosophical conversation around whether this car is an illusion Titania created," I said. "Let's just get on the road before something else goes horribly wrong."

"Your hospitality has been impeccable, and my house owes you a great debt," said August. She curtseyed to Theron, deeply. "If there's ever anything you need, you only have to call on us."

"Much appreciated," said Theron. He looked to Simon. "You taught this one manners."

"I did my best," Simon agreed. "August, get in the car."

"The doors on the back open," I supplied. "Once inside, pull the strap to your left across your chest and insert the tab into the buckle. In the event of an accident, that belt will keep you from being expelled from the vehicle."

There ended the bulk of my automotive knowledge, and I was proud of myself for being able to convey even that much. August and Garm got into the back seat and fastened their seatbelts. I relaxed, very slightly, and watched as Simon offered his own bow to Theron and got behind the wheel.

This was it, then: the place where I could show just how brave I was capable of being for my beloved's sake. I took a deep, uneasy breath and got into the front passenger seat, fastening my belt and resting my hands against the dashboard.

"I believe we're ready," I informed Simon.

"You know where we're going?"

"Oh, that's easy," said Theron. "Tell the car GPS where you want to go."

"The what?" Simon and I asked, in unison.

Theron leaned in the open driver's-side door, tapping a display on the console. "Where did you say you were meeting your friends?" he asked.

"Muir Beach," I said.

"All right." He kept tapping. A list of names appeared, Muir Beach among them, and he selected it from the display.

"Calculating route," announced the car.

"How . . . novel," I said, stiffly.

Theron withdrew. "Just do what the car says," he said. "It'll get you there."

"I will follow its instructions assiduously," promised Simon, and turned the key, looking somewhat surprised when the engine actually responded. He began pulling away from the parking area, and I was relieved when he didn't hit the King and cause a new problem for us to deal with.

Remaining in human form as Simon drove was difficult, although slightly simplified by the fact that he drove with a degree of exquisite care that October had never demonstrated in her life. Even when she was driving normally, she had a certain disregard for safety that never failed to put my teeth on edge. Simon, on the other hand, drove as if he had just learned the art, coming to a complete stop whenever indicated, observing speed limits, and signaling every lane change. It was almost pleasant in comparison to what I'd been expecting.

Garm and August goggled out the windows, eyes wide, absorbing absolutely everything around us.

"Human police arrest people for driving poorly, do they not?" asked Simon.

"I believe that's a part of their purpose, yes."

"What happens if they decide I'm driving poorly? It's too close to sunrise to safely spin a human disguise and expect it to hold up."

"October frequently casts don't-look-here spells over her car while she drives."

Simon looked alarmed. "That's dangerous! The other drivers won't be able to see me!"

"She says they automatically avoid the space her car occupies, and as she's yet to have a fatal accident, I'm inclined to believe her."

"All right," he said uncertainly. He came to a stop at the next corner, waving a hand and muttering something under his breath. The smell of smoke and cider filled the car, with no trace of oranges, and he sighed before he resumed driving.

"That should do," he said.

"One hopes." I glanced at the dial which displayed our speed. "You can go a little faster."

"Is that safe?"

"No. But the best chance our allies have of making it to the surface comes at sunrise, and if they make it through, they may not be able to stay for long before Titania's spell reasserts itself and puts them back below. If they *can* make it, and stay, that gives us one of Titania's own Firstborn. Even if they can't stay this time, being able to surface once means she might be able to join us later. I'd rather risk collision than missing them."

"Do you even know for sure that they'll be there?"

"No. The wild, unfounded hope is normally October's department, and it feels odd to depend upon it now. Still, if hope is what we have, then hope must be what we cling to."

Simon looked thoughtful, and pressed down harder on the gas.

According to the car's map, which helpfully provided verbal instructions every time we needed to do something, we had started almost five hours' driving distance from Muir Beach. Even with Simon going as fast as he was comfortable, making it by sunrise was going to be a close thing.

Time isn't always aligned between the mortal world and the Summerlands, but the duration of holidays and celebrations tends to be set to the mortal clock. We had departed from Golden Shore about an hour after midnight. If we encountered no difficulties and didn't stop for any reason, we might be able to reach the beach before the dawn arrived and tore down or eroded all standing illusions.

And if we didn't, we could just hope that anyone who managed to make it to the surface would also be able to stay, at least long enough for us to reach them.

I continued to grip the dashboard, trying not to look out the windows, trying not to think about how much I hated cars. Oh, October was going to laugh and laugh when she heard about this. She was going to consider it the funniest thing that had ever happened, worthy of being commemorated in story and in song. After the number of times

I had insisted on taking the shadows rather than allowing her to drive me, when she remembered knowing how to drive and had an actual license, this was going to be endlessly delightful.

I smiled a little, relaxing as I considered her with her memory restored, laughing uproariously at my predicament. Oh, so much of this was going to be funny in retrospect, even as so much of it might rouse her to towering heights of rage.

Human transport was comfortable, certainly. There was air, and light, and no need to keep pouring magic into the journey. That was where the advantages, such as they were, stopped. Human transport was *slow*. We had gone little more than an hour before August began to snippily ask how much farther we had to go, and less than an hour after that, Garm joined in, the two of them turning the car into a symphony of discontent. The roads were clear; we passed human cities and dark farmsteads without a whisper or a trace. What few other cars we saw were mostly heading in the opposite direction, headlights slashing through the night for a few seconds before they, too, were gone.

And still we weren't fast enough, and still they endlessly complained, until I slumped down in my seat and muttered to Simon, "Sometimes I am reminded that having children is not always the blessing we would make it out to be."

He laughed, sounding merry and almost startled, like he hadn't been expecting me to speak to him. I looked at him more thoughtfully.

"What did you see in the blood?"

"I focused on the driving, to regain those memories," he said, keeping his eyes on the road. "But the driving came with some other aspects of the life you say I once lived. I still served my lady, but she felt more free to use me cruelly."

"More free? You mean she uses you cruelly here?"

Simon looked uncomfortable. "I mean I have felt, at times, that she was constrained by outside factors to keep her ambitions curtailed, and as a consequence, did not put me to all the uses she desired. I saw myself in the car, driving as you said, on my way to sow her influence in the fertile soil of distant courts. I seemed to have no family ties to bind me? And at times a strange woman rode with me, unfamiliar in the present but all too familiar in memory."

"Oleander," I supplied.

"The assassin?"

"You kept close company with her in my Faerie, at the command of your patron," I said. "It wasn't the most pleasant period in your life."

"I can't say I'm eager to know more," he said, sourly. Then: "I saw

October, but only from a distance, as if I had no excuse for approaching her, and I didn't see August at all."

"She was missing for much of the time those memories would be drawn from," I said.

"Ah. And I saw you, beside October. You looked devoted to her; if you found a way to lie to me via your own memory, it seems you also found a way to lie through mine. I suspect not, however. I suspect you are exactly who you've claimed to be. I'm sorry this is happening."

"Is that why you didn't expect me to talk to you?"

"In part, yes. I don't think we have the best relationship in your Faerie."

"No, not precisely, but it's not as bad as it once was, either." I was very aware that the muttering in the back had stopped, August now paying close attention to every word I said. "You were a boy when we first met, as was I, children in Londinium, wild things running feral through your family's estate. We weren't close as we grew, and when we met again as adults, you were a married man, a father, and quite content with where your life had gone. You had no need for your frustrating childhood companion, and Amy was . . . less than enamored with any reminders of those days. I let you be, and remained at a distance as the life you'd built so carefully began to crumble. First your best friend married a mermaid and went to the sea, and then—"

"My best friend—you mean Patrick? Patrick Twycross?"

"Yes. You know him in this Faerie as well?"

"I did. He died in the Earthquake, crushed when King Gilad's knowe collapsed. If he'd been willing to take my lady's offer of a place in Goldengreen, he might have lived. But instead, he was lost."

Oh, wasn't the real world going to be a revelation for this version of Simon? "Things didn't follow that precise path in the world I know," I said, delicately evading the topic. "But he left, and your service to the woman you call 'patron' became more intense and frequent, until it seemed to strain your relationship with Amy. Things might have recovered, had August not vanished during the Earthquake, leaving you desperate to find her. Your patron offered support and aid, if only you would give yourself over to her will completely. So you did."

I stopped there. Simon's hands tightened on the wheel.

"And?"

"She lied. The aid she gave was minimal at best, designed to keep you in her service as long as possible. She gave you as a pet to her favorite assassin, Oleander de Merelands, and together, the two of you terrorized the Mists in her name for decades. You broke your brother's heart. Your wife did not divorce you, for Amy never gives up what she owns, but for a long time, you were estranged from her, and my October grew to adulthood not knowing your relationship to one another. She has only recently begun to acknowledge you as any sort of presence in her life."

"All of which combined would explain the way you looked at me in those memories, like I was a danger who needed to be kept as far as possible from your family." Simon sighed. "More and more, I come to believe that you're right—your Faerie, being the original, needs to be restored, or many more will suffer than already have. But there are aspects of it that wound me, even held at such remove."

"I don't see why we *have* to put their Faerie back," said August from the backseat, voice low and dangerous. "Can't we just make Titania stop hurting people, and then fix the Faerie we have?"

"There are aspects of this Faerie that are entirely incompatible with the real one," I said, slowly. "Even if we could, as you so naively suggest, somehow make Titania stop, we would no longer belong to the same reality as the Faerie outside the range of her enchantment. What would happen to us when we inevitably came into contact with the world unchanged? With the nobles who expected us to honor agreements we no longer remembered, or with the Firstborn furious that their descendant lines had been erased within this bubble? We would become a thorn jammed into the lion's paw. Infection would follow, and rot, and we would inevitably be pulled loose. It's better that we end this quickly and of our own volition, when there remains a chance that we might heal."

"I hate it," said August.

"That's fair enough," I allowed. "No one is asking you to feel otherwise. And at the same time, you can hate something—you can hate something with every fiber of your being, rage against it in every possible way—and still see it for the best choice in a bad situation. I've been forced to agree to things I hated on a fairly frequent basis, because of that terrible truism."

"It's not fair."

I laughed. "Now I *do* believe you for my October's sister. She makes that complaint with far more commonality than anyone else I've ever known."

August slumped back in her seat, arms crossed, sulking. Garm frowned and watched her, but didn't say anything.

As that had quieted their endless complaining, I didn't object. We rode the rest of the way to Muir Beach in silence, reaching the parking lot reserved for beach-goers as the sky was beginning to grow light around the edges, darkness fading into a deep, plummy blue as the stars winked out of view.

Simon pulled into an open space even as the console announced our arrival at our destination, turning off the engine and getting out of the car. The rest of us followed him. August pointed at a sign.

"This says the beach isn't open yet," she said. "Is that going to be a problem?"

"According to October, the human authorities are unlikely to patrol this area so close to sunrise. If they see the car at all, they may issue a ticket, which it will fall upon Theron to pay. We won't be here."

"Where are we going?"

"There." I pointed to the waterline. It wasn't far, maybe five hundred feet or so by walkway, which was open and clear, the wood lightly dusted with sand. "Simple don't-look-here spells will keep anyone from seeing us when we don't want them to."

"Or I could throw up a screen to keep any humans who chance by from noticing us," offered Garm. He shrugged when we all turned to look at him. "Illusions are sort of my thing. Let me feel useful."

"All right," I said. "Shield us."

Garm closed his eyes and lifted his hands. We were in sight of the sea, but for a moment, all that rose around us was marsh, the smell of moss and stagnant water. Nothing changed. Garm lowered his hands again.

"There," he said, with some satisfaction. "Anyone looking in our direction won't see anything out of the ordinary, and we'll be able to conduct our business."

"Assuming these allies of yours show up," said August. "Are you sure they got your message?"

"Quite," I said, and started down the walkway, forcing the others to follow or be left behind. "Whether they'll be able to reach the surface is another question, and open for discussion until the sunrise passes."

"If they don't show up, what happens then?" asked Simon.

"We head for the Library of Stars," I said. "Magdaleana will be able to confirm the truth of what I've told you. The Library's nature prevents Titania's enchantment from reaching past the doors, and those who dwell there do so all unchanged."

Really, we would be keeping ourselves occupied until Ginevra and October returned with the sea witch. It would prevent us—prevent *me*—from dwelling too deeply on the situation at hand, and that could only be to our benefit. It never does to wallow. As these past four months had provided me with plenty of time for wallowing, I was quite happy to play at purposefulness for the benefit of October's family, keeping them from joining me in fretting themselves into despair.

The walkway was as smooth and stable as it appeared, bearing us down to the sandy shore without misstep. A few early beachcombers were already out, walking the tideline, scanning for shells and washed-up treasures. None of them so much as glanced in our direction, which could have been Garm's magic, but could honestly just have been human self-absorption. I am forever impressed by how well they can close out the rest of the world.

Gulls and ravens wheeled far overhead, and I spared a thought for Jasmine, whose whereabouts were still unknown. I should have asked after her while we were in Golden Shore, just for my own peace of mind, but what good would that have done, really? Knowing she was there wouldn't bring her back to us, or let May out of the Library.

No. It was better to focus on finishing this. We walked down to the edge of the water, watching the waves crash against the shore, and stopped.

"Okay, now what?" asked August.

"I passed the message along," I said. "They have one of the First-born among their number. She's been testing the barriers between land and sea since this all began. If anyone can find a way through, it's her."

"How will she find you?" asked August.

I looked at her flatly. "Magic."

August had the grace to look mildly embarrassed as she turned her attention back to the sea. "I guess it just seems a little impossible that the Undersea still exists. It's been lost for longer than I've been alive. Could it really have been out there this whole time?"

"You thought the Cait Sidhe were lost as well," I said.

Above us, the sky continued to grow lighter, and between one breath and the next, sunrise hit like a hammer. The air blazed with the smell of ashes, magic dissolving around us, and I saw Garm grit his teeth as he fought to keep the screen which shielded us from dissolving. Not many can hold an illusion through the dawn. I suppose the Gwragen are among that fabled number, because as the pressure of the dawn began to fade, the humans who walked the shore continued to ignore us.

August gasped, staggering backward, and I realized this version of her might never have experienced a mortal dawn before. What cause would Amandine have for taking her perfect toy of a daughter out among the humans at sunrise? What benefit could it bring her?

There was so much about the world that August had yet to learn, and some of it would hurt.

That thought made me stand a little straighter, another thought occurring to me. I had asked Raj to tell Peter where I would be and when, and asked for Amphitrite by name. I hadn't asked that she come alone, if it was possible for her to come at all. If she did come, she might well come with company.

"Simon," I said, voice low.

"Look!" He pointed to the water, where a blue-silver glow was starting to form beneath the surface, glimmering and effervescent. It was like looking through a hundred sheets of diamond gauze, each invisible on its own, all combining to form something of breathtaking beauty.

"*Simon*," I said again. He glanced at me, clearly startled, as the glow intensified, moving swiftly upward like a falling star in reverse.

It was moving too fast. My heart sank, and I bit off an oath because I should have realized my omission sooner; now there was no more time.

Still, I had to try. "The Merrow Firstborn may not come—" I began.

The glow struck the surface and kept rising, bulging upward until it became a gleaming pearl of force, pure magic held together by Amphitrite, who stood at its center with her arms straight out to her sides, framing the space through sheer force of will. Ripples of distortion raced across its surface, like oil shimmering atop clear water, and it was obvious that the world was trying to repel her creation, at least to some degree. With an expression of intense concentration, she gave a mighty shove, and the bubble burst, popping in a glittering hail of droplets that left three people standing at the surface.

Amphitrite slumped forward almost instantly, resting her hands against her knees as she breathed heavily in and out, trying to compose herself. It didn't seem to be going well for her. She looked shaken, to a degree that was frankly terrifying in one of the Firstborn, who are supposed to be endless wells of power. But then, she had just squeezed her way through a spell originally cast by Titania herself: maybe a little bit of unsteadiness was warranted. She didn't fall down, which was probably a good sign.

Behind her, Patrick and Dianda looked around with eyes full of awe and wonder. They hadn't been sure she'd get them to the surface. They'd decided to come along, willing to take the risk for the sake of their missing loved ones, but that didn't mean they'd been *sure*.

Simon made a choked-off sound. I grimaced.

"—alone," I finished. "You remember, I told you, my version of you was heartbroken when his best friend left him to marry a mermaid and live in the sea."

Simon took a stumbling, unsteady step forward. I caught his arm, preventing him from wading out into the water, and he shot me a poisonous glance.

"Let go," he said.

"Simon, you don't understand," I said.

"I understand well enough," said Simon. He yanked his arm out of my grasp. "I understand that Patrick is not dead, and I haven't seen him in over a hundred years, and I don't intend to go another minute without embracing him."

"That's good to hear," said Patrick, walking across the surface of the water toward us. They had come up close enough to the shore that the water should have reached their knees at the very most, but instead, all three of them balanced atop it, light as soap bubbles, even the clearly exhausted Amphitrite.

Simon watched his approach with wide eyes and, when Patrick was close enough, threw himself into the other man's embrace, the two of them holding each other so tightly that I would have been hard-pressed to work a sigh between them.

"Oh, I missed you," murmured Patrick, and kissed him.

And all hell broke loose.

TWENTY-THREE

SIMON RECOILED, AN EXPRESSION of shock and abject horror on his face. "*Sir*," he said, in a strangled tone. "I am a *married man*."

"Tybalt, what is this?" asked Patrick, mingled pain and anger in his eyes as he looked past Simon to me. "When you called for us to come, we thought—"

"Technically, I only called for Amphitrite," I said. "I wasn't sure she'd be able to make the journey, even alone, much less with passengers."

Dianda was storming toward us across the water, a look of burning fury on her face. She stopped when she reached Patrick, putting an arm protectively around his shoulders and directing a glare in our direction. "What, we weren't suffering enough, so you had to make sure we felt every bit of the rejection and isolation you did?"

"It wasn't my intention," I said.

Simon was still moving backward, away from Patrick, seeming utterly mortified. His hand shook as he touched his lips, and in that gesture I could see the love he'd pushed so carefully away, lest it anger the woman he had already pledged to honor all his days. Simon had loved Patrick long before they were parted, or their current relationship would never have been able to work.

Dianda, on the other hand, was only now learning to love the strange and slippery man whose heart had accompanied her first husband beneath the sea, and from the way she was glaring now, endlessly fierce in the defense of her family, it seemed that love might not long survive. I stepped forward, holding up my hands in a placating gesture.

"Dianda, I'm sorry," I said. "I should have guessed sooner that you would come to the surface with Amphitrite; I should have asked Simon and August to wait in the car, or at least warned them in more detail of how you might react to seeing them."

"How would you expect us to react?" demanded Dianda. "They're our *family*!"

"They don't remember that," I said. "If it helps at all, October is just as mistrustful of me. Titania took care to split up families when she thought she could get away with it. You aren't unique."

"But we're the ones who fought our way here from the bottom of the sea," said Dianda sourly. "Why did you even call us here?"

"October and Ginevra have gone to find the sea witch," I said. "We believe Titania intends to Ride at midnight on Hallows' Eve, as is traditional. I had hoped Amphitrite, as her daughter, might be able to help us stop her. If we can't break Titania's Ride, she'll lock Faerie into this form, and sunder the Undersea from the land forever."

"That might be better for your survival," said Dianda. "Hard to drown a man without the depths."

"Simon didn't mean to hurt you," I said.

She shrugged, glaring at me with hopeless rage. "Who said I was talking about him? And why should I believe you?"

"You can't drown Tybalt," said Pete. "That would be death by water."

"There's one way we can prove it," said August, shaking off her shock and stepping forward. She eyed Patrick and Dianda warily, like they were dangerous beasts of a variety she had never seen before. I turned to look at her. She met my eyes, and shrugged. "You keep telling me I can do it. Maybe now's when we need to prove it."

"I thought you were concerned that memories of this world might be lost in restoring memories of the other," I said.

"Everything you've said about that other world tells me that my father still knows and loves me there; that my father will *always* know and love me, no matter what," she said. "You can't say the same for my sister. The situation isn't the same."

Simon turned toward her, naked desperation on his face. "Please," he said, in a half-strangled voice. "Please, do it."

"I'll need a knife," said August.

Amphitrite pushed herself upright and plucked one of the scales from the outside of her thigh, lobbing it underhand toward the shore. It stretched and grew as it flew through the air, finally embedding itself in the sand as a blade easily six inches long, with a handle of unpolished shell. August bent to pull it loose. The blade gleamed oil-dark and filled with rainbows, like the rest of Amphitrite's scales.

August glanced at her in surprise. Amphitrite shrugged.

"Your mother is my sister on the paternal side, and I didn't attend the presentation of your birth, which means I never gave you a proper gift. Call this a birthday present with several decades of accumulated interest on top, and mind the edge. It's sharp." She grimaced then, putting her hands back on her knees. "And whatever you kids are planning to do, get around to doing it, okay? Mom's trying to put me back where she thinks I belong. It's not guided—if she were doing this consciously, I'd already be five fathoms down and dropping—but even a reflex is going to push me out sooner or later, and without me to play anchor, we're all going down. Hurry it up."

August nodded, looking at the knife in her hand. She looked back up at Simon, paling slightly at the thought of what she was about to do.

"Please," he repeated.

She nodded with sudden resolve, and slashed the knife across the palm of her free hand. Like October, she cut with no concern for muscle or tendon; she would heal too quickly for any permanent damage to be done, and cutting her palm meant she could cup her fingers and capture some measure of the blood before it dripped away. Raising her hand to her mouth, she began to gulp down the blood, quickly, not allowing herself to hesitate.

Then she lifted her head and looked at Simon, reaching out with her bloodied, already-healed hand as if she were grabbing something hanging in the air between them, something the rest of us couldn't see. Simon stiffened but didn't scream. One more argument for memories that couldn't be enchanted away.

So far as I was aware, Eira had never touched him physically. Oleander, however, had been more than commonly fond of pain, and there was no way she'd have been able to restrain herself for all their years together. He had been trained not to make a sound when he was suffering, even if he didn't remember that training in any conscious way.

Sometimes I rather thought it was a pity that Oleander had died so quickly and relatively easily. Her poisons had not been kind. She had still deserved much worse.

Tears appeared at the corners of Simon's eyes as he continued to stand rigid, staring at his daughter. August was nowhere near so stoic. Even as she increased her pulling gestures, she began to keen, a high, pained sound that rose and fell like a Banshee's wail, lacking only its magical pull to complete the comparison. She kept pulling, the knife falling from her hand as she transferred to a two-handed grip, until suddenly she stumbled backward and began shaking her hands frantically, like she was trying to chase away a terrible case of frostbite.

Simon took an unsteady step forward before collapsing into the sand, barely managing to catch himself. Patrick pulled away from Dianda and rushed to help him up, while Dianda followed more cautiously, staying close enough to defend, but not close enough to interfere.

Simon moaned as Patrick pulled him upright, clutching at the other man's arms like they were a lifeline, or an anchor that could keep him from blowing away in the storm that now raged in his expression. He lifted his face to Patrick's, and for just a moment, his eyes cleared.

"Patrick," he said, in a voice so filled with love and relief that I had to turn away. I longed to hear his daughter speak my own name in that tone.

Speaking of daughters, August was still shaking her hands frantically. I walked over to her and took one of them in my own, hissing at the feeling of her frigid fingers. "You're freezing," I said. "August, what . . . ?"

"Pulling the spell away was like trying to juggle snowflakes with my bare hands," she said, fingers tightening around mine as she sought my warmth. There was nothing inappropriate or intimate about the gesture: she was a wounded animal, trying frantically not to freeze. "It *hurt*."

Dianda had reached Simon and Patrick, and the three of them were clinging to each other, swaying slightly, like none of them were entirely confident in their ability to stay upright. Dianda murmured a question, and Simon answered, neither letting either of the other two go. It seemed, for the moment, that they were well-content as they were.

Which left only the exhausted, irritated Firstborn in need of my attention. I straightened, still allowing August to cling to my arm and leech my warmth as I turned to Amphitrite.

The water around her was starting to shimmer again, although the light this time was less silver-white and more petaled pink, like something red as roses was rising from the deeps. The glitter rose in a spray every time a wave broke nearby, scintillating in the air. It was a beautiful effect. It would have been easier to admire if I hadn't been quite sure it presaged something dire.

Amphitrite met my eyes. "Did you call me here for a reason, cat, or did you simply want to facilitate the world's most awkward and temporary reunion?"

"I wanted to tell you that we'd managed to locate October, and she and Ginevra are off to find your sister," I said. "They have a Summer Roads key, and were able to open the door onto the Thorn Road, so they're running somewhere in the dark now, trying to locate the sea witch wherever she's been sealed away."

"You sound remarkably calm about all this."

"Oh, I'm not." The admission came easy, and was possibly the most honest thing I'd ever said. "I am nothing but endless screaming and the sack of Gaul inside. She doesn't know me. She looks at me and doesn't know me. She doesn't *trust* me, which shouldn't be a shock when I'm a stranger, and yet hurts in a way I could never have anticipated. And still. Losing my temper does nothing to hasten this toward its end, and can do much to slow it. If I seem calm, it's because I am reserving my rage for those who deserve to receive it, and while you, lady, deserve all good things in this world, I do not count my anger among them."

Amphitrite threw back her head and laughed. It was something of a bittersweet joy, to realize that I could still make the Firstborn laugh.

When she calmed herself, she looked to me. "That's the only reason you called me here?"

"I truly did hope you would be able to break the shell on the sea and assist us in stopping your mother. Beyond that, I must remain busy, and must keep my allies busy, or we'll all go mad with fretting over the quests we can't be part of, the dangers we can't be shields against. I should have realized you would bring the Lordens. That I didn't is entirely my error, and you have my apologies."

"It seems to have worked out for the best," she said, jerking her chin toward the trio.

"It may help convince August to unbind her sister, if nothing else," I said. "She was afraid the enchanted would lose their memories of the world that never was if the spell was broken."

"And she and October never had time in the real world to get to know each other," said Amphitrite, with what sounded like genuine understanding. I blinked. She shrugged. "I'm the rejected daughter of possibly the worst mother to have ever lived—and it's not like Faerie encouraged good parenting skills. I grew up with a few dozen of my stepsiblings to answer when I cried, and most of my mother's other kids won't even acknowledge me. They're assholes, it's not like I *want* a solid relationship with most of them, and yet it still hurts when they don't want me. August has a shitty mom and only one sister, and in this world, that sister loves her. She wants to know her sister's going to keep loving her when things go back to what you say is normal. It's completely understandable."

I glanced at August, who turned her face away, cheeks burning red.

"Everyone wants to be loved, Tybalt. You're climbing the walls because your wife doesn't love you here. This whole fake Faerie is just my mom trying to make people forget that she's a shitty person and a shittier parent long enough to love her for a while. Well, August's afraid that if October loves *you*, there won't be enough love left for *her*." Amphitrite stopped and grimaced, expression going pained. "Patrick, Dianda, bus is about to go back down below. I'm not sure I can leave you here, and if I'm not with you to blunt the impact, when Mom's spell shoves you back to the bottom, it's going to hit like an iceberg."

"Wait, please—please, wait," said Simon, as they began to pull regretfully away from him. "Take me with you. I want to go home. I don't want to stay here with . . ." He grimaced. "If either of the women who think they hold my fealty calls upon me, I'm not sure I'll be able to answer believably."

"Simon, I need you to tell me something right now, and tell me truthfully," said Dianda, putting a hand on his shoulder. "Has either of them touched you? At all? Even if you thought you wanted it at the time, if either of them has touched you, I'll . . . I don't even know. Amy is presumably as enchanted as everyone else, but I don't know if that will let me forgive her."

"Tybalt says the spell began four months ago," said Simon. "That matches the texture of my memories. Everything before four months ago runs parallel to the things I know really happened, the things I lived through. *Those* memories have texture and weight. The memories Titania created are more like a film being projected on the wall. They're still accessible, still mine, but they didn't *happen* the same way. My memories of the last four months have the same texture and weight as my real ones."

"You're not answering me," said Dianda.

"I'm trying to," said Simon. "Please, love. Patience."

The "love" seemed to calm her. She relaxed a little, still watching him.

"In the last few years, Amandine has been called more and more often to fiefdoms outside the Mists, to attend upon their changelings. I'm not sure what benefit Titania found in seeding discontent within her fictional ideal, but she did, and so Amy has been very busy. She has been at the tower very little these past four months, and when she was there, she was too tired and distracted by her duties to call me to the marital bed. Indeed, in my memory of that other world, she hadn't called me so since October's birth. I had begun to fear that carrying another man's child, even a human man's child, had soured her love for me. Now it seems that Titania was simply clever enough not to cross certain boundaries where I was concerned."

"She's not smart enough to leave my family alone, but she's smart enough to know I'd kill her," said Dianda.

Simon touched her cheek. She leaned in, then, and kissed him like she thought she might never see him again, not in all the time the world had remaining. Patrick stayed close, putting his hands on both their shoulders, keeping their circle intact. I looked away. This felt too personal for me to share.

If I hadn't turned my head, I might not have seen the people now coming down the beach toward us. It was a small group, maybe ten in all, but they were moving directly toward where we were gathered, and the fact that none of the other beachgoers seemed to see them told me without question that they were fae.

"And that's our cue," said Amphitrite. "Dianda, I can't hold us here." The rosy glow in the water around her was getting brighter and brighter, shining above the surface now, glittering like a crystalline shell that extended almost to her knees. She was looking more strained by the second.

"We're coming," said Dianda.

"I am your *First*, and I am telling you to come *faster*," said Amphitrite tightly.

"Can we take him with us?" asked Dianda.

August made a wordless sound of dismay, finally pulling her hands from mine. Her fingers no longer felt like icicles, which was something; they were still too cold, but the worst of it seemed to have passed.

"No!" she half-shouted, half-yelped.

Dianda and Patrick both looked at her and grimaced, unhappily. "Can't you give yourself your memories back?"

"It doesn't work like that," said August. "I'd need October to break the enchantment. And I'm still not sure I want to."

"You will," said Patrick. "I promise, you will. Simon, even if Amphitrite could take you down with us—"

"Big 'if,'" said Amphitrite. "He belongs here, we don't. Come *on*."

"Even *if* she could, we couldn't force August to go. Do you want to leave her alone up here?"

"No," said Simon, voice very small. He turned to look at August, repeating, with more strength, "No. I'm sorry, but no."

"Sweetheart, that's the right answer," said Dianda. "We'll be back as soon as we can. It should be easier now that we know it's possible."

Amphitrite grimaced, making me wonder how true that statement really was. Dianda and Patrick gave Simon one last quick hug before retreating across the water to the increasingly bright pink glow. Amphitrite looked at me and nodded, an acknowledgment and gesture of respect.

"Stay safe," she said. "Try, at least."

The light got brighter. Then it flashed, and they were gone, leaving the surface of the water smooth and undisturbed.

Simon stared at the place where they had been, tears running down his cheeks as he put one hand over his mouth. August moved to stand beside him, putting a hand on his arm, and he whirled around, burying his face in her shoulder as he pulled her tight against him.

"Um, Tybalt?" Garm shifted to stand closer to me, glancing uneasily at the approaching group. They were still too far out for me to see any details, but they appeared to be moving in some sort of formation, and I could tell they were all wearing the same thing, a combination of dark gray trousers and lighter-colored tops. Beyond that, nothing was clear.

"We should go," I said. "Simon, August, come. We're going back to the car."

I started back across the beach, heading for the pedestrian walkway. The others moved with me, Simon leaning against August, both of them clearly shaken by what they had just seen. At least there was no question left of whether they believed me, and now we knew that August's magic extended to the same unweaving trick as her sister. We would be able to release October, once she granted her consent.

I would have her back again.

As soon as we started to move, the people who'd been approaching changed trajectory to intercept us, moving faster, still attracting no notice from the people around them. "Garm?" I asked, tightly.

"Yes?"

"Illusion?"

"Let me check." He squinted at the group for a moment, then nodded. "Yes. A strong one. Not as good as mine, but then, it doesn't need to be. They're still obscured, and that's what matters."

"Can you hide us from them?"

"Not while they're looking right at us. I'm good. I'm not so good that they wouldn't notice the people they're moving toward blinking out of existence."

Out of . . . "I have an idea," I said. "It's going to be dreadful, and you're all going to hate it, but it might get us away from here. Simon, take my hand."

I reached behind myself, and was relieved when I felt Simon's hand in mine, clammy but grasping me firmly.

"Hold on to August," I instructed. "Garm, grab her sleeve."

Bemused, he did as I said, and we continued walking, now joined in a rough chain.

"Everyone, take a deep breath," I said.

The beach was littered with driftwood, clumps of kelp, and the remains of bonfires, black char standing out against the pebbled sand. Nothing tall enough to cast a massive shadow, but then, I have never needed a *massive* shadow.

Garm, who had been Grianne's friend and comrade before I entered the picture, realized what I was about to do even before I did it. He inhaled and exhaled several times in quick succession before taking a massive breath. Simon and August were slower to catch on, but I waited until I heard them both inhale sharply, then stepped forward into the nearest shadow.

It was small, cast by a piece of half-burnt driftwood. That, combined with the strain of pulling three people in my wake, made the transition less like a simple step into the dark and more like pitching forward, a moment in terrible freefall before my feet hit the ground. Simon's hand slipped in mine. I clamped down, holding on as tightly as I could, and had to hope the others had the sense to do the same.

Distance is different in the shadows. It still exists, but much as the Summerlands are smaller than the mortal world, the shadows are smaller than the Summerlands. Traveling from one place to another happens more quickly in the dark, if it happens at all. We didn't need to go far, or I would never have attempted this.

Exhaustion is a risk when you run too hard along the Shadow Roads. Cait Sidhe have died there, pushing themselves too hard and collapsing in the dark, where their bodies may go unfound forever. Royal cats are blessed with more than the standard number of lives, although that number is far from infinite, and I had exhausted myself to the point of death at least once before. I got better. There was no guarantee that it would happen again, or for any of my semi-willing passengers, none of whom fully understood the risk they were taking.

I used the fear of something going wrong to push myself as far as I could safely go, then toppled out of the shadows and onto the soft, dense, evergreen-scented mat of fallen needles covering the ground. I rolled onto my back, gasping for air, and tried to count the equally winded voices around me, verifying that no one had been left behind.

One, two . . . and there was three. I didn't need to go back into the dark to hunt for a lost companion. I felt an obligation to Garm, who had been my first unexpected ally in this strange new version of our world; if I'd managed to lose August or Simon, October would murder me. So really, I would have returned to the shadows no matter which of them had managed to lose their hold.

All the better that I didn't need to. I stared up at the redwoods looming all around us, trying to steady my breathing and figure out where the hell we were at the same time.

August, unsurprisingly, was the first to recover. I heard her scramble to her feet, kicking needles in all directions. "Father?" she asked. Then, in a voice gone shrill with panic: "*Father!*"

Simon coughed as she dropped back to her knees, presumably beside him. "I'm fine, August, I'm fine. That was just a longer run with less breathing than I'm used to . . . Squeezing the air out of me won't make it better."

"Oh, *Father*, you frightened me," August moaned.

"I'm sorry, my dear." He wasn't coughing anymore, although he was still wheezing. Then he chuckled, sounding a little strained. "It's very odd to hear you call me that, even with four months of memory telling me it's correct. I've always been 'Papa' to you. Amy hated it so much that I allowed you to be informal with me . . ."

His voice trailed off, tone turning perplexed.

Garm groaned. "Tybalt? You alive over there?"

"Sadly, yes." I pushed myself into a sitting position, shaking frost and redwood needles out of my hair, and looked around. We were in the clearing that should have housed Arden's knowe. A reasonable destination for me to have landed upon, all things considered. At least it was someplace I knew.

"I didn't know you could *do* that!"

"Technically, I can't," I said. "The Shadow Roads are difficult to traverse with one passenger. Three is beyond even my capabilities. If we hadn't been going such a short distance, this would have had a very different outcome."

Garm blanched. "You mean you weren't sure?"

"I was sure those people were coming for us, and that if I didn't do something, we were going to be taken." I pushed myself to my feet, relieved when the world only spun a little in response. "Further, I was sure that once my strength began to flag, I'd be able to throw us out of the shadows. I only had to hope we'd find sufficient distance first."

"Well done," said Simon, looking at me over the top of August's head. She was clinging to him like she had no intention of ever letting go.

"It would have been better if not needed," I said. "How were we followed here?"

The answer would have to wait, as the sound of boots marching through the undergrowth reached us. I looked to Garm, gesturing frantically. He nodded and began waving his hands, the haze of an illusion settling over us and erasing my companions from sight. I was sure that from their perspective, the same had happened to me; we were, for the moment, invisible.

None too soon. Four men in the livery of the Mists emerged from the wood, looking around the clearing with wary eyes.

"Any sign of them?" asked one.

"No," said another.

"But we know they came this way," said the first.

I narrowed my eyes. How did they *know*? None among their number appeared to be Candela, and even if they had been, Grianne had given no indication of being able to follow my movements through the shadows. If they were tracking us somehow, it would have to be through other means.

More motion in the trees presaged three more guards entering the clearing. I knew one of them: Lowri, a Glastig who had been serving the false Queen when first I made her acquaintance. Her clothing was shabbier than that of her companions, her hooves unpolished and her gear generally run-down. They were doubtless offering her the treatment they felt she deserved as a descendant of Maeve, something that seemed confirmed when she ducked her head and waited to be addressed.

"Yes?" asked the first guard, brusquely.

"All pardon, milord; the beach approach is clear," said Lowri. "They aren't there."

"They must be here." The man strode to the center of the clearing, placing his hands on his hips. "Attention! You are commanded to surrender yourselves, in the name of the Queen of the Mists!"

What name? The woman he served had given up her name in exchange for a crown, a bargain she had never seemed to regret in the time that I had known her.

He held his stance for several seconds, turning slowly to glower at every inch of the clearing. "Her Majesty understands that some of you may have been led astray by undesirable elements, and will be merciful if you surrender yourselves. I, however, am standing in a filthy forest surrounded by the least of Her guard, and have no desire to return to the Rose of Winter with empty hands."

Wait. Did these guards serve the false Queen, or Evening? And in this world, was there truly any difference? If Evening felt herself free to live as a Firstborn daughter of Titania, what was the point of even pretending that the false Queen held authority?

"All right, if you'd prefer to do this the hard way." The first man turned to one of the new arrivals. "They're here. Flush them out," he said, sternly.

The man he had addressed nodded, moving toward the vacated center of the clearing. He reached into his pocket as he did, pulling out a delicate silver chain with a tear-shaped red glass pendant at its end. He held it up, and smiled as it flashed bright.

"All right," he said, taking several steps forward and reaching into the air, seeming to grab hold of something. He made a yanking motion, and suddenly Simon Torquill was there, disillusioned and blinking in surprise verging on panic. "Your lady worries about you so," said the guard.

Simon gaped at him, saying nothing.

"She worries when you miss an appointment to serve her, and more when your ungrateful changeling child has impossibly disappeared from the Queen's own dungeon. She worries so deeply that she would grant a tracking charm keyed to your blood to those tasked with finding you."

The other guards had produced short bows from inside their jerkins, and were aiming arrows at random points around the clearing. At least two would hit me where I currently stood. I didn't know about any of the others. Garm's illusions were too good.

"Here's what's going to happen now," said the first man, and moved to take Simon's other arm. "We know you're not alone. We tracked you to Golden Shore, and we already confirmed that there are four of you. If you all come out and surrender, we don't open fire. If you don't, we fill this clearing with elf-shot, and we leave you where you fall. The choice is yours."

In this world, there was no cure for elf-shot. Why would they have wanted to pursue one? Once we got our real world back, we'd have access to it, but that required getting there. If August was elf-shot, we couldn't unbind October. If I was elf-shot, my Court would fall. And if Garm was elf-shot, the illusions concealing us would probably collapse, meaning we would have chosen bravery for no meaningful gain.

I took a deep breath and snapped my fingers. All the men immediately pivoted in my direction, arrows wavering as they searched the empty air for me.

"Garm, if you would," I said.

The illusion dropped away.

The guard lowered their bows.

"Well?" I asked. "Were you going to arrest us?"

TWENTY-FOUR

THEY GRABBED US QUICKLY and efficiently, binding our hands with rosewood-and-rowan cuffs that snapped shut with an ominous clicking sound. The man who'd been doing most of the speaking sneered as he looked at us.

"So you're the terrifying rebels carrying out a plot against the most wonderful woman Faerie has ever known?"

"Which one?" I asked, mildly.

He paused. "What?"

"Well, I was under the impression that you served the woman who calls herself Queen of the Mists. But you found us using a blood charm created by Eira Rosynhwyr, or the person currently pretending to be her," I said. "Both of them serve Titania. That's three women. Which one are we supposedly plotting against?"

He scowled at me. I shrugged, trying to look guileless.

"I simply want to understand the charges against me, since so far as I'm aware, I've done nothing wrong. None of us here were involved in a jailbreak, and even if we had been, your own words would put us in Golden Shore at the time, where, I believe, any crimes we committed wouldn't fall under the authority of the Queen of the Mists. So I ask you, who are we plotting against?"

"Oh, you're a clever one, aren't you?" He grinned at me, and kept grinning as something struck me in the back of the head, knocking me once again to the forest floor.

August shrieked something. Several more of the men grabbed her as she kicked and fought, apparently enraged. It wasn't my problem, however. My problem, which was somewhat more immediately press-ing, was my sudden inability to keep my eyes open. Bit by bit, they drifted closed, and my last coherent thought was that I would need to apologize to October: it was more difficult to carry out heroism-adjacent acts without being knocked insensate than I had ever anticipated.

I don't know what happened for a time after that. We were moved, somehow, whether into a mortal vehicle or via some other means, and when my eyes opened next, I was on my side on a hard marble floor, a layer of heavy fog above me and the rowan-and-rosewood cuffs no longer clasping my wrists. My head ached as if I had been drinking all day with my old theater fellows from long-lost Londinium, and when I tried to sit up, it spun and rang, awakening a fierce nausea in my belly. Concussion? Quite possibly.

That was something I had never taken into account when scolding my wife for her tropism toward injury: when she got hit in the head, she was perfectly fine inside of the hour. I, on the other hand, felt as if I were going to throw up all over the polished marble around me. At least if I did that, the fog would cover it.

I'd been here before, I was sure of it. It had been a while, but this place was too familiar to be entirely new to me. But between the dis-orientation and the throbbing in my head, I couldn't quite place where I was. Ah, well. I was quite sure something dreadful would happen soon enough to ground me in my location.

I must have made a noise when I woke up, because someone moved in the nearby fog, moving toward me. I tried to tense away from it, and only succeeded in squirming slightly, uncomfortable on the cold stone. I was, effectively, helpless.

"Tybalt? Is that you?"

The voice belong to Garm. I released what little tension I had man-aged to muster, licked my lips, and croaked, "Aye."

"A little archaic, don't you think?" Garm bent, hands breaking through the fog as he reached for me. Oddly, his cuffs were as missing as my own, presumably removed by our captors once they considered us fully in their power. They no longer thought we posed them any threat. In the moment, I couldn't say that they were wrong. I grasped hold of Garm's hands and let him pull me to my feet, the motion mak-ing my head spin even worse. "That looked like a pretty nasty hit you took. You all right?"

"I feel very much as if I've been drinking for the past several weeks and am about to pay the consequence," I said gravely, and was impressed with myself when I didn't slur. "Still, I believe I'll live, and at the moment, that seems to be of more importance than anything else. Where are we?"

Garm raised his eyebrows. "Every time I think I'm used to the idea that things are different in your world, you go and say something that reminds me just *how* different we're talking here. This is the Queen's knowe."

Of course. It hadn't occurred to me right away because where I was from, this place was sealed and half-dissolved, lost back to the firmament of Faerie. What's more, I had only ever seen this room when it was being used for the Queen's Court, which had been a very monochrome affair, lacking the pomp and circumstance of some royal courts, but had made up for it by being filled with light despite the ever-present fog, sourceless illumination piercing through the sheets of mist and turning everything into a magical parade of people appearing and disappearing within the gray.

I looked around. Simon and August were nearby, the former weeping, the latter apparently trying to comfort him. She shot me a venomous glare when she saw me looking their way, and I wondered what I could possibly have done to earn her ire while I was unconscious on the floor. I dismissed it as irrelevant for the moment, and spent the time I had before the next inevitable crisis finishing my study of the space around us.

The ballroom—what was it with nobles of the Divided Courts and ballrooms? Did they think I was going to be impressed by their heating bills?—was vast, too large to have been constructed by any mortal means, the floor and ceiling both hidden by choking layers of water vapor, fog above us, mist swirling to our knees. Tall pillars of filigreed marble presented a game attempt at seeming to hold up the unseen ceiling, but couldn't possibly have provided enough structural support to do the job. This was a place woven from and sustained by magic alone, called back from nothing when Titania decided she had need of it.

There were no walls. There was no furniture. Only foggy endlessness stretching on in all directions. That, too, was a magical effect; no space is truly limitless, whether inside a knowe or deep below the sea. It was clear, however, that we were meant to be awed, and so I shifted a little closer to Garm, lowering my voice.

"Can you seem impressed?"

"I don't know. Is pants-wetting terror in the right family of emotional responses?"

I managed, barely, not to laugh at his tone, which skirted the line between sarcasm and terror with elegant ease. "If there's anything I'll take from this world and be grateful for, it's your friendship, Garm. I don't know that we'd have ever gotten to know each other better in our own reality, and I have enjoyed coming to know you better."

"Am I . . ." He hesitated. "Am I a good person in your world?"

"A little suspicious of my lady, at times, and very protective of your liege, as is right and proper," I said. "But not cruel or capricious or inclined to deceit according to any accounting I have ever heard. Those who have served with you speak well of you."

"Grianne?"

"I can't say she speaks well of you, because I can't say she speaks," I said. "She is, in my world as well as this one, a proper Candela, and communicates through other means than words."

Garm looked relieved. I looked around again.

"Pleasant as it is to have a moment to catch our breaths, it seems odd that we were taken prisoner and then abandoned," I said. "Where are the guards?"

"They brought us here, said we'd be sorry to have conspired against their lady, and left," said August. "What they intend to do with us from here, I do not know."

"Intimidation tactics," I said. "They're trying to awe and impress us with their power. After all, if they can uncuff us and leave us to our own devices, doesn't that mean we're powerless to do anything against them? Surely they'd feel compelled to keep us bound and under guard if we had any power, or any potential to cause real harm. We're not alone, of course. We're being monitored closely."

"You sound very sure of yourself," said August.

"It's what I would do, and I've been a King for longer than the mewling whelp who claims this Court has known what a crown was, much less that she would trade her name to have one."

"Names are such protean things, but we place so much import upon them," said a familiar female voice, lilting and light, and painted with an accent I hadn't heard her use in centuries. Londinium laced through every word she spoke, like she was a child of that Kingdom, like she had grown up there and not in the deepest reaches of Faerie itself.

"The humans say they can capture us with our true names," I said, turning toward the sound of Eira's voice.

"Oh? And what would your true name be, then? Rand, son of Ainmire, Prince of Cats? Tybalt, temporary King of uncounted courts? Or is it the name your mother gave you before she sold you to the man you would call 'father'? What name would I use to put an arrow in your heart and bind you to my will?"

"Nothing, for I will not serve you," I said, trying to sound braver than I felt.

"October," she breathed, and finally stepped out into the open. "That's the name I'd use. That's the name that binds you. Your true name isn't your own, and never was; it's your heart, ringing like a bell when someone else strikes it."

"Then you have no true name."

"No, and I'm stronger for it." She smiled, sweet as poisoned honey, and I remembered that Oleander had been attracted to her service for good reason. There had always been fellowship between them.

Behind me, Simon made a pained noise. I glanced back. He had moved to stand halfway behind his daughter, trembling, eyes darting to Eira's face and then quickly away, as if it hurt to look directly at her.

Eira Rosynhwyr moved to stand directly before us, looking us each up and down with undistilled disdain. She wore a dress that appeared to have been cut from a single sheet of silver birch bark, growing around her like she was the tree and her limbs its branches, hugging her every curve. Boughs of branches dripping with leaves in spring green and autumn flame were braided into her long black hair, which danced with opal flashes of color. Her skin was white as snow, her lips red as blood, and her eyes blue as flawless sapphire. It was easy to look at her and see how she had shaped beauty standards in both Faerie and the human world, and equally easy to be repulsed by the thought.

"Naughty boy," she said. For a moment, I thought she was talking to me; then I saw that she had switched her attention to Simon. "Naughty, naughty boy. You were supposed to stay as you were even to the end, so that you would never know anything other than peace and paradise. Why do you refuse such good gifts as we have given you?"

"You *stole* me from my family!" Simon stood up straighter as he snarled at her, but didn't move away from August. "You put me back in a place I had left of my own free will, and for what purpose?"

"You belonged with Amy," said Eira. "You belonged with the mother of your children. We let you have them both, together, as you had always wished they were. We gave you everything, and you rejected it for a mermaid and a man with no ambitions. Why?"

"I left your service, even before I left my wife," said Simon. "The things I did in your name were cruel and villainous, and I was no longer that man. I should never have become him to begin with. For you to force me back into it was a crime, even if no law has been written against such an act."

"You can't break the law when you control it," said Eira. She looked around at the four of us one more time, then sighed, heavily. "You're boring. You're all boring. Mother promised me you wouldn't be boring, but you are. You can go now."

She flicked her fingers at us, like she was dismissing a particularly irritating servant. Any hopes that this meant we were being released were short-lived, as the floor dropped out from under us and we plunged down into fog-choked darkness.

Falling with a spinning, aching head is not pleasant, and I do not recommend it. Landing isn't much better. All four of us hit the ground hard when our fall came to an end, slamming into the stone floor of the Queen's dungeon without a chance to catch ourselves or even try to soften the landing. I managed, barely, to avoid cracking my head a second time upon the ground.

Not that I'm sure it would actually have made things that much worse. The air was thick with the scent of iron and rotting yarrow, the latter coming from the heaps of decaying straw pushed up against the edges of our newly-shared cell. The door was solid, and banded with enough iron that I wouldn't stand a chance at forcing it open. There were no other restraints. With so much iron, none were needed. Thus free to move about our cell, we settled against the walls farthest from the iron-banded door, August beside Simon, Garm and I well apart from one another, and didn't speak. It seemed there was nothing left to say.

Then a thick fog began to gather in the middle of the room, swirling until it formed a pillar, which burst to reveal October, the Luidaeg, Dean, and Rayseline. The sight of the sea witch was almost enough of a relief to counter the despair of seeing my wife once more surrounded by iron. Dean and Rayseline collapsed as the Luidaeg slumped. October dropped to her knees, looking utterly broken by whatever they had experienced in coming here.

"Toby!" shouted August, the nickname an unfamiliarity strong enough to bring my head whipping around to stare at her. I watched as she rose from the corner she'd retreated to and ran, half-stumbling on the uneven floor to drop to her knees in front of October. She ran her hand over October's face and shoulders, charting every inch, reassuring herself.

When she began to pull back, October made a choking sound and grabbed hold of her, pulling her close and holding on.

I knew I should hold my tongue. I could only make things worse. And yet, I couldn't do it, not when a member of their party was missing. "So, you finally got caught," I said. "Where is Ginevra?"

"The guards took her; she was injured in our arrest, but they bandaged her wounds, at least," said the Luidaeg.

"If she dies . . ."

"If she dies, you'll still know better than to pick a fight with me, kitty-cat," said the Luidaeg, tone bitterly cold and unforgiving. "Now. How many of us have they taken?"

"It's an 'us' now, is it?" I asked. "Myself, clearly. Sylvester's knight. The renegade Torquills."

October sniffled, pulling away from August. "Father's here?" she asked.

August nodded, looking back toward the corner where Simon still huddled, weeping. "He is," she said, in a soft voice. "He's . . . not well at the moment."

"The amount of iron in here would do that to anyone," said October, moving to rise.

August grabbed her arms, pulling her back down. She turned to blink at her sister, who shook her head. "No, it's not the iron," she said. "He's *not well*."

"Is he hurt?"

I sighed, shifting slightly away from the wall. "They took us in Muir Woods," I said. "We had gone there to meet with our allies from the Undersea. Your father believed his best friend to have died in the Earthquake, not gone below the waves to marry a mermaid and shelter in the deeps. He was overjoyed and, in his joy, embraced the man."

October turned to frown at me. "Why should that render him unwell?"

Dean helped Rayseline off the floor, the two of them moving silently off to the side as they allowed the rest of us to speak. I kept my focus on October.

"Patrick forgot that Simon still labored under the memories of another world, and met an embrace from his husband with a kiss, which Simon was not prepared for," I said. "He reacted with shock and shame, and in the interests of avoiding a diplomatic incident, your sister unbound his memory. It was the only way to quell Dianda's wrath."

"That woman has a lot of wrath to go around," said the Luidaeg.

"Even so," I agreed. "Your father has handled the revelation of the true world . . . poorly."

"But he knows us?" asked October. "He remembers August, and myself, and who he is? Nothing was lost by restoring his memory?"

"He was a happy man before I did this to him," said August fiercely. "He loved our mother and his patron, and he was content to spend his life in service to our family. Now he's lost. He knows himself, but believes his place is beneath the sea, and weeps for things he did willingly and with joy in service to his ladies! How can you not see this for harm?"

"Because you gave him back what was taken from him against his will," said October. She grabbed hold of August's arms, holding her where she was. "August, you can *do* it. You can see and snap the threads. You can release *my* memory!"

"I won't." August shook her head before turning to glare at me. "Threaten all you like, you can't force me. I refuse to risk losing my sister as I fear to have already lost my father, as he swears I will lose my mother before this all comes to an end."

"I'm not on the tower wards," said October.

August stiffened.

"Mother removed me, in the other Faerie, after the divorce," said October. "She took me off the wards, and it seems she never added me back on, because I went there when neither you nor Father was in residence, and I couldn't get inside. Whether she remembers it or not, I'm not her family. *You* are my family. You, and Father, and several other people, some in this room, who I don't currently remember the way I should. You don't want to unbind me because it might cause you pain. Well, you're causing *them* pain by leaving me as I am. And I think . . . I think you might be causing *me* pain, too. Please, August. This is something you can do. This is something *only* you can do. We know the last four months were real, even if everything before it was a dream. For four months, I have loved you desperately, with every waking hour. That doesn't go away just because I remember who else I love."

"There's so much iron here . . ." said August.

"Here." October pulled what looked like half a dozen large garnets out of her pocket, offering them to August. "The sea witch made them for me. They make my blood magic stronger. I assume they would do the same for you."

She paused then, looking at the Luidaeg, who said nothing. I rose in that pause, wanting to reach for my wife, unable to force myself to move any closer. If she rebuffed me again, I thought I might die.

"*Please*, August." October turned to look at me, and continued: "If you've ever loved me as I've always loved you, let me remember."

August took half the stones out of October's hand, tears starting in her eyes. "Am I not enough for you?" she asked. "Is my love not sufficient to feed your hungering heart?"

"I don't think anyone should depend on just one person to love them," said October. "From what Dean tells me, I'm not the only person who loves you. You don't need to keep me bound to have my affections, August. Please."

I started to step toward her. The Luidaeg put her hand on my arm, stopping me.

"Let them," she said, softly. "They're getting where you want them to be, you just need to trust Toby to take it the rest of the way. This is what she does. Every version of her. She convinces people to do the things that don't seem like they should work."

August turned back to Toby, a tear running down her cheek. "Promise me," she said. "Promise me that no matter who we were to each other in that other world, no matter what neither one of us remembers right now, you'll still be my sister, and you'll still love me."

"I'll always be your sister, you walnut. If that were something that could be changed, I would have changed it long before now."

She laughed, the sound thick and half-swallowed, and closed her eyes as she tossed the red stones into her mouth. October tensed.

August reached out with both hands this time, seeming to hook her fingers into something I couldn't see, and made a hard pulling gesture. October screamed.

It was one of the worst sounds I'd ever heard in my life. I flinched away as she bent forward and dug her fingers into the floor, breaking a nail and releasing a single drop of blood before she healed from the small wound, recovering as she always did, without a scar left behind. Well, not all scars can be seen, and if she wouldn't carry these, I would, for her sake, and for my own. I wanted to move toward her, to support her. I couldn't move, and had to glance down to be sure my feet weren't rooted to the floor.

The Luidaeg put a sympathetic hand on my shoulder. "I'll go," she said, softly. "You stay."

She moved to October, then, kneeling and holding her upright as she screamed and fought against the spell. It seemed to go on forever, agonized howling without end, her voice growing strained and then clearing again as she stripped the skin from her throat and regrew it, over and over.

Finally, she sagged, screams coming to an end, and the Luidaeg caught her before she could fall. August fell forward, catching herself on her hands, and stared at her sister, hair stuck to her cheeks and forehead with sweat, panting from the effort of what she'd just done.

October groaned, then raised her head, attention going to the woman in front of her. "Hey, Aug," she said, weakly. "You okay?"

August stared at her. "It hurts."

"Every time," agreed October. "Thank you."

August blinked. "I . . . I don't . . ."

"You can always thank family, August," said October. "Don't be ridiculous, you walnut, it's not polite."

August relaxed. "I'm only impolite because you were rotten *first*," she said, throwing herself at October and embracing her as tightly as she could. "I thought I was going to lose you," she whispered.

October patted her back with one hand. "Things are going to be different now," she admitted, "but you were always my sister. We just never had the chance to find out what that meant for us as a pair. Now that we know, not even Titania herself is taking me away from you. I promise."

August pulled away, sniffling, and October turned to look behind herself for the first time. Her face fell when she saw the Luidaeg standing there, and hope leapt in my chest. The Luidaeg nodded, gesturing toward my position with her chin.

"He couldn't bear to come any closer," she said. "Might want to go make sure he's okay."

"Right." Toby stood, legs shaking from the effort. She looked to August, who smiled unsteadily and stayed where she was, watching her sister go. Toby hesitated, then turned to face the corner where I was standing, away from the screaming and suffering, away from *her*. Fighting the urge to help had been almost more than I could handle.

She took a step toward me. I looked away.

"Tybalt?" she said, and under her hesitancy and fear, for the first time, she sounded like she knew who I was—like my name was more than just a word.

I didn't answer her. My voice refused to come.

"It worked. She broke Titania's illusions. I know who I am now." She paused. "I know who you are. I'm so sorry I wasn't strong enough to break it on my own."

"I couldn't have asked that of you," I replied, even though every fiber of my being was screaming at me that I could have asked exactly that. If she'd been willing to listen, I could have demanded it.

"But you're hurt because I didn't somehow do it anyway," she said. "You're not looking at me, and you only do that when you're really upset."

"I know . . . I have no right to be angry that you were captured in a spell cast by one of the founders of all Faerie, especially not one which I knew to be tailored specifically to do you harm," I said, choosing my words with exquisite care. "I know you are not to blame, and in all honesty, I feel a relief so vast that it aches behind my breastbone right now, like an injury in and of itself. But I'm still angry. I'm so angry I could scream and throw myself against the walls of the world raging at the injustice of it all." I finally allowed myself to look at her. She looked wrung-out and exhausted, a smear of blood at one corner of her mouth, and she had never been more beautiful. "I don't know what to do with these feelings. I thought I had already experienced every form of anxiety you were able to inspire."

"Pretty sure there's always another form of anxiety." She kept moving toward me, closer and closer, finally stopping barely an arm's length away. "That's what loving someone means."

"It was like you were dead, and someone else was walking around in your body." I finally allowed myself to reach for her, unable to stop my hands from shaking. "You looked at me, and you didn't see me."

"I see you now," she said.

I stepped forward, sweeping her into my arms without pausing to see whether she would welcome the gesture. I could think of no other answer to her much-wanted words. She wrapped her arms around me and clung to me as if I were her very lifeline, as if she had never wanted anything more than she wanted this moment.

Pulling her tight, I held her close against me, breathing in the scent of her, the side of my face resting against the side of her head, smelling her unfamiliar shampoo.

Finally, she began to pull away, apparently ready to resume the matter of getting us out of here. I didn't let go. I wasn't ready. While we had been apart for the same amount of time, she had been aware of our separation much more briefly. I held fast, and when she had leaned back far enough to see my face, I didn't say anything. Just looked at her, silent and solemn. She stilled, looking into my eyes, waiting to see what I was going to do next.

"If you ever do anything like that again . . ." I said.

"You'll have to get in line," she said, and leaned in, and kissed me.

I kissed her like I'd been without her for four months, running through the world and—worse, even—waiting for the moment when we could find each other again. If it had all been running, it would have been fine. It would have hurt, but I would have been too busy trying to survive to count the days and hours. It was the waiting that had come far too close to breaking me, and it was the waiting that meant I would never be letting go of her again. Not that it had been very likely before that.

To my joy and relief, she kissed me back, and there was no real change in the way she kissed me. She kissed me like she loved me more than anything else, like I was the home she had been trying to find for her entire life. She kissed me like she was never going to leave me again, and I kissed her back like I was accepting her promise. I kissed her like I believed her.

When we finally broke the kiss, I let her go, and she stepped back, smiling at me. I answered her expression with a smile of my own. "I missed you, little fish," I said.

She shuddered for some reason, but kept smiling as she put a hand against the side of my neck, fingers tightening possessively. "I wish I could say the same," she said. "But fuck, it's good to have you back."

"Yes," I said. Then the other thought occurred to me once again. I hesitated, trying to find the words, but my involuntary glance at her belly told her my thoughts. I swallowed hard. "October . . ."

"Yeah. I know."

She extended her hand, palm toward the ceiling and fingers curled loosely toward her palm, save for her index finger, which pointed at the far wall. "I know one of the things you're worried about, and I'm worried about it too, and if we're going to get out of here, you need to not be worried," she said. "Prick my finger."

I jerked away from her, eyes going wide as I fully processed her request. Then, understanding that the first thing she'd asked of me upon recovering her memory was not a kiss but an assault, I glared at her. "I will *not* hurt you."

"I'm not asking you to hurt me, just to draw blood," she said, stubbornly. "I could bite my own cheek, but I don't think that's a good idea right now. I've had other people's blood in my mouth and I haven't brushed my teeth. So please, prick my finger."

If I didn't do as she asked, she had a dozen ways to make herself bleed. I knew it, and she knew I knew. I still didn't understand why this was so important to her, but my claws were the safest option, and so I nodded, grudgingly, before I reached out and tapped the tip of her finger with one claw, breaking the skin. Quickly, she stuck her finger in her mouth. The wound would already be healed by that point, but I wasn't willing to cut her any deeper.

She closed her eyes for a long, long moment, the scent of her magic rising around her and doing . . . nothing. No spells were cast or unwoven, nothing changed. Until, finally, she opened her eyes and smiled at me, warm and relieved and as loving as she had ever been.

My stomach unclenched. My heart, suddenly released from a fear that had been weighing it down for months, keeping it from ever feeling as if it were free to beat, as if I were ever free to breathe, contracted and let go in a feeling of relief so immense that it was dizzying. I swallowed hard, watching for any sign that I was misinterpreting the look on her face.

"Truly?"

Silent, she nodded.

I raised my hand, resting it beneath her chin, nudging her head ever so slightly higher. Once she was looking me squarely in the eyes, I pulled my hand away, cupping her cheek with my fingers as I ran them softly down the curve of her jaw. She shivered, pressing herself tighter against me.

"It wouldn't have mattered," I said. "I would never have blamed you. But I would have set myself to destroying her."

"Here I thought we were going to do that anyway," she quipped. I smiled at the lightness in her tone, and before she could say anything about how important it was for us to get on with that, I pulled her close once more, lowered my mouth to hers, and kissed her again.

"If you two are finished trying to suck each other's faces off like a pair of hormonal teenagers, there *is* the little matter of being locked in an iron-barred dungeon while Titania is preparing to Ride for the Heart," said the Luidaeg. She didn't sound amused.

October turned to face her, moving closer to me as she did, leaning back to rest against my chest. I put my hands on her upper arms, holding her where she was, honestly rejoicing in being allowed to touch her at all. The Luidaeg looked at the two of us with the tolerantly annoyed expression of a mother cat finding her kittens engaged in some sort of ill-timed mischief. I wanted to laugh and swing her around, asking whether she'd thought there was any other way this could have gone. If not for October's pregnancy and the iron in the room, I would already have grabbed her, pulled her onto the shadow roads, and been gone.

"How *are* we getting out of here?" asked October. "The last time I had to escape from an iron-laced dungeon, I had a Tuatha de Dannan's blood to borrow. Or, I guess, technically, the *last* time, a pair of Tuatha came and got me. I'm thinking of the time before that. How did they manage that, anyway?"

"I helped them," said Simon. He sounded exhausted, like a man broken, and I hoped he would be able to recover from all of this. "We knew you'd been arrested, and had gone to Golden Shore hoping we could claim clemency on your behalf. There is no extradition between the Mists and the Golden Shore. I wanted your freedom more than I wanted my own safety. I was able to brew a draught that helped the Windermeres to overcome their normal issues with distance and break through the dungeon wards. I don't have access to my equipment, or to the Windermeres."

"So that's out," said October. She tilted her head back so she could look at me. "Tybalt?"

"Much as I would love being your savior in this matter, little fish, I couldn't carry this many people through the shadows, even were I inclined to make the attempt. The roads degrade when unused, and most of my Court has been unable to access them for months. They are unsafe for passage."

"Ginevra took me via the Shadow Roads," said October.

I tried my best to control my reaction. I'm afraid I did a poor job of it. "And we'll be discussing that, once she has been recovered from wherever she's being held. She should have known better than to risk you so."

October turned to the Luidaeg. "I still have the Summer Roads key," she said, almost pleading. "Could we take one of the old roads?"

"Accessing them with this much iron nearby would be a complicated trick, and not one that I'm sure would play out the way we want it to," she said. "There are a *lot* of roads under the heading of 'old roads.' We could wind up on the Road of Rust, that was opened for the Gremlins, and die in a place where our bodies would never be found. I have a slightly better idea." She gestured toward the door. "Does that thing look like it contains any silver to you?"

Sensibly, October hesitated before she answered, "No. Why?"

"Because bound and limited as I am, I remain Firstborn, and I know how the Firstborn die," said the Luidaeg. She held up her right hand, and her fingernails grew long and wickedly pointed, transforming into talons. "We die by iron *and* silver. We don't die by iron alone. Go comfort your father-failure. He thinks he's lost you all over again."

The Luidaeg turned away from us, moving toward the cell door with a purposeful stride that dared anyone to get in her way. October looked over her shoulder at me. Loath as I was to allow her out of reach, I took my hands from her arms and nodded my assent. She stepped away from me, and as I felt the sudden aching absence of her, walked toward Simon in the corner where he huddled.

There was nothing I could do to ease that conversation, which seemed as likely to be confrontation as reunion, now that they both knew the truth about what had been done to them, and what they had done during their time under Titania's spell. I couldn't help them.

Maybe I could help someone else. I turned and followed the Luidaeg's path to the cell door.

She had turned her hands to wicked-looking talons, and had already inserted her first claw into the lock when I arrived, working it back and forth as she tried to trigger the internal mechanisms. Wisps of smoke were starting to rise from the keyhole as the metal scorched her.

"I am sorry this falls to you," I said, solemnly. "It seems you are forever drawn into the chaos we create."

"Not like I was ever going to have a peaceful life, and your chaos has its good sides," she said, still working at the lock. "Never forget that you and that walking degree in chaos theory you call a wife are the reason I have my descendant line back. They're not my children, but *their* children will be my grandchildren, and my great-grandchildren, and that woman who calls herself my sister will never touch them again. People talk to me now. Not always with the awe and deference I deserve, but still. They talk to me when they don't want something. I have no idea where my stepmother put Poppy. I know she has to be okay, because Aes Sidhe are descendants of Maeve, but I don't know where she is. She's been a good friend to me. Weird and loud, and a little annoying, but good." She looked at me, and I could see the strain around her eyes. "You have plenty to apologize for, Child of Malvic. Everyone does. But involving me in this situation is not among those things. I know who I blame for this, and it's not you."

"That's something of a relief." I glanced across the cell to where October was kneeling next to Simon, talking to him quietly. "He seemed to think their relationship was a strong one, and she showed no reluctance to run to him."

"That's probably a good thing. They're both going to be traumatized by this—I mean, everyone is, they're not special, my stepmother is what happens when you give a narcissist infinite cosmic powers and no one who can tell her 'no,' she's basically a mass traumatic event with legs—but they don't need to be hurt by each other on top of that.

Simon hasn't always been my favorite person. Honestly, neither has October. That doesn't mean he deserves the crap he's been through. There's a *reason* the Firstborn withdrew when we did."

"Forgive me, but I've never quite managed to understand it."

She shot me a thin, strained smile. "Our parents were gods. We were demigods, to steal the term from the Greeks. We made mountains. Our parents made *worlds*. And then our children, our wonderful, strange, varied children . . . you were powerful, yes, and glorious in ways we couldn't have predicted, but you weren't *divine*. Compared to us, you were so fragile, so easily destroyed. You lived faster, moved faster, added more urgency to everything you did, because you couldn't imagine eternity the way we could. And that was fine. You didn't resent us or hate us for being more than you were, because we were less than our parents. We weren't the summit of everything. And then Maeve's Ride was broken."

Her smile faded, and she hissed with pain as she pulled her smoking claw from the lock and inserted the next one in the line. "Those of us who were her descendants lost our mother and our protector that night. My stepmother saw her opportunity, and allowed her own children new freedom to harry and attack us, driving us to the edges of the world, and while that was happening, *our* children began to resent the fact that we couldn't protect them, and they couldn't protect themselves. They started to hate us. Father didn't actually help by sealing Stepmother away. Her kids stopped attacking us without knowing they had her to back them up, so he saved a lot of lives, but the resentment was there, and growing. Then *he* left, and there was nothing in Faerie more powerful than we were. We weren't supposed to be running Faerie! We weren't kids, but we weren't heirs, either. We didn't have the training. And all our kids were getting madder and madder about the things we could do and they couldn't. So those of us who were still around got together and agreed that we'd do like our parents had done. We'd fade, and let our kids be the most important things in the room. Maybe then they'd sort their shit out. We're too powerful to go around making problems for our descendants."

"You never vanished."

The Luidaeg grimaced. "I'm bound. And someone ordered me to stay accessible, so that I could become a proper monster. Some of us went into hiding, as you know, while others fucked off completely. And some of us died, of course. But Simon, man. That poor boy's been the target of two Firstborn, off and on, for most of his life. It's not a pleasant place to be. With those two fighting over him, it's no wonder he's messed up in the head."

"What's so special about him?"

"Amy had him, which meant he got a little more practice at telling us 'no' than most fae tend to have, Cait Sidhe notwithstanding, you stubborn assholes," she said, and gave her claw a vicious twist. Something clicked. She withdrew that claw, and inserted the next. "And so when he ran into sister *dearest*, he told her 'no' to her face. That was unusual enough to be charming, and to be something she had to destroy. So she started trying to take him away from Amy. There's nothing special about the poor bastard, except for the fact that he's managed to survive. Like father, like daughter, I guess."

My attempt at a smile came out somewhat twisted. Positive as it was for October to have people she cared about in her life, I still wasn't sure how I felt about one of those people being Simon Torquill. Well, there were worse people she could have adopted and brought home with her. This experience could have left her with a new appreciation of her mother, for example. I probably couldn't have been calm about that.

October was offering Simon her hand. When he took it, she pulled him to his feet, and they embraced, quickly, before turning to head toward us. August rose and trailed along behind, looking as if she wasn't entirely sure of her own welcome. Raysel watched the Luidaeg with hopeful intensity, while Dean leaned against the wall near Garm, merely waiting.

When October came close enough to see what the Luidaeg had done to her hands, she blanched, asking, "Luidaeg, are you—?"

"I'm *fine*," snapped the Luidaeg. "This hurts like a fucking bitch and a half, but it's nothing I can't handle, and if you just shut up and let me—get—this!"

There was a loud click from inside the lock, and the door swung open, apparently weighted so that it didn't need anyone to touch it when it wasn't locked. She made a triumphant sound and took a half-step back, shaking her blistered hands in front of herself. This close, I could see how badly burnt the skin on her fingers was, charred and blackened by the proximity to the iron in the door. She glanced at me, and I nodded. I'd keep my mouth shut about how badly hurt she was, at least until she wanted to say something.

"We're out," said the Luidaeg, voice bitter-bright with pain and irritation. "Now we storm the castle with . . . no weapons, not enough fighters, and two people who still think this is the way the world is supposed to be. Isn't this going to be fun?"

"No," said Dean, opening his eyes.

"I do some of my best work while dramatically underprepared," said October. "Good job on the door."

The Luidaeg looked at October without responding, expression going neutral before she nodded once, tilting the gesture upward instead of down, so that it was an acknowledgment rather than an agreement, and stepped out of the cell to the waiting hall.

The rest of us followed her. I waited until October was by my side again before I moved, pacing her, unwilling to let her out of arm's reach while we walked into danger, and to her credit, she didn't try to motion me away, but seemed to understand the reasons for my anxious closeness, and bumped her shoulder against my arm as we walked, acknowledging my presence. The hall was long and narrow, lined with iron doors and lacking any living guards. This wasn't where you put people to wait for trial. This was where you put people so you could forget about them.

I sniffed the air, searching for the scent of Cait Sidhe under the rotting straw and iron. I didn't find it, and while the iron was beginning to confuse my senses, it wasn't yet so far along that I wouldn't have been able to detect her presence. Wherever they had put Ginevra, it was, mercifully, not here.

I could feel the iron settling in my joints, making them ache, now that we were out of the cell and moving relatively freely. The others seemed to be feeling the effects in their own ways. October and August looked entirely fine, while Garm and Dean moved a little stiffly yet didn't seem to be actively suffering.

Simon and Raysel, on the other hand, were breathing heavily and moving slowly, their discomfort visible and pronounced. After the second time Simon stumbled, October stopped and frowned at him.

"Hey, are you okay?" she asked.

His smile was terrible, the rictus of a dying man. His voice, however, was steady enough as he said, "So much better than I was yesterday, or the day before, or four months ago, when you pressed the blood back into my body and compelled my heart to beat. Truly, October, I'm fine, and will only improve from here. I have never had this much to live for."

I stayed where I was as the Luidaeg moved to stand next to her, mirroring her concern. "The Daoine Sidhe have always been more sensitive to iron," she said. "I never worked out exactly why it should be so, only that it is. It does their First no more damage than it does to the rest of us, but her descendants burn with it. Dean's Merrow heritage will have shielded him, at least a little. Simon will suffer."

"I'm as Daoine Sidhe as my uncle," muttered Raysel, voice too low for anyone else to hear. I turned. She was beside me, face pale and pinched, wincing with every breath she took. "But *he's* the one who tortured *me*. Why is everyone so concerned about him?"

"People are complicated, Raysel," I said. "Are you well, apart from the iron? Did October unbind your memories?"

"They were never bound," said Raysel, bitterly. "Apparently I don't get to exist in a 'perfect' Faerie, since Mother would never have fled her parents, and so I got tossed onto the family estate to rot where no one would remember me."

I blinked slowly to cover my shock. "Blind Michael's lands?"

She nodded, expression grim.

"You've been there this whole time?"

"Dean and I, and a bunch of other people Titania didn't think needed to exist. We've been exiled and fully aware of what that means, for *months*. And now we're back, and no one knows us, and I have to travel with the man who ruined my life."

On a small, bitter level, I had to appreciate the fact that the number of people in my company who despised Simon Torquill had remained constant. In the moment, I patted Raysel on the shoulder. "We promised you the hospitality of our house, and you still have it. I'll protect you if necessary."

Raysel smiled at me, gratefully, even as the Luidaeg's voice cut across the scene.

"Right now, we need to find Titania and stop her from Riding," she said.

"If this place is modeled off the false Queen's knowe, there should be a stable," replied October.

"Great." The Luidaeg looked at her expectantly. "Where is it?"

October took a step back, clearly startled, although it was a reasonable question under the circumstances. "I have no idea," she protested. "You think she invited me to go hunting with her? She would have been happier having an excuse to turn me into a rabbit and go hunting for *me*."

The Luidaeg scoffed. "Oh, please, Toby. Think a little more highly of yourself. She'd have turned you into a coyote at the very least. Something she could call vermin and feel good about killing."

October scowled. "I can't tell if that was supposed to be a compliment or not."

"Good."

"Excuse me."

We all turned to face Simon Torquill. He was half-leaning on Dean, one hand pressed against his side and a look on his face like he was about to be sick. "I may be able to help."

"That would be a first," muttered Raysel.

I said nothing. Their relationship was theirs to repair.

"How?" asked the Luidaeg.

Simon shrugged. "I served my patron for a very long time, and she often sent me to attend functions at the High Court on her behalf. Assuming this place follows even a portion of the original floor plan, I should be able to find the stables. Although it would be very much appreciated if we could stop by the kitchens first, to let me get a glass of water."

"Getting something in their stomachs will help them shake off the iron," said the Luidaeg, looking to October. As always seemed to be the case, we were all deferring to her as our leader. "Water would be good. Milk would be better. Milk, bread, and chocolate would be best, if we can't crash an alchemy lab and get some anti-iron treatments." She looked speculatively at Simon, who shook his head.

"I never had access to the royal alchemy labs. If they exist in this iteration of the knowe, I won't be able to get inside."

"Pity. Kitchens it is. Lead the way."

She gestured grandly down the hall. Simon started to walk again, Dean alongside him, and the rest of us followed.

TWENTY-FIVE

TRUE TO HIS WORD, Simon led us down a series of eerily silent halls to the kitchens, which were warm, well lit, and utterly deserted. He looked briefly nonplussed when we stepped inside to the crackle of the fires and the soft sound of simmering pots on the hob, only to find that no one was there. Then he shrugged, gesturing for Dean to help him toward the cold closet.

"She must not have bothered to recreate or relocate servants no one would ever see," he said. "Anyone who worked here has moved on, and not many settled with Queen Windermere. Those who have are probably somewhere in the knowe, such as it is."

"She's treating people like dolls," said Raysel sourly. "It's not right."

"None of this is right," I agreed. "Is the food safe?"

The Luidaeg spread her blistered hands in surrender. "Your guess is as good as mine. I want to say anything we find here was created with my stepmother's magic, but my hands wouldn't feel like this if I just *thought* I'd been exposed to iron, which means there's real iron in those dungeons. Maybe the food is real and stolen from someplace else, maybe it's magical and make-believe, maybe it's whatever was in the false Queen's larder when the knowe collapsed, enchanted to seem edible even though it's all ashes and mold. I have no way of knowing."

"Maybe I do?" volunteered August, timidly. She raised one hand, like she was waiting to be called on.

The Luidaeg took pity on her. "How?" she asked.

"We need . . . Toby needs to keep her strength, she can't be disenchanting loaves of bread or whatever," said August. "But I can see the spells too, now, and if there's one on the food, I can break it."

The Luidaeg blinked, looking briefly impressed. "That is not the worst idea I've ever heard," she said. "We'll go with that. Simon?"

"Yes?" He had reached the cold closet and opened the door, releasing a gust of frigid air. He paused in the act of reaching inside to look back at the Luidaeg.

"Let August look at anything you plan to put in your mouth before you do."

He nodded, and went back to looking through the cold closet.

I took advantage of the pause to catch October's arm and guide her to an open chair at a nearby table, gesturing for her to sit. She laughed a little as she did, grimacing.

"Sorry," she said. "I feel mostly fine, but my head hurts. It's been doing that a lot since I started ripping down illusions cast by one of the Three."

"Overachiever," I said, fondly. "We should be going home soon. You're sure the iron isn't—?"

"I'm sure I want to see Walther, or Jin, or both, as soon as I can," she said. "This much iron isn't good for anyone, and I doubt it's good for the baby."

I felt a small thrill at having her refer to her pregnancy so casually. I would never take living in the same reality as my beloved for granted again. "No, likely not," I agreed. "But as long as the iron did you no lasting harm, we should be able to repair any damage that's been done."

"I am so tired of this bullshit." She leaned over, resting her forehead against my side and closing her eyes.

On the other side of the kitchen, Simon had produced several bottles of milk and some chickpea mash, and was stirring the two together into a sort of unpleasant pudding, mixing it with some mint and cilantro taken from the herb garden in the windowsill. His purpose was less than clear, but I assumed he was calling on some alchemical sympathy of those four ingredients, blending them into something that might actually help.

Once he was done, he began dishing up the mixture, speaking quietly to Dean for a moment before handing the boy two bowls and gesturing him toward Raysel. Interesting. Well, he knew she didn't like him—he was no fool, and was well aware of what he'd done to her. This accomplished, he dished up two more bowls and shuffled across the kitchen to settle in a chair near to October, passing one of the bowls to her.

"There's more, if you feel unwell," he said, looking at me. "All these things are useful for the drawing out of iron. Mixed and granted a speck of magic, their sympathy should act as a poor man's antitoxin. Not good enough to constitute true medical care, enough better than nothing as to trade day for night."

"Indeed," I said, and didn't object to his choice to treat himself and October before me. He was suffering as I was not, and she mattered more than either of us. I decided to show my trust in him by leaving them alone, crossing to the bowl where the remains of his mixture resided, an unappetizing beige lump speckled with green.

"You getting some of that?" asked the Luidaeg. I looked at her, nodding. "Cool. Pour me a glass and find me a straw?"

My confusion must have shown in my expression. She raised her hands, waving taloned fingers at me.

"Not going to be spoon-fed, can't really hold a utensil like this," she said. "But a straw should work, and even if iron can't kill me, that doesn't mean it feels amazing."

I grimaced. "My apologies. I didn't consider—"

"Less apologize-y, more find a straw-y."

While the Queen's knowe seemed unlikely to have anything as modern as a plastic or paper straw, I found a container of bucatini while digging around the shelf above the cutlery, and took a fistful of noodles with me as I brought the Luidaeg her glass of mash.

"Will this suffice?"

She eyed the pasta critically, then nodded. "Better than nothing, I guess. Put it down on the edge of the counter. I have enough dexterity to swap the noodles as they get soggy."

I did as she bid, then returned to my own bowl, picking it up as I moved to return to October. August had joined them, and was sitting at her sister's other side, talking quietly, shoulders low as she compared their versions of reality. No one was crying. That struck me as a good sign.

"Is everyone feeling better?" I asked, and took a bite of my own mash. It tasted like . . . nothing, really. Like blandness and the color green. There was a faint trace of mulled cider—Simon's magic flavoring the mixture—but not a hint of mint, which was impressive. I gave the bowl a critical look before I took another bite. At least it wasn't unpleasant, unlike most alchemical treatments.

"Better, no, like I'll live, yes," said Simon. "We'll all need proper treatment when this is done. You can't cobble together a full counter to iron poisoning. You can only leaven the effects."

"But you did that, Simon," said October. "Be proud of yourself. We're going to get through this."

He ducked his head, looking embarrassed and pleased at the same time. I turned away from them, eating my mash as I watched the rest of the room.

Dean and Raysel were their own corner, isolated from the rest of us, but joined by their common experience, which couldn't have been easy on them, given their past. The Luidaeg was on her third hollow noodle, sucking up greenish goo with the enthusiasm of a woman I had once seen eat a bowl of slugs with chocolate syrup. Texture didn't seem to be an issue for her, thankfully. And the small family group behind me was quiet and seemingly stable, nursing their wounds as they treated what they could.

It was nice to have a pause while nothing was collapsing in on us. But the clock was still running, and when my spoon clinked against the bottom of my bowl, I knew it was time to move along.

"Is everyone ready?" I asked, looking around the room.

One by one, everyone nodded, putting their own dishes away. October twitched like she was going to start gathering and carrying them to the sink, and Simon set his hand on her shoulder before she could, stopping her. She shot him a wry, half-grateful look, then offered me her hands. I tugged her to her feet, and she embraced me quickly before turning to help August up. It was natural and easy and I found it didn't bother me in the least. Yes, I'd missed her and wanted to cling until we both ran out of breath, but that didn't mean the rest of the world stopped existing.

We needed to help each other. And I needed to find Ginevra, as soon as reasonably possible.

We resumed our trek through the knowe, Simon leading the way. Everyone was still slow and unsteady, the mixture Simon had made blunting some of the worst effects of the iron exposure without actually removing the iron from our systems. Only the Luidaeg seemed to be genuinely shaking off the effects of her time in the cell, although her hands had yet to return to what I thought of as her normal. It was a bit unsettling, with the rest of her looking so mortal, to have her walking among us with the hands of some taloned sea-beast.

As we walked, we began to find ourselves confronted with places where the knowe simply ceased to exist, an ordinary hall turning a corner and becoming an expanse of emptiness. I felt for the shadow roads when we reached those spans, and while I could find them, they were distant, insecure. I didn't try to access them. Losing myself in an endless void when I was this close to going home seemed like foolishness.

Every time this happened, Simon would make a sound of displeasure, turn around, and take us via another route, resulting in an increasingly circuitous journey. We had been walking for what felt like well over an hour when October leaned closer to the Luidaeg and asked, in a low voice, "Is this going to work?"

"Titania isn't creating new spaces, which means she's working with whatever collapsed and wasn't somehow reclassified as 'lost,'" she said. "I don't understand how that magic works. I don't think anyone does." She turned to look at me as she spoke, clearly waiting for me to tell her that no, no, the Cait Sidhe understood perfectly, and always had.

Sadly, I couldn't do that. Instead, I said, "The magic that takes the lost things to our Court is very old. It may be older than the Cait Sidhe ourselves. I don't even know if Oberon actually put it in place; it may have simply arisen from the void, a necessary part of Faerie maintaining its own structural integrity. Or maybe it's a spell so ancient and complex that we no longer understand it, and so we dismiss it as the way things have always worked. The knowing of the difference is beyond me."

"So no one knows," said October, frustration evident. "Swell. Is there a reason Titania's not making new spaces?"

"She's always been more about refinement than creation," said the Luidaeg. "Mom did most of the intentional creation, back when it was the going thing. And what Mom didn't make, Dad had a tendency to cobble together, to make sure everything kept working properly."

October frowned. "If Titania didn't create, what did she add to Faerie?"

"She bore many of the First, and her children were by and large successful, if only because they were so good at killing off the competition," said the Luidaeg, tone going flat. "And they shaped Faerie in her image. Mom could build a bench. Titania would decorate it, turn it into something people would fight and die to protect. Creation isn't the only worthwhile pursuit, and right now, we should be glad of that, because if she were more inclined to make her own things instead of repurposing what belongs to others, we'd be in even more trouble than we already are."

Simon had moved to the head of our group as we walked, and was now approaching a plain wooden door, simpler than most of those that lined the halls. A somewhat ominous pattern of repeating briars and thorns was carved along the doorframe. He paused and turned back to the rest of us.

"If she was able to recover anything of the grounds, they should be here," he said. "If not . . ."

"The grounds were in the Summerlands, and even as the knowe collapsed, they should have been stable enough to remain," said the Luidaeg, clearly trying to sound reassuring, and doing a frankly terrible job of it. "Go ahead."

Taking a deep breath, Simon turned again, and opened the door to reveal the grounds of the royal knowe.

It was a wide stretch of green, apparently modeled off the hunting fields behind a European country estate. It was beautiful and dated at the same time, both wild and absolutely cultivated, with not a single strand of grass out of place. Fog swirled thick around the edges of the scene, framing it in gray. The sky was blocked out by more fog, or possibly clouds in the same color, making it difficult to tell the time of day; there was neither sun nor moon, but there was light, bright enough that I would have guessed at early afternoon if I'd been pressed to name an hour. Simon sighed relief and stepped outside. The ground didn't collapse out from beneath him or vanish to leave him standing in the void, and so the rest of us followed, trailing out into the open air, which was sweet and tasted slightly of loam.

After going from the iron-laced dungeon to the lifeless, empty halls, being outside and in good air again was a huge relief, and I watched it spread through our party, everyone relaxing and untensing just a little as they realized we had made it out.

"This way," said Simon, and set out across the green, already moving better now that we were out in the fresh air.

"Has this always been here?" asked October, hurrying to match his pace.

I matched hers with less trouble, but then, I hadn't spent the last four months locked in a tower, comparatively inactive.

"For as long as I've known the knowe," said Simon. "I'm a bit surprised you're not familiar, given the story of how you found this place."

"I found it, I didn't claim it," said October, somewhat sourly. "And it's not like I was exactly welcome to wander around and explore after I surrendered it to the Queen."

I swallowed the urge to laugh. She sounded so genuinely annoyed that the Queen, who had famously never liked her, hadn't thought to invite her over to explore the grounds. Sometimes my little fish was even more of a delight than I expected her to be. Here we were, walking toward what might well be a confrontation with the Summer Queen, and she was still mad at someone she'd never liked in the first place for treating her inconsiderately.

That woman can hold a grudge like a cat, and I have very few higher compliments that I can give.

My amusement didn't last. The fog was getting thicker, reducing visibility in all directions to perhaps twenty feet, and swallowing up the crumbling shape of the false Queen's knowe as we moved further into the green. If there was a standing stable, it had yet to make an appearance; we could just be wandering away into the wilds to lose ourselves forever. I reached again for the Shadow Roads, and was relieved when I found them strong, present, and close. If I needed to grab October and run, I could.

Maybe that was a cowardly way to think, but I was well past concern for cowardice. What I cared about at this point was survival, and the survival of my wife and child. If that meant we ran, then we ran. I was only waiting because she'd never forgive me if I moved too soon. Sometimes, balancing my natural desire to keep my family out of danger with the reality of loving October is a quest in and of itself.

October frowned as we walked, clearly pondering the situation. Finally, she looked to the Luidaeg, and asked the one question that was prying at us all, to one degree or another: "Who could she be using as a sacrifice?"

"Can't be a child of Oberon, which means May's safe," said the Luidaeg. "The night-haunts came from a daughter of his and Mom's. May's been around long enough at this point that she has some Titania-descendant memories mixed up with everything else in that nightmare she calls a head, but while that gives Titania a claim, it doesn't change who she belongs to. Jazz is protected for the same reason."

That caused me to think of something I didn't care for in the least. "Raj is of Erda's line," I said. "Are the children of Titania so protected?"

"No," said the Luidaeg, glancing in my direction before looking firmly back at October. "He could be a candidate. So could Quentin. She wants this one to hurt you, Toby, and that means she's going to be looking at the people you actually care about."

"So Mom's in the clear," said October bitterly, as August winced and Simon grimaced.

"Probably," agreed the Luidaeg. "Taking Amandine wouldn't hurt you enough. Neglectful parenting as a form of self-protection isn't

TWENTY-EIGHT

SIMON, WHO WAS NAKED save for October's leather jacket wrapped around his shoulders, staggered to his feet. October stayed on the ground, grabbing August by the shoulders and shaking her fiercely.

"August? August?! Wake up, you *walnut*," she snapped, then looked up, at me, expression pleading. "What happened? Why did they fall down?"

"If I had to guess, given who was impacted, I'd say that breaking Titania's Ride broke her spell, and when she went to pay the sacrifice herself, it shattered and rebounded on everyone who was still enchanted," said Simon. "They should have their memories back when they wake, if I'm correct."

"And the Luidaeg?" asked October. "I already unbound her."

"I can't speak to the Luidaeg," said Simon. "Given the way my own head is pounding, it may be as simple as the iron poisoning catching up with her."

"There are five of us and four of them," I said. "That means we can carry them as needed, without October having to lift anyone by herself."

She looked like she was about to object. I glared at her, and she quelled.

"You are *pregnant*," I said. "I'm not fool enough to try to order you to stillness, but I won't have you exerting yourself without cause."

I moved to scoop the also-naked Quentin off the ground, leading to

Dean objecting and fluttering around me, trying to take his boyfriend back. I glared at him, much as I had glared at October.

"Get Garm," I said. "He's lighter, and we need to do this sensibly."

"I'm not seeing how this is sensible," said Dean.

"I am a King, and you will do as you are told," I snapped.

"You're not *my* King," he snapped back.

"You spend half your time in my house, I have this much authority."

Raysel, having picked up on the numbers and the fact that someone would have to carry the sea witch, hurried to lever August up, wrapping the unconscious woman's arm around her shoulders. Simon looked unimpressed but didn't object, not wanting to scare the girl. He moved to lift the Luidaeg, October looking like she couldn't decide between helping him and helping Raysel.

In the end, the Luidaeg won out, and she stepped over to help him.

Between the five of us, we were able to get our four fallen off the ground. We were, however, still in the middle of nowhere. I reached for the Shadow Roads, finding them easily, then turned to Dean.

"You carry one of those mobile phones, yes?"

"Yes," said Dean uncertainly.

"Do you have it with you?"

"Yes," he said again, and shifted his grip on Garm so that he could reach one hand into his pocket, producing a small metal-and-glass rectangle. "The battery's half-dead."

"It's been *four months*," said Simon.

"April wanted to make sure we didn't lose touch just because Toby dragged us off on a wild goose chase," said Dean. "My phone's good for almost a year, if I'm not doing anything major with it. All I've been doing since this started is taking pictures and reading things I already had downloaded."

"Please don't explain what that means," I said. "Can you send a text to Raj, please?"

"Sure?" Dean lowered Garm carefully back to the ground, then began tapping away. A moment later, his phone buzzed, and he raised his eyebrows. "Okay, Raj says Ginevra just came back, and all the other cats are unconscious. He seems pretty freaked out."

"As he should be," I said. "Tell him the Ride is broken and that we're somewhere deep in the Summerlands. I can't transport you all via the Shadow Roads. It's not safe to take anyone unconscious through that route, and I refuse to take October into the cold."

"Hey," she objected.

I ignored her. "So we're going to have to walk until we find a way out of here, which may take a while. Please let him know that we're all alive."

I wasn't going to claim that we were all okay. Not yet. That status was reserved for some point in the future, when we were all safe in our homes and no longer dealing with the aftermath of chaos.

Dean resumed tapping at the screen, then glanced up. "Raj asks if there's anything he can do."

"Not unless he knows someone who can perform a location spell powerful enough to find us in the deep wilds," I said. "Does anyone have the key?"

"The Luidaeg had it last," said Raysel. "I didn't see what happened to it."

"And as I doubt any of us wants to search her pockets, that means no," I said. "Fine. Let's go."

We started walking, slow and unsteady. Everyone was still dealing with iron poisoning; the spell's aftereffects rendering half our number unconscious didn't make this any easier. Quentin was a dead weight in my arms, and I wished I had a blanket or something to cover him with; he deserved more dignity than this. At least he was breathing normally. While we might not know how long the backlash of Titania's spell would last, it didn't seem to have done any physical damage.

I was honestly more concerned about the Luidaeg. She had been more affected by the iron in the dungeons than she'd admitted to any of us, and I would have been willing to wager that her current state had more to do with how much magic she'd performed without a chance to clear the poison from her system. Firstborn are hard to kill. How hard are they to damage, really? It wasn't a question I'd had much cause to contemplate.

Although it was going to be a question in the future. Amandine had to die for what she'd done. Not just Simon, but Quentin, and telling Titania that she'd be willing to raise my child as her own. She had signed her own death warrant with that decision, and if she had any sense at all, she knew it.

We staggered on, across the seemingly endless fields, the sky shining dark above us, until we reached the forest's edge. I paused there, sniffing the air.

Yes, I still smelled bonfires in the distance. We might be far from any habitations, but not so far the wind couldn't reach. And if the wind could reach, we could get there.

"This way," I said, trying to sound confident, and kept walking.

The nature of our respective burdens meant that October couldn't pace me, not without leaving Simon to carry the Luidaeg alone. I was, in all honesty, grateful for the silence. Once we were alone, we would have a great deal to discuss, beginning with how much I had missed her and ending with how angry I was that the moment she had been restored to herself, she had gone charging right back into danger. I didn't expect her to change. I expected her to remember that she was endangering more than just herself, no matter how good she believed her reasons to be.

On and on we walked. The journey was simultaneously nerve-racking and uneventful. The sky was black and endless. The forest was dark and filled with shifting shadows and strange noises, owls calling out across the miles and foxes cackling in the deep distance. What forms those creatures would actually take remained unrevealed, as they avoided us much as we avoided them.

Garm, who had been able to perceive the changed world if not break through the changes on his own, was the first to start to stir. He groaned and twitched, becoming harder to carry, until finally he opened his eyes and began to stumble along, trying to regain his footing. Dean stopped walking, letting Garm steady himself. Garm groaned, rubbing his face with one hand.

"I feel like I just took a brick to the head," he said, sourly.

"Spell backlash," I said. "Not quite the same, but close enough."

His eyes snapped open and his head snapped up as he processed what I'd said. "Wait—backlash?"

"Yes. We broke the Ride. We won, such as it is." I shifted my grip on Quentin, gesturing to the forest around us. "And now we're lost in the Summerlands with a bunch of unconscious people, so if you can walk on your own, or better, help Raysel carry August, that would be a great advantage."

Garm nodded, staggering away from Dean and moving, as requested, to assist with August. Dean, as I had very much expected, moved toward me, and I relinquished Quentin to him in order to shift over and nudge October out of the way, taking the Luidaeg's weight onto my own shoulders.

"How much farther?" asked Raysel.

"I'm sorry, child, but I don't know," I said.

The ground was starting to soften underfoot, turning swampy. That made me feel somewhat better about our chances, since the Summerland's access to the Luidaeg's residence had a tendency to manifest in marshy areas.

"Look for any sort of standing structure," I said, to the group in general, as I scanned the trees around us for anything that might support a door.

We kept walking. Quentin woke up, looked at Dean, and immediately burst into tears, which only intensified when October moved to join the pair of them. That slowed our progress considerably, and as they were still trying to collect themselves, the Luidaeg came to long enough to mumble something and pass out again.

The next turn we made left us looking at a crumbling brick wall, alone against a border of briars. There was a door right in the middle of it. I shifted the Luidaeg's weight back onto Simon and cautiously approached, finally knocking.

Someone on the other side of the door knocked something over with an audible clang, and then it was opening, and Poppy was there, hair askew, wings hanging limp, staring at us.

"Here you are!" she cried. "Here you are, and here I am, and come in, come in! Home's been waiting long and long for your returning!"

We went inside, and while we weren't home yet, we were finally almost there.

TWENTY-NINE

THREE MONTHS LATER, OCTOBER and I stood at the entrance to Muir Woods. The sun had long since set; the mortals who worked the gate during the day were gone home, and the trees were alight with pixies. I swept her into my arms before she could protest, starting to walk toward the trees.

"I'm pregnant, not injured," she complained, half-laughing.

"No, and I won't *allow* you to become injured tonight," I replied, walking onward. "Arden wishes to see you, and you cannot refuse. But I *can* insist that you be escorted at all times."

"I love you, you nerd," she said, resting her head against my shoulder and otherwise offering no resistance.

This was the first full Court Arden had called since "the incident," and she had made it very clear that October was expected to attend, whether or not I wanted her traipsing around the woods in January. I wasn't thrilled by the timing, but I was still grateful for the reprieve, even if it had been a consequence of Arden needing her own period to adjust to the real, fully restored world.

Arden and Nolan were among the lucky few whose lives had been in some way materially better under Titania's enchantment, and both of them had found the return to normalcy unexpectedly rough. So far as I was aware, they were still in close contact with the monarchs on the Golden Shore, and I had little doubt that our Kingdoms would be closer allies going forward.

Breaking Titania's Ride had restored people's memories and, in the case of places like the home I shared with October, removed the illusions that kept us from our homes. When we'd gone back to the house, it had been waiting for us. Bridget, on the other hand, had returned to the house in Berkeley where she'd been living for the duration of Titania's spell, only to find it occupied by the human family who had been renting it from her since her relocation to Shadowed Hills. It wasn't a perfect system, by any means.

Not least because that human family had been living as enchanted furniture for the previous four months. Titania remained a fan of the classics, it seemed.

What it had not done was put anyone back where they belonged. Walther found himself in Silences; much of Arden's Court had snapped out of the spell still on the Golden Shore. The chaos of getting everyone back to their proper places had lasted much of the first month.

Simon had been correct about the Luidaeg: her collapse was brought on by iron poisoning rather than the breaking of Titania's Ride. Poppy and Oberon had been sealed inside her apartment through the whole ordeal, and had been happy to provide us with counteragents for iron poisoning once they'd realized what was going on. Thankfully.

Patrick and Dianda had been waiting for us when we'd finally left the apartment, having come to the surface the moment it was possible to do so, and had taken their family home with them, not looking back. I hadn't seen Simon since then. August, on the other hand, was visiting regularly, spending time with her sister—sisters, really, since May was teaching her how to bake. It seemed she was going to be a permanent fixture in our household going forward. She still disliked Quentin for his part in Titania's fantasy, and Quentin didn't blame her; he was quieter now, more subdued, and rarely left the house when not forced to do so. His healing would be long, but it would happen.

Raysel continued to insist that four months in an enchanted alternate reality didn't count against her term of service, and still fully intended to live with us for a full year. To my surprise, Sylvester had agreed, and Luna hadn't argued. Things were calming down.

The Brown children had resurfaced after the spell collapsed. October had apparently located Anthony and Andrew during her own chaotic journey through the Summerlands; Karen had been playing the role of Eira, and while all three were racked with guilt over the actions they'd taken, no one seemed to be blaming them. Where Cassandra had been, she would not say, only turned her haunted eyes away in silence.

The part of the false Queen had been played, apparently, by the woman herself. Sometime during the first month, she'd been found in hiding and arrested once more, and resided once again in Arden's prisons.

All my subjects were well, as was Ginevra. We were going to be all right.

I climbed the hillside, October in my arms, holding her close as we made the transition into the Summerlands. The gates to Arden's knowe were standing open, Lowri and another guard keeping watch outside. October began trying to sit up.

"Put me down," she said.

I did as I was asked, setting her carefully on her feet. She leaned up, kissing my cheek, and the curve of her belly pressed against my side, a reminder that for all we'd paid, we hadn't lost what mattered.

Dropping back to the flats of her feet, she said, "Let's go visit the queen."

"As long as it's only this one," I said, smiling as I reached over to brush her hair away from her eyes. "No more Summer Queens for us."

"No," she agreed. "I quite like the one we have. Come on."

I took her hand, and we walked into the knowe side by side, neither of us looking back or letting go. We were back in the world the way it was meant to be, and we were close enough to home that we could feel it in the air.

Titania would be back. Of that, there was no question.

But she would never be able to offer us a perfection better than the one we already had.

Read on for
a brand new novella
by Seanan McGuire:

DOUBTLESS AND SECURE

I'll fill these dogged spies with false reports:
And, pretty child, sleep doubtless and secure . . .
—William Shakespeare, *King John IV.*

ONE

Summer, 1612

SHE ARRIVED IN A carriage pulled by greater hippocampi, their coats bright and tropical in their garish rainbow array. Compared to the spectacle of her conveyance, all of Saltmist must seem shabby and monochrome, for all that it was not a Duchy without its own natural beauties. It was just that the wonders of the Pacific were more slow to show themselves, more inclined toward shades of silver and brown and russet than the richly pigmented rainbow of Chantara's retinue.

The carriage stopped on a level with the highest arrival platform of the palace, door swinging open, and a series of Cephali emerged, four in all, ranging from two large individuals whose patterned sashes marked them as guards and explained the large knives belted at what served as their hips, to the smaller lady's maid who followed, her hair in an elaborate braid and an adolescent girl riding on her back. The four swam to the platform and anchored themselves there, the guards at the front, the maid and her charge locking their tentacles around the rail, all of them watching their surroundings with wary eyes.

They expected an attack, it seemed, or were at the very least prepared for one if it were to come.

The carriage door, which had swung shut after the Cephali emerged, opened again, and Chantara pulled herself cautiously free. She was a lovely woman, as befitted a Merrow noble, with long, iridescently hued fins that gleamed rose pink and opal in the light coming off the palace, moon-white scales that trended toward a delicate mother-of-pearl across the front of her tail, and skin the color of a brown tang's scales that cast all the rest of her even more deeply into contrast. Her hair was purest black, braided with loops of shell and pearl, and bracelets ornamented the length of her arms, which were long and corded with muscle, marked by the thin white scars of a dozen successful combats. She swam to position herself behind her guards but in front of her maid, waiting in frozen silence.

Morcan, who had watched their arrival from the safety of the palace window, looked at the frozen ferocity on her face and wished, not for the first time, that Amphitrite had not bid the Merrow to be fearless. She was frightened: he could see it in the stiffness of her shoulders, the iciness of her eyes. But fear was not allowed, and never had been; for a Merrow, especially a daughter of a noble house, fear was a transgression greater than dalliance with a mortal, or bargaining with the Almere in the deepest dark. Her parents and his bartered for her life, and while he did not know what fee had been asked for her presence, he knew it was his duty to see it well-paid.

Regretting more than he could ever say, Morcan rose from his place and swam out the window to meet his bride for the first time.

The first I remember of the man who bartered for my mother's mistress is his voice. He spoke loudly, as many among the Merrow did, but with him, there was always the impression that he understood he was doing it to perform for an audience as yet unnamed: he didn't feel his voice deserved the bulk of the space in the sea, only that custom demanded he take it. When he came before my mother's mistress, his eyes were gentle.

Mistress Chantara had spoken direly for our entire trip from her birthplace in the waters of Suvannamaccha, saying that she had heard Saltmist was a backwater, too yoked to the land, which was underdeveloped and hostile to the Undersea. She would surely live a life of privation while she was here, denied art and culture and decent food, and she would never have agreed to come had she not been the third of three daughters, unable to inherit from her parents, with no prospects any closer to home. Suvannamaccha was a wonder and a jewel of the sea, and she would miss her homeland even more than she would miss the company of her sisters, one of whom would claim the Duchy and one of whom would very likely die when the time came for their parents to step away from their domain and leave its guardianship to their daughters.

"You Cephali are fortunate, not to have been tasked to rulership," she said to my mother, on many occasions, as Mother rested behind her and braided her hair or adjusted her ornamentations. "It is a burden such as should not be set upon the shoulders of any in the sea."

"Yes, mistress," Mother would reply, and continue at her duties, for the Cephali inherited no desire to rule from our Firstborn. Instead, Chryseis left us with a great desire for order, and the understanding that order is best found by placating the Merrow, who may enjoy their games of king and kingdom, but who have no skill for the organization of their own households or the doing of their own laundry.

It is a noble calling, to bring order to the sea, which seems to have no interest in our art, and indeed rejects it at every turn. We will fight to tame the waters until our bloodline is no more, and we will stop our dancing content that we have done a great service for Faerie. Mother had been chosen to accompany Chantara after her parents announced that she was to wed a Duke in far-off Leucothea.

I say "chosen" as if anyone, anywhere, has ever been able to compel a Cephali to do something we didn't want to do. Mother didn't volunteer, but when the task fell upon her, she did not change her shade and vanish into the walls, and when she asked me if I wished to see the world, I came willingly. I was young, but I was not so young that I could not see both the temptations and the dangers of Suvannamaccha.

The kingdom was large and ancient, well established, thronging with demesnes and noble houses, and each of them had their own staff of Cephali bringing order to their halls. The duchy where I had been born was no exception. Chantara's sisters had staffs of their own, who would be looked to first when the time came to assign such duties as were needed, and Cephali of Chantara's staff who had chosen to remain behind would find themselves scrambling to be useful.

It's not good for us, mentally, to be idle. And so I had gone with my mother to this new place, where the water tasted of unfamiliar currents and the weather shifted without warning, where the people were as pale as I was, when I allowed my colors to relax into the shades they self-selected, the ones that were as natural to me as the shimmer of Mistress Chantara's fins was to her: red, bright as a betta, from my waist downward, with hair to match, and pale as a snapper's belly in between tentacles and tresses. I matched these people quite well. I would blend into the background of their lives with ease.

It is better, for a Cephali, to blend in than to stand out. Faerie would not have made us masters of camouflage if we were intended to be seen when we didn't wish it: everything about us is designed to disappear. I had spent most of our journey hidden from the eye, compressing myself against the carriage walls and changing my hue to blend perfectly with their design.

Mother and Mistress Chantara's guards had watched me with indulgent grace, not calling attention to my brief flickers of visibility. I was yet young on that journey, scarce twelve full tides of age, and experimentation was how I would learn. We lived among noble households then as we do now, in part to bring order, and in part to give our children time to grow into their potential, unafraid of the dangers of the open water. If I behaved as a child, it was a sign that they had provided for me sufficiently.

And then we were in Saltmist, and Duke Morcan was emerging to greet us. His parents had been more clever than Mistress Chantara's, and less fortunate: while they had stopped at a single child rather than cast their lines of inheritance into question, they had been drawn into a rebellion against King Elynas of Leucothea, and when their rebellion had been unsuccessful, as most such must be, they had painted the tides with their blood. Elynas ruled yet, and was a kind-enough king that he had not ordered their only son executed for his parents' crimes, only asked that Morcan tend to Saltmist and find a bride from outside the Kingdom to continue his family line.

It was a more clever command than it might seem, for King Elynas had a daughter, and it was murmured among the Merrow that Duke Morcan was a well-formed man. I looked upon him and didn't see it; he had far too few limbs, and was always the same colors, which was dull and would surely cost him the interest of any partner he chanced to take. But Mistress Chantara looked upon him and seemed not to be displeased, and so perhaps it was a truth that he could catch the eye of a Merrow-maid seeking for a mate.

King Elynas had no interest in losing his throne to the son of those who tried to take it, and so his hand had been behind the offer which reached across the seas, all the way to Suvannamaccha, to land in the ear of Mistress Chantara's parents and bring her to Morcan's side, with her retinue in tow.

The night of our arrival there was a grand banquet, and a musical performance by the Duchy's Selkies, during which the Duke and his bride-to-be slipped away. Mother and the guard were occupied with meeting the Duchy's Cephali, none of whom were so young as I was, and so I had taken it upon myself to follow them and listen to see if I needed to report poor treatment of our mistress to my mother.

She was not my mistress then, for I was too young, and she was not my mistress later, for I had another come to claim that position, but in the moment, I had been more than willing to believe myself in her service, if it meant I could play at serving a Cephali's role. I could watch, and listen, and, as needed, defend.

"I know you do not love me, and I do not love you," said Morcan, once they were alone. Mistress Chantara drew back, feigning offense. She lacked the ability to change her colors, or she might have done so more believably. Morcan snorted. "You've just *met* me. If you fell in love so quickly, it would be without value, and I can tell by looking at you that you are a woman who understands the value of things. Our marriage gains allies for your parents, and removes a potential problem for my king. Do you agree?"

"I do," said Mistress Chantara, cautiously. "Such things are not often spoken of so openly. Do you tell me this to shame me, or to push me to the side while you dally with some lover you prefer to cleave to?"

"No lover," he said. "I am a simple man, in that I find the Merrow to be the finest jewels of the sea, and there have been no Merrow suitable for courtship in my demesne for some time. My parents, you see, labored long before they came here, established Saltmist, and welcomed me to their keeping."

Mistress Chantara frowned. "I do not understand."

"My father made poor choices, but he was a clever man," said Morcan. "When my mother yearned for a child to call her own, he went seeking the sea witch, and from her he bartered the secret of why children come so slowly to us. Like sings to like, you see, and when enough are gathered in one place, the song drowns out all others."

"Forgive me, but I still—"

"We are the only Merrow now remaining in Saltmist, my lady, and if you will be my wife, I will give you children more quickly than you can possibly believe." His expression was earnest; his voice, equally so. "I am willing to make it a condition of our marriage. If no child has blessed our bed by the seventh tide of our union, then I will release you without complaint or dishonor, to swim where you will. And when our second child is born, an heir for each of us, if you are not happy here—if Saltmist has not become your heart's home—then we will wait for the children to reach their majority and, upon that happy occasion, divorce without reluctance. You will have your freedom. You can find love, if you so choose. Do we have an accord?"

It was an audacious proposal, bold and sincere and all but unheard-of.

Mistress Chantara considered it for some time before she nodded.

"Yes," she said. "I will marry you. But I get my heir first."

And how he smiled.

Winter, 1614

Lady Chantara, Ducal Consort of Saltmist, howled in furious pain, clutching at the loops of seaweed that kept her from drifting free of her birthing bed. There was a note of triumph in the sound: this was a battle reserved for her and her alone, which none other could fight on her behalf, and she was winning.

Cephali swarmed around her, Mother and three others, who had become trusted members of the Lady's retinue in the two years we had spent so far in Saltmist. They were a beautiful dance of tentacles and bodies, moving with a grace and practiced elegance that made it look as if they attended upon the birth of a noble Merrow every day.

The lady howled again, and the water around her darkened with blood as her firstborn son slid into the sea. The Naiad who had been waiting by the door, watching this process, waved her hands and the blood compressed itself into three small spheres, almost like jewels, which floated to nestle in her palms. She would take them to the Asrai, who would use the blood to enhance the Duchy's wards, tying them ever more closely to the Lady and thus, through the power of inheritance, to her children.

As the Naiad slipped from the room, Duke Morcan swam into it, having been drawn by the cessation of his wife's screams. The babe had yet to begin to cry, nestled as he was in a cradle formed of Mother's tentacles, the tip of one in his mouth, where he sucked at it curiously as he looked around the room with unfocused dark-blue eyes. Like every other baby I'd seen, he looked nothing like his parents, and more like the unpleasant blend of a salmon and a drowned human.

"Helmi, come see the baby," said my mother, as Morcan went to Lady Chantara and stroked her tangled hair, beaming ear to ear. She had borne her heir. Half their marital duties were done, and they had been wed less than a tide.

She might yet return to Suvannamaccha.

Spring, 1619
"But *I* want to be with Mother!" protested the boy, lip jutting outward and fins flared in challenge.

I was no longer a child of twelve, but a long and lanky young woman approaching my own adulthood. I kept my tentacles spread, blocking the door from passage, and stared him down from my greater height. He could swim above me if he so chose, seeking the higher ground, but to do so would be to admit that I had begun our conflict by getting the better of him. His pride would take a bruise if he chose that path, and young Torin was nothing if not a prideful boy.

His fins relaxed as he abandoned the pretense of a challenge, and he sulked at me. "My baby brother or sister is coming right now, and you won't let me into the room," he accused.

"A new approach," I said. "I can't say I think any more of it than I did of your attempts to intimidate, but it's certainly more polite."

He glared.

"Do you think you can take me?" I asked, with genuine interest. He was only five, but he was quick, and had a wicked temper. He'd managed to bite some of the other Cephali when he didn't want them cleaning his quarters or telling him to finish his supper, and I had no doubt he would rule in the fine Merrow tradition when the time came.

Fortunately for me, he would be doing it far from here. He was to be the Lady Chantara's heir, which was part of the reason behind his continual viciousness; while his parents couldn't compel who he chose in the eventual divorce, they could encourage his choice. Since his birth, the lady had doted upon him and encouraged his every whim, while his father offered discipline and dire tales of the weight of rulership in a coastal demesne. When she left, he would very likely accompany her, and I had already made the decision to stay here, in Saltmist, where the currents had become familiar and the people were the same.

I liked this place. I liked the taste of the water and the forests of towering kelp on the mortal side of the world. And of course, I enjoyed the company of the giant Pacific octopuses, which often moved into the lower levels of the palace during the stormy season, their bodies so like my own in color, their eyes so wise.

Saltmist was my home. I would not leave when he did. And I would not weep to see him gone.

As on the occasion of Torin's own birth, the lady's wails stopped, and silence fell. Duke Morcan pulled himself through the nearest window, having been swimming laps outside to distract himself from the battle he could neither join nor win for his wife's protection, rushing toward the door.

"Helmi, let me pass," he commanded.

I drew myself a little higher, limbs as rigidly extended as I could manage, and answered, "Hydor has not yet emerged. The lady is not ready for you."

"She has borne my heir!" he snarled. Any other outcome was not to be considered, however possible it was. Death in childbed is more common for Merrow women than for Cephali, due to the rigidity of their bones, although it is still not a common thing.

"Perhaps she has, but she is still duchess here, and we will not enter her chambers until she shows herself ready."

Behind me, the door opened. I looked over my shoulder, and Hydor was there, globes of blood resting in her palms like strange, dark fruits. I untensed my limbs and dropped to the floor, allowing her to pass me by.

Before I could resume my post, Duke Morcan was past me and into the room, with Torin on his fins. I sighed, watching them go. I might be scolded for allowing them through, but I wouldn't be punished, not on such a grand and celebratory day.

The wail of an infant rose from the room, and I followed the two Merrow inside to find my mother rocking a fresh-born Merrow in her arms, trying to convince the babe to settle. The babe, who already had a full head of thick black hair to go with her mazed blue eyes, was having none of it. She flailed her fists and thrashed her tail, and continued to do so until Mother surrendered her to Morcan, who tapped her nose with the tip of his finger.

"Be still, my limpet," he said, and she was, staring up at her father with judgmental confusion.

Torin was ignoring the baby entirely, seeking instead the company of his mother, even as I moved to seek the company of mine. She slipped her arm around my shoulders.

"Your liege, my Helmi," she said. "Oh, how I shall miss you."

I think that was the moment I realized we were set to swim in different seas, my mother and I, and more, that while I might regret it, I wouldn't change it. My future was here, in Saltmist, with the furious child Duke Morcan cradled in his arms.

"What's her name?" he asked, glancing at his wife.

Lady Chantara sighed, satisfied and pained. "Dianda," she said, and all the sea bore witness.

Summer, 1625
The summer tides were high and strong, the waters warm and rich with foreign currents, each carrying its own wealth of secrets. The nets were full, the fields fertile, and I was beginning to consider how severe the penalties for breaking Oberon's Law could truly be. Surely the Undersea was at war, somewhere in all its great and drowning depth! Surely I could claim to have been acting under the orders of some far-off prince or unidentified princess, and thus have acted maliciously, but not illegally.

Alas, I could think of no currently declared wars, and while I could claim all I wanted, there were ways of having the truth of people if it was needed. And surely Lady Chantara would demand the truth if I was found disposing of the body of her beloved boy, no matter how much he deserved it.

At five, he had been a terror. At eleven, he was a nightmare, and to none greater than his younger sister, who doted upon him for all his cruelties. I had stopped him on multiple occasions from cutting her hair and stealing her things, and once from cutting her fins, which he had likened to a haircut, not seeming to care that it was one in which the "hair" would never grow back or recover.

Each time I attempted to punish him or have him held accountable for his actions, he laughed at me, called me increasingly unkind names, and swam off, Duke's son, untouchable and growing crueler by the day. Dianda did not lack for bravery, but seemed determined to express it by attempting to convince her beloved older brother to play with her, not understanding that nothing she could do would dim his temper.

He was old enough now to understand the arrangement his parents had made before he was born, and more, that as his mother's heir, he would keep her company, which was of the utmost importance to him, but he would lose the Duchy. Until quite recently, he had managed to believe that he would be able to go away with his mother when the time came, but still inherit his father's title. Learning that he wouldn't had raised a great and terrible fury in him. Some nights I feared that if he wasn't controlled, he would see his sister dead in a bid to keep what he believed belonged to him by right.

I had been assigned as Dianda's nursemaid and companion almost from the moment of her birth. When she no longer needed a nurse's care, I had transitioned into a more general sort of service, and would be continuing to serve until she had no more need of me or one of us was dead. Given her general incompetence when it came to managing her own wardrobe, I expected it to be the latter. Which might come more quickly if Torin was not brought firmly to fin.

I swam back and forth outside the receiving-room door, waiting for the moment when I would be called into the presence of the Duke and Ducal Consort. Torin had been found trying to bait his sister into swimming down to tweak the tails of the Almere, which was a death sentence by a softer name. Duke Morcan and Lady Chantara were debating his punishment now.

Traditionally, Merrow children are encouraged to begin disposing of their rivals at as early an age as possible, which explains why most Merrow parents raise their offspring in solitude, rather than favoring teeming nurseries, as the Cephali are more wont to do. For Torin and Dianda, the expectation was that they would each emerge from childhood dominant and secure, something that would be difficult to achieve if they weren't permitted to fight. But the arrangement between their parents both meant that it was essential Torin not torment his sister too dramatically, and that Dianda be alive and able to take the Duchy after he had swum away. They would live too distant from one another as adults to be considered rivals.

Punishing Torin too harshly would discourage him from the normal ways of his descendant line, and might disadvantage him when he was older. At the same time, refusal to punish him would leave Dianda vulnerable to his abuse, and would weaken the Duchy over time. As I circled, waiting for the summons, I was grateful that I was not inside that room. The decision was not mine to make.

Merrow court and marry in the ways of the land courts, having been encouraged to keep that custom by their First, who had been asked to do so by Titania herself, or so the stories go. The Cephali First was, perhaps, more aware of her environment, and that we would never be predictable, stationary creatures of fixed points and gravitational constraints. The rules were different for us because *we* were different. Torin and Dianda would both be raised knowing that it was their duty to one day wed and continue the Merrow bloodline, while I would be free to spend as many centuries as I liked in solitude, tending my own garden, until someone came along to sway my fancy.

Really, the Cephali have it easier in almost all ways worth charting, save one: unlike the Merrow, we have to *deal* with the Merrow, and they're exhausting.

The door swung open, and Mother's head emerged. "Helmi, they'll see you now," she called.

I nodded, pulling my tentacles together in rough parody of a Merrow's single tail, and swam into the room with the up-and-down kicking motion they used to propel themselves through the sea, stopping before the raised platform where the ducal thrones were settled. That, too, was an element kept in common with the Courts of the land, which I had been assured followed much the same design. Morcan looked exhausted. Chantara looked enraged.

"Maid Helmi," said Morcan, with a deep nod. "I understand you were witness to the disagreement. Can you enlighten us on the truth between the two tales we've been told today?"

It would have been easier had the Lady Chantara not been in the room. Of the pair, she was the more likely to insist upon titles and niceties. Mother said it was because they had been more like a land court in Suvannamaccha, for all that I had been too young to attend on such protocols when yet we lived there.

It felt odd, attaching titles to children, like I was tying stones to the tails of salmon spawn, but what must be done must be done, and so I bowed my own head and said, "The Lady Dianda was playing with her counting stones in the sand pit when Lord Torin sought to make mischief. He came and swept her stones aside, and, when she objected, told her that his lady mother would believe him when he said she had been throwing the stones at his eyes. He called her cruel names and pulled her hair, and, when she rose to his taunts, told her she was no true Merrow, and would not be, until she had performed an act of great bravery. She asked what manner of bravery could be found in these waters, and he told her to go down and tease the Almere, that none would doubt her courage if she were to do so. He was quite insistent. When he didn't choose to stop and swim away, I alerted the guard, lest the young miss head for the undertow."

"Which she did," said Duke Morcan. "Hence this meeting."

What he didn't say was that if I hadn't been there to overhear and then inform the guard, she might have made it down to the lightless deeps, and never come to light again. He could have been left without his daughter, the Duchy left without an heir. Would that change the agreement he had with the Lady? Would she have to bind herself to Saltmist long enough to get another child to leave behind when she swam away?

The ways of nobles are complicated and confusing, and I was well glad to be free of them.

"Yes," I agreed. "Which she did."

"Torin can't be allowed to go about risking his sister's life because it amuses him to do so," said Morcan slowly. "But she can't be sheltered to the point where she becomes other than Merrow, or she'll never be able to hold the Duchy when I'm gone. The boy will go three tides without desserts, and be otherwise unpunished. And you, Maid Helmi, will be Dianda's companion."

"Me?" I squeaked.

"You already attend on the children with admirable frequency, and she approaches the time when she'll need a nursemaid no longer but instead a lady's maid to call her own." He nodded gravely. "It is a simple solution, but I think an elegant one, and you will be able to intercede with my blessing if our son begins to push the bounds of what is permissible for one of his station. Do you understand?"

I had been intending for some time to remain in Saltmist when the Lady Chantara gathered her retinue and swam away, but this would solidify that choice; there would be no going back if I threw in my lot with the Duke's daughter.

But then, it is Chryseis's will that we should bring order to the sea in whatever way we can, and if my path to order was through a child too convinced of her own indestructability to know where she should and should not swim, well. Stranger tides have been set before us, and we rise to the occasion as we must.

"I do, Your Grace," I replied, and my course was set.

Winter, 1636

The less spoken of Chalerm, the better. His birth was a surprise; none had realized the Duke and his consort still dallied with one another, much less that they did so with a frequency that might get them a third child. That stopped with his arrival, for he represented not only an extension of the Lady Chantara's time in Saltmist, his majority being eleven years later than Dianda's, but a complication in dire need of addressing. Who would he decide for? As the marriage had been a negotiation, who did he belong to? Torin resented his brother from the moment of his birth, assuming that he must decide one day for their mother, who was, in Torin's eyes, the most wonderful woman in all the sea. And Dianda doted upon her younger brother, encouraged him to swim with her everywhere, and assumed far too openly that he would choose to stay in Saltmist.

Given the chance to secure his mother's full affections for himself *and* harm the sister he had come to despise, seeing her as the thief of what should have been his own, Torin moved with what might have been admirable forethought, had the death of his younger brother not been the goal toward which he swam. He waited for the day when Chalerm was old enough to swim unaided and unattended, then went to mock and taunt his brother much as he had once mocked his sister, until Chalerm rose to the bait and allowed himself to be led into the depths.

Torin returned. Chalerm did not.

Torin's punishment for what I could only regard as the calculated murder of his younger brother was a week with no treats or exercises in the open sea. Chalerm's punishment for believing in his beloved older brother was an eternity in the dark below, among the Almere. Such is the cruelty of the deep.

After that day, I took care that Torin and Dianda should never be alone, not even for an instant, out of the fear that Torin would try again and her anger would be too great to stop her from listening. If she had one towering flaw, my charge, it was that her temper could at times erase her reason, leaving her vulnerable to anyone with a more level head. Morcan had already lost a son. I wouldn't see him lose a daughter, not if there were any other way.

Chalerm's verse was a short one in the song of Saltmist, and his loss left unkind silence behind.

Spring, 1650

Dianda's thirty-first birthday had arrived, and with it, two great milestones that would change the Duchy around us forever: her majority, and her parents' divorce. Lady Chantara had spoken of nothing else for tides—and while it was forbidden by custom, if not any true law, for her to order her children in their choosing, both Torin and Dianda knew what was expected of them. Duke Morcan had been quiet and reserved since the discussions of divorce became an impending deadline and not a theoretical future possibility.

For the first time I realized that, despite the arrangement having been his suggestion to begin with, he had been hoping for a different outcome. Hoping that his arranged marriage would blossom into actual love, and his lady wife would choose to stay beside him when their heirs were raised and ready. But alas, that happy ending was not his to have, and as Dianda swam to present herself before the court that would one day be hers, he floated motionless at the back of the great reception hall, eyes on his daughter, fists balled at his sides.

"Sire?" I asked, coming to a stop beside him. "Are you well?"

"My lady intends to bring her call for divorce before me at midnight," he replied, in a soft, almost dull voice. "Both our children have their lines well set to memory by now. They've been rehearsing our separation since they were old enough to understand it—I think it's the only game they've ever enjoyed playing together. The one where they get to swim away from one another as an ending, and both can call themselves victorious. I shall have Saltmist, and she shall have all the damned sea."

"Sire, you could ask her to refrain," I said, for all that I was aware that only the divorce would have Torin away from Saltmist. Dianda still could not be trusted alone with him, nor he with her; the longer he remained, the more chance there was that I would slip in my supervision, and I would lose her.

Duke Morcan shook his head, solemnly. "If I have to ask, it's not meant to endure," he said. "I'll seek her when Dianda is old enough to take my title as her own, and leave my Duchy to less heartbroken hands."

"Saltmist will weep to see you go." I wasn't sure of that, but it seemed the proper thing to say.

He glanced my way, amused. "It won't, though. My girl will be twice the regent I've ever been, and as she won't have made the mistake of falling in love with one who won't stay, she'll be able to remain so much longer than I ever could. When the time comes for her to fight for her home, she'll fight like a demon. You and I both know that for what's true."

Dianda had finished presenting herself, and now floated at the center of a school of admirers and courtiers, all of them looking to curry favor before her currents were set and more difficult to change. There were even a few Merrow near her age among the number, attired in their finest, flirting and flashing their fins in her direction. She paid them no attention, but cast a smile across the hall at her father and myself, serene and untouchable as she always was when she presented herself in public.

There's no such thing as perfect order in the sea, and yet I had all faith that Dianda would bring truer order to Saltmist than it had ever known before.

Winter, 1740

I had never considered, before Dianda, that the Merrow must learn their ferocity and fighting somewhere. It couldn't all be them working things out on their own, wrestling with Cephali and stabbing at sharks. We had been afforded ninety years after the divorce of Duke Morcan and the Lady Chantara, ninety years of peace and comfort, during which Dianda had been the heir apparent to her father's holdings, and I her faithful companion.

Those years had been the true span of her childhood, a period during which she could explore every inch of the Duchy that would one day be her own, uncover every treasure and try her wit at every mystery. Oh, she had been a wild thing in the waters, my Di, and how the waves had rung with her laughter and her rage.

Away from Torin's constant, dampening presence, she had finally come into blossom as the curious, chaotic creature she had been born to be, quick to anger and quick to calm, protective of the things she cared for to a degree unusual even for one among the Merrow. The Duchy was her first and truest love, and I had no doubt she would protect it against any who might try its bounds.

But protection required that she know the *how* of that protection, the military strategy that went into each decision to move guards along the border, the economic plans that planted the fields and gathered the

crops. If she was going to rule one day, she needed to know *how* to
rule, or her reign would be punishingly short, and nothing I or anyone
else did would be enough to save her. I knew all this. These things
were truths, and like all truths, they had little concern for what I
thought of them.

Her schooling had begun the day after her parents' divorce, in a
local cove where two old Merrow soldiers who had fought a dozen
wars taught the children of local nobles how to defend themselves, and
the basics of tactical thinking. Morcan had quickly seen that it wouldn't
be enough, although it had taken him these past ninety years to barter
and blackmail her into a position at the school where he had taken his
education.

A school that was very far from Dianda's home waters.

"Stop your complaining and your caterwauling," I said, with a
fierceness I didn't feel, as I packed the last of her wardrobe into the
trunks that would be accompanying her to school. Most of her baggage
was filled with weaponry, knives and nets and throwing darts shaped
to fly straight and true beneath the sea. The rest was an even divide
between weaponry and medical supplies. I had heard that the school
had healers, but that new students weren't permitted to enjoy their
attentions without first withdrawing their enrollment until they had
made it through three full tides of classes. While I wanted Dianda to
learn the ways of her station, I was far more interested in knowing that
when I had her back, it would be with the full complement of fingers
and fins.

"But they won't let me take you *with* me!" she said, almost petu-
lantly enough for me to class it as a wail. I gave her a dubious look,
shading my hair toward a deeper red, until the tips looked virtually
black in the bedchamber's light.

"Not much of a combat school, if all the little nobles came swanning
in with their servants right behind them, so sorry, sir, did you want me
to swim after your kidney before it could drift too far astray, oh, my
apologies, miss, my little killer didn't realize this was your current
when she dumped all that chum into it, we'll find another spot to lay
our ambush. Can't go with you unless they all get to bring their versions of me with them, and that won't prepare you lot for much of
anything."

Dianda snorted a laugh and cracked a brief smile—the first one I'd
seen from her in days. "No one has a version of you except for me,
Helmi, and I'll fight anyone who tries to take you away from me."

"Since I'm not a bauble to be stolen, you'd be fighting me first of all, and don't think you can do that and win until you've finished your time at that fancy combat school you're going off to." I closed the trunk with a snap, and began undulating my way up the wall, suckers finding purchase in every crack and cranny. "I'll miss you dearly while you're away. See to it that you make your father and your Duchy proud; we'll be waiting for you to return crowned in glory to tell us that we're no longer vast enough to suit your ambitions, or with a whole school of suitors following on your fins, ready to swear their hearts to you in eternal devotion."

She snorted again. "And where am I meant to find these suitors, Helmi? I'm going off to a school meant to teach me the best ways of stabbing someone so they fall down and stop their dancing. I'm not going to be gossiping and making friends, much less looking for lovers amidst the competition."

"An instructor, perhaps, or a member of the school staff?"

She made a face.

"No? Well, then, you'll have to get creative."

"I'm not looking for a lover," she said staunchly. "If I ever marry, it will be for love, and it won't end as my parents' marriage did. Nor will I negotiate the futures of my children before they even slide into the sea."

"From your lips to Amphitrite's ears," I said, warmly. "Swim along now, girl. You have a carriage to catch."

The detachment that would see her to the school had been ready since tide-turn, and would guarantee her safe delivery to campus. After that, there were no guarantees. Many Merrow never returned to their home fiefdoms, either because they had found the love Dianda so derided, or because they had died during their lessons. I had to let her go, and hope that she'd come swimming home to me.

She blew me a kiss and swam out of the room, vanishing in a flurry of fins. I stayed where I was, color slowly fading to match the wall. Perhaps Mother had the right of it, tying herself to a Merrow she didn't care for as anything other than a mess to be tidied and put away. It's hard to mourn for a liege you don't care about.

I was still sticking to the wall when Morcan swam mournfully into the room and settled himself on the edge of what had been Dianda's bed. "She was sorry when you didn't come to say goodbye, but it was the right choice," he said, to what should have seemed an empty chamber. "It would have made her look tender, to be saying farewell to a servant, and some other incoming students had already joined the detachment. They would have seen her as easy prey once they got to school. You honor her with your discretion."

Slowly, I uncurled myself from the wall and dropped to the floor, my coloration returning to its default state as I did. "My lord is too kind," I said, bowing until I faced the floor.

"She's gone," he said. "You can find another position, if you like."

"I am Dianda Lorden's handmaid," I said, voice stiff. "I serve until she dismisses me, and after, if she dismisses me against her will."

"You know, no one used our surname until you came along and teased it out of the Asrai," he said, with a trace of amusement.

"A name is a thing to wear with honor," I replied. "It shows that once, your line was clever and quick enough to seduce a human into the depths, and keep them breathing long enough to pass their lineage along. To do this, and then to cleanse the mortality from your descendants, is a badge of honor so great that I'm astounded it ever fell from favor!"

Morcan looked at me, expression mild. "The mother of the Merrow is a daughter of Titania, who looked with less favor upon such escapades, but I would prefer my own daughter be proud of where she came from. I won't take you from her service, Helmi, but it may be a long while before she returns."

"A hundred years," I said staunchly.

"If she lasts to graduation."

I lifted my head and looked him dead in the eye. "A hundred years," I repeated.

"And may it be even so," he said, and rose from the bed, swimming for the exit.

I said nothing, but I watched him go.

Summer, 1840

Time is a curious thing. To the young, a night is an eternity. I remembered nights that had lasted decades in the innocent eye of my mind, stretching out into an infinity of possibilities and paths as yet untaken. After youth comes experience, and a jadedness that slows the infinite nights to a crawl. When I had been in my sixties, afternoons had been my bane. Awake, but unhappy about it, with all the night's chores as yet ahead of me, unstarted and looming, and no desire to do them. I have often thought the ways in which time can pass explain much about the humans. Like us, they start their lives as young things, and move into the jaded languor of experience. Unlike us, they never graduate from there into true age.

Age comes after a hundred years or more—most often more—and brings with it the knowledge that a night is a moment, a blinking of an eye, and unless there is a young thing to slow it down and render it important, it can be all but disregarded without fear. So I had passed the better part of a hundred years in the happy haze of nights that flared and faded almost before I knew they had begun, busying my hands with the work of running a duchy, busying my heart with the occasional slow evening spent among the Cephali children of the local nursery, regaling them with tales of other demesnes and far-off waters.

I had doubtless inspired some number of them to seek their fortunes far from home, and while I might regret the loss on the part of their parents, that was as it was meant to be, in clement waters. Breed and prosper where the seas are welcoming, and spread to where they aren't. They would untangle their own tales to tell.

And I? I was waiting.

A hundred years is no small thing, even for the ageless, but no great thing for one who has reached the calm and ease of age. I rose, I did my work, I rested, and I listened for news from the school where Dianda learned to be a better Merrow.

It came with reasonable frequency. We love to gossip, beneath the sea, and there are few topics as interesting as dead heirs who aren't your own. Word of deaths came every full tide or so, this minor noble and that second son cut down on the dueling fields, this duke's only heir gutted and left to the sharks. But never did I hear Dianda's name among the lists of the dead, and hope grew in my bones like a pernicious weed, refusing to be uprooted or denied. She was surviving. She was thriving, a shark among sharks, and she would come back to us, and she would still be my Dianda, or the true test of her education would be a poisoned knife at the highest point of the day.

Her father knew my intentions, and didn't dismiss me from his halls, which was as good as an endorsement. He had sent his daughter off to become a better killer because he knew his duty to the Duchy and his people. He had released his wife to the wider sea in exchange for an heir; if he lost this one, he would be forced to marry again, or to hold his title against the endless crashing of the waves, alone and unchanging. But his desire to have an escape from his duties didn't mean he was prepared to surrender Saltmist to a monster.

If she returned to us a graduate and a hardened Merrow noble, but still essentially the same loving, loyal woman she had been when she swam away, he would welcome her and begin the preparations for his own stepping aside. If she returned to us as an exemplar of the worst the Merrow could become, bloodthirsty and cruel, he wouldn't blame the school, which he himself had once survived. He would blame some essential failing in her character, and he would look away as I removed her from my orderly sea.

It would destroy all three of us if I was called upon to act in such a way. I knew it, and Morcan knew it, and neither of us discussed it, even as the hour of her graduation and return drew closer tide by tide, until I was engaged in reopening and preparing her chambers for her homecoming.

Assuming it was a matter of more than a moment, she would need to redecorate all but entirely; these were the rooms of a young woman, still accented here and there with the rooms of a child, and she was coming home a proper adult. Like her father, she would no doubt want her own armory close to hand, and she'd need a wardrobe, so I could dress her properly to attend upon her own Courts, as well as visit those of the land. Picturing the fine gowns I would commission for her passed many an evening, a pleasant activity, even as it ran in parallel to thoughts of her burial shroud. If we were to send her down to the Almere, it would be in silk and pearls, as she deserved.

If we were to send her down.

The night began as any other, calm waters and salt-sharp currents. The Cetacae and Easgann were in the fields, bringing the harvest in before the tides turned, and I was flitting about the halls, tidying things that had already been tidied half a dozen times or more. Had I not been Dianda's companion since childhood, I think Duke Morcan would have put me out to join the harvesters, citing a lack of work for me to do, and he wouldn't have been wrong to do so. A lady's maid with no lady to attend upon crosses the line from affectation into indulgence, and he already risked rumor that we were indulged in some sort of passionate affair. As if I would ever have dallied with a man with so few limbs, and those he had so rigid with bone. The thought was repulsive, but amusing enough to tease a smile from my lips as I worked.

I was collecting an assortment of shells left behind by one of the resident children when a commotion erupted ahead of me. I dropped them at once to free my hands and jetted toward the sound, stopping as I reached the final doorway between myself and the source. There, I plastered myself to the wall and changed colors to match it, becoming white and gray and mother-of-pearl. Thus camouflaged, I crept around the door's edge and into the wide-open space of the reception hall.

There, Duke Morcan circled high in the center of the room, a knife in each hand, as a smaller, lither Merrow struck at him again and again with the vicious hooks she held, their hilts curved around her fingers as guard as well as anchor. Neither was bleeding yet, but it was clearly only a matter of time.

Morcan could see that as well. Discarding one of his knives, he grabbed the floating cloud of her hair, yanking her forward and stabbing at the same time, only to miss the meaty center of her tail as she was abruptly a two-legged creature, her face already strained with the effort of holding her breath. She jackknifed upward in the water and wrapped her legs around his neck, squeezing as she pulled herself close and pressed the tip of one hook to his temple.

Morcan roared laughter and threw his other knife aside, wrapping his arms around his daughter. Dianda unwound her legs and returned to her proper fins and scales, exhaling as she embraced him.

"A risky move," he scolded her. "If you'd failed to take me at once, you would have been in a bad position from the lack of breath."

"I can shift fast enough that it wouldn't have mattered, old man," she replied. There was a new hardness to her tone, but there was laughter there as well. She sounded happy to be home. I stayed where I was, still watching. There would be time for our own reunion soon enough, when I was sure that we were to be companions once again, and not a butcher and her beast.

"Have you graduated, then? Are you home?"

"Or have I escaped from the school, and do you need to send me back in disgrace?" Dianda disentangled herself from her father, swimming a short distance away before she busied herself with sheathing her hooks in the webbing around her waist. It appeared to be some sort of salvaged mortal fishing net, doubtless all but unbreakable, braided together and strung with bits of shell and pearl. "I'm a full graduate, and your little killer." There was a bitterness in her last word that made me pause, stiffening.

Morcan's face fell. "I'm sorry I had to send you away."

"I understand why it was necessary, and I don't hold it against you as much as some do; how many Merrow die because their children return from those torture camps and set them to the knife at once?"

"Too many," Morcan admitted.

"I suppose it keeps our numbers low," said Dianda, almost philosophically. Then she shrugged. "But I was quick and clever, and willing to be cruel when the curriculum demanded it of me, and I survived long enough to be declared a full graduate. And now I'm here, and home, and all I need is for you to tell me what happens next."

Morcan hesitated, studying her, and I tensed. He was closer to her than I was, had known her better than I ever could, and his love for her was as fathomless and forgiving as my own. If he saw something wrong . . .

But then he smiled, slow and sincere, and said, "What happens next is you give your father another hug, and Helmi comes out of whatever corner she's been lurking in, and we begin the preparations to hand this old beast over to the new regent."

Dianda lifted her eyebrows. "So quickly?"

"I've been waiting a hundred years for you to finish and return," he said. "There's nothing quick about this in the slightest."

That seemed to be my cue. I detached from the wall and swam toward them, recovering my normal coloration as I entered the center of the room. Dianda laughed and swept me into her arms, radiant in her gladness, and I wrapped my tentacles around her, glad the sea stole away my tears. She was back, my girl, and there would be no need to end her. She was home.

Autumn, 1840

It had taken a hundred years for Dianda to win her graduation and cross the ocean to come back to us. It took the span of a season for her father to inform his allies and his peers that he was swimming aside and Saltmist would have a new Duchess before the winter storms began. How slowly things occur in Faerie! How blazingly, brutally fast. It seemed impossible, but a few scant months after her return, the King on the land—Gilad Windermere, one of their teleporting kind, who could open passages through open air with a wave of his hand—had bade them both to come ashore, to attend a gala in the old duke's honor and to present the new duchess to the land courts.

It was an opportunity to show Saltmist at our very finest, to remind the land courts that we were as fae and fearsome as anything the open air could offer. And naturally, Dianda didn't want to go.

She had been forcing me to chase her through the palace for most of the evening, constantly darting into the next room when I came to ask her about her gown for the evening, or when she would be ready for me to prepare her hair, or any number of other small, essential questions that had to be answered before she could surface.

Finally, in desperation, I retreated to her rooms and settled on the bed, shifting my colors until I disappeared into the background. And then I waited.

Her reasons for not wanting to go ashore were valid ones, and even ones I shared; the land fae were inclined to treat us poorly when given the opportunity, to see us as lesser because we had all the seas to ourselves while they had to find and master ways of sharing their environment with the humans. The challenge of coexistence supposedly proved their superiority, as if that were anything other than an excuse! Anyone with a scrap of thought to their name could easily see the self-aggrandizing nonsense for what it was, but the land believed it, and when we had cause to brush against them, they tried to make us believe it, too.

Dianda was still adjusting to life in the court, to a daily existence where no one tried to kill her on her way to meals. The school had been hard on her, that was clear in her every choice, and she didn't want to spend an evening being made to feel inferior by soft, bloodless land dwellers.

It was understandable. It was reasonable, even. And it was a true pity that she couldn't be allowed to sit home and weave, or scale fish, or otherwise pass her time as she chose. But she and I were not the same, and she was to be the duchess here, which meant she needed to attend on diplomatic duties.

True enough, I had not been mirroring the bed for long before Dianda swam into the room, glancing back over her shoulder to be sure I did not follow. When she saw no sign of me, she flipped over in the water and dropped herself victoriously into the tangle of weighted blankets and pillows she had created for her own comfort.

That was when I wrapped all six of my tentacles around her body, and my arms around her shoulders, pinning her down. She thrashed, but before she could produce a weapon or do me proper harm, I hissed, "I've caught you, Dianda Lorden, and you'll be going to the surface tonight, or I'll harry you from one side of this Duchy to the other. And don't say you'll stop me. You don't have the authority to do that until you take your father's position, and the dance to that day begins with tonight."

Dianda sagged and huffed. "I thought you were on my side," she complained.

I disentangled myself from her and slithered out from underneath her, floating at eye-level with the seated Merrow. "I am," I said. "You have the potential to be a glorious leader, to bring Saltmist closer to the land than it has ever been, and to be a strong ally to the people you deem worthy of your efforts. But you do none of that as a stranger to them. You must meet the ones who will need to accept your authority, must look them in the eye and assert that you are every bit as good as they are. You are a daughter of Amphitrite, a descendant of Titania, and tonight you go among people who will see those facts as opposite in importance, as if you shouldn't consider yourself first born to the deeps. But you will be glorious before them all the same, and they will remember why they fear the sea."

She sighed, put-upon and petulant as a child centuries her junior. "Must I?"

"You must. For your father's sake, you must. But cheer up. You might enjoy yourself."

Dianda scoffed. "What enjoyment could I possibly find on the *land*?"

Spring, 1841

Dianda had found the greatest enjoyment of them all on the land: young love, and doomed enough to make a lovely ballad as soon as she came to her senses and the bards set to scavenging the carcass of her failed romance. For a Merrow to love one among the Daoine Sidhe was foolish enough to be almost amusing, rather than alarming as it might have been had there been any chance their courtship could succeed. No Merrow known had ever taken a spouse from the courts of the land. Dalliances had occurred, but nothing of any true seriousness. I smiled indulgently as I watched her settle into both her ducal role and her fresh courtship, exchanging letters with her swain, choosing gowns she thought would please him . . . all until the day the man was fool enough to let his lady liege write to *my* lady with a dismissal of her affections. She was beneath him in the eyes of the land, it seemed, condemned to a second-class existence because her natural state included gills.

Oh, how I hated them, those soft and pampered children of the land, Titania's favorites, who walked in air and struggled in an endless garden, rather than facing the pressures of the deep. How dare they make my charge feel so belittled, so unwanted? She fell into a time of deep despair, and it was during this depression that the Kingdom of Arkticheskiy reached out to us. They had a princeling in need of a bride, the third son of their royal house, who would never inherit if he remained home among his kin. He was said to be a pleasant sort, less violent than many of his kind; his position as a second spare meant that he had never been called upon to attend a school such as Dianda had done, or indeed to train in the art of combat at all.

He was a diplomat, this prince from far-off waters, trained from birth to flirt and flatter, and they were offering him to her on a platter, intended to be her husband and her helper, and she had no reason not to accept. So it was that Inna of Arkticheskiy came to our waters, arriving by carriage, much as the Lady Chantara had so many years before, but unlike the Lady Chantara, he looked about himself and saw not a dismal backwater worthy of his scorn, but a bay of nightmares to be feared.

We were too close to the land, our ties too tight for his comfort; we were too loud, we moved too quickly, and my Dianda, pearl that she was, was too trained in the arts of murder to be civilized. He seemed to have come to us from some fantasy of the sea, some idealized waters that had never known storm or slaughter. I could envy him that, even as I attributed it to a sheltered upbringing and an unrealistic view of the world.

What I could neither envy nor forgive was the way he cringed whenever Dianda came too close to him, hiding his reaction as quickly as he could behind a practiced, polished smile, but flinching all the same if she so much as reached to take his hand during a court function. He was meant to wed her. How would they ever get the Duchy an heir if he couldn't stand her presence? It wasn't fair to Saltmist. It wasn't fair to him. Most of all, it wasn't fair to *her*, who was my first concern.

Gilad was hosting another ball, this one intended to celebrate her engagement. I had seen them off with the proper smiles and circumstance, waving them off to spend the night on land, dancing their dreams away. I was taking advantage of their absence to properly clean their rooms, both connected to the cluster of chambers that had belonged to Dianda since her childhood. Inna's fear of my lady transferred at least somewhat to me, and convincing him to let me in had proven to be more difficult than I could ever have supposed it would be. What manner of noble doesn't want their every need attended to? It was a mystery worth solving only in that I was sure he couldn't be as innocent and untested as the façade he tried to show the world, and might be plotting to take the Duchy somehow, possibly upon my lady's death.

An hour of searching his room had proven fruitless. Either he was as innocent as he appeared, or he was canny enough to have concealed his true intentions even from a thorough investigation. It was vexing, either way.

More vexing still, as dawn approached, Inna returned alone. He was bright-eyed and smiling as I had yet to see him smile, and he swam straight toward me, not shying away in the least. "My fair Maid Helmi!" he cried, accent making his words strangely shaped and enticing. "I am to bid you help me pack!"

"I beg your pardon?"

"It seems the fair Duchess Lorden finds no comfort in the promise of my embrace, and would far rather court another, if she were allowed to do so. Being a gentleman, I shall not stand in the path of true love, truly loved, and have agreed to stand aside. Your waters are a poor match for me, I think. I much prefer the calm and cold of home, and will be more than glad to return there. Better a third son with no crown to his name than a forgotten shadow sacrificed to court an unwilling current, eh?"

I blinked at him then, and nodded in slow agreement. The lack of my lady was undeniable, and put truth behind the rest of his words, or at least, the potential of truth, if not truth's actuality. "Who has she chosen to court?" I asked, keeping my voice seafoam-light and frothy as the tip of a wave.

"A land-born man. I hope there is no shame to that in these waters, as there would be in the waters from which I come—at home, that would surely bruise the lady's reputation beyond all redemption, and leave her easy pickings for her enemies, for an air-breather can never aid her in defense of her domain. But then, who am I to judge?" His laugh was as deep and rich as it was unexpected. "I would have been almost as little help, and with far less cause than an allergy to the world around me. I wish her all the joy of him, and him all the joy of her; there is no offense between our houses."

I blinked again, more slowly than before. "Does this man have a name?"

Inna waved a hand lazily. "Peter? Padraig? One such as that— Patrick, I think. It feels right in the mouth, and the shape is much like the name I heard her utter."

So Patrick Twycross had recovered from his bout of cold fins and found his way clear to court her after all? It would never work out, would never last, but in the moment, if he brought her joy, I could see little reason to discourage it. What man born to the land would choose to leave it behind for the deeps? What son of Eira Rosynhwyr could even dream to humble himself in such a way? Let her have her courtship. Another marriage could be arranged when it inevitably collapsed around her, and a better one, one that would bring to her the joy she so deserved. Inna made his apologies and swam off to gather his possessions and his retinue, and I turned to wait for my lady's return, for this temporary disruption in the way of things to begin.

Autumn, 1901
Less temporary, perhaps, than I originally assumed; after sixty years of courtship, they still found joy in one another's company, and now she floated before me, my lady, the woman to whom I had pledged my life, with an alchemist's art in her hands and an anxious expression on her face.

"What if he refuses me?" she asked. "I might destroy everything we have together by asking him for more, and find myself alone in the shadows of the sea."

"You have never been alone in your life, and you won't start now," I replied. "I won't go anywhere, whether he accepts your suit or no. And if he refuses you, he never deserved you to begin with."

She looked at me with clear anxiety in her eyes, and I knew two things without question: that she truly loved him, loved him as the tales tell us we should all aspire to love, and that if he declined her, a part of her would remain on the shore forevermore, grieving the life she didn't have the chance to live beside him. I have never thought much of the intersection between land and sea, but looking at the hope in her eyes, I knew that it was an essential boundary line, intended to be crossed with care, but still intended to be crossed.

This was good. This was right and proper. This was *orderly*, and by uniting their two states of being, they would only improve the world in which we lived.

"Oh, my lady . . ." I moved toward her, wrapping my two front tentacles around her wrists and holding her fast in a momentary embrace. "If he is half as clever as you have made him out to be, he'll greet your proposal with all the joy the land has to offer. And if he's not, you're better off without him."

She laughed, looking at me. "I always thought you didn't approve."

"I don't. A ducal consort is meant to assist in the protection of the demesne, should it be required, and he'll be scarcely this side of useless. Even Inna would have been better suited to taking up arms in our defense. But he makes you happy, and your joy has always come first for me, before the Duchy, before all the damned sea. So let him make you happy, and come back to us with a ducal consort-to-be, so I can plan a wedding such as shakes the seas for years to come."

She laughed again, radiant in her joy, and swam away, bound for the surface, where her land-bound love was waiting.

I didn't properly take into account that proposing to a man of the air would mean bringing him back with her to the palace, or that I would find myself making greetings to a Daoine Sidhe. To his credit, he looked at me with awe rather than revulsion, although he seemed to find Hydor amusingly distressing, and tracked her motions at all times when she was nearby. Somehow she was more terrifying in her liquidity than I was in my solid presence. The land had its own share of hybrid bloodlines, fae who were one thing from the waist up and another from the waist down. I was simply one more variation on a familiar theme. Hydor, though—she was something entirely unknown.

Naiads are such a common sight in the Undersea that I had stopped noticing the strangeness of having a hive entity made of living water sharing the palace halls with the rest of us. Hydor enabled us to keep the dry places dry, for the sake of those fae who enjoyed their coffee undiluted or their teacakes undampened, and for the sake of Dianda's increasingly extensive land wardrobe. And now that Patrick Lorden was to join us on a long-term basis, I supposed, for the sake of rebuilding my lady's living quarters, as they would need to be con-figured to suit the needs of an air-breathing lover. It seemed a terri-ble inconvenience, but then I saw the way she looked at him, and thought that she would suffer any inconvenience necessary to keep him by her side.

The humans have tales of mermaids turning themselves mortal to be with human princes, and those romances are almost always short-lived and brutal. My lady did nothing of the sort. She brought her prince home with her, and neither of them was to change to suit the other. It seemed much more balanced and reasonable, and Patrick agreed to make his life beneath the sea with remarkable speed and willingness. There were aspects of life on land that he would regret, of this I was more than certain, and first among them a man named Simon Torquill, who had been his close companion for quite some time, but it seemed that his heart had been given, and now that the deed was done, he considered the matter settled. He was ours to keep and care for, and that meant making the palace safe for him—or as safe as the sea was ever likely to be for a man of the land.

Hydor was kept busy with opening new air-filled chambers and moving the water about inside the palace proper, increasing the spaces Patrick could safely occupy tide by tide. Patrick proved to be a dab hand with a hammer, and with the sculpting spells that allowed our architects to manipulate living coral. He set to building furniture and assisting in the design of new chambers, busying himself as he waited for the wedding date to be settled upon.

It was a more complicated matter than it should have been. King Windermere had insisted upon the honor of hosting the celebration, but before my lady could take a husband from the land, custom first required that she solicit consent from the reigning monarch in Leucothea. Not the easiest task to perform, given that the new queen was yet in the process of seizing power from her father. War reigned in many parts of the kingdom, Queen Palatyne's forces subduing the old king's with a viciousness that made many feel she would be a good ruler, or at the very least, a stable one. People who seize their thrones with sufficient bloodshed tend to keep them, if only because all possible challengers know there will be no hesitation to kill if pressed. And so that happy day was delayed as we waited for the conflict to settle long enough to get a messenger through, someone who could make the journey successfully and return to us alive.

"I don't understand," said Patrick, after the second week of waiting had come limping to a close. "She just decided she was at war with her father, and then she was?"

"Wars are a lot like pregnancies," I replied. "You need two people to get one going—unless you're Maeve or Titania, to be truly technical—but once you have, the person who carries it is the only one who matters. Palatyne has been asking her father to stand aside for a century, and he's been refusing just as long. When she said that now she must be at war with him, I believe he thought she was expressing a childish fit of fancy, for all that she's near three hundred years old." My tone turned wistful then. "Of course, he realized far too late that she had assembled an army from among his malcontents, those who were tired of power being static and locked in others' hands. Power passes below the sea in two ways. Either a peaceful transition from one regent to the next, by mutual agreement, or through bloodshed in time of formally declared war. This is to be the latter."

Patrick sighed, heavily. "I realize the land's traditions are not your own, and are in no way superior, only different, but how long is this supposed to take?"

"Why? Eager to return to your home on the shore?"

He grimaced, as if he had bitten into something sour. "More concerned that I'll be given no choice. The King in the Mists is a good man, and cares more for my happiness than many in his position would. But among his vassals he counts a woman of high position among the Daoine Sidhe, who has tried once before to sunder me from Dianda. The Countess Evening Winterrose believes in our First's command that we should breed true and fill Faerie with the Daoine Sidhe before all others. Until I am wed to my lady and formally set aside the titles of the land, she has some degree of authority over me."

"And how would her word reach this far below the waves?"

"Do not the Selkies come and go as they please? I've seen familiar faces in the court, people I recognize from the colony in Roan Rathad."

"The Ryans have been there for the better part of a century, and they serve their master on the land as well as they serve my lady here in the sea," I allowed. "They will not carry commands you have no desire to answer."

"Oh, but they might," he said darkly. "Baron Aberforth has never been known to stand up against the Countess Winterrose. He's not Daoine Sidhe, or she could command him directly, but he still bows to her demands. He commands Roan Rathad."

"I see." Selkies are unusual in the Undersea, if not entirely unique. They serve both sea and shore, and answer to authorities in each domain. Once in the water, they were my lady's to command, but in their rookeries, where they went to raise their children and dry their skins, they answered to the Baron Patrick had named. I frowned, looking down at the intricate knots of my tentacles for a moment before glancing up again, an attempt at reassurance in my expression. "That would be a convoluted course to denial. I am sure the Countess already thinks you lost to her, surrendered to the sea, and will attempt no such intercession."

"May the root and the branch see it so," he said, firmly. He glanced up then, at the ceiling but more, I thought, at the land so far above. "Until this is sorted and we rise for the marriage, I don't dare go ashore. It's too great a risk to take."

"Why would you need to . . . ?"

"Simon."

He spoke the name with love such as I had only heard when he spoke of my lady, with true and abiding affection. I cocked my head.

"A friend? A brother?"

"A friend, yes, a brother, no. I harbored a crush on him for quite some time, unrequited and unrequitable—*his* lady is not one who knows the way of sharing what she believes she owns, and she would have killed us both. Not that it could ever have been necessary: part of why I love him so is his loyalty to the people he chooses to put his trust in. He could no more betray her than I could betray my own lady, now that she's mine to hold. He was a sweet dream, for a time, and a dear friend, forever. I miss his company."

I touched his wrist delicately with one tentacle. "You understand that you will be missing him much longer than this, if you go through with the marriage, yes? Passage will be possible, but complicated. It's not as if you can attend on Court functions above simply for the sake of doing so."

"I know," he said. "I have accepted what it costs me to remain below, and judged it worth paying. But there's a difference between 'difficult' and 'forbidden,' and the latter is more difficult to lift."

"I understand," I said. "He'll dance at your wedding, I'm sure."

"Will you?"

I paused. "Me?"

"We're to wed at the court of King Windermere, by his request and by Dianda's willing agreement. I've never seen your kind on the land. When this war is over and we can finally be wed, will you come to attend upon your lady? From what she tells me, you've been present for her entire life. You've been her protector and her companion, and you deserve to witness her pledge her heart. If she had married Inna, there would have been no question."

"I . . . I hadn't considered that," I said. It was true. I had never considered that Dianda might court and come to care for someone from the land; it had always been my expectation that she would wed in Saltmist, as her parents had before her. Even during the long years of her courtship with Patrick, I had believed on some level that she would change her mind. It was nothing against the man, who was quite pleasant, and increasingly good company. It was just that he was of a different world, and must inevitably drift away from hers.

Was I willing to go up into the heavy air of the surface, where gravity would pin me to a single plane of motion, for the sake of my lady's wedding? I wanted to be brave. I wanted to be bold. I wanted to believe there was no true question there. Sadly, the question was clear. Even for my lady, could I do this?

Spring, 1903
I could.

King Windermere had been delighted by my appearance, claiming with gleeful enthusiasm that I was proof Faerie's wonders were without limit or end; here he was, a king in his own knowe, and I was something he had never seen before being presented to him on a day when he was meant to be giving the gifts, not receiving them. His laughter was larger than he was, and the acoustics of the air meant that it bounced and billowed like a rolling storm, loud as anything.

My lady's gown was the finest the seamstresses of the sea could weave, floating, diaphanous silk in white, cream, and the very palest pink—the fashion on the land was for white wedding gowns, and so a white gown she should have, to prove that she was every bit the bride a daughter of the air could have woven, decorated with strings of pearl and bits of polished glass from the bottom of the sea that shone like clouded jewels in the light cast by the swarm of pixies that constantly attended on her groom. How anyone was meant to tell the color of her gown when it was a dozen candied shades, I had no idea, but there had been a gratifying intake of breath among the court when she entered, and so I accepted that our message had been sent.

I was not the only member of her court in attendance, but I was the only Cephali to have chosen to make the ascent, and I clung to the wall like it was an anchor in a raging storm, my tentacles spread to keep me from slipping as I dangled some feet above the floor.

I was hanging there, watching as Patrick led my laughing lady through the steps of a simple dance I didn't know, when a Daoine Sidhe man with hair almost as red as my own came to stand beside me, a goblet of something sweetly floral in his hand. He nodded toward the pair circling the floor. "I suppose I needn't ask which side of the happy couple you've accompanied this evening," he said, and it wasn't mockery, but a pleasant greeting from someone who believed we shared a secret of some sort.

I turned to look at him, keeping my expression neutral. Like all Daoine Sidhe, he looked like a tropical Merrow in their bipedal form, his fins and scales traded for aggressively bright colors that would warn off any potential predators. His hair was red, his eyes were gold, and his expression was as politely noncommittal as my own.

"I suppose I could say the same to you," I said. "The groom's side of the guest list?"

"You wound me, Lady Cephali, with the accuracy of your assumptions," he said, and took a sip from his goblet before setting it on the tray of a passing server, allowing it to be whisked aside.

I, meanwhile, stared at him in confusion. He looked at me, waiting for me to say something, and I finally shook myself out of my silence.

"Forgive me," I said. "No one else I've met outside the sea has been acquainted with my descendant line."

"I have made a study of Faerie's many forms, and how they fit together, one unto the other," he said. "It seems a mean trick, to be surrounded by such wonders and refuse to see them for what they are. I have learned something worth knowing from every descendant line I've encountered, and dream of the day when I'll be at leisure to meet the rest of us."

"In that case, it's a pleasure to make your acquaintance." I extended one tentacle as Dianda might extend a hand, and was somehow unsurprised when he took it and kissed it, exactly as he would have that hypothetical hand. "My name is Helmi, and I am of the Court of Saltmist."

"And I am Simon Torquill of Goldengreen, Baron of Kettled Time and husband to Amandine."

He didn't give her surname. That was interesting. Surnames are reasonably uncommon in the Undersea, being a mark of human heritage somewhere further back, but as a rule, when I've encountered someone with both a surname and a spouse, they tend to combine the two.

Simon, Simon . . . I brightened, looking at him more closely. "You're Patrick's Simon!"

"Would that it were so, but alas, that happy outcome was not to be my own, for I am a happily married man, and knew my wife long before the Baron Twycross came into my life," he said, without a flicker of surprise. "But he is a fine man, and your lady could search a lifetime without finding any better. She is a fortunate one, to have him by her side."

I tilted my head to the side, considering him for a moment. He looked back at me, seemingly entirely earnest, and I decided that while I might not believe him, he at least believed what he was saying. Friends, nothing more, with no love lost between them.

Were all men of the land so good at lying to themselves?

His eyes had returned to the couple circling the floor as I considered his words. Other couples had started to join them, few enough that they were not yet quite a crowd, but enough that none stood out in specific. He turned back to me, a twinkle in his eye that I should have seen for mischief in the making, and extended his other hand to me, the first of them still holding my tentacle.

"May I have this dance, Lady Helmi?" he asked.

I raised an eyebrow. "I lack some of the anatomical features the steps assume," I said.

"And I don't know the steps," he replied. "We can fumble through together, you and I, and celebrate two hearts we both love dearly."

It seemed cruel to refuse him, and so I laughed and descended from the wall, reclaiming my tentacle in order to slide my hands into his. "Very well, then, Baron Torquill," I said. "Take me dancing."

And so he did.

Spring, 1906

The sea was shaking as it had never shaken before, rolling as if a wave so great that it swept away the very ocean had managed to rise out of nowhere. The ground beneath the palace shook, rattling its foundations, and great rocks fell from above, knocked loose from canyon walls in both the Summerlands and the mortal seas.

Within the palace, Hydor had called all her sisters together, gathering in the Ducal chambers, which would normally be forbidden to any save for the Duchess and her consort, where they stood with hands raised and eyes open wide, holding back the pressure of the deeps that threatened to pour in through the shattering wards. Dianda was trying to get a bottle of the water-breathing potion past Patrick's lips, as he scrambled to stay upright in the horrible, endless rolling.

And then, as if it had never happened at all, it was over. Only the shaking—the damages remained. Cracks were racing through the palace walls, spreading into webs that would soon give way. Patrick finally snatched the bottle out of Dianda's hand and drank deeply, only to begin choking as the air turned against him. Hydor lowered her hands, and the rest of the Naiads did the same, allowing the water to flow into the room through countless tiny cracks. Patrick sank to his knees, expression grateful as he inhaled.

"What *happened*?" demanded Dianda.

"Earthquake," I replied.

"But so large? And extending this deeply into Faerie?" She shook her head, looking out the remains of the window upon the palace grounds, which were pocked with massive fallen stones and riddled with cracks in the soil. The fields would be even worse, I knew, the new-planted crops lost to the devastation. "How is this possible?"

"I don't know," I replied. "It's never happened before that I'm aware of." The water flowing through the cracks tasted of strange magic, roses and woodsmoke, like someone had managed to light a bonfire deep below the waves. Patrick inhaled and began to choke, spitting the water from his mouth like it had somehow offended him.

I turned. Dianda was holding him up, her tail back in place, her flukes wrapped protectively around his leg like she thought she could protect him from all the sea at once. By the panic in her eyes, I supposed this was the first time she had truly realized how fragile he was, how easily he could drown.

That might have been a better revelation before the marriage, but I couldn't blame her fully for refusing to allow it any sooner. It had to be terrifying, to understand so abruptly how easily she could lose him.

The taste of magic in the water was fading. I pushed myself away from the wall and swam toward her, pausing to bow while still floating some distance above the floor.

"Your orders, my lady," I said.

This was a test, of sorts. If she could remember her place and her people, the loyalties she was expected to put before the man she'd married, then she was still and always suited to serve as Duchess of Saltmist. She was still the woman I had pledged my life to, a bond truer and more enduring than any marriage. And if she couldn't . . .

Power changes hands easily in the Undersea, especially when a Duchess goes missing in the aftermath of an impossible earthquake. This could be settled here and now, and I would love her anyway, even as I would hate her for putting my hands on the blade.

She stared at me for a span of several seconds before snapping out of it and saying, in a clear, commanding tone, "Guards to the far fields, to check the damages. If we're going to be importing food this fall, we should know sooner than later, if only to get in with our bids before the prices start going up. Hydor, take your sisters and start checking the other rooms of the palace. We need to know if anyone's trapped or hurt. Helmi, can you rally the rest of the Cephali to check the surrounding homes? There are children there, or should have been, given the time. We need to understand the scope of the damages."

"Of course, my lady," I said, and joined the others in swimming away to begin the long, slow work of repairing the damage that had come so suddenly, and so out of nowhere.

It would be weeks before we learned that the ground above had shaken even worse than the sea below, or that half the city of San Francisco had been burnt to the ground, lost to flames before anyone could react. It would be months before any passage to the surface could be opened even long enough to allow the Selkies to return to their homes, and years before stable passage to the land could be reestablished.

By then, King Gilad was dead and a woman none of us had ever heard of was in his place, a nameless woman who carried Siren and Sea Wight in her veins, yet seemed to loathe the Undersea. She banned us from her Courts, citing our absence during the devastation as good reason to take our voice in the management of the shores away, and she drove the Selkies to the coasts, denying them homes in more in-land demesnes.

It was during her mistreatment of the seal-kin that Mary first came to Saltmist.

She was a skinny, moon-eyed creature in a white shift dress that clung to her skin, transparent and dripping as she stood in the arrival room, her hair already beginning to dry enough to stand up in snarled wisps. It took me a moment to realize what was wrong with her. Her eyes, while massive, were green rather than dark brown or black, as I would have expected, and she had no sealskin either tied around her shoulders or braided into her hair. In fact, no matter how closely I looked, I couldn't find any sign of it.

She blinked as she turned to face me, then tilted her head to the side, and said, "Your garden grows as well as any may, with silver bells and cockleshells all down beneath the bay. I've come to serve, although the Duchess hasn't asked me yet. But she will. She will. And I will have my cakes and corner of the sea."

"Roane," I breathed.

The children of the sea witch were rare enough to be a mystery to me, all but never seen in these waters, phantoms of the tide. To have one standing before me and informing me that she had come to serve my lady was a shock and a fearsome obligation, for if the sea witch ever returned to us, she would want to know who had cared for her children in her absence—and who had been unkind to them.

Footsteps behind me alerted me to Patrick's approach, and I turned, but not quickly enough to wave him off. He stepped into the room, stopping as he saw that I was not alone.

"Oh, hello," he said. "I don't believe we've met."

The woman lit up, smiling as brightly as I had ever seen anyone smile. "Not yet and always, my Pat, and I'm so glad we're finally living in the same tide, that I may come to entirely know you."

He blinked. "Er?" he ventured.

His recovery was, at least, admirably quick. "I'm afraid you have the advantage of me, milady, as I don't know your name."

"No one does, really, but I use 'Mary' when I must," she said. "The Lady Cephali can explain. I'm going to my room. It already knows where it is, and I know as well, but no one else does, so I shan't need an escort."

She turned then, wandering out of the room. I watched her go, mouth hanging slightly open, but didn't move to stop her. Much as she didn't need an escort, there would have been no point in my trying to intercede. She didn't need me.

Clearly baffled, Patrick turned in my direction. "What just happened?" he asked.

"She—that woman—Mary, I suppose, isn't a Selkie," I said. "She's Roane."

He frowned. "But they're extinct."

The Roane had been largely wiped out as a descendant line centuries ago, shortly before the sea witch created the Selkies to keep her company in the open sea. I've often wondered why she would answer the deaths of her children by making herself a parody of what they'd been, but I am not Firstborn, nor would I wish to be, and their ways are quite beyond me in comprehension. It's common in the great book of Faerie for descendant lines to fail; there have been so many, and most never had more than one or two members. It's rarer for a line to become established enough to be known and then vanish. It made sense that Patrick would know of the Roane. They belonged to the Undersea, but like the Selkies who followed them, they were as much creatures of shallow and shore as the depths.

I smiled at him, as warmly as I could manage through my own confusion, and said, "They're *almost* extinct. Most of them died, and those who remain are slow to reproduce themselves, as if they want to keep their own numbers low. Most types of fae, if dealt a harsh blow, will turn to rebuilding. Not the Roane. They set to disappearing."

"Roane . . ." he said, looking after Mary with wonder in his eyes. "I never thought I'd see one. But how did she know my name?"

"The Roane are Seers," I said. "The only thing they failed to See was their own destruction. If she knows your name, it's because she's Seen it somehow, and knows you as important to her."

He blinked, slowly. "I see. Will Dianda let her stay?"

"We have no Court Seer, and it would be foolish to refuse one among the Roane who agreed to keep the position," I said. "I think that Miss Mary will be with us for quite some time."

"Well, then, we should go and greet the newest member of the Court," he said, and started in the direction Mary had gone. I followed. With Selkies arriving by the night to seek sanctuary from the abuses of the land, it was best if we presented a united front to the Duchess on the matter of new members of our household.

Summer, 1993

It felt as if I had fallen backward through time as Lady Dianda, Duchess of Saltmist, howled in furious pain, clutching at the loops of seaweed that kept her from drifting free of her birthing bed. Like her mother before her, there was a note of triumph in her screaming, a fierce joy at the battle she faced, and would inevitably win. No other outcome could be considered, by herself, or by those of us who attended upon her.

The hall outside had been emptied of water, and Patrick paced there. I knew from the moments before my departure that he had Mary by his side as she so often was, stroking his arm and murmuring quiet words of comfort. There had been some among the Court who worried that the Roane Seer was attempting to seduce him, but Dianda had laughed their concerns aside. Mary saw the future, and had already spoken to Dianda of children yet to come, with the calm assurance of someone who had no questions about their existence.

"The boys are guaranteed," she'd told me once, when I was bold enough to ask her what she'd Seen. "Two of them, bright and perfect and flawed as anything, and one will stay and one will go, but both will be a joy to you all the days of their lives. The girl who follows after, she comes and goes—right now she's not to be born, but yesterday she was, and tomorrow she might be. They'll be here soon enough, so gather rosebuds while ye may, and set their rooms to order."

She had no romantic interest in Patrick, or intent to interfere in his marriage. If anything, she was as excited to meet the children she'd Seen as the rest of us were, and on the evening when Dianda had finally been confident enough to disclose her pregnancy, Mary had been at the lead of the dancing. But her affection for "her Pat" remained undimmed, and only seemed to grow night on night. For his part, he was puzzled by the strange Seer, but as time passed, he came to find more and more comfort in her presence—such as now, when Dianda howled in her flooded chamber and he could only pace outside, denied a presence in the room.

He would have been there if he could have been. But Dianda needed submersion for the birth to go properly, and with no way to estimate how long the process would take, it was impossible to brew him a safely extended dose of his potion. Once the babe was born, the room would be drained, and he would be allowed to enter, to see his child for the first time.

It was imperfect at best. But it was what we had, as Dianda screamed and Mary walked, doing what she could to distract him from the howling.

Then, abruptly, Dianda stopped screaming. I rushed forward to catch the baby as it slid into the water, realizing as I did that something was wrong with the shape of it. It looked more like a newborn Siren than a Merrow, skin peppered with small scales but lower body split right down the middle into two distinct limbs, rather than one tail. Hydor waved her hands, gathering the blood, as two of her sisters moved to begin draining the room.

Dianda screamed again, this time in terror rather than pain. "He can't *breathe*!" she shouted, and I saw that she was right.

The infant was drowning.

All three Naiads abandoned what they were doing, and from the hall I heard Mary yell, "Grab hold of something!" a bare instant before Hydor and her sisters shoved the water out of the room with a brutal finality that left me dry down to the roots of my hair, and left Dianda, now unwieldy in her fins and scales, lying beached on the bed, reaching for the baby in my arms. Freed of the smothering tide, he took several hitching, shocked-sounding breaths and then began to wail, the sound loud enough to pierce through the walls.

The door slammed open, and a sodden, dripping Patrick staggered inside, Mary drifting blissfully along in his wake. She didn't look distressed at all about the wave of water that must have slammed into her when Hydor pushed it out of the room. Then again, based on her yell for Patrick to grab hold, she'd seen it coming, and had been ready to keep them both from being swept away. Life with a Seer in residence could be like that sometimes; she wouldn't say anything about the future for weeks, and then her predictions would come in a cascade of small requests to grab this or move away from that, preventing small injuries and inconveniences as easily as breathing.

Patrick staggered to Dianda's bedside, dropping to his knees beside the marooned Merrow, and I finally surrendered to her silently pleading expression and handed the baby over. He continued to wail even as Dianda got him positioned in her arms and guided his mouth to her breast, where he thankfully latched on without further complaint. Patrick stared at him in awe, then looked up at his wife's exhausted, relieved face.

"What happened?" he asked.

"Our son takes after his father," she said. "Merrow are born in the water, so we can open our gills immediately and start breathing properly. We should have guessed that this one might need something different, given that Daoine Sidhe are prone to drowning, but somehow, it slipped all our minds." She shot a hard look at Mary, raising an eyebrow in silent indication that the Roane Seer should have said something.

Mary shrugged, serene as ever. "I made sure I was with my Pat, to tell him to catch hold of something when the time came, and telling you to birth the babe by air would only have left you to wonder if he would have been able to breathe the currents in, had he been born in the customary manner. This saved him, and you, the agony of not knowing. The boy is born to the sea, but not of the sea, and never shall be; when he leaves you, he must go without asking himself if he could have tried just that slight bit harder to remain."

Dianda leaned away from her, holding her newly born child just that tiny bit more closely, and scowled. "He's not going *anywhere*."

"Boys may not. Men may, in time. Many do. When the time comes, he'll know the choice is his to make." Mary turned to go, pausing before she left the room. "Flood the room next time as well. The boy will need to breathe."

Then she was gone, leaving Patrick to soothe a distressed Dianda while their child, who was born to the sea if not of it, took his first meal, all unaware of what had just happened.

Winter, 1996

As before, the room was flooded, and Dianda held tight to the loops of seaweed that dangled above the bed, keeping herself in place as she howled and writhed. Also as before, Patrick was not present, waiting in the air-filled hall, although this time he waited alone; Mary had swum off to spend a week with the Selkie clans, which I couldn't help but take as an omen of an easy, uncomplicated birth. Seers are their own form of natural disaster: they change everything around them simply through their presence, and it was difficult not to approach any event which Mary chose to attend with caution and with some small degree of fear.

Dean had been intended to wait with his father, but his mother's firm refusal to let him be in the room to meet his baby brother as soon as the boy arrived had driven him to a small tantrum. He was too young yet to be skilled at regulating his emotional responses, and his air-breathing nature meant that he was already excluded from much that went on around the palace. Being shut out of the room while his brother was born was a denial too far for his capabilities, and after crying himself into exhaustion, he had fallen asleep and been carried off to bed.

We'd wake him once his brother came, but for the moment, Dianda was screaming enough to keep me more than occupied. I didn't need a second set of lungs contributing to the din, especially not from the air-filled hall, where the sound would be amplified beyond all common reason.

With a final wail, Dianda pushed and her second son slid into the water, gills already opening to let him breathe the waters all around him. Unlike Dean, he was finned and scaled as I expected a Merrow babe to be, and he looked around himself with wide, dark-blue eyes, webbed fingers balled into involuntary fists. He waved them, nearly punching himself in the nose. I wrapped my tentacles around him and pulled him close as Hydor cleaned the blood out of the water. She gathered it into a red globe above her hands, then walked out of the room to deliver it to the court alchemists. Her sisters remained, waving their own hands in front of themselves. There was a thick gurgling sound and the water began to drain away, until what remained came barely to cover the bed.

Dianda reached for her son, and I surrendered him to her arms, remembering the birth of another second child of this household. There had been a brother there as well, barred from the delivery room, although in his case it had been less care for his health than it was fear of him creating a distraction. Tentacles finding easy purchase in the water, I moved back, opening space even as the door opened again and Patrick entered, looking around the chamber until his eyes settled on the scaled boy in his mother's arms.

He looked at his second son with the same awe and reverence he had brought to the first, and waded across the flooded chamber to settle on the bed next to his wife, not appearing to notice the fact that he was getting soaked. Then again, he'd had plenty of time to grow accustomed to the continual wetness of life below the sea.

"I'll go fetch Dean, if the three of you can do without me," I said politely.

Neither looked up from their reverent inspection of the baby, and I chuckled as I left the room, off to fetch our newly elevated older brother to see how much his life had changed. They would be the best of friends, if I had anything to say about it. I had failed to keep Torin from hating his sister. I would do better this time.

I would.

Summer, 2011
My boys were gone.

They had been taken. A stranger had come in and spirited them away, and it wasn't Blind Michael, for he had stopped his dancing; all the seas had rung with *that* news, when it came. A changeling girl, the long-lost Simon's honorary daughter, had put the blade into his heart and left him to rot in whatever terrible prison he had been stealing children away to for as long as I'd been alive, and longer—Blind Michael was a monster from the dawn of Faerie, and for him to be gone was a miracle.

But my boys were also gone, Dean and Peter both, and Mary had been gone for months, having left with a smile and a sigh at the start of spring. Whether she could have warned us was something we might never know, for she rarely seemed able to dwell on the past, living only in the present scaling blithely into the future. It was a difficult way to live, free of regrets, but also free of lingering bonds. I could remember every moment of my time in the halls of Saltmist, and my memories were normally a comfort, even if right now they lurked in corners, ready to strike and bite. Mary had the people she'd seen as important to her in the future, which often made me question whether they were important only because she had seen them so.

Well, she hadn't seen this. Dianda was angrier than I had ever seen her, so furious she could barely hold a two-legged form, but swam wildly from one end of the palace to the other, her colors flushed dark with rage. The sky above her territory was dark with clouds, and the waves were whipped into a frenzy as great as her own. So it has always been, when the Merrow are pushed beyond reason.

Patrick was the calmer of the two—calmer than I was, by a fair depth. He had been the one receiving the ominous messages the Selkies carried for the past several tides, and while he seemed weighted down by what had happened, he was still standing as straight as ever he had, lending what support he could to Dianda, when she came close enough for him to reach. The depths of the palace were still sealed off to him, and always would be.

"We have to go to the surface, of course," he said, turning away from the window he'd been staring through.

I paused in circling the room to look at him quizzically. "Why?"

"Because no one from the sea took our children," he said. "If they had, we'd already have an army at the gates, and war would be properly declared. No, whatever mischief this is, it began on the land. It's been a long while since I was back again." His expression was grim, unforgiving. "It seems the time has come for my return."

"But how . . . ?"

"I'll send word through the Selkies to the shore, tell that pretender Queen who holds the throne that we're to come and discuss the situation. She won't like being ordered around by a man who gave up his title and chance at power to marry a mermaid, but she's clever enough to understand that she'd like war even less. I'll bring them home." His voice broke then, cracking on the word "home" like a ship's mast breaking down the middle. "I promise you, I'll bring them home."

"See to it you do," I said, and turned away. "I'll fetch a messenger."

My boys were gone.

We were going to bring them back.

Autumn, 2011

We didn't, of course—not both of them. Dean had been traumatized by his experience in the open air, to be sure, as traumatized as his brother, but in a very different way. For the first time in his life, he had moved through a world that wasn't constantly trying to suffocate him, and unlike his father, he never chose the sea. He was born to it, but not of it, and I had always known that one day he would leave us for a world more suited to his nature. I'd never needed Mary to tell me that the elder of my beloved boys was only with us until he wasn't, and when he declared his intention to accept the position of Count of Goldengreen and stay ashore, I had managed not to weep or demand he change his mind. He was growing up. He deserved a world where he could thrive.

Besides, there was a certain beautiful symmetry to him taking ownership of the knowe that once belonged to the woman who had put Patrick into fear for his marriage, who would have seen his parents split apart before he could even be born. If Evening Winterrose had been given her way, the man who now walked what were once her halls and reshaped them to his whims would never have existed. There was an undeniable beauty in that.

We would all miss him. But he deserved this chance to prove himself, and to be happy, if he could. And on some level, I was grateful.
Neither of my boys could inherit: if Dianda ever wanted to step aside,
she would need to adopt or entice an heir from somewhere else. It
wouldn't be that difficult, really; there were always second sons and
extra daughters somewhere in the sea, or she could reach out to see if
her own parents—who had remarried after they were both free of
other duties, and now lived a nomadic life on the other side of the
kingdom, moving from fiefdom to fiefdom with the tides—had ever
had another child. Four children of one marriage would be unusual,
but not unheard-of, and it would let her keep the Duchy in the family,
if that was what she wanted.

Dean had always been destined for the land, and Peter for the sea.
At least Goldengreen was coastal. Should my lady ever choose to set
her demesne aside, Peter could go to his brother as once Patrick had
come to the sea, and things would continue in the strange peace we
had worked so hard to develop.

One thing was sure: our ties to the Mists would be tighter now that
Dean was counted among their nobility, and now that October Daye—
the changeling girl who killed Blind Michael—was counted among our
allies. Her presence brought with it many stories, and many complica-
tions, including news of Simon Torquill, who I had thought gone from
our lives forever.

Perhaps it was better that he were, as he had apparently become a
villain of towering cruelty in the absence of his friend . . . and of his
daughter. The girl's disappearance had been the catalyst for the earthquake in 1906, the one which sealed us from the land and began our
current isolation. Without her, and without Patrick to anchor him, he
had descended into a pit from which he might never emerge.

October had been one of his victims, as had Rayseline, the girl responsible for stealing our boys from their beds and beginning this
whole disaster. His own daughter and his own niece, both damaged
beyond repair by his actions.

It pained Patrick to return to the land and not immediately seek his
friend, but he was wise enough to see that it was for the best. Our new
allies mattered more than his old friendships. Still, I could see how he
ached to begin searching for the man, and it was only Dianda's constant intercession and distraction that prevented him from giving in to
the impulse.

Mary came around more and more frequently during those days,
seeming brighter, more focused, and more alert. She Saw a single

future approaching, and it seemed to be one which pleased her, for all that it had its dangers and its risks. She coached Peter, again and again, on how to respond if a strange Cephali came anywhere near him, and began coaching me as well. I listened more out of politeness than any need for education—might as well teach her grandmother to shuck oysters!

Until Torin returned from his long and semi-voluntary exile to challenge for ownership of what had never once been his, endangering Peter in the process and calling Dianda's marriage into question. Peter survived to come home to us, at least in part due to Mary's careful warnings, and she was rewarded by the restoration of her species to the sea, and the return of the sea witch to the Roane. These new Roane were not the originals; they looked upon the Luidaeg without seeing their mother come back to them at last. Mary, however . . . Mary was much older than any of us had guessed she was.

She wasn't there with us, in the Duchy of Ships, when the Luidaeg stood with Amphitrite and October and called the Roane back from their place in the deeps. But she might as well have been, from the way she wept when we returned home to her, and confirmed what she already knew to have transpired. She wasn't there. I think she might have burst if she had been.

Family reunions harm as much as they heal, even when all parties involved mean as well as can be meant. Still, she was a part of our family, and I was glad for her, strange creature that she was.

And time marched on.

Autumn, 2014
What is there to say about Simon Torquill? He was a villain, of that much there seemed to be no question. Everyone who had ever known the man agreed that he was a villain, even Patrick, who still harbored more affection for him than seemed wise by any means. Dianda, too, was soft-hearted where he was concerned, willing to accept that he might have done the things he did out of necessity. They had told me of their intentions before they went to the surface, and for all that I had not been a part of the discussion which led them to that point, I could no more fault their conclusions than I could shame Dianda for loving Patrick as she did, or myself for choosing Saltmist all those centuries ago.

Patrick loved Simon. He always had, and he always would. Dianda loved Patrick, truly and deeply as I had always known she had the potential to love, and she loved her memories of Simon, the man who had helped her to her happy ending at the expense of his own. Her love for Simon was perhaps more shallow than Patrick's, less rooted in shared time and more in the possibility of more, but it was real all the same, and so when they informed me that they were going to propose marriage to the man in order to save him from the consequences of his own actions, I had no true objections. So they had gone, and as they hoped, they had returned below with a husband in tow.

A husband who was a far cry from the silver-tongued flirt I'd met at their wedding, so many years before. This man was scared and scarred, flinching away from any hint of either kindness or censure, which meant that he was flinching almost constantly, afraid to be touched, afraid to be alone. Whatever he had been through—and I knew only the boldest strokes of it, the outlines of villainy and deceit—it had been enough to wound him deeply enough that I had no way of knowing if he would ever be fully recovered. My lady's latest suitor was a broken man, and hence he posed no threat that I could see, only moved through the knowe like a terribly polite shadow.

The girl Mary had foreseen and told me of accompanied him below—or at least, what I assumed was the girl, as Simon's daughter, August, had chosen his bloodline when he divorced her mother, and was now his child alone. The marriage to my lady and her consort hadn't made her a Lorden—she would be a Torquill until she took a spouse of her own, or found some other means to set the name aside— but it had made her family, and the sequence of events which had brought her to us was too convoluted and confusing to have ever been guaranteed. Mary had been speaking of her. I was almost sure.

August was quick to defend her father against all slights, real and imagined, interposing herself between him and anything she perceived as a threat, however inaccurately. I respected her dedication to him, even as I questioned its origins; she was as damaged as he was, in her own ways, and while much of her story was neither mine to seek nor share, I had to wonder what shape she would hold when she was finished healing. They would both recover, of that I was sure; we had removed them from the deepest dangers to their safety, giving them a safe place to rest and recover, and they were taking full advantage.

I watched Simon more closely than I did August, at least in the early days, for he was positioned to easily do harm to my lady and her consort, both of whom had my love and my loyalty, built over many years, and both of whom I would put before him if the situation arose where I had to choose between them. And to his credit, Simon seemed to feel much the same; if there was a chance to make one of them happy, he leapt for it, sometimes with more enthusiasm than was entirely wise.

Still, his presence seemed to make Patrick and Dianda happier than otherwise, and both of them moved through their days with a hopeful-ness I hadn't seen in years, like they were standing at the edge of some glorious new beginning, ready to see where they were going to travel from here. Our neighbors had long since written my lady off as a fool for marrying one Daoine Sidhe; adding a second did nothing to change their minds, and, if anything, only made them more sure that one day her fiefdom would come available for someone else to claim. A noble who persists in refusing to produce an heir can seem an easy target, although none of them were foolish enough to try our borders, recog-nizing that Saltmist was well defended whether or not the lines of suc-cession were clear.

Simon went about the business of healing, with Patrick and Dianda doing what they could to lend him their support. He began seeing a doctor of the mind, what the humans called a "therapist," via video call; whatever benefit he took from those sessions was invisible to the eye, but visible in the way he gradually began to socialize more freely among the court, meeting people and cajoling details of their lives out of them with the skill of a master who had allowed his skills to lie for some time fallow.

Peter, who had initially been terrified of allowing a Torquill into the palace, was quickly enamored of August, and could be found following her through the knowe at almost all times, choosing her company above all others, preferring her as a playmate and companion. It made sense, in many ways; she was as limited in her movements as he was, being unable to leave the knowe without alchemical aid, and unwilling to return to the land without an escort, out of fear for her mother. She was older than he by a full century and more, but her experience had been limited such that she fell easily into the role of child of the house, putting them on an equal social footing. He had been lonely since his brother left us for the land. In August's company, he blossomed, and I grew grateful for our new residents.

I wasn't quite ready to call them family, not yet, but they were bring-ing more joy to our household than they were trouble, and so I was glad to have them. I was willing to let them stay.

I was also far too aware of their bedding arrangements, without trying to pry. My duties included tidying their shared sitting room every evening, and setting out light refreshments to sustain them until they could reach the dining room and properly break their fast. I was thus continually informed as to who was sleeping where, and with whom.

The nature of their physical limitations meant that my lady and her consort had always maintained separate bedchambers: while they slept together two nights out of three, it was bad for Dianda to sleep dry and in scales, and she was unable to remain on two legs continually enough to sleep with him every night. It was bad for Patrick, meanwhile, to sleep submerged: even when he found a clever means of propping his head above the water to avoid drowning, his skin would become bloated and soft, absorbing an unhealthy amount of the sea around him. No, they had to sometimes sleep apart.

In the beginning, Simon slept with them, although he would as often as not come staggering back to his room while I was cleaning up, his eyes wide and his shoulders hunched, retreating into the privacy of his own space. After the third such encounter, I had gone to my lady, ready to defend him against her, odd as that thought felt to form; this was her domain, and she could do no wrong here. Still, if she was harming the man, she needed to stop. The honor of her house demanded no less.

She had met my arrival with sorrow in her eyes, sitting on the edge of the bed she shared with Patrick in her two-legged form, the air seeming to press down upon her shoulders such that she looked wilted, smaller than she was meant to be.

"I know why you're here," she said. "You saw Simon running away this morning, and wanted to caution me not to damage him. It would look unkind for me to be seducing Daoine Sidhe beneath the waves only to torment them, and would lessen us in the eyes of ally and enemy alike. Am I close enough to your lecture, Helmi, or shall I let you deliver it yourself? I'm sure you'd do a better job."

"You're quite close enough, and it's not my place, so if you'd like to continue lecturing yourself and spare me the trouble, I'd actually appreciate it." I folded my arms, watching her carefully. "This can't go on."

"He insists on sharing a room with us, but if we so much as brush against him in our sleep, he panics," she replied. "Neither of us has attempted to push him toward anything he doesn't want to do. We don't even reach for each other when he's present. But he seems to feel he must come to us, and then his demons follow him, as I fear they always will."

"Ah, my poor lady," I said, understanding. "Perhaps this is all a part of how he heals himself, if he comes to you and runs when he feels he must. If nothing else, it means he feels safe enough to run. He is taming himself, like a wild thing remembering how to eat from a friendly hand."

"I never thought this would be easy, but I told myself it was worth it," she said, miserably. "To save him from *those women* . . . ugh. Two of the Firstborn had him as a plaything for longer than I can consider without losing my temper. Even if we were marrying him as a friend, it would have been worth it. But he seems to think he has to live up to some expectation that exists only in his head, and pushes himself so that I fear he'll do harm."

"I can speak with him, if you'd like."

She brightened. "Oh, *would* you, Helmi? It's outside your duties—I was loath to ask . . ."

"All things pertaining to your health and happiness fall within my duties, milady. They always have, and always shall, unless you cast me from your service." I didn't particularly want to act as marriage counselor for my liege, but if she asked it of me, or simply needed it, it was my honor to serve.

Simon had left his private chambers by then, trading them for the security of his workshop. Had there been any question in my heart as to the sincerity of my lady's suit, it would have been answered by that workshop. It was an alchemist's dream, designed to suit every need her new husband could possibly have, and she and Patrick had seen to its outfitting as one, filling every jar and polishing every piece of equipment until it shone.

I knocked, measuring the hesitation before Simon called, with forced joviality, "Come in." Thus granted his consent, I undulated inside, tentacles slapping the floor with a sound that is unique, even in the Undersea; no one moves like the Cephali except for the Cephali, and no one ever will.

He both brightened and deflated a bit when he saw that it was me. He had settled himself at the workbench; the air smelled of unfamiliar herbs and flowers, but judging by his lack of safety equipment, it was nothing that would be dangerous to inhale.

"You have to stop this," I said.

"Lady Helmi." He set aside the small knife and tongs he had been holding, frowning at me. "Do you dislike this recipe? I can change—"

"I don't mean your alchemy. I mean insisting on sharing a bed with my lady and your husband when you know you'll have to flee before the evening bell. You do them harm. I fear you do yourself the same."

Simon stilled. It was easy to overlook the way the man was normally in constant motion until that motion stopped. Frozen as a stone, he looked at me with those yellow eyes of his, and I almost wanted to apologize and leave the room, sorry to have disturbed him.

I resisted the urge, and the following urge to climb up the wall and put myself into a superior position. Remaining where I was, I crossed my arms and watched him, waiting for the silence between us to break.

Finally, he turned his face away, plucking nervously at the already-chopped flowers in front of him. "I'm sure you have better things to concern yourself with than my wellbeing."

"Your wellbeing is my lady's wellbeing, and her wellbeing is the wellbeing of the Duchy," I said, voice sharp. "I have *nothing* better to worry about, as well you know."

"I am . . . sorry."

I frowned. "There's no need for sorrow. Only stop forcing yourself to do something you're not ready for."

"I owe them a vast debt—"

"No." The word was cold, implacable, and final. I would not allow this man—this man, who had been a hero to our household and a villain to all of Faerie—to transform my lady's bridal bed to the transactional thing it had been when it was shared by her father and my mother's lady. Saltmist had grown beyond those days of equal exchange. There were no debts here, not among our family.

"No?"

"There is no debt. They wed you because they love you, and yes, because they wanted to protect you from the world above, which seems to have been unaccountably cruel in its dealings with you. They know who and what you are, Simon, and they love you. They'll love you if you stay away until you're healed enough to come to them because you want to, and not out of some obligation that can only hurt you all."

He blinked, slowly. "I didn't know you cared."

"I don't. But August is happy here, and it would break Peter's heart if you were to take her away, and it would break Patrick's heart if you were to take yourself away," I said, briskly. "I would say my lady's heart was safe as yet, but you can't go breaking so many hearts she cares for and not do her damage in the process. And she *does* care for you, more deeply than perhaps she realizes. You need to be more careful."

"So what, I should refuse their company until I've accomplished a recovery which may never come?"

"No. But you should stop pushing yourself for the sake of what you assume is expected of you. Nothing is expected of you. Only that you continue to heal until you heal no further, and that you try to discover the life you want to lead, now that you have the freedom to lead it."

Slowly, he nodded. "I will try, Lady Helmi."

"I'm not a lady."

"No, but 'Miss' seems rude, and we're not close enough for me to call you by your name all unadorned."

I snorted. "Very well, then, Lord Simon. What are you working on?"

Eyes bright, he gestured me closer. "Ah, this is very interesting, and I think you'll agree once I explain . . ."

I smiled, thinking of Patrick and equally nonsensical explanations of incomprehensible machines that did nothing of value save for making him happy.

My lady's heart had a type, it seemed, and not merely Daoine Sidhe.

Spring, 2015

Simon and Patrick had returned from October's wedding hand-in-hand and all but weeping for joy, and I knew even before I came to clean their rooms in the morning that something had changed within him. Some old pocket of close-held trauma had been effectively lanced by the journey, and so it was less of a surprise than it might have been when I came to see to my duties and found his bedchamber already empty, as was his workshop. Patrick's private room was likewise unoccupied, while the door to the chamber the three were meant to share was closed and locked, the wards glowing warning to any who came too close.

I didn't need to see that. I saw to the rooms and left, privately glad that this step had been taken. If it were going to happen, better that it happen while the marriage was yet young enough to be malleable, not hardened into the shape it would hold forever after.

The three of them came to second meal together, having missed the first entirely. They were all of them disheveled and giggling, Patrick wearing a shirt I was quite sure belonged to Simon, Simon sitting a little too close to Dianda, allowing her to play her fingers through his hair. Subtle they were not, in the slightest, but as they were already wed and Dianda was mistress in these halls, they had no cause to be.

I smirked at her as I cleared their dishes away, and she huffed very slightly, rolling her eyes at my expression. "Shall I fetch you anything more?" I asked, keeping my tone stiff and proper.

"I think we shall retire to our rooms," she said. "It's been a long week. I'll see you at dinner, Helmi."

I knew a dismissal when I heard one, especially from her. I still paused long enough to ask, "And the children? Shall I tell them you're not to be disturbed?"

"Ask August if she can keep Peter amused for the night," she said. "I'll find her some pleasant reward if she agrees." And she *would* agree. August was not so eager to please as her father, but that was like saying a lake was not quite so deep as the sea. It was still suited to drowning the unwary.

"Indeed, my lady," I said, and took my leave, the sound of giggles and hushed whispers following me out of the room.

I had been hoping for this night, hoping they would find peace and balance between the three of them. I hadn't considered how *annoying* it might be.

Mary found me halfway between the dining room and the kitchen. She looked smug.

"What now?" I asked.

"She's coming," she said. "Not right away, but the tides have shifted, and it's no longer a maybe that the girl will arrive. We've been waiting to find out her answer for so long."

I raised an eyebrow. "Are you sure?"

She looked at me flatly.

"Of course you're sure. Well, that will be a nice surprise for everyone." I paused. "Do you know who the father is?"

"They both are," said Mary. "But I can tell you her magic smells of whitebeam flowers and water lilies, and that we'll be very glad to have her."

"Will you tell us when she's on her way?"

Mary looked at me, eyes twinkling. "Now, where would be the fun in that?"

Summer, 2015
The land was being overly dramatic again. They seemed to specialize in that, especially when Sir Daye was involved, and my greatest concern over Simon's marrying into the household was the fact that now she was, technically, part of the family. She was his daughter, and he was married to my lady, which made her adjunct to Saltmist. I generally did my best not to think about that.

At the moment, it was impossible not to think about that. The reports coming from the shore were wild and unbelievable. Titania, the Mother of Flowers, the Summer Queen, Fairest in Faerie, had been found. She had been returned to us. And all it had cost was the woman whose identity she had been wearing, and a little girl who had been her youngest daughter, who had been Firstborn in her own right and hadn't run fast enough when her own mother came to her with murder in her eyes.

The Undersea has always known that of the two Queens, Maeve was the darker but Titania was the wicked. How could we fail to know it, when so few of Titania's descendants had bothered to come below to preach her poisoned philosophies to us? Of our number, the Merrow are the closest to following her teachings, and even they deny the bulk of them, much as she denied their Firstborn when Amphitrite was born with fins and scales and terrible teeth.

And October, of course, was right at the center of it all. Simon had been ashore when the chaos began, and had been sending regular updates home throughout, both via traditional messenger and by instructing Quentin and Dean to text Peter, who had been taking an unpleasant glee in telling the rest of us how terrible things were getting. October had apparently attempted to fight Titania single-handed, which seemed like a terrible idea, no matter how I looked at it.

Simon's most recent message had been brief, asking that we not listen to anything anyone else might say before he could get home to explain himself, and August had been dispatched to retrieve him. Dianda and Patrick were both worried about what Simon might not want them to hear from someone else, which struck me as a sensible concern.

Then, as we waited, the sea shook. At first, I feared another earthquake—a hundred years had not been long enough to forget the destruction of the quake which marked August's disappearance. Then the shaking stopped, and everything was normal.

I frowned at Dianda, who frowned back at me, and we were settling in to wait as the receiving room abruptly filled with Roane and the scant few Selkies who still lived in the local sea. They were all confused, looking wildly around themselves, and had barely appeared before they were talking rapidly to one another, some of them on the verge of panic. I recognized a dark-haired figure pushing through the crowd toward Patrick, and lashed out, wrapping a tentacle around her wrist and pulling her toward me.

"Gillian," I exclaimed. "What is going on?"

"I don't *know*," she said. "I was in Half Moon Bay, it's my weekend with Diva, and suddenly I was here, and I don't know how. Did Mom do something?"

I sighed. "Probably." As October's daughter, Gillian had been given plenty of time to learn that when things go catastrophically wrong, her mother is normally right at the center of the chaos.

Dianda was shouting, trying to silence the din. I didn't think it was helping. If anything, it was just making things worse. I let go of Gillian's wrist and retreated to the wall, climbing up it to dangle from the ceiling in a position of tactical superiority.

The seal-shifters did eventually calm, just in time for other members of the Court to begin pouring through the arrivals pool with dire news. The passage to the surface had been closed, magically. Anyone attempting to swim beyond a certain point found themselves turned around and shoved back down into the depths.

And the water, as I breathed it in, began to taste of roses.

Patrick lost his composure as the ramifications sank in, shouting for someone to find a way out, to find a way to bring his family home. Dianda simply became more and more calm, lips thinning to a hard line as she directed her subjects—those who were customarily in the deeps and those who hadn't expected to be here—to safe chambers where they could pass the night. The palace staff was already at work on sufficient food to satiate them all, and I knew I would soon be called upon to join them.

I crossed the ceiling to drop down next to Dianda, who didn't flinch at my sudden appearance. "May I get my lady anything?"

"I want one of those sponge cakes they sell on the surface—a Twinkie. Wrapped in pickled kelp." She continued glaring at the room. "I don't know what's going on, but I'm not going to find out on an empty stomach."

"I'll have to get the Twinkie from Peter, but I'm sure he'll share," I said. "Shall I bring it here?"

"I think that might be best," she said, and sighed.

I rolled out of the room, off to check in with the kitchen staff and gather sponge cakes and seaweed for my lady. The order we had made for ourselves here in Saltmist was a strange and shaky one, but it held together. People came and went, but my lady remained, and I remained beside her, and that was quite enough for me.

That was always and would remain quite enough for me.